MORE THAN FATE

MORE THAN FATE

TAMZIN L. BURCH

ANDREA J. SEVERSON

*To all the relationships that
have been, could've been, and are yet to be.*

AUTHOR'S NOTE

Please be aware that this book covers some sensitive topics, such as sexual harassment and emotional abuse. We, the authors, understand that these depictions may be triggering for some, please proceed with care. We hope we have treated Macey and Isla's stories sensitively.

CHAPTER 1 - MACEY

We were meant to be leaving in ten minutes and I was nowhere near ready yet. There were boxes everywhere possible, except in the car where they should be, and as usual, Dad was having a meltdown over the amount of stuff I have.

"Have you been managing your emotions effectively recently Macey?" he asked. "Where has all of this come from? You had about half this amount in the first year. I thought your belongings would dissipate over your student life with all the moving involved."

"John Bowlby didn't spend years developing his attachment theory for you to use it against me in an argument about over packing." I said, with only a slight sass.

I have a lot of stuff, but I am not a hoarder. My parents are psychologists, which meant they liked to psychoanalyse everything, including why the amount of online shopping I do has increased significantly, as of recently. I have been dreading going back to university, hence why my procrastination levels have been sky high and packing has been left until just now. I was studying psychology, as you might have guessed. I have little idea why though.

As we eventually pulled out of my hometown of Glossop and began the five-hour drive to Plymouth, I buried my head in my jumper against the window and reflected on the summer I just had. I couldn't believe it was September again, and for once in my life, I didn't want to leave home. I had spent the past few months outside, making the most out of being in the countryside, exploring with my best friend Sam. We were either hiking around Kinder Scout or hopping on a train to Manchester or sometimes Sheffield to relish in city life. We'd spent hours having picnics in Manor Park and even more time sunbathing at Melandra Castle, basking in the sun on the old Roman fort.

I never appreciated living in a small town when I was younger, but now that I'm an adult, I really love being out in the sticks and breathing that fresh, country air. I suddenly felt some tears form, so I quickly pushed my glasses out of the way and rubbed my eyes with my sleeve. We're not big criers in my family, and I wasn't in the mood for Mum to ask a million questions and then tell me to just *breathe*. I guess it was just the realisation that I wasn't going to be home for a while, which sucks more when the future feels so uncertain.

I absolutely adore Plymouth though. Being down by the sea, breathing that crisp, sea air, aimlessly wandering around the seaside stalls on a Sunday, browsing the trinkets and collectables they house. I love sitting in Liner Lookout cafe, reading or writing whilst watching the waves creep in and swallow the scattered rocks down below. I've missed the hours I would spend people watching, analysing each eager tourist as they walk past my flat window, making up stories in my head about why they're in Plymouth, what they're there to see and do. I may have lived down south for less than a year, but it certainly felt like home. At least a second home, with its pretty coastlines and lush country parks. I will always be Northern at heart, as uni peers like to remind me whenever they claim I pronounce something "wrong." Overall I am so happy in Plymouth, you couldn't beat this new life I've begun to pave for myself. Although, there's one tiny thing. I really, really, really dislike studying psychology.

Psychology is in my flesh and blood. If you were to cut me open, you'd see the words of Sigmud Freud etched onto my bones and his personality development theory running through my veins. We aren't religious in my household, the only god we pay homage to is Freud himself. When I tell you my parents squealed when I was born on my due date, Freud's birthday... I am convinced they planned that somehow. I am not quite sure how they pulled it off, but I am sure they were more pleased about it than my actual existence. I could name the five founding fathers of psychology at the same time I was learning to count to ten. You see, there's never been anything else on the cards for me. My main hobby, writing, just became my escape, a way to get away from hearing about the seven stages of grief at every opportunity. The "interesting" dinner table conversations do in fact, become boring after twenty years.

It's been my dream since I was a little girl to be a writer. I never thought too much about what I would write exactly, all I knew was that I wanted to write. And create. Create stories, fantasy lands, worlds that I could get lost in. Even when I wasn't penning my ideas, I was daydreaming about the worlds I had made. Or I was reading, living on other people's planets. I loved nothing more than burying my head in a book and forgetting that the real world existed. My favourite genre is definitely romance. Love stories. I love love! Yet, I am still waiting for my own epic love tale.

I am sceptical that they even exist on planet Earth though. My whole life has been benchmarked by disastrous attempts at love stories. From my parent's divorce to my high school relationship with Owen that I felt trapped in from the get-go. I just wanted to experience love in its purest form. I didn't want to be like my parents at 55, living in different rooms in the same house because they just can't seem to settle on their separation terms. I want the kind of love story that flips your world upside down, in the best possible way. The kind of love that makes you feel dizzy with excitement. And I want to write about them. But I've never felt adequate enough. My parents always squashed my dreams, claiming that being a writer is not a concrete career choice, and I'd be better off doing something "useful."

I knew I wanted to go to university regardless of what I did. The idea of a new life, away from high school peers (including Owen of course) and being able to break away from my small town. I always dreamt of being by the sea, somewhere I could listen to the ocean splash against the shore and feel the salty breeze sneak in when I cracked my window in the morning. If I couldn't study Literature or Creative Writing, at least I could be in a place that inspired me to create in my own time, for fun. Writing had become my hobby, yet the disapproval from my parents still hung over my head, meaning it just didn't feel that enjoyable a lot of the time.

Three hours into the journey and I've done enough thinking to last a lifetime. Including the important topic, what is it about service stations that's so magical? I know that sounds bizarre, as who really cares so much for often soggy sandwiches and toilets that definitely haven't seen bleach in a long time? To me, there's just something about them, it's like time doesn't exist within those walls. Maybe it's because you'll see people eating a Whopper from Burger King at 6:30am, trudging around in their workwear, or maybe it's because they are what someone once called "the airports of the road," and we all love airports and the fact having a beer before your early flight is considered the norm. I have loved service stations since I was a kid, so as soon as we approached our trusty Michaelwood Welcome Break, I felt the excitement rise. A stroll around Waitrose picking up a magazine and some overpriced snacks was my idea of bliss.

I hopped out the car as we pulled up and Dad passed me a £10 note out of the window.

"Not coming in?" I asked, questioning his odd behaviour.

He's typically as eager as me to venture into the services, so I wasn't sure why he wasn't so keen today.

"I will follow you shortly. I need to talk to your mother."

Whenever he says that, it's typically about me, so I took the £10 and made myself scarce for twenty minutes. I don't know what it could be this time, probably something to do with my reluctance to go back to University. I was trying to be subtle with that, but going off Dad's hints recently, I was failing. Every so often he'd ask me about my course, and how "university was treating me." I get being a concerned parent, but he was going a little overboard, which made me think he was onto me about my degree doubts. My parents' overbearingness could be draining, but I understood why they are like that, given their past, so I understand and let it go. Most of the time, anyway.

I wandered directly to the fridge section of the Waitrose franchise and picked up a bottle of fruit juice and a pack of vegetable sushi, before meandering over to the magazines, browsing each title carefully. I finally settled on *Vogue*, a classic, and took all of my items over to the till.

The woman serving shot me a smile before asking where I was headed today.

"Just back to university," I explained, smiling back.

"Oh to be young and free again!" she replied, laughing as she said each word.

"It isn't like it's cracked up to be," I said, clarifying that it's equally as stressful as being a "proper adult" and the looming future is very scary.

"What do you study?"

I hesitated. "Psychology," I said, looking glum.

"Do you not enjoy it?" she replied, reading my expression.

"I just wish I did something else."

"If I can give you one piece of advice," she continued in a whispered tone, "It's better to regret the things you do, than the things you don't do. I'd say, follow your heart always and study what you want to study!"

She emphasised the last part, before adding some sweets to my pile and giving me a wink. "Don't ever forget what it's like to be care-free."

I nodded, thanked her for her kind gesture and gathered up my purchases in my tote. I exited the shop, bumping into Dad on the way out.

"I thought you weren't coming in?"

"I needed to use the bathroom," he said, in a hurry, almost as if he was flustered.

"I'll meet you in the car," I told him, before heading back to see what had obviously gone down between him and Mum.

"He was just getting all het up. Stressed that you're stressed about going back to university," Mum told me as I collapsed onto the back seat once again. "I don't know what all the fuss is about, you're fine," she added.

I agreed, that I was indeed fine, even if I didn't feel fine, and began to flick through the copy of *Vogue* that I just bought.

"Why'd you waste money on that Macey? You could have gotten *Psychology Today* or something informative. Instead you just read trash."

"An article about Timothée Chalamet's recent clothing choices is not trash, Mum. It's an essential read," I murmured as my eyes rolled so far back that I could see my brain.

As we began the final stretch to Plymouth, I felt that horrible, sickening feeling rise inside of me. I was too familiar with it. I'd felt it numerous times over the past few years. It started when Owen and I split and after that, it happened whenever I experienced any big, gut wrenching moment. I'd feel lightheaded, and very overwhelmed, to the point where I couldn't think clearly. I was so apprehensive about going back because it meant that I had to face reality. I had been ignoring it over the summer, putting off making any kind of decisions about my future. Now was the time to face the music and this week was going to be a big one. I had one week to get settled back into life in Plymouth before the term would officially start and I had a lot more thinking to do. Knowing me though, nothing will change.

I like my routines too much. I am a creature of habit and a lover of familiarity. The quote "life starts outside of your comfort zone" makes me feel sick every time I hear it. I hate any sort of change. It's caused several problems throughout my life, and I do wish I could change myself sometimes, though I am far too stubborn to. I am a typical Taurus, through and through, and I drive myself up the wall with how much any sort of personal shift affects me.

My parent's divorce, Owen and I's breakup, were both things I had no control over. They both stopped me right in my tracks and changed the course of my life. I blame both of them for contributing to the way I am, as now I tend to keep things even more simple, refusing to make any major changes, just so I can continue to feel as settled as I can be. I always thought Owen and I would get married, I always thought I'd have both my parents there, happy, hand in hand, just as in love as I thought Owen and I were. When everything began to fall apart, I clung onto the things I knew were bound to happen in the future. Studying for a degree in Psych was a part of that. So was living by the sea. And staying single for the foreseeable because I was absolutely terrified of dating again. This, I have stuck to for the past year and a bit. I think I'd quite happily live alone forever now. I have fully come to terms with it.

Well, I go through phases. Some days I think I'd be happy living in a little cottage on a cliff, overlooking a harbour, populated by boats and bustling with jolly fishermen and their latest catches. Other days, usually just after finishing yet another romance novel, I dream of being swept off my feet by a real-life Prince Charming. In the summer, we'd go on lovey-dovey dates and I'd wear cute sundresses and sandals, and in the winter, we'd cosy up by the fire and share our love for poetry as the sun set outside. The latter sounds idyllic, but then I remember my track record with guys is not ideal and the thought of having to go through both getting to know someone and trusting them again is way too daunting. I may only be 20, but I've lived through enough already to tell me that.

As we finally pulled up outside of my new house in Plymouth, I actually felt a sense of relief that we had got there safe and sound. At one point, about an hour ago, I thought we were all going to die as Mum accidentally ran a red light whilst snapping at Dad for eating his crisps too loudly. I didn't think I would feel relieved, as I have been so worried about coming back, but just being able to get out of the car and away from my parents is bringing me a newfound sense of peace. It's hard being with them both when they're like this, and if I'm honest, I would rather them finally officialise their divorce and begin living separately. I don't see any chance of reconciliation and they are just dragging it out now. It's sad, because who wants to see their parents apart? However, anything would be better, not just for me, but for them also, than what it's like at the moment. They must be so unhappy too, so I do have empathy, even if I complain about them a lot. It's just been a long two years.

I got lucky with my house this year. I decided to live privately and not in university provided accommodation again, and I am so glad I did. I was scrolling through Facebook last semester when I came across an advert for a room in a Victorian terrace, down by the shore. I knew I had to snap it up, and when I spoke to my potential housemates, I knew it would be the perfect fit. They were all studying creative subjects, so they were my kind of people anyway, and the girl who they were meant to be living with initially, was doing the course I'd love to do, English and Creative Writing. She only gave up her tenancy due to moving in with her boyfriend, and the other girls seemed more than happy to have someone like me take her place. It felt meant to be.

My room is at the back of the house, overlooking the garden, and if you stick your head out of the window far enough, you can see the sea. When I viewed the property initially, I was so excited by that fact, that I almost fell out of said window. I'd have to make sure not to do that too often, and instead just look out of it like a normal person.

I began to unpack the car with the help of Mum and Dad, box by box, constantly reminding Dad to be gentler with the boxes marked "FRAGILE" as he could be rather rough. We placed all the boxes by the front door, as my parents had already kindly told me they couldn't stick around. Apparently, they had to "dash off" and embark on the five hour drive back. I gave them both a hug and said goodbye, whilst reaching for the door handle and attempting to let myself in. Before I could make it through the entrance, a fair haired, petite girl came skipping towards me.

"Heyyyyyy!" she squealed, with a big smile painted across her face. "I'm Charlotte! It is so nice to meet you. Macey, right?"

I nodded, to confirm that Macey was in fact my name, and began shuffling the rest of my belongings into the hallway.

"You look like a Charlotte," I said, without much thought, yet with immediate regret after. Despite being a reasonably intelligent person, I have this ability to say dumb things when I first meet people.

"Thank you! I think," Charlotte said with a slightly confused look on her face. She was still smiling though, and I decided that she must just be one of those high energy, constantly positive girls. I also concluded that she must have sore cheeks from grinning so much. She bobbed down and looked me in the eye as I was picking my stuff up from the floor.

"Welcome to the family," she announced, her perfect blonde curls bouncing as she spoke each word. She was wearing tight leather leggings with a frilly white cropped blouse on top, which accentuated her petite frame.

"Thank you, Charlotte," I replied, attempting to match her kind demeanour. It wasn't a department I was skilled in, though I was trying to improve. She started to help carry my boxes upstairs, even after I insisted that I was more than capable of doing it by myself. I let her continue however, as I thought it'd be a good opportunity to get to know her.

"Ruby and Liberty are out at the moment. They nipped to the shops to get some ingredients for dinner. We thought it would be an idea to welcome you properly with a nice meal. Is that ok?"

I blushed. I wasn't used to people being so nice to me. I wasn't even used to having female company or friends, I always just hung around with Sam before university and last year I kept myself to myself most of the time.

"That would be lovely, thank you so much," I replied, with a genuine smile on my face.

"Yay! Libby's girlfriend Anna is going to join us as well."

"Great. I can't wait to meet them all. What was it that you girls study again? Forgive me for blanking," I added.

"My degree is Drama and Theatre Practise; Ruby's is Fine Art and Libby's is Marketing. Anna does that as well. You're Psychology, right? The new brains of the house," she chirped.

"Yes, Psychology. Though, I wish I did something else."

"How come?" she queried, as she slid the last box into my room.

"I decided to honour my parent's wishes. My dad's a criminal psychologist and my mum's a forensic psychologist. I chose to study Psychology with the idea that I'd focus on Developmental Psychology. It does interest me how people become who they are," I explained, before going on to tell her that I wish I had done a creative subject like them, ideally something in the writing realm.

"It's never too late," Charlotte suggested gently, as she vacated the room, slowly closing the door behind her. She paused, before peeking through the remaining crack.

"Dinner's at six. I'd get a wiggle on with the unpacking if I was you," she added, with her signature smile and pleasant tone.

I nodded, acknowledging what she said, before I crashed on my bed and listened to her singing a song from *The Lion King* as she made her way downstairs. Twice in one day, two separate people have told me to follow my heart. Is this universe trying to tell me something?

CHAPTER 2 - ISLA

I logged off my last video conference of the morning and checked my watch. Just past eleven o'clock. *Perfect*, I thought. Still plenty of time to get some writing done today before the book club I'm attending later.

I dashed around the house, gathering the essentials. Laptop? Check. Tablet? Check. Phone and earbuds? Check and check. I put my notebook for my current project in my tote bag as well, along with my small pen case, and slipped into my ankle boots that were sitting by the welcome mat. I wound a scarf around my neck and looked at myself in the mirror that hung next to the front door.

My dark auburn hair appeared dull, more brown than red at the moment and I could see bits of grey coming in again. *Time to book in at the salon*, I thought. I've earned my grey hairs, but I didn't particularly want to see them just yet, so I dyed them into submission. I had circles under my green eyes, from a few too many sleepless nights. I made a mental note to stop at Boots to pick up my go-to under eye concealer that I ran out of.

"I should do that before the book club meeting," I muttered aloud to myself.

I tugged at the bottom of my blouse under my blazer and

fidgeted with my scarf. I wouldn't have time to come back to the house, so I guessed this will just have to do. Thank goodness the book club is a casual affair. It's not that I think I'm terribly unattractive right now, it's just been a crazy year. Turning 40 will mess with the head of even the most well adjusted person, and well, I struggle to think of myself as that well adjusted. But "normal" is overrated, right?

I locked the door behind me and jogged down the front steps, waving over the low hedge to my neighbour.

"Hello Isla!" she called out to me.

"Hello Mrs. Russell! Lovely weather, isn't it?"

"It is. Good to see the sun for a bit," she replied.

She's been my neighbour since I moved in here a couple years ago. I love this house so much, I saved for years from my book advances and royalties until I was finally able to purchase a property. I fell in love with it from the first viewing. When I moved in, I instantly fell in love with my neighbour, Mrs. Jacqueline Russell. I already knew her from my past, but we hadn't seen each other in decades. She brought over a casserole my first night in the house and we've been friends ever since.

"We should have a chat later on this evening if you're free," she called out as I let myself out the small gate at the end of my front garden.

"We will, I promise," I called back and then started walking down the road. I love this whole area, I was slightly tucked away from the hustle and bustle, but once I was on the main road it only took me ten minutes to get to the centre of Bath. I soon crossed the River Avon and admired the views as always. After living in the States for a bit, and then in Cambridge and London, it was nice to be back in Bath where I grew up.

I quickly checked my watch to make sure I was still doing ok for time. The book club wasn't until four o'clock, but I wanted to get a fair bit of writing done first. I walked past Bath Abbey, a sight I never got tired of or stopped being mesmerised by. The architecture was so inspiring and it was a great area for people watching, which is probably why I favoured a selection of coffee shops and cafes in this part of town to write.

I walked into one of my favorite coffee shops and waited in the queue to order my usual cappuccino and pastry. Today I chose a croissant, and found a quiet spot to sit. I got out my laptop and notebook. Another check of the watch showed I had at least three solid hours to write.

I started working on my current book, which will be my sixteenth. I've been publishing for twelve years and have been lucky to publish some special pieces that allowed me to have two books out in one year, something that didn't usually happen. My publisher jokes that they don't know what to do with me, they can't keep up with how quickly I write, but I can't help it. Ideas aren't the problem, time is. I have more ideas than I have time to write and I always worry that one of these years my readers will tire of me, so I have to get the ideas out and published as quickly as I can. You don't stay the darling of the romance publishing world forever. There's always some newer, younger, hipper writer coming up on your heels. At least that's what my agent likes to remind me.

I've been lucky. I have a very active, very vocal, and very supportive fan base. Every book does better than the previous one, so I'm not really worried. Not much. But any creative person struggles with insecurities and I'm no exception.

About an hour or so into, my writing session, my back and wrists started to ache, and my coffee was gone. I leaned back in my chair and stretched my arms over my head, then lowered my arms and flexed my wrists. My head was starting to swim in my plot line and my characters felt stuck. It was time to wander. I left the coffee shop and started walking. I walked past the Pump Room and the Roman Baths and then over to the Parade Gardens and walked around there for a bit, admiring the gardens and the beautiful weather. I sat on a bench and watched tourists go by as I jotted down notes in my little notebook. Tourist season was almost over, schools will be back in session any day now. I love summer and the increased crowds but I also love when Bath gets a little quieter in the autumn. Eventually, I walked to Pulteney Bridge and spotted some open seats in Bridge Coffee Shop so I dashed in and ordered quickly before a tourist could steal a spot. I sat near the window and got my laptop back out to continue writing. I had just over an hour before I needed to walk to where the book club was meeting.

My second writing session was more productive. The characters were actually getting somewhere and I think I might have fixed a plot issue that was driving me bonkers yesterday. The second cappuccino was clearly helping. I've been ignoring my phone but I decided to check it now. An email from my agent. *I'll respond later*, I thought. A text from my assistant, Beth, confirming the time and location for the book club. I don't know what I'd do without her. If I'm the creative right-brained thinker, she's the logistical left-brain of our little team. She handles all the administrative aspects of my day to day, like my schedule and making sure I get to the right place at the right time. She's also a genius with tech, so she helps keep my laptop and other devices in proper working order. We have a shared calendar where she adds appointments and sets alerts, meaning between her and my phone, I usually get to where I'm supposed to be. It's not that I'm flighty. But more often than not, I get lost in my work and forget what time it is.

I checked my watch again, twenty minutes to spare, great. I popped into Boots and grabbed my concealer, waited in the queue to pay, and then took a moment outside to touch up my makeup and tone down the dark circles under my eyes. With five minutes left I walked into the Caffè Nero where the book club was meeting and soon spotted the host, who Beth and I had been talking to over email.

"Jessica?" I asked as I tapped her on the shoulder.

Jessica turned around, "Oh my gosh, Isla, hi! It's so good to finally meet you, thank you soooooo much for coming to speak to our group, we're all just so pleased to meet you!"

I was touched by how sincere and enthusiastic she was. "Thank you, it's absolutely my pleasure! Thank you so much for choosing *Bold and Bright* as your book choice for the month."

"We're all so excited, it was such a good book, probably my favourite so far and I love all of your books!"

I laughed kindly, "That's high praise, I'm glad to know I can still impress."

"Oh you definitely can. Now, what can I get you? You sit down, maybe in the middle there, everyone will be here any minute. I'll go get you something to drink."

"Thank you, I've had a lot of coffee already today, so maybe a peppermint tea?"

"Coming right up," Jessica replied eagerly.

Jessica hurried over to the counter to place our order, and I could see other women come in and join her in the queue. There was some whispering and finger pointing in my direction and I could tell there was a growing buzz over by the counter as my presence was being noted by the new arrivals. Jessica came back with my tea and her coffee and was followed soon by a couple women who'd finished getting their drinks. Everyone sat down and we made introductions and small talk until the whole group had arrived.

It was a small book club, only about eight people, but I lived for moments like these. To get to sit down and really talk with some of my readers. The large book launch events and book signings were amazing, but getting to talk one on one with small groups like this were so valuable to me as a writer. My latest book, *Bold and Bright* had just been released a month ago. This group very smartly reached out well in advance of the launch to say they wanted to read the book, and could I come talk to them. Since we were all local it worked out and they were the first book club I was talking since the release. The online comments and reviews were positive, but this would be the first time I really talked face to face with a small group to hear their thoughts. I was a little nervous, even though it was my fifteenth novel to be published. People always gush at the book launches and signings, even if they haven't read the book yet. This would be different. And important.

Once everyone sat down, we started talking. Jessica had shared with me the list of questions they would lead off with, and from there I could guess what several of the follow-up questions would be. I told them about my inspiration for the book and how I came up with the characters. Then we walked through the key points of the plot. I deftly swerved the conversation when they asked if the characters were based on any real experiences, giving my standard line of...

"It's important for writers to write what they know, but also important to give themselves permission to write some things outside of their own specific experiences."

I think they bought it. If they only knew.

———

AFTER THE BOOK club was done, I said goodbye to everyone and promised to keep in touch. They were a great group and it would be fun to meet them again when my next book comes out. It was now nearly six o'clock and I was getting tired and hungry. I hadn't eaten enough. My mum would be cross with me if she knew. I'd had a muffin at Bridge Coffee but that was the last thing I ate. Breakfast was at seven o'clock this morning, and then just a croissant at the coffee shop near the Abbey just before noon. Other than that, it was just the muffin, two cappuccinos, and a peppermint tea that I'd had today.

"Brilliant Isla," I muttered under my breath as I crossed the river again and walked back up the road to my place. I got home in less than fifteen minutes and let myself in the front door. I ran upstairs to my office to set my stuff down and changed into something more comfy, choosing an old pair of jogging bottoms and a cosy jumper. Going into the kitchen I got out some pots and pans and started to whip up a basic pasta dish. While it cooked, I nibbled on some crisps I had in the cupboard. Tomorrow I would be working from home all day, so I'd be able to eat better.

As I cooked, I put my phone on speaker and called Georgiana, my best friend.

"Hi!" she said as soon as the call connected.

"Hiya! How's it going?"

"It's going well, how about you? How'd the writing go today?" she asked kindly.

"It went fine, still lots to do. I don't know, I just need to work on it. I had some meetings today, but tomorrow I can just stay home and write all day."

"That's good. You'll get there. So, are you going to come out this weekend? We all want to see you. It should be the last really nice weekend before the weather turns."

"Yeah, I should be able to make it. A picnic would be fun and you're right, this will be our last chance this summer."

"We were thinking of the meadow near you, our usual spot?"

"Well that would be easy enough for me then, it will be lovely to see you all!"

"Great! We'll see you then!" she said excitedly.

I've been staying home working so much, it would be good to get out and see Georgie and the rest of the group.

An hour later I was fed and happy. I grabbed the novel I'm currently reading and a cup of tea and sat in the chair in my living room in the large bay window. The bay window was a selling point of the house, there's one downstairs in the living room and one in the upstairs front room, my bedroom. I love a bay window. After a few minutes, I saw movement out the window and noticed Mrs. Russell in her garden. I put my book down and went outside to join her.

"Good evening, Mrs. Russell," I said. For some reason, even though I've known her for years, she's always been Mrs. Russell. Her first name is Jacqueline, which I found out when our mail once got mixed up. There's just something teacherly about her, not surprising since she used to be a teacher. You just don't call your teachers by their first name, do you?

"Good evening, Isla dear," she replied. "How was your day darling?"

Dear and darling, two more of my favourite things about Mrs.

Russell. She was only a little older than my mother, but she reminded me of my grandmothers in the way she talked to me. I loved it. Mum's parents lived in the States and Dad's lived in Scotland, so I didn't see my grandparents very often. Mrs. Russell had become my stand in for that kind of love, support and often a sounding board that you get from a grandmother or a favourite aunt, for those times when you need someone to talk to but you're too afraid to talk to your parents.

"My day was good, a few meetings, lots of writing in town, and then I was a guest at a book club meeting, which was a lot of fun," I replied as I sat down on the wooden bench I'd put in the front garden after my third long evening conversation with Mrs. Russell. She sat down in her rocking chair on the other side of the hedge and we both settled in for one of our regular evening chats.

We didn't do this every night, but most nights. In the winter or when the weather was bad, we usually met at one another's home. You read stories about people with wonderful neighbours, but I never thought they actually existed until I met Mrs. Russell.

"That's nice dear, were they reading your latest one? I've been telling my book club they need to read *Bold and Bright*, I do think it's one of my favourites you've ever written! Such a wonderful story," she said dreamily.

"You are so nice, Mrs. Russell," I said with a blush. "Yes, they were talking about that one. They were really lovely about it, lots of thoughtful questions and good chat."

"How's your current work going?"

I sighed, "It's coming along. I got a lot written today but I'm still slogging through it. It's taking longer than usual."

"What are you struggling with?" Mrs. Russell asked with concern.

"It's just different from the rest of my books. Three points of view, three different time periods and timelines, lots of historical references. I'm beginning to think I bit off more than I can chew."

"I'm sure you'll be fine. Just take your time. It will come to you," Mrs. Russell nodded confidently.

"Thanks," I said kindly. Her support was great. I had a good support network overall, but no one else that lived so close. Mrs. Russell was always there with a cuppa and a kind ear to listen if I needed it. She previously taught literature and writing too, so she knew what she was talking about.

"I know you're a very busy woman, but you deserve to have some respite every now and then, have you met anyone lately?" She asked, raising an eyebrow suggestively.

"Mrs. Russell!" I laughed. "You know I don't date. It's just not for me anymore."

"Nonsense, everyone deserves to find love, regardless of what point they are at in their lives. Considering it's what you write about, it's criminal that you're still single."

I frowned slightly, "You know why I don't date," I said pointedly.

"Not every man will treat you like the last one did," Mrs. Russell said, mimicking my frown, which made me laugh.

"I know, I just…I'm so busy with work, my friends and family, and my evening chats with you of course," I said with a wink. She smiled. "I don't feel like I'm missing anything."

"You can't miss something you never really had, and by the sound of it, I don't think you've had true love. You don't miss being in a relationship because your last one didn't add to your life, it only took from it."

Damn. She had me there. "You have a point, but I'm happy right now. Finally. I don't want to mess that up."

"You're just like Henry. He refuses to date anyone too."

"Oh?" I asked politely. "How's he doing in San Francisco?" Mrs. Russell hadn't mentioned her son Henry in a while, I couldn't help but be curious. I hadn't seen him since we were at school together when we were 16.

"Haven't I told you? He's moved back to Bath!" Mrs. Russell said excitedly.

I froze. Henry? Back in Bath? After all these years, I could hardly believe it. I tried to focus on what Mrs. Russell was saying.

"He's been ever so busy lately, so I've hardly had the chance to see him. He works terribly late most nights and hasn't been able to come over for dinner more than once since he moved back. I would have had you over dear, but it was last minute and when I knocked on your door you weren't in."

I quickly replied, "Oh what bad luck, it would have been nice to see him again." Understatement of the year.

"We'll definitely arrange something soon. His schedule is getting better now that the business is up and running, so I hope to see him more often. He's had me over to his new place, one of those fancy new buildings on the other side of town, all glass windows and such. But it's very nice and homely on the inside. Needs a woman's touch though if you ask me."

I laughed. "I'm sure it suits Henry just fine."

"Oh, but I wonder if your charming friend Georgie might take a look. She's a genius at interiors, I still love how she did over my front room for me last year. Do you think she'd mind if I contacted her?"

"I'm sure she'd be delighted," I replied. "But what has brought Henry back to Bath? I thought you said he was happy in San Francisco."

"Oh for certain, he was. Much happier than he'd been in London with that woman," she said with a shudder. "But I shouldn't tell tales. Forget I said that Isla dear."

"It's forgotten," I replied, thinking at the same time that I really wanted to know more.

"The two of you should meet up. All of his old friends have grown up and moved on. You're probably the only person he still knows."

"I'm sure he has more friends left here than just me, but I'd be happy to meet up with him."

"Oh that would be wonderful. I'll try to get him to come for dinner soon and you can join us, I'd love to have you both over, it will be so nice!"

She seemed so excited, I agreed that it would be nice and we continued chatting, about work and gardening, what we were reading and autumn slowly arriving. After about an hour we said goodnight and went inside, the sun was down and the air was getting chilly.

Back in my house, my mind started to wander as I cleaned up downstairs and turned off the lights, taking my book and a fresh mug of mint tea upstairs. I tried to read but all I could think about was Henry. After all these years, and we're both back in Bath, and single by the sound of it. I swore off dating ages ago, but somehow this felt like it changed things. All those years and all that heartbreak and I've always wondered if things would have been different if Henry and I had had a chance. If we'd just stayed in Bath and not gone our separate ways. Sighing, I finished my tea and padded barefoot into the ensuite, determined to rinse my persistent thoughts down the drain, at least for the rest of the evening.

After a long shower, I climbed into bed with my book, all fresh faced with my evening skincare routine dutifully applied. I finally managed to read for a while, getting lost in the novel I was reading. Being an author, I got sent so many advanced copies of new work, hoping for a great quote they can use for marketing. I always considered it a professional courtesy, though sometimes, like with the book I'm reading now, there are some real gems. I was transported to sunny LA and the life of a trendy fashion blogger who meets a sexy musician. Such a different life from my quiet one in Bath.

Such a different life from anything I'd known, I thought to myself. I have traveled, I studied in the States. But nothing ever seemed to work out, and moving back to Bath twelve years ago wasn't really a choice, more of a necessity. Yet it had all worked out for the best and I'm happier now than I ever was. Which is why the thought of meeting a guy is a bit silly. Why upset things? Don't fix something that isn't broken, isn't that how the saying goes?

I could feel myself frowning, so I reached up and tried in vain to smooth out the wrinkle between my eyes. I swear it gets deeper by the week and no amount of creams are helping. I need to get to a yoga class soon. I reach for my phone beside the bed, I'm one of those ghastly people you hear about who can't sleep if my phone isn't right beside me. Leave it charging in another room? Never! Not me.

I pulled up the text thread for Beth, who *does* sleep with her phone on silent and charging in the other room, so I know my text won't bother her.

I need to be booked in at the salon ASAP for a colour. Also, can you find a good yoga studio near me and look up times of classes? The one I used to go to has closed and I don't know where to try now. I need to get back into a class, trying at home isn't cutting it.

I put the phone back on the charger on the nightstand and set my book beside it before turning off the light. I was looking forward to a whole day writing tomorrow, at home and then the picnic at the weekend. And sometime soon, seeing Henry again.

CHAPTER 3 - MACEY

E vening rolled around and I subsequently rolled out of bed. I hadn't managed to do any unpacking, as I had fallen asleep shortly after I crashed. I blamed the long day of travelling, as well as the emotional exhaustion. Thinking really takes it out of you. I strolled over to the mirror that was fixed onto my wall already and made sure I looked at least presentable, before chucking on a cardigan and heading downstairs for dinner.

"Rise and shine!" Charlotte laughed as I entered the kitchen.

"You knew I was asleep?" I questioned sheepishly.

"Well, we assumed. We hadn't heard a peep from you in the last two hours," she replied.

Charlotte went on to introduce me to each of my new housemates individually, each of them telling me their names and courses again. I had spoken to Libby briefly when I viewed the house, and exchanged a few messages with Ruby, but that was about it. It was a relief to meet them all properly, including Anna, and be reassured that they were indeed my kind of people. Ruby looked over at me from the behind the kitchen counter. She was tall, with long honey braids and deep brown eyes. She was wearing a pair of light wash mom jeans, similar to my own, with a strappy yellow crop top and matching bandana. I admired her style for a second, already concluding that I was going to have to ask her for some fashion advice.

"I'm head chef today," she said eagerly, as her elegant hands chopped each carrot. "I'm cooking the girls' favourite, a vegan Maafe, a West African peanut stew. Worked out pretty well that we're all plant based! My grandma is Ivorian and taught me how to make it."

"Sounds delicious! Do you usually all cook together?" I asked curiously.

"Most of the time," Libby confirmed. "We love it. Of course, you're welcome to cook with us too now." Libby was perched at the bar, flicking through a recipe book which was laid on the counter. She had mousy brown hair, cut into a bob, and eyes of a similar colour. She was a little taller than Charlotte and I, but shorter than Ruby. She was wearing black skinny jeans and white t-shirt, with a checkered overshirt comfortably over the top. I liked her style too.

"I'd love that," I said with a grin of my own. It's so affirming to meet people similar to me for once.

After dinner I helped tidy up and clean the dishes, whilst continuing to chat to the girls.

"Who did you hang around with last year?" Charlotte asked as I moved each dish to the sink. "Plymouth is a pretty small place, so we probably know them," she continued.

"No one, really," I said slowly. "I didn't get on with my flat-mates and I just spent most of my time reading in my bedroom. My friend Sam from home came to visit when he could though."

"Ah! That's fair. Sometimes it just takes longer to find your people at university, that's completely normal. Despite the fact some claim you can find your bestie or the love of your life in first year!"

We all laughed. "So is Sam just a friend then?" Anna asked.

I nodded. "I've known him since we were babies basically! He's great. We do have a marriage pact, that if we're single by the time we're 35 we'll have kids together, but he's adamant on finding a boyfriend before then and I'd quite like to find one too!"

When we finished the clean-up effort, Charlotte and Ruby announced they were going for a run whilst Libby and Anna said they were going to watch a movie. They offered for me to join them, but not wanting to intrude, I politely declined and explained that I should really start unpacking. I thanked them again for a great first evening and headed back to my bedroom.

Back upstairs, I faced the mess I had left earlier. The number of boxes was overwhelming. I knew that sorting through them and arranging my belongings was going to be a big task. My bedroom luckily had a lot of storage space, including shelves that surrounded an unused fireplace. The first time I saw my bedroom, I fell head over heels for it. I absolutely adored all of the open shelving and couldn't wait to house all my books. At home, I often kept my collection hidden, as my parents didn't approve of my obsession with reading romance. For Mum, it's more the fact I am not reading world-class psychology journals, and for Dad, it's more because he thinks I spend too much money on novels.

I slowly started the process of removing each book from the boxes, dusting them down, and adding them to the shelf in colour order. I was going to do alphabetical, but I decided that putting them in colour order was more aesthetically pleasing. I lined them all up carefully, ensuring they wouldn't topple, and added some cute ornaments throughout to break up the shelves slightly.

After about an hour, I had finished the shelves, whilst listening to Ten Tonnes. I had my clothes to tackle next, which was bound to take at least two more hours, but given that I had napped earlier, I was actually feeling quite energised. Once again, I decided to organise my vast wardrobe in colour order, taking the time to neatly hang all of my dungarees, smock dresses and mom jeans. I placed my shoes in the bottom of the wardrobe, lining up each pair of Vans and Converse. I decided to hang my trusty burgundy Kanken rucksack on the back of my door, for easy access, as I used it most days. I felt a sense of relief again, once I'd finished organising my room. The house felt like home already, and the girls showing so much kindness to me really had helped. I headed over to my windowsill, grabbed my phone, and snapped a photo of my finished room before sending it to Sam and my parents. Once they replied, I tossed my phone down, ready to get cosy and have no distractions.

I grabbed my favourite book, *A Courageous Beginning* by Isla Stewart, and curled up on my bed with a thousand throw cushions surrounding me. I had read this book at least six times and it was practically falling apart. I never got tired of it though. Isla Stewart was my favourite author for that reason, her love stories were so intricate, that every time I reread one, I would discover another detail or something new about a character. *A Courageous Beginning* was the story of a woman who overcame so much on her quest to find the one, and rumour has it that it's based on Isla herself.

———

I AWOKE as the sun began to peer into my windows and the seagulls began their daily squawks. I was pretty much used to the constant gull sounds after living in Plymouth last academic year but readjusting to their ongoing tune after the Summer at home was a bit of a culture shock. Today was Tuesday, I've been back in Plymouth for almost a week now, and the term was due to begin tomorrow. I'd spent the last week getting back into my usual university routines, giving myself the opportunity to settle in and get used to life by the sea once more. I had missed it so much.

The girls and I had visited the beach almost every day, either to eat lunch, go for a stroll or to watch the sunset. I'd spent the last week getting to know them all properly, baking cupcakes on rainy afternoons and playing board games in the dim evenings. We'd had endless conversations about our favourite topics, including astrology and all of their signs, as well as boys and girls and our love lives – or attempts at them. Despite studying psychology myself, and being brought up constantly discussing it, I have always believed in astrology as well. I cannot deny that it makes sense, though it makes my parents cringe with disgust.

Over the past couple of days, we've browsed charity shops in town, looking for vintage treasures, and we upset our neighbours on Saturday evening by having a dance party which was a little too loud. As much as I looked forward to getting back to some sort of normality, attending classes and having work to do again, I was still apprehensive about the future, and possible decisions I had to make. I was also going to miss spending so much time with the girls. They were all out running errands today, ready for the start of term, and I felt a bit lost already.

I decided that instead of dwelling on being on my own for the day, I'd attempt to enjoy my own company again, just like I used to. It felt strange, resenting being alone, as that's pretty much how I spent all of my time last year.

I checked the time and decided if I was to get into town by early afternoon, I should hurry up and actually get dressed. I brushed my hair, added some light makeup, threw on a red, floral smock dress, some white ankle socks and my trusty black Old Skool Vans. I grabbed my rucksack, stuffed it with my MacBook, my phone, money, keys and earphone case, after placing each earphone into its respective ear. I shuffled a random playlist and locked the front door behind me. It was actually a rather mild day, so I turned back around to go and grab my trusty beige knitted cardigan, grimacing as I tried to find my keys whilst stood in the wind. I keep forgetting it's not summer anymore, which is painful, but I looked forward to the cosy aspect that autumn brings.

Town was a short walk from the house, so it wasn't long before I arrived at Drake Circus, Plymouth's go-to shopping venue. I navigated my way to Waterstones and headed straight for the fiction section, despite the fact I had come here to pick up my recommended reading textbooks for the year. I always get distracted by the novels, as I am sure I'm not the only one who doesn't want to browse the boring sections, with their plain covers and equally as dry descriptions.

I meandered over to Isla Stewart's shelf, carefully caressing each cover as they took their pride of place on the wall. I hovered over *A Courageous Beginning* for a few moments, internally debating whether I should pick up a fresh copy, considering my version is battered now, and I do love a fresh book. Just as I went to pick it up, another hand brushed my own.

"Hey!" I exclaimed, impulsively whacking the hand away from the book.

"There's one copy left, and I really need it!" a young, masculine, yet soft voice exclaimed pleadingly. "It's for my sister's birthday and she is a huge fan of the author, but this one is missing from her collection."

I immediately felt guilty as I do already own the book, but I was desperate for another copy, with that crisp new book scent and perfectly ironed pages. I pondered how to play this for a quick second - do I lie and make up an elaborate excuse for why I need the book too? Or do I let him have it? For all I know however, he could be lying as well.

"Do you really have a sister?" I sputtered out, without a second thought.

He laughs. "No, I just wanted the book for myself," he responded, in a bashful manner.

I immediately felt worse, but before I could say anything, he added, "I kid. It's honestly for my sister, but you should take it. I personally don't see what all the fuss is about with this author, but she must be good if you're fighting me for the remaining copy."

It was that last part that made me feel like I should take it, as no one disrespects Isla Stewart like that!

"You really shouldn't bad mouth the greatest romance novelist of our generation, especially when you know nothing about literature."

"I know nothing about literature?" he replied with a glare.

"Yes, or you wouldn't be bad mouthing the greatest romance novelist of our generation," I reiterate with even more confidence this time.

"I guess I should ask for a refund on my literature degree then…and pack the Masters in whilst I am at it."

Only me, Macey Banks, could trash talk a good looking, literature studying, book buying guy.

"I'm sorry. I guess I should take back what I said."

"No need, honest mistake," he protested, with a bit too much enthusiasm for my liking. "I'm Ted, a Lit grad and soon to be Creative Writing Masters student at Plymouth."

"Macey, Psych undergrad at Plymouth."

"Psych? You came to a seaside town, the perfect place to write, to study Psych? *And* you claim to know enough about literature to assign the title of greatest romance novelist of our generation?"

I couldn't get a word in edgeways. He wasn't wrong. A stranger just completely owned me.

"It's a long story." I say, in an attempt to shut him up. At this point, all I wanted to do was go home, back to my bedroom, and snuggle up with a book—any, seeing as I couldn't get a new copy of *A Courageous Beginning*—and forget about one of the most embarrassing encounters of my existence.

"Good job I have a lot of time to spare then. Fancy a coffee?" Ted smiled as he stared directly into my eyes, almost searching for the answer without me having to say anything at all.

"A coffee? With you? How do I know that you're not an axe murderer?" was the only thing that came to mind. And unfortunately, yes, I said it. Ted laughed at me, again.

"Come on. We all know it's the Maths students who are the real criminals."

I smirked, smiling up at him, whilst inside I was freaking out. Who was this guy and why was he talking to me? And why on earth was he asking me for a coffee? Was he asking me for a coffee, as in just a coffee, or was he asking me for a *coffee*? You know, the date kind? The, let's grab a coffee and get to know each other kinda coffee? We'd literally just met. He couldn't fancy me already, surely? Not that he fancies me. But if he didn't, why would he be asking me for *coffee*? If it is, the *coffee* kind of coffee. I kept smiling up at him, probably for far too long, before he broke the silence and asked if I had been to Prime Café before.

"I haven't. Are you wanting to go, like, now?" I asked, looking as perplexed as I felt this time.

"Yes. Unless you have some other pressing plans?" he quizzed.

I shook my head, after deciding it was best if I kept my mouth closed for the time being.

"Great, it's a date then," he declared.

————

"So, why aren't you studying literature?" Ted asked as he put down the two coffees he had just ordered for us on the table.

"Mainly, my parents. They're high flying psychologists. I felt like I couldn't stray from family tradition. They wouldn't approve," I told him, still confused as to how I had ended up in this situation.

"The best kind of creativity is born when those who don't typically rebel, rebel," Ted murmured.

"Who said that?" I replied, confused.

Ted laughed. "Me," he said, raising his hand shyly.

"I should have known, with you being a writer. It is true though," I sighed.

"Then why do you care what your parents think? Why not do what makes you happiest?"

"It's too late now. I'm starting second year tomorrow!"

"It's never too late. Call the University Admissions Department. My friend changed courses after a year, smooth as silk. Luckily I have always just marched to the beat of my own drum."

"If only we were all like you!" I added coyly.

He nodded and said sarcastically, "It's a hard task, I get it."

"You're not the first person to tell me that it isn't too late recently. I just feel like it is, you know? Like I'm on this path now for a reason. Changing would be too scary."

"Life should scare you a little," Ted said wisely, winking at me from under his sweeping fringe.

We then spent the next almost three hours talking about all things literature, writing and what the correct pronunciation of scone is, after I ordered one for a snack. Ted was originally from Exeter, and was adamant that scone rhymes with gone, which is obviously wrong. Being Northern, it rhymes with bone, as it should. The North/South divide is a constant source of debate at University. The extensive mix of people creates an interesting basis for any conversation, especially of those surrounding dialect. I spent my days explaining that I don't have a solid answer to what a bap/barmcake/breadcake is actually called, seeing as Glossop is close to Manchester, Derbyshire and South Yorkshire, and to many people's disgust, I would accept any of the three. "Just choose!" I have had screamed at me several times. It's a life-and-death situation apparently, you have to pick a side.

After explaining this to Ted, he scoffed.

"Well, it's a roll."

I rolled my eyes. "Whatever."

"You're stubborn, aren't you?" he muttered, as if it had taken him the whole three hours to establish that.

"Stubborn has too many negative connotations. I'm a woman who knows who she is and what she wants."

"I see," he said, taking another sip of his coffee.

I peered over at him, attempting to check him out whilst he was distracted. His medium length, light brown hair fell softly on his shoulders. It wasn't long enough to tie back, but long enough to give him that effortless look. His eyebrows were bushy, but not dark, and whenever he raised them, which seemed like a common occurrence, his widened eyes became the main feature. They were light brown too, but when the sun caught them, they glistened a warmer, almost golden tone. You know the phrase, "a smile that could light up a room"? I feel like that would describe his accurately, despite how overused, cliché, and cringey that term is. His smile was just infectious, every time he beamed, I felt the need to as well. He had the friendliest demeanour to match. His warmth didn't seem forced, or fake. He oozed a general confidence that wasn't overbearing, nor uncomfortable. He seemed like he just lived with a sense of ease, as if he was never nervous, never feeling any sort of anxiety.

As soon as we had arrived in the café, he was chatting with all the staff as if he'd known them for years, thanking each one for their service on this surprisingly chilly Wednesday, throwing a £5 note into their collective tip jar before we'd even sat down. He was one of those people that just looked kind, even though he stood at six-foot-two and had strong, broad shoulders, ones that you'd get lost in, if you ever had the pleasure of him hugging you. I wasn't intentionally objectifying, but he really was beautiful. His aura was reassuring, I hadn't felt this comfortable in someone's presence for a long time, especially someone I had just met. We seemed to have "hit it off" as they say, connected almost instantly.

"Macey? Maceeey?" he teased, snapping his fingers to get my attention. "Did you zone out or something?" he said, scoffing at my apparent ditziness.

"Kinda," I laughed back, taking a sip of my own coffee, which was cold now, due to all the talking.

"How old are you?" Ted wondered aloud.

"Twenty. Though sometimes I feel 75, with all the reading and lack of partying that I do. "

Ted laughed. "So if you're twenty…that means…"

I could see him attempting mental calculations.

"I took a gap year," I interrupted. "After my A-Levels, things were a little crazy at home. So I deferred my place at Plymouth for a year and worked in a farm shop. Saved up some money before heading down here last September."

"I see," Ted responded. "I'm 22. I kind of dived straight into the whole education thing. On reflection, I wish I had taken a gap year too. I came to uni at 18, straight after my A-Levels, did two years of my course, a placement year, then my third year, this past year. Now I'm starting the Masters. I feel like I've been studying forever," he sighed.

"What did you do for your placement?" I asked curiously.

"I was a publishing assistant for Bloomsbury in London," he responded, casually.

I blinked repeatedly. "Wow!" I was impressed.

Ted smiled, "It was certainly an experience." He looked around, before turning back to me. "Would you like to take a walk on the beach?" he asked politely.

As much as I wanted to, I quickly declined. "I'd love to Ted, I really would," I said, sincerely. "But there's something I really have to do." Speaking with Ted was the last push I needed to make the decision that had been bothering me for a while. I needed to act upon it before I lost my nerve.

He nodded, accepting my rejection with the utmost respect. "I understand. Is it okay if I take your number? I'd love to do this again sometime, if you'd be happy to arrange it?"

I grabbed his coffee receipt, and a pen out of my bag, and scrawled my digits down on the back.

"Old fashioned. I like it," he chirped.

"Bye Ted," I smirked, looking up at him again, as he gathered his belongings from around the table.

"At least let me walk you to wherever you need to go? I know it's only half four but it's getting quite dim outside, now it's September and Winter Equinox is on the horizon. Apparently, a few of the streetlights on Charles Street are dodgy—"

I cut him off before he could continue.

"I'm fine, honestly. I need to do a bit of thinking before I get to my destination, clear my head a little."

"Okay," he said, the slight disappointment apparent in his golden eyes. "I'll be in touch."

"Catch you later!" I sang, flashing a friendly smile, before quickly heading out of the door, conscious of the time. Ted's eagerness had somewhat taken me aback. I felt like I was living in a story I'd read, or on one of the planets I'd dreamt of when I was a kid. A guy was interested in me, I think. He was showing it. Usually guys mumble something incoherent, about wanting to ask you out. I wasn't used to this kind of clear affection, or forwardness. It didn't feel pushy though, it wasn't unwanted. It just felt right. Not wanting to give too much away, I didn't turn back to look at him as I left. It was only when I was outside, I glanced at him through the window. He had sat back down, smiling to himself, his gaze telling me he was happy with our meeting and the fact he'd bagged my number. Here's to hoping I wasn't wrong.

————

"You want to switch degrees?" the woman behind the desk questioned as she peered up at me. "The new academic year starts tomorrow. Don't you think it's a little late in the day? Bearing in mind I am meant to be going home in fifteen minutes?" She fired the questions at me with some agitation.

"I'm really sorry. I know it's late. I was told by a friend it wouldn't take long. He actually said that the process is as smooth as silk!" I giggled, thoughts of Ted entering my brain.

The laughs were not reciprocated. "What is your current area of study?"

"Psychology. BSc. I want to switch to English and Creative Writing. BA."

"Quite the change," she commented.

"Not for me. It's what I've always dreamt of doing," I clarified, but she didn't seem to care.

"Luckily for you, this looks like it will actually be rather straightforward. I can begin the process on my computer now, but you will need to speak to the head of your new department first. He has authority and I cannot give you approval until he has. His office is just down the hall. He will talk to you about the decision and advise on where on the course you can begin. That's if he likes you, of course," the lady said, smiling this time.

"Fabulous," I said, almost bursting with excitement. It felt surreal that I was finally doing this. I headed over to the head of the department's office, with a spring in my step all the way. When I finally figured out which door he was behind, I knocked, and patiently waited to be called in.

"Macey Banks?" he queried.

"That's me!" I answered enthusiastically.

"Donna from Admissions just called to inform me that she is currently processing your request to join my discipline. Cutting it fine, aren't you?"

I nodded, before going on to explain that I don't usually display such haphazard traits.

"The best writers are all a little unhinged," he said, stacking up the papers on his desk. "I just glanced over your personal statement from when you applied to do Psychology. Reading it felt like you were applying for an English degree. I can see that you're passionate about English, and you must be if you are switching degrees the evening before a new term. I'm assuming you have experience already, am I right?"

"Yep. I am actually a published poet, as well as a creative writer in my spare time," I explained. "I have written several manuscripts that hopefully I'll get to publish one day."

"I trust that Macey. Your commitment to this decision, albeit a little rushed, obviously demonstrates that you have thought this through. I would be delighted to have you join us. I have authorised the transition and allowed you to join the English and Creative Writing BA in the second year, meaning you won't be behind at all. I can see that you're ready. I believe you're more than capable. Do you think that you're ready?"

"I do!" I blurted out, before grabbing the signed papers and thanking him for his help, as well as his belief in me.

"See you tomorrow, Macey. Nine o'clock sharp. I am giving your first lecture," he added as I left.

Papers in hand and his words ringing in my ears, I dashed back to the admissions department, and flung said papers down onto Donna's desk, just as she was getting up to leave.

"I'm sorry!" I cried out again. "It's all done now!" I added, the desperation in my voice. "I just need you to tick the authorisation box on the digital form. He did everything else."

"I've already done it," Donna said pointedly. "I could hear your joy from down the way. I didn't think you'd be that happy if he'd have said no. It's sorted. I'm going home now."

"Thank you!" I gushed. All I had to do now was tell my parents. I think their enthusiasm may just mimic Donna's. Just as I was leaving uni, my phone pinged with a text. It was an unknown number, and it read:

> **The most important decision we have to make in life is how to make ourselves the happiest. Hope that head of yours cleared up and you did what you needed to do. Ted**

> **A quick internet search brought back no results for that quote. Who said it? Courses have been switched. Macey (English and Creative Writing, BA)**

> **Macey, do you not trust that I conjure up these lines myself? Because I do! Give me some credit! LOL! Glad to hear, it's a good job I distracted you from buying textbooks for a course you are no longer studying. It must have been fate. Well done M. Ted x**

CHAPTER 4 - ISLA

Wednesday flew by, I had a whole day at home to myself to just focus on writing. I loved days like those. No calls, no meetings, no pressing errands. Just home all day writing. I went through endless cups of coffee throughout the day, then switched to herbal tea in the late afternoon. I was still struggling with my current book.

Thursday went much the same, then on Friday, Beth came over to work. When I first moved into this house, a few people asked why a single woman needed a four bedroom house, but when you're self-employed and work from home, space is a necessity. Downstairs is the living room, kitchen and dining room, and an office space. The house had previously been used as a bed and breakfast so that had been the reception office. It had tons of storage space so it worked as a common office and conference room for Beth to come work and for us to have space to talk. My private office, guest room, and main bedroom are upstairs. All in all, it's the perfect home for a writer. The views from my office upstairs were gorgeous too and provided plenty of inspiration.

I was still working upstairs when I heard Beth let herself in through the kitchen. I grabbed my now empty coffee mug and jogged down the stairs to greet her.

"Hiya Beth!" I said cheerily. After a few days working at home, I was happy for some company.

"Hi, how are you today? Making progress?"

"Some, at least on the current chapter."

I made us both some coffee and then followed her into the office. We had some business to go over before I could go back upstairs and get back to writing.

Beth took me through everything in her usual no nonsense manner. To look at her, you wouldn't think she'd be so businesslike and focused. She's a few years younger than me, only 36, and a classic English rose, petite with creamy pale skin, blonde bouncing curls that come to just below her shoulders, and always positive and smiling. Until it's time to get to business, then that smile gets set in a firm line, her shoulders thrown back and she directs her laser focus on whatever problem she's tackling. It's a little intimidating to watch, until you get to know her. But heaven help anyone who tries to dismiss her as just a pretty blonde. She's brilliant with my readers at events but she can hold her own with my agent or any of my business contacts if they try to take advantage of me or monopolise my time. Honestly, it helped having an assistant who liked your work. She always prioritised writing time in my schedule, because she always wanted to read my next book!

We worked for almost two hours, going over plans for the next few weeks, my schedule, people who wanted time with me, either for book club meetings like the other day or for interviews or potential collaborations. We're also looking for a new printing company to produce and distribute the small collection of products I sold through my website, cute mugs and t-shirts related to my books. Because royalties alone don't make you a financially independent author. If people only knew the various income streams it takes to be successful in this business.

Eventually, I left Beth to her work downstairs, and I went back up to my private office to write. I'm struggling again, so I took a

notebook from my desk and went to sit in the cosy reading nook
I've set up in the corner of my office. A plush, deep wingback arm
chair, with a matching footstool and a throw blanket to wrap
around me if it's cold. Plus a side table for my coffee and a view out
the window to the hillside just beyond my row of houses. I spent
the rest of the afternoon freewriting in the notebook. I don't know if
I've solved the problem, but Monday I'll type up my notes and see
if I can make something of it.

———

THE NEXT DAY was Saturday and I woke up late, I needed a lie in so
badly. I had a text from Georgie, confirming that we were
picnicking in the park near my house, so I packed up a small bag of
food and a blanket and headed out to the spot the group had
decided on. I got there a little while after the rest had arrived. It
was a small group, Georgie and her husband Grant, Ingrid and her
wife Chelsea, then there was Lin, Anirudh, and Will. Grant works
with Ingrid and Anirudh, so they often were included in social
events like this, along with Chelsea and if Anirudh was dating
someone they would join too, but he was currently single. Georgie
and I had gone to school together, way back when, and by the time
uni rolled around we were more like sisters, so even when I left
Bath for several years, we stayed close. She's an estate agent and
property developer, so she was more than happy to help me find a
place to purchase once I was ready. Grant runs a start up, Ingrid
and Anirudh are his partners. Chelsea works in event planning,
and Lin went to uni with Georgie and is a lecturer at the university,
teaching literature.

Will was Grant's best friend from uni, and there was a really
awkward attempt to set us up when I first moved back. He's
divorced and has a ten year old son who he has for half the week.
Georgie loved the idea of me falling in love with her husband's best
friend, she thought it would be like something out of one of my
novels. But real life isn't fiction, and halfway through our first date

we both had to admit that it wasn't going to work out, we're far too different. Will is a great guy, and has turned into a good friend, and that's where it ends. He's not dating anyone seriously but always seems to have a date planned each weekend. Lin was a single girl, like me, and she and I bonded immediately over our mutual focus on our careers. Georgie and I think Anirudh has a crush on Lin, but he has yet to make a move.

"Isla, you made it!" Georgie cried out. She got up and rushed over to me to give me a hug. Grant was close behind, with a hug for me as well. I exchanged greetings with everyone else as I spread out my blanket, connecting it with the patchwork of blankets everyone else was sitting on, and unpacked my food and drink. Chelsea and Ingrid's two little girls were running around beyond us in the meadow with Will's son. We all were honorary aunties and uncles to the kids and they often came along to these sorts of daytime outings.

As usual, Georgie and Grant brought plenty of nibbly bits and champers for us to share, the rest of us brought our own sandwiches and a few other things we wanted. From where we sat you could see the skyline of Bath, which hadn't really changed much since the days of Jane Austen. This was one of my favorite places to go for a walk when I needed to clear my head. But it was also a favourite picnic spot for our group.

Georgie came to sit by me for a little while, bringing the champagne to fill up a glass for me. Georgie and I were very similar in some ways and polar opposites in others. She was blonde to my dark auburn, stylish and trendy while I was traditional and classic. She had legs for days, while I was an average height, bordering on the shorter side of things. She loved anything designer and I was happy with a deal at Primark. Her picnic hamper was from Fortnum & Mason and would make for a lovely Instagram pic, while I was content with an old rucksack that had some leather cords to tie my picnic blanket on. She was bubbly and outgoing, I was shy and introverted, happy to sit back and observe a get together like this, while she was born to be the center of attention.

You would think our differences would have led us to outgrow our friendship but instead our differences complemented each other. I helped ground her and brought out the quiet, thoughtful side of her personality. She brought me out of my shell and helped me shop when I needed a smart wardrobe for all my author appearances. I never thought of her as vain and superficial and she never saw me as boring and stuffy, things that others have often thought about each of us.

And more importantly, after years apart, keeping in contact first by email and phone then eventually social media and video calls, she welcomed me back to Bath with open arms when I came crawling home, whimpering and tail tucked firmly between my legs. Those were dark days and Georgie was by my side through it all. In fact, it had been Georgie who showed up at my flat in London with Grant to help me load up my few possessions and drive me back to Bath. Everyone needed a Georgie in their life.

The day was gorgeous, a truly beautiful late summer day with high puffy white clouds like cotton balls in a crystal blue sky. The meadow was a vibrant green and sparkled in the sunlight. We all talked and laughed for hours. Grant, Ingrid, and Anirudh caught us up on how the business was going. Lin filled us in on her visit to her parents in Beijing and moaned about the new school year being about to start and feeling buried under all of her lesson planning and prep. I sympathised because it was similar to all the work that went into publishing a new book, so I felt her pain. I filled them in on my writing and Will chatted about his work at the bank, he always had good stories about the customers. Georgie told stories about some of the recent viewings she's been on and told us about some of the amazing properties around town she'd been looking at.

"I found this great two bed, one bath flat in an old Georgian building not far from the Royal Crescent Isla, I think you'd love it!" She said enthusiastically. "Just under four hundred grand, it's a steal! Needs a little bit of work but not much."

I laughed, "I already have a house Georgie, remember? You helped me buy it?"

Everyone else laughed, Georgie included.

"Yes, but this could be an investment property. The location is perfect, you could rent it out to pay the mortgage, either as a vacation rental or a regular lease. In a few years or so you could sell it for almost double what it's going for now, especially if we do it up nicely."

"We?" I asked, raising an eyebrow.

"Careful Isla," Grant said with a laugh. "I think Georgie's fixing for a new project."

It was a common debate we had. Georgie was always falling in love with properties. She already had a few she'd purchased, renovated, and resold as investments, and a couple she rented out. She did know what she was talking about. But the last several months she'd been on me about investing in something myself. She argued that she would do all the work of renovating and renting, but I would be the main investor. Basically, I'd be the money and she'd do the work. It wasn't a bad idea, but I wasn't totally sold yet.

"Send me the information, I'll think about it," I said diplomatically. I've looked at a few properties she'd sent, and none had stuck yet. But none had been near the Royal Crescent and that was a good location. Georgie was enthusiastic about property but she was also very smart and deliberate. She was 40 like me and already a successful estate agent and property developer.

The rest of the picnic went well, we ate and joked around and laid on our backs pointing out shapes in the clouds. Every so often we'd get up and form new groups of conversation partners on the blankets. A perfect Saturday picnic indeed.

———

THE NEXT DAY I got on my bicycle and rode over towards the University of Bath, where my parents lived, for a Sunday roast. I didn't have a car, so one of the selling points of my house was that it was an easy walk to the city centre and a short bike ride to my parents. The house where they live is the one I grew up in. It's an old Georgian stone building and I loved living there. When I had to come back to Bath several years ago, after my life in London disintegrated, it was comforting to come back here and my parents were amazing. I still see them every week, either for lunch or dinner one day on the weekend and sometimes I'll meet Mum in town for tea during the week if she has meetings in town.

Dad is a professor at the uni, he teaches history and researches the Roman times in Bath. I've literally lost count of how many times he took me to the Roman baths in town and lectured me on the history. But he's brilliant, he knows so much about so many different things and always had a way of bringing history to life for me when I was little. Mum loves history too, and she knows all about the Georgian era in Bath since she's a huge Jane Austen fan. She studied history too, they met at uni in Cambridge, but she works for a historical nonprofit, applying her historical knowledge to the business side of preservation and educational outreach. It was because of her that I got into reading novels at a young age, starting with Jane Austen and Charlotte Brontë and eventually moving on to Daphne de Maurier and Baroness Orczy. There was also a lot of Dickens mixed in. My parents were big on the classics.

I arrived at my parent's house and parked my bike against the wall by the front door. I let myself in and immediately smelled the roast cooking and the Yorkshire puddings in the oven. The scent of the food was incredible.

"Hello sweetheart," Mum said as I walked into the kitchen.

I went over and gave her a kiss, "Hi Mum. Smells fantastic in here!"

"It will be ready soon, can you go lay the table and then find your dad? I think he's gone back to his study."

I nod and quickly went to set the table in the dining room off the kitchen. Through the windows I could see the cows in the field behind their house. I loved living so close to open land and having neighbouring farm fields that I could wander around as a kid. I was always running off into the wooded areas and playing around the streams that ran through them.

Smiling at the memory I went through to the back end of the house, a little bit that was added on in Victorian times that Dad had taken over as his library and office. I was always amazed at his book collection. He had even more in his office at the uni. But as a child I felt like I'd wandered into a fairytale library whenever I came in here.

He was working at his desk when I knocked quietly at the door. "Hey Dad," I said softly.

Dad had that usual far off look in his face. Mum and Beth say I both get the same look when I'm writing or reading. Like I'm there, but not really. That's how Dad was now. His head moved as if to look up at me but his eyes stayed on the page he was studying, half in the room with me and half in whatever world he was reading about. After a few seconds, his eyes finally broke from the page and looked up at me.

"Oh, Isla dear, I thought you were your mum. When did you get here?" Dad asked with a smile.

I moved to sit in the arm chair across from his desk. It had been my favourite place as a kid, and even now I still sometimes come in here with a notebook or my laptop and worked or wrote while he was working or reading. "I just got here a few minutes ago. I've just set the table and Mum sent me to find you. Food is almost ready. What are you working on?" I asked with interest.

"Just some scans of primary sources I'm researching for a new journal article I'm working on. Might also test it out first as a conference paper. Pre-Georgian attitudes towards healing baths."

"Sounds fascinating," I said pleasantly. I don't totally love Dad's research, but I loved how excited he could get about really specific aspects of it.

"I think so," he agreed amiably. "But that's enough for today, we mustn't keep your mum waiting."

Dinner was a quiet but cosy affair. They asked me about my writing and how things were going on the next book, as well as how sales were going for *Bold and Bright*. They are so supportive, it makes my heart melt sometimes. I asked them about work. Dad was getting ready for the new academic year to start and getting his classes prepped for the new term. Mum was working on a fundraising gala, so I offered to donate a complete autographed set of my collected works and agreed to offer afternoon tea with me as silent auction items. It baffled me that anyone would want to pay money to go out to tea with me, but over the last several years that my books have really taken off, I've become something of a home-town celebrity. Even if they don't recognise my face, everyone knows about "that writer, Isla Stewart," so I often got asked to help out with different charities. I'm happy to help, even if it confuses me why I'm all that helpful.

After dinner we had tea and a honey cake Mum had made and continued talking about random things. It's nice to just sit with them and have time together. The older I get the more conscious I am of time moving and them getting older. They were now in their early 70s. Both should be retired but they liked working and their jobs weren't that physically demanding, so it seemed like a good thing to help them stay active, even though they didn't need to work anymore.

Eventually I said goodnight and got on my bike to cycle home, promising to meet up with Mum during the week.

———

THE REST of the week went smoothly. Mum and I met for tea at the Pump Room after she had a meeting there for the fundraiser. It's always a treat to do afternoon tea there, the atmosphere was so lovely. I had a couple days working at home on my own and a couple days where Beth came over to work as well.

On Friday, I wrote at home in the morning and then I had to nip to a local independent bookstore I had recently done an event at. They'd gotten a new shipment of a bunch of my latest book and they needed my autograph in them for a contest they were running on their social media accounts. Afterwards I would be meeting with a reporter from a local magazine for dinner and a casual interview about the latest book. Sally had interviewed me many times before so I was looking forward to it.

I got to the bookstore and enjoyed the sudden hush of quiet as I closed the door behind me. I found the store manager and we chatted for a few minutes while she walked me to her office in the back where they'd set up my books, alongside a pile of marker pens for me to use. The next couple hours went by quickly as I posed for some pictures for the store's social media and chatted with the employees who were helping open the book covers to the right page and stack the signed books. We had a good time and I took some selfies with the employees when it was done.

After I finished signing, I still had some time to kill so I decided to have a wander through the shop. I headed up to the Fiction & Literature section and moved aimlessly up and down the rows of shelves. I turned down the next row and stopped suddenly when I saw a man at the other end of the row. I recognised him immediately, even though it felt like a lifetime since I last saw him in person.

He must have sensed my presence because he looked up from the book he was looking at and turned to look at me. Recognition lit up his face as he began to smile. He walked towards me and stopped just a few feet away. I could feel his closeness and had to look up to look into his eyes. He was taller than I remembered, well over 6-foot. At 5-foot-5-inches myself, I wasn't particularly short, but he seemed almost a foot taller than me. I could smell his cologne, notes of sandalwood with something spicy. His thick hair was still a dark espresso brown, but now had slight bits of grey coming in at his temples, and his eyes were a piercing blue that seemed to be staring straight into my soul.

"Isla Stewart, you haven't changed a bit," he said smoothly, his voice was like velvet.

I smiled and could feel myself blushing. "Don't lie Henry Russell. You haven't seen me since I was sixteen. I know I've picked up at least a few wrinkles since then."

He closed the gap between us and leaned in for a hug and

kissed my cheek. "Maybe, but I would recognise you anywhere. You look good Isla."

"Thanks Henry," I replied, I was definitely blushing now. "You look good too. Must be all that California sunshine."

He laughed, "San Francisco isn't as sunny as LA, but yeah, it was pretty nice. For a time."

"But now you're back," I said, suddenly feeling a little shy.

"Now I'm back. And so are you. When Mum told me you were neighbours now I couldn't believe it."

"Yeah, it was a pleasant surprise. She's amazing. It's been so nice getting to know her better," I replied. I had known her a little bit when we were teens but she was always "Henry's mum". My friendship with her had really taken off when we became neighbours.

"So how are you? How's the writing going? Mum loves your books. I tried keeping up when I found out you were a writer now but work was crazy and I never had time to read for fun. I read your first book though, and loved it."

Henry sounded so sincere and enthusiastic, just as he'd been in school, and I was reminded of why I enjoyed being friends with him. He was the most genuine person I've ever met.

"I'm doing well, the writing is going great. I have a lot of fun with it," I replied with a smile.

"We really need a proper catch up. Are you free now? We could have dinner?"

"I wish I could!" I said regretfully. "I'm actually on my way to a dinner meeting, I was just wandering the bookstore to kill time, but I need to be there in about twenty minutes."

"Can I walk you there?" he asked hopefully.

"That would be nice," I replied, feeling my heart beat a little faster. I wasn't in a rush to say goodbye to him.

We walked downstairs and I waited while he paid for his books. I noticed one of my books was in the stack.

As we walked out of the bookstore I said, laughing, "You know, if you wanted a copy of my book I could have given you one. I've got loads at my house."

"Yeah, but then you wouldn't get the royalty," Henry said winking.

"Good point," I laughed. "Thanks for the one pound, forty-three pence."

"Forty-three? That's oddly specific. And less than two quid per book? Is that all you make?"

I laughed again, "Well, when you sell as many books as I do, it adds up pretty quick."

"I suppose so, but still, that's what, ten percent?"

"Yep, I get a higher percentage on my more recent books, I renegotiated my contract about five books ago."

"Good for you. I had no idea that's what authors make."

"Well, everyone's different. It also depends on the format, like paperback, eBook, audiobook, as well as how many copies have sold so far. I get a higher royalty on some books because I've sold so many. But the big money is more in the licensing and film rights," I said simply.

"Have you had any of your books made into films?!" Henry asked excitedly.

"Not yet, I had one of them optioned a couple years ago, but the film industry moves slowly. They'll buy stuff up and then not produce them for ages. So we'll see."

"Well, I think you should make more," Henry said laughing.

"No, it's alright," I laughed. "It's actually standard. And my publishers deserve their cut. I wouldn't have a career without them. Although, they wouldn't be what they are without me, so it kind of balances out in the end. They have more salaries to pay so it makes sense they keep more."

"Now that sounds like a longer story," Henry said with interest.

We rounded the corner and I could see the restaurant where I was meeting Sally in the distance.

"Not really, just my publishers were really small, only a few dozen authors when they offered me my first book deal. Then it took off and so did the next one and the next one. Now they're a bigger player in the publishing world and have a number of massive authors on their roster. They took a chance on a small first time author and I took a chance on what was then a small indie publisher. It worked out for both of us."

"Wow, that sounds amazing."

"I'm very lucky," I said with a smile. "So did you buy my book for yourself or someone else?" I asked curiously.

"It's for a coworker, it's her birthday coming up and she mentioned she's a fan of your books and didn't have this one."

"Well, tell her thank you for reading my books!" I said happily.

Henry looked at me a bit sheepishly, "I don't suppose...I mean, I wouldn't want to be presumptuous."

"Would you like me to sign it for her?" I asked pleasantly. It was charming that he seemed nervous to ask.

His eyes brightened, "If you wouldn't mind? I know she'd be beside herself. It's my finance manager in the office, she's a bit terrifying, if I'm honest. Wickedly smart and great at her job but I feel like I'm in school again trying to impress the headmaster. A signed copy would definitely put me in her good books." He laughed as he pulled the book out of the carrier bag.

"Aren't you the boss?"

"Don't tell her," he laughed.

I fished a pen out of my handbag, I always carry some for this purpose, you never know when you're going to run into someone and signing copies is such an easy way to make someone's day. I took the book from his hand and flipped open to the title page. He told me her name and I wrote it with a small message and signed my name and then waited a few moments for the ink to dry before handing it back to Henry.

"There, all set. Tell her thank you and I hope she enjoys it," I told him with a smile.

"You really are the best Isla," he smiled back.

We walked a little further in companionable silence until I

stopped in front of the little Italian restaurant. I could see Sally already sitting inside.

"Well this is me," I told Henry, suddenly wishing the walk to the restaurant had taken longer or that I didn't have to meet with Sally, but she had just waved at me through the window, so it would be rude to cancel now.

"Can I see you again? Soon?" Henry asked. He looked so hopeful, I nearly melted right into the pavement.

"Yeah, that would be great," I replied quickly. "I mean, you know where I live," I said with a grin. "I'm home most weekends, so next time you visit your mum just let me know."

"I'm having dinner at her place this weekend, Sunday I think. I'll check with her, but I'm sure she'd love to have you."

"Sounds perfect."

He leaned down and gave me a kiss on the cheek and squeezed my arm gently.

"See you soon Isla." He turned and began walking away, hands shoved deep in his pockets. I watched him leave but wished he could stay. The old butterflies in my stomach had awakened after years of sleeping. Henry Russell had just walked back into my life and I didn't know what to do. Suddenly I felt like everything was changing.

CHAPTER 5 - MACEY

Plymouth at dusk was always so pretty. The pastel shades that filled the sky, the gorgeous colours that already looked filtered by the naked eye. As the sunset crept in over the horizon, the sea front was so peaceful as I strolled over to an empty bench, to sit with my thoughts for a while longer. I looked over at Smeaton's Tower just along the coast and spotted a couple of gulls circling it. I could hear other birds singing their evening praise, as I sat and felt the cool evening air embrace me. As it did, I felt stress lift, almost as if the wind was carrying the weight on my shoulders away. I no longer had to panic about the future, as I had just begun to pave the route I knew I was always meant to take. It was comforting, whilst also being exhilarating. Like a different kind of roller coaster, as thrilling as they are, I was locked in safe. I wasn't going to fall. I was right on track.

By the time I got home, it was six o'clock. Along with my rest stop, I had walked the long way home, giving myself time to process everything that had happened. I was also subsequently planning how I was going to tell my parents; which I still hadn't figured out by the time I was standing on my doorstep. I unlocked the front door, to be greeted with Charlotte, who could tell that something was kind of off. I was still ecstatic of course, yet, the thought of having to have the conversation with Mum and Dad was slowly draining the happiness out of me. It's the fact I know they'll be displeased that I didn't consult them first and I know they'll give me a very long lecture on why psychology is the most sensible path to take. I can already hear the line "*Mental health problems in society are only becoming more apparent Macey. There's always going to be a need for psychologists.*" It's been said before, and I was as sure as anything that it'd be said again.

"I have a lot to update you all on," I proclaimed to Charlotte as I kicked my trainers off. "Like a lot," I added, to really get my point across. "But first, I need to make a call."

"Okay?" she responded, looking concerned. "Dinner's at seven. Libby's making lentil Spag Bol again. You can tell us then."

"Again? What is it with her and that lentil Spag Bol?" I said, managing a laugh.

"Who knows, just eat it and smile," Charlotte replied, laughing too.

———

"Is Mum there?" I asked, as Dad picked up his phone. I was sat, crossed legged, on my bed. My phone was on speaker phone, about an arm's length away. For some reason, the distance was reassuring. This way, they couldn't scream directly into my ear.

"She's just gotten out of the shower, I think. Why Macey? What's wrong?"

"I need to speak to the both of you. Urgently."

"Let me grab her."

The next two minutes whilst Dad went on his quest to locate Mum felt like the longest two minutes of my life. I glanced around my room, suddenly feeling five again.

I flashbacked to a time when I could hear my parents arguing, which wasn't an uncommon occurrence to be honest. This one occasion, I was sitting in my bedroom, in the house in Glossop. We've lived there since I was two. They were shouting so loud, and I remember feeling so scared to go and speak to them. I really wanted some supper but didn't want to ask in case it made them angrier. When I finally plucked up the courage to do so, Dad scooped me up in his arms and took me downstairs for some porridge. Sat at the breakfast bar, he looked at me, matching my eye line and grabbing my hands. "Don't you ever be scared to talk to me, Macey," he said, after I had explained how I had felt. "I will always listen and help in whatever way I can. Even if it's just a bowl of porridge you need." Remembering those comforting words, I felt more at ease.

"You're switching courses?!" Mum screeched after I had explained to her the events of the day.

"No. I have already switched courses," I emphasised. "I decided that enough was enough. I wasn't happy doing Psychology and it had taken me until today to take the leap. I had been thinking about it for a while. All summer in fact."

"You were thinking about it all summer, and you said nothing?" Dad contributed. I could hear Mum ranting in the background.

"I'm sorry. I know I should have said something sooner. But you know what, I am actually tired of apologising to everyone. I made this decision for my own happiness and wellbeing. I truly hope you can support that."

"Macey. You know we will support you know matter what. But it's really important that you are honest and open with us. Tell us when you're feeling doubtful. Remember how we said no secrets? Talk to us and we can then figure something out, together," Dad said, calmly, and rationally, almost as if he had seen this coming.

Mum interjected, sneering, "Speak for yourself! Macey Genevieve. I am so disappointed. We have done nothing but aid you in your journey to becoming a Psychologist. Encouraging you through your GCSEs and A-Levels, arranging appropriate work experience with our colleagues, helping to fund your education. All because you said that this is what you wanted. And now, you want to throw it all away to write some stories that will probably never go anywhere. You'll make no money and live a sad life Macey."

"Expectation is the root of all heartache. What you may be failing to realise, though I am sure you do, maybe deep down or to a certain extent, is that your high expectations of me caused this. You aiding my journey only caused feelings of guilt within me. Yes, I've had an interest in Psychology from a young age, but that's because I knew of nothing else! That's all I had been told. I was led to believe that it was the only career I could ever undertake. Do you realise how much stress I was under, every time I had to take an exam? I was petrified I would fail and therefore fail you and fail the choices you had made for me. I never wanted it. You wanted it for me. I have wanted to be a writer for years Mum. You know that. Dad does too. It was just suppressed under the weight of theories and practises and methods and cases. This is me finally doing what I want to do. I will write some stories, or maybe some poems, or maybe I'll be a copywriter, or a publicist, or a journalist, or a teacher. I still have options that don't include writing stories or a sad life. I know that by following my dream, I'll be happy." I took a breath. "And I hope that by me being happy, you'll be happy too."

"Macey—" Dad started, taking a heavy breath of his own.

"Don't bother Simon, she won't listen to us. We know what is best and she has completely disregarded that, and in turn, disrespected us. You know we love you, no matter what, but this is ridiculous. What you're saying, is ridiculous."

I could almost see her scowling at the telephone. I was glad we weren't on a video call.

"No, actually, I disagree Valerie. I agree with Macey. If she's truly unhappy, then why wouldn't we want her to do what makes her the happiest? We, more than anyone, should understand the impacts of this on her mental health. It must have been draining for you Macey. I am sorry that you felt like you couldn't address this sooner. Of course, I would have loved for you to follow in my, our footsteps. But if that won't be the case, that's okay too."

I could hear some shuffling in the background of their call.

"Your Mother just got up and left. I think she just needs some time. Let her have it. I will continue to support you no matter what, my strawberry lace."

He only calls me that on rare occasions, usually when he's trying to get on my good side. He says it stemmed from me having auburn hair, and his love for sweets. Oh, and plus the fact my name is Macey, as it rhymes. I remember the day when he called it me for the first time, and I thought it was hilarious that my pet name wasn't of the regular kind. It was never honey, or blossom in a birthday card, it was strawberry lace. Of course Mum hated it, but it was mine and Dad's thing.

I sighed, "I just wish she got it Dad."

"I'll talk to her. She'll come around. For now though, just be reassured that you did make the right decision, regardless of how your mum reacted. Try and talk to her again in a few days. And don't go in all guns blazing. You know that rarely works with her."

"Thanks Dad." I replied, somewhat surprised at his pleasant reaction and offer to mediate. "I really appreciate it."

I hung up and sank further into my bedsheets than I already was. I knew telling my parents was going to be rough, and although I was surprised that my dad reacted as positively as he did, I wasn't surprised that my mum was so upset. I held out hope that she would be a little more supportive, but I couldn't have expected anything less from the woman who lives and breathes her career, and apparently her daughter's future one too.

"How was it?" Charlotte asked as I arrived in the kitchen.

"How was what?" Ruby chimed in, Libby too distracted with the Italian feast she was preparing. I could see the concentration on her face from the other side of the room. She murmured something to do with the pasta not being al dente yet.

"She had to make a call," Charlotte explained to Ruby. Turning to me, Charlotte asked, "Who did you call?"

"My parents. I switched degrees earlier. I am now doing English and Creative Writing and they've allowed me to start on Year 2," I announced.

"That's amazing!" All the girls said in chorus, even Libby as she was tasting the red sauce.

"More wine," she added.

The girls laughed.

"More wine, always," I agreed with a wink, reaching for the bottle of Rosé in the fridge, and the four glasses on the side. "My parents weren't happy though. Well, Dad was okay, but Mum was livid."

"Don't let that ruin your high. You made the right choice Macey," Libby said to comfort me.

"I know. Everyone keeps telling me that, which is nice," I replied.

"You mentioned that you had a lot to tell us. Was there something else?" Charlotte exclaimed as we sat down to dinner. I poured all the girls their wine as I considered how to answer the question.

"Umm. Yes. I met a boy," I responded nervously.

"Like a BOY, boy?!" Charlotte squealed with excitement.

Ruby and Libby rolled their eyes at her.

"She hasn't even said yet Charlotte. She might just be referring to that neighbour that keeps asking us round for drinks," Ruby shrugged.

"No," I stuttered. "I did go on a date," I said, giggling.

Charlotte's face lit up. "See!" she shouted. "Oh my gosh!!! Tell us everything! Who? What? Where? When?" she added, unable to contain herself.

I've concluded over the past week that Charlotte is a self-proclaimed romantic, like me in a lot of ways. Whilst Ruby doesn't care much for romance and is much more invested in her art. Libby and Anna have been together for over a year now, so I guess Charlotte, with her being single (and looking) is the only one who would freak out at this news.

"His name is Ted," I confirmed. "I met him in Waterstones earlier, of all places."

Charlotte's face began to gleam with anticipation.

"We went for a coffee afterwards and chatted for over three hours. He is about to start his Masters in Creative Writing. It was all a bit crazy and out of nowhere to be honest. Like something out of a movie!"

"Ted Leakes?" Ruby eventually interjected, a puzzled look on her face.

"I don't know his surname. But it was so lovely. He was so lovely. I gave him my number afterwards and he messaged me just as I switched courses. I told him that I'd done it, thanks to his encouragement, and he said well done. It was really sweet."

Ruby continued to stare at me, baffled. "Ted Leakes," she said slowly, her jaw dropping as she did. "The most eligible, and sought after, bachelor in the whole of Plymouth Uni. You're really out here securing the goods Macey." She burst out laughing, "Proud of you, sis."

Charlotte glared at her. "What are you saying Ruby? That it's a surprise that Macey pulled a hot dude?"

"Of course not. I'm saying it's a surprise that Ted Leakes took a girl on a date. I've heard a lot about him through Issac. Apparently, he is very low-key with all that kind of stuff, persistent that he isn't looking for anyone or anything, after turning down all the girls on his course. Ted must be really interested in you Macey," Ruby explained.

Issac is Ruby's "thing". They aren't official, as she is "focusing" on her art. But they may as well be. I just think she's afraid of commitment, and wants to be single, even if she likes someone. Which she does by the way, she's obsessed with Issac, but she'll never admit that.

"Are you going to text him again?" Libby asked.

"I'm not sure. I guess I'll just wait to see if I hear anything from him?"

"Good idea. Treat 'em mean, keep 'em keen!" Charlotte hollered.

I shook my head. I didn't agree with that whole premise. I just wanted to give it some time, to make sure it wasn't a one off thing, and that he was still interested in me. Who knows, maybe he was just bored and wanted some company for the day? I felt as if the date went well, but I have misjudged similar interactions before. He was dreamy, but I didn't want to get too caught up in any feelings I may have developed over the last five hours. After all, that was all it had been. It was too soon to make any moves. I needed to wait it out, just a bit longer. I explained all of this to the girls, whilst we finished off the Spag Bol.

"Delicious again Libby. You're really mastering that recipe!" I told her, as I got up to clear the dishes away.

"Thanks. You're not getting sick of it yet? I think it needs a few more tweaks before it's perfect."

"Not at all," I smiled. I could sense Charlotte glaring at me from behind. I spun around to face her and gave her a wink.

"Why don't you cook the next meal Macey? Give Libby a break and show us what you've got?" Charlotte insisted.

"Of course. I'll head to the shops tomorrow and whip something up after my lecture."

"Sounds like a plan!" Libby responded, whilst the other girls nodded in unison.

After the kitchen was tidied, I headed upstairs to relax and took some time to mull over the events from today. I switched courses and met a guy. The latter I could not stop thinking about, especially after Ruby's confession. I felt like Ted and I did get on really well, but if he isn't the "dating type", I do not want to go there. I have spent far too much time in my relatively short life stuck in a relationship that I shouldn't have got myself stuck in. I was with Owen, my one serious boyfriend, throughout school, up until the summer before I went to uni.

After a lot of intense therapy, I finally came to the realisation that it wasn't what I wanted. All of the back and forth with him, all of the ups and downs, it wasn't making me happy. I had gotten far too comfortable with someone who just didn't love me the way I loved him. Effort is a two-way street and I gave my all, to which he didn't. He knew I was comfortable and used that to his advantage, not treating me well because he thought I'd never leave him. I mistook him staying with me as love, as I thought he must love me after being with me for so long. I think he was just comfortable too, though I believe I naively mistook, or purposely claimed, my "comfortability" as being scared. I was scared of leaving as I thought no one else would want me.

I wasn't self-confident back then and I had so little self-worth. Him ending it, was in fact the best thing he could have ever done for me. That summer was a major time of self-development for me. As well as all of the therapy, and promising my parents that I wouldn't hide anything from them anymore—they hadn't known the extent of what Owen had put me through—I met a different guy.

He was a summer temp at the farm shop I was working at during my gap year. It was at the beginning of August that year, about two months after Owen and I's breakup, and though things didn't work out between me and him, he taught me so much about myself, and what I want in my next relationship. I became confident because I realised I was capable, and worthy, of another person's admiration.

I have become so cut-throat when it comes to what I want in my life now, and if something isn't bringing me joy anymore, I eradicate it. Marie Kondo style. I applied the same logic to my degree, mulling it over in the summer just gone. I had started to realise that I had to do things for me, even if I still procrastinated those things until the day before term began. I have the good ideas; it just takes a lot for me to follow through. I think it's the mixture of stubbornness and laziness. Typical Taurus things.

Today with Ted might have seemed as if it came straight out of an Isla Stewart romance novel, but I must not wear rose tinted glasses this time. As romantic as I am, I need to stay level-headed.

It was one date, with one guy. The guy happened to be very similar to me, and very endearing. And extremely likeable and courteous, but I must not be blind-sighted. I won't. Honestly, I won't. I am making that promise to myself, whether Ted decides to text me again or not. I'm telling the universe that the ball is in Ted's court now, and if whichever higher power wants me to message him, they are going to have to give me some sort of sign.

CHAPTER 6 - ISLA

My interview with Sally went well. We had a good chat but I left thinking about Henry. It's not like me to be consumed with thoughts of a guy. I'm not interested in dating anymore. At all. But then again, Henry's not just *any guy*.

Saturday came and I let myself sleep in. I pottered around the house all morning. The weekends are strictly off limits for work, unless there's a book event at some bookshop or something, and those are only allowed once a month and then I get a weekday off in compensation. I've tried working and writing on the weekends but my brain just won't have it. When I moved back to Bath, establishing some kind of work/life balance became my primary goal and weekends off were nonnegotiable. My brain needed time away from my characters or the words stopped coming. Time off usually helped me to avoid writer's block during the week.

I spent the morning reading and doing yoga, drinking lots of tea and reading some more. In the afternoon I went out to the front garden and did some gardening whilst the sun was still out. I was cutting flowers to bring inside when Mrs. Russell came outside.

"Hello Isla, how was your Friday? I didn't get to see you yesterday."

"It was a busy day, I saw you in your front room as I dashed out to go into town in the morning and I was there all day until evening. I'm happy to have a quiet day at home today," I said with a smile.

"I'm glad you're getting to relax today," Mrs. Russell said sincerely. "Henry said he saw you in town yesterday."

"Yes, we ran into each other, it was lovely to see him. We tried chatting but I was on my way to a meeting."

"He said your time was limited. Such a shame. But he told me he invited you to join us for dinner tomorrow, I'm so glad," she said warmly. "I hope you'll still be able to make it? I'm making lasagna."

"Yes, Henry was kind enough to invite me, so if you're okay with it, I'd be delighted to join you and catch up with Henry. And if I get to enjoy your amazing lasagna, well then that's even more reason to come over," I said with a smile.

"Fantastic! It will be so much fun," Mrs. Russell said, her hands clasped together gleefully.

We chatted for a bit longer before we each went back inside to relax and enjoy the rest of our Saturday.

———

ON SUNDAY, I went for a long walk in the morning and then cycled over to see my parents around one o'clock. We chatted about our week and had a good catch up. Then they felt like going for a walk so they walked me part way home and I cycled the rest of the way. I got back to my place an hour before I was due to go next door, so I read for a bit and then went upstairs to change.

I didn't want to overdress, it was just a dinner with an old friend. But I didn't want to go over in the outfit I'd just worn cycling halfway across the countryside and back in. In the end I opted for a simple denim shirt dress with an oversized cable knit cardigan. I freshened my hair and makeup and went back downstairs. I slipped my phone and lip gloss into the pocket of my dress and grabbed the box of chocolates and flowers from my garden that I'd cut earlier that day for a bouquet for Mrs. Russell. The ones I cut yesterday looked so nice in my kitchen I wanted to make a similar bouquet for her.

I locked up and walked down through my front gate and walked a few steps down to her gate, went up her small path, and knocked on her door.

Henry opened it, smiling widely. "You made it! I'm so glad you could join us, now we can catch up properly and talk about the good old days."

I laughed, "Watch it with the old references, those days are not *that* old."

Henry laughed, his eyes crinkling as he did.

"How did your finance manager like her signed copy of my book," I asked.

Henry smiled, "It went down a treat. I'm a hero in her eyes now. She keeps asking me how I managed to get it."

"Are you going to tell her you know me?" I laughed.

"I might," he replied mischievously. "But fair warning if I do, you might end up signing more copies for her."

"I'd be more than happy to," I replied with a smile.

"Henry, I taught you better, don't keep her standing on the front step. Isla! Come in, come in! We're all cosy in the kitchen tonight," Mrs. Russell came bustling out into the foyer and herded Henry and I into the kitchen.

Mrs. Russell's house had been renovated differently from mine over the years, so she had formal living and dining rooms and then a larger open plan kitchen compared to mine. It was very cosy. There was a small fire going in the log burner in the corner. I gave her the chocolates and the flowers, which she placed in the middle of the table as Henry and I sat down. She wouldn't let either of us help her and I could tell she was enjoying being hostess for the evening.

There was a large salad to start with while the lasagna finished in the oven, and white wine that Henry had brought over. The conversation flowed easily and to start with I just sat back and listened as he and his mum shared stories of his time in San Francisco. She was clearly so proud of him. She kept telling me all about his recent successes and his current work here in Bath. While in San Francisco he worked for a big consultancy firm. He was now setting up his own firm here in Bath to serve the whole of southern England. It sounded complicated but very impressive. Which didn't surprise me. Henry was always so smart, even back in school we all knew he'd end up doing something cool.

I kept glancing between him and his mum and I could tell that he loved how proud she was of him, but also that he was getting a little embarrassed from all the attention. When the salads were done and Mrs. Russell got up to get the lasagna, Henry turned to me.

"You must be getting tired of hearing us talk about me," he said with a sheepish grin.

"Not at all," I replied sincerely. "It's great hearing what you've been up to since school."

"Still, I feel it's your turn. I want to hear more about what you've been up to and the novels you're writing. Romance right?"

I took a sip of my wine. "They're more contemporary women's fiction. They all have romance plots but also a lot of self-discovery, of women who are creating the life they want."

"Wow, sounds very interesting. I loved the one I read, I need to read more of them."

"Her books are fantastic, Henry," Mrs. Russell said as she brought the lasagna to the table. "I've read all of them, they're on the shelf in the living room."

"Your mum is a little biased," I said with a small laugh. "But she's also been a great test reader, so if my books are good, especially the last five books since I moved in next door, it's because of the great feedback she gave me during the editing process."

Mrs. Russell smiled widely, "Well I'm just so happy that I could help you. I really do enjoy reading your work." Turning to Henry, "She is an excellent writer."

Henry and I both smiled.

"I'll have to borrow one of them to read Mum. I'm probably not your typical demographic though, am I?" he said, looking at me questioningly.

"I suppose it depends on how open people are to reading about different life experiences. When a male author writes a book about male characters, they call it fiction. But when a female author writes a book about a female character, they call it women's fiction, or chick lit, as if only women would enjoy it. I don't really think of myself as writing women's stories. I write stories, that's it. They just happen to be about women because that's the experience I live. My publishers will say I have a certain demographic of readers, but I just write stories for me and hope that someone will like them."

"Well said," Mrs. Russell said emphatically, slapping her hand lightly on the table.

Henry laughed, "Well after that explanation, now I really want to read one, if you write like you speak, I'm sure I'll love it."

I could tell I was blushing, so I took another sip of my wine. I can definitely get worked up about my writing and my readers. I never want to feel like there's someone who thinks they can't or shouldn't read my books. Why do romance novels only have to be for women? But I also don't want to freak out Henry by getting on my soap box about it. But this isn't a date so I guess it doesn't matter?

"It's just a shame that someone who writes such beautiful romances, isn't open to a little romance in her own life," Mrs. Russell said a bit wistfully, looking off into the distance, carefully avoiding looking at either me or Henry.

Henry laughed, "Mum, Isla is a grown woman, if she wants to be single that's her business."

"You're just as bad as she is Henry, all this business about being happy as a bachelor. When I was your age I was already married with a child," she said firmly.

"Yes, well, thankfully, Isla and I were raised in a generation that gave us other opportunities," Henry said with a laugh, softening his statement.

"Mrs. Russell, I think Henry and I are both happy, just as we are. Maybe one day that will change, maybe it won't, but that doesn't make either of our lives less fulfilling," I said gently.

Mrs. Russell sighed and conceded, "Of course not. You're two of the most successful, brilliant people I know. And I'm very proud of you both."

Henry leaned over and gave his mother a kiss on the cheek and she patted his hand in return. They really were adorable. We ate our lasagna, which was delicious and cooked to perfection, and talked about memories from school. We'd gone to different colleges for A-levels and lost track of each other by the time we each went off to university. We'd never been best mates but had a lot of friends in common and hung out in the same social group. I'd always wanted to date someone like Henry. He'd always been so nice to me, never let me just fade into the background in group situations. In school there were always girls braver than I was who would approach him and make their interest known, while I'd always secretly crushed on him. In the years that followed, I'd often wondered how different life would have been if I'd only said something. Now that I was sitting across from him, my mind was reeling with new possibilities.

After dinner we had coffee and biscotti in the living room. I could see Henry noticing my books on Mrs. Russell's shelf. I wondered if he would read one, and if so, which one he would pick.

After a little while Mrs. Russell started to seem tired, I saw that Henry noticed it too.

"Mum, we should let you go to sleep."

"Oh, no. I hate for you to leave already," she replied, followed immediately by a yawn.

"I'm afraid I'm going to have to insist Mum. I'll come by sometime this week for lunch if I can get away from the office."

Henry got on his coat and we said goodbye to his mum. I could tell she wanted to say something more, but she didn't. I thanked her for a lovely evening and then Henry and I left. We walked out of Mrs. Russell's front gate and Henry walked me the few steps to my gate.

"I'd offer to walk you home but I guess I already have," he said with a chuckle.

"Yes, you have," I said laughing.

"I've had a good night, it was nice to catch up after all this time." He shoved his hands in his coat pockets and looked at the ground with uncertainty. "Look, I know it's been ages and your last memories of me are probably as a gangly, awkward 16-year-old," he said laughing. "But I really did enjoy talking with you tonight, and I don't really know many people in Bath anymore. So, would you like to meet again sometime? Lunch or coffee maybe? Just as friends…or as a date? I know we both just told Mum we're happy being single, and I wouldn't want either of us to rush into anything, but it kind of feels…I don't know. Just, running into you again after all these years, we're both settled in our careers and happy and back in Bath. It's like…" his voice drifted off.

"Like fate," I said simply.

"Yeah," he said slowly, his eyes lit up with understanding. "You feel it too?" He looked so hesitant and unsure, it was kind of endearing.

I thought about how I'd felt at dinner. "I do. I was thinking about it while we were talking over dinner. You're just as I remembered you, but all grown up," I said smiling.

Henry laughed.

"Listen, my life is complicated, the past…well, it hasn't always been easy. And while your mum has never shared the details, she has let some things slip and from what I gather it sounds like you've had your share of complications. I can't just dive headfirst into something right now, but I do want to get to know you again. So, lunch or coffee, as friends-for-now? If that makes sense?" I said smiling.

Henry smiled brightly then, "It makes perfect sense. Friends-for-now sounds great." He took out his phone and tapped a few times to open a new contact page.

"Here, put in your number, and I'll call you tomorrow after I've looked at my schedule."

I entered my number and handed his phone back, "Great, I look forward to hearing from you."

Henry smiled and hugged me goodbye. As I opened my front door, I looked back and he was still standing there, watching to make sure I got inside. He waved and I waved back.

When I got in the door, I locked it behind me and then pressed my back against it. This whole night had been lovely, but I felt like the ground beneath me was slowly starting to shift. The solid lines of my life were starting to shimmer with new opportunities.

Friends-for-now or something more, either way I suddenly felt out of my depth a little. I wrote about romance. I didn't live it. My books may as well be fantasy, compared to my real life.

"Oh Isla. Don't get carried away. He's Henry and it's just lunch."

Giggling, and feeling a bit giddy, I went upstairs and got ready for bed. As I drifted off to sleep, I could hear Henry's light laughter in my head.

————

THE NEXT DAY Beth came over to discuss plans for the week. There was a meet and greet coming up scheduled this coming Saturday, at a Waterstones in Bristol. Thankfully Beth would be coming with me, I hate having to do these things on my own. It's one thing when it's something here in Bath, but when I have to travel some-where else, I'm grateful for the company.

I was in the middle of writing upstairs while Beth was working downstairs when my phone rang from an unknown number. I nearly let it go to voicemail but I remembered it might be Henry.

"Hello?" I said questioningly.

"Isla? It's Henry, how are you?"

"Hi, I'm well, how are you?"

"Things are good, busy at work today, but I didn't want to let the whole day slip by without calling. I have a few spots on my schedule this week, would you be able to get away from your writing either Tuesday or Wednesday?"

I quickly thought back over my schedule that Beth and I had just sorted out, "Yes, I'm just working at home all day Wednesday. It's a writing day for me, and I usually spend part of that time writing somewhere in town, so I could meet you while I'm out. Whereabouts is your office?"

"Not far from the city centre, so I could meet you anywhere."

"Okay, did you have a place in mind, lunch? Or afternoon coffee?"

"If you have time, lunch would be great. There's a nice little bistro on the other side of Pulteney Bridge that does a good lunch."

"I know the one. Would noon work?"

"Noon would be perfect, I'll meet you out front."

"Great, see you then."

We said goodbye and put down the phone.

"Who are you meeting for lunch and why are you scheduling things without running them by me?"

I jumped in my seat.

"Beth, my god, how long have you been standing there?"

"Long enough to hear you schedule lunch at noon, but not long enough to know which day."

"Wednesday. Which is my day to work at home and do what I want. And you weren't consulted because it's not a business lunch," I said with a wink and a laugh.

"But your parents and your friends usually call me to schedule to meet you during the week?"

"It's someone else," I said sheepishly.

Beth knows me too well, so she read my expression. "Oh. My. God. Are you going on a date?!"

"Stop it, it's just lunch with an old friend. He's the son of Mrs.

Russell next door. We knew each other in school and he's recently moved back to Bath."

"Right." Beth said, looking unconvinced that it wasn't a proper date. She just smiled and went back downstairs.

"It's just lunch," I laughed to myself before focusing on my writing again.

————

On Wednesday I forced myself to just get dressed for a regular day of coffee shop writing, not wanting to overdo it for lunch with Henry. I spent the morning writing near the Abbey again and then just before noon I packed up my laptop and headed towards Pulteney Bridge. As I approached the cafe I saw Henry leaning against a lamppost reading a book.

I tilted my head to try to see what he was reading, and stumbled slightly in surprise when I realised it was one of my books. He must have caught my movement in his periphery because he suddenly looked up, a wide smile lighting up his face. I smiled to cover my surprise that he was actually reading my book, but he seemed to read my mind.

He closed the book and held it up in one hand, "I started last night thinking I'd skim through since I've read this one already, but I can't put it down."

"*A Courageous Beginning,*" I noted. "Are you starting at the beginning of my back catalogue?"

"I do like to start at the beginning, although your new one sounds interesting too, Mum raved about *Bold and Bright*. But I wanted to read *Courageous With You*, I just thought it would be good to read this one again first, since it's been years since I read it. I wanted to reacquaint myself with the characters."

"Well, I'm waiting with baited breath to hear what you think. I'm pleased it's got your attention so much that you're reading it whilst waiting for me. I hope I'm not late?"

"Not at all, right on time, shall we go in?"

We went in and found a table near the window, the transition from September to October last week had brought autumn in full force. It was hard to believe a little over a week ago I was having a picnic on the hill, sipping champagne in the sun. Today was overcast and very chilly and I was bundled up in a coat and scarf. Thankfully the bistro was warm and cosy, and we settled in and ordered our lunch.

"I really do like your writing style," Henry said, as he sipped his tea. "You have a way with words and getting into the character's minds."

"Thank you," I said, trying not to blush. It was always hard for me to be complimented on my writing.

"I thought I would just skim this one, since I've read it before, but I got sucked right back in. You really root for the main character, I'm nearly half way through and I'm already desperately hoping that everything works out for Elizabeth, even though I already know it does, at least in this one. I hope her dreams don't get dashed in the next book."

"You'll just have to keep reading and find out," I said with a grin. He really did seem invested in the story, which was always a great feeling.

We talked for a little bit about work. He told me about his consultancy firm and more about the work they did. I explained what my typical day as a writer was like and about having Beth helping me these days.

"She keeps me sane and keeps my agent off my back," I said with a laugh. "But seriously, I was never organised when I was on my own. Ever since she came to work for me, it's changed the whole work flow of the day, it's been amazing."

"I feel the same way about my assistant, he's a genius with task management and scheduling. It's incredible the way the right people can make your business flow so much better. So, tell me more about this meet and greet event you have coming up. Are you excited?"

"It's this Saturday. I am excited. Thankfully Beth is coming, so that will help things go more smoothly. She always makes sure I get to the right place at the right time. I haven't been to Bristol in a while. The book has only been out for a month. We're not doing an official book tour, I don't have the energy for making a big fuss and doing ten cities in ten days or something like we did with the first few books. Now we do something every week or so. I just recently met with a local book club, which was amazing. Book clubs are basically small focus groups for me. This meet and greet will be bigger, a lot more people, I'll give a small talk about the book and my other projects, answer questions, and then we'll do a book signing. It should be fun!"

"It must be amazing to interact with your readers like that," Henry said, sounding awed.

"It's an honour, and a huge privilege. You spend all this time writing this thing, and then you put it out in the world, desperately hoping it will find its way to the hands of someone who will love it as much as you do. Once you finish writing, it's not solely yours anymore, you share ownership with the reader. Everyone will connect with my writing differently and some people will see things a different way than I might have intended. Characters that I think are more secondary will become a favourite character for some readers because they'll latch on to a small aspect of the character that they relate to. Or a plot line will impact them differently because of their own personal experiences. Book clubs and meet and greets are where I get to hear how everyone has connected with the book. It's definitely the most interesting part of the business side of writing."

"Well I'm impressed. I can kind of relate, I always enjoy following up with companies we've worked with a year or so down the road to see how they're doing. Seeing how they take our advice and implement it, how they've got through their growing pains and are thriving."

"That must be amazing though, being able to help companies and help founders achieve their dreams. So many businesses fail in the first few years but you help them succeed, that's brilliant," I said sincerely.

"I won't lie, it's a seriously awesome feeling, and I'm lucky to have a team with me that is just as passionate about my vision as I am," he said warmly.

At the end of lunch, we walked out together, wrapping ourselves back up in our coats against the cold. The hour had flown by.

"I had a great time," he said. "Thank you for meeting me."

"It was great," I agreed sincerely.

"Would you be up for doing it again some time? Maybe after your meet and greet, I'd love to hear how it went."

"I should be free at the same time next week if that would work?"

"Wednesday lunch next week sounds great, I'll have my assistant put it in my diary."

"Fantastic, I'll see you then."

We said goodbye and I watched as Henry headed back to his office before I headed home to do more writing in my living room, I was definitely going to get a fire going in the fireplace and snuggle in! I was looking forward to Saturday for the meet and greet, and for next week to tell Henry how it went.

CHAPTER 7 - MACEY

It's now been ten days since I met Ted and I haven't heard a peep from him. The universe hasn't even given me a sign, and I've started to settle on the fact that maybe it was just a one-time thing, a fun date, even if the connection between us was undeniable. To me anyway, who knows if he felt the same. I was probably way overthinking it, as usual. I can literally hear myself spiraling. I hadn't texted him because I had been so busy with the start of the university term, but also, I didn't want to chase. After all, I was happy being single. Even if I did run to check my phone, every time it pinged, thinking it could be him.

As a matter of fact, the term was off to a great start. I had quickly settled right into my new course, the same way I had with the house and with the girls. I felt comfortable straight away and all of the lecturers had helped as well, making the transition as smooth as possible. None of them could believe I had spent a year doing Psychology before, a few claimed that I was a natural born writer, and I was totally up to speed already. I was spending all of my free time reading last year's materials, so that might be why. I was determined to excel this year and prove to Mum that my newly chosen degree was the best fit for me. She and I haven't spoken since I told her and Dad the news, but we've arranged a call for later on this evening to catch up. It was Friday night, and to be honest, I didn't have any better plans.

"Hi Mum," I muttered as she picked up the phone.

"Hi Macey," she murmured, in a similar tone. "Your dad said your new term has started well. I'm assuming you haven't changed your mind then. No Psychology degree for definite?"

I couldn't help but laugh. "No Mum. No Psych degree. Honestly, I am so much more content now. It feels so right. Even my lecturers have said that I am a natural born writer, and I am doing so well given the change. I hoped that would help you understand that this was the right move for me."

"I am starting to get it," she acknowledged, even if I could hear the grimace behind her words. "I do want whatever is right for you Macey. I do. I'm in Weston Super Mare next week to provide training at a clinic there. I'm travelling down tomorrow if you wanted to meet there? I'm only really free tomorrow though, next week I'm stacked."

"I'm going to a book signing tomorrow Mum, for my favourite author. I haven't been able to go to any of her other ones and I am so excited. I'm really sorry. If I was free, I would have."

"Of course you're going to a book thing!" she laughed. "It's okay. I am sure we can sort something out for another time. Which book will be signed?"

"*Bold and Bright*. It's Isla's latest one. It came out a recently and she's doing a signing for it in Bristol. It's such a good book, probably my second favourite of her's after *A Courageous Beginning*. I can't wait to meet her!" I exclaimed.

"I'll have to Google it. And her," Mum responded, which to me, was a sign of improvement. If she was willing to Google a book that I liked *and* an author that I liked, well, that was a start. Considering I used to hide my books from her and now we're talking about them, it's definitely progress.

"I have to go, Macey. I need to pack. Speak soon though. Send me the information about the book and the author and let me know how it goes. I love you!"

I told her I loved her too, before hanging up the call and quickly texted her the info, to which she replied with a smiley face.

———

I WOKE up bright and early, giving myself enough time to get ready for the day and head to the station to get my train. The meet and greet was at one o'clock, and it was going to take me about two hours to get there. I booked the 10:30am train, in order to give me enough time, which meant I had to leave to get to the station no later than ten o'clock. I wasn't a morning person, so being awake at eight o'clock on Saturday felt like purgatory. I finally managed to get out of bed, after wrestling with the snooze button. I threw on my dressing gown, as the temperatures had suddenly dropped now we're well into October. The cooler temperatures only made it so much harder to get up in the mornings, every battle with my alarm felt harder than the previous day. I am definitely a night owl, not one to be awoken before sunrise, for all man fears a grumpy Macey.

I headed straight for the kettle once I was in the kitchen, desperate for my morning coffee. To get to it, I had to step over Charlotte who was already up and doing her morning yoga. I sighed. "How do you have that much energy, at this time?" I asked her. "The gulls aren't even squawking yet."

"They are Macey! The whole world wakes up way before you do. Happy Saturday anyway. Do you have your book thing today?"

I laughed. Why does everyone keep referring to it as a "book thing", despite me explaining over and over that I'm going to meet my favourite author?

"It's an Isla Stewart meet and greet, and yes, it's today."

"Ah. Have fun!" Charlotte sang whilst in downward dog, not flinching in the slightest.

"Where are the others?" I asked, looking around.

"Libby's gone to Winchester with Anna and Ruby stayed at Issac's last night. I don't think we're meant to know that though," she sighed. "I wish Ruby would just admit to herself that she likes him, and they could live happily ever after. Like the characters in those books you read."

"They don't all have happy endings, Charlotte. Take Romeo and Juliet for example. Have you read any romance novels at all?" I teased.

"No, I've looked at them though and read the blurbs. Told me all I need to know."

"Hmmm. How does that famous saying go?" I giggled.

"Ha-ha. I'm not judging. I'm making an educated guess with the limited time I have." She went on to add, "I wait for the movies most of the time. They tend to be better. I like to actually see how fit the Prince Charming is, if you get me? I don't want to have to do the hard work myself, conjuring one up in my imagination."

It took me a minute to digest her reply. There were a lot of issues at hand here. I couldn't hide the dismayed look on my face.

"No offence, obvs. The only books I read are self-help ones."

I shrugged. I didn't have time to run through all of the points that were bubbling up inside me, however desperate I was to do so.

"Movies are rarely better than the books. Movies use imagery, yes, but it's lazy if you ask me. Books capture the essence of a story so much better due to the intimate detail they include. Movies lack that. It's fun to use your imagination Charlotte. Everyone's interpretation of a character can be so vastly different. It's what makes books so personable, yet they form a sense of community as everyone has a common investment. You're a musical theatre student, you literally spend all your time acting, hasn't that shown the importance of how an author creates a character? And how you interpret that?"

"Did you pull that speech from an essay you wrote?" Charlotte chuckled. "No, it's just showed me that I prefer to watch films."

"I'll get you to read a romance novel one day," I laughed.

"If you say so," she said, bowing her head as she entered her final stretch. "I'll get you to try yoga one day then. Namaste!"

I finished my coffee and grabbed a granola bar for my bag from the cupboard. The next task was deciding on what to wear, eventually deciding on the red floral smock dress I wore the day I met Ted. I paired it with tights and some Doc Martens this time, as it was certainly much colder. I put on a pleather jacket and some gold jewellery to accessorize, including a pair of hoops. I threw my hair up into a messy top knot, tucking the remaining strands behind my ears and out of my face. I did my usual makeup routine, a few coats of both concealer and mascara, lots of rosy blush, warm bronzer and soft highlighter, and of course, a pale nude lip. I don't like to go too heavy on the coverage as I prefer my freckles to peek through, plus, who likes to wear that much heavy makeup on a daily basis anyway?

I brushed my brows up using some gel, they are so thick and dark, and often unruly, that a gel is all they need. Once I was somewhat happy with my appearance, I grabbed my trusty tote and headed for the door. To my surprise, I was on time. I shouted goodbye to Charlotte, who was now in the lounge doing a HIIT workout. She never stops. That could never be me. I swiftly left, popping my wireless earphones in as usual. I got about halfway down the street when I was stopped by a young man, who looked somewhat familiar.

"It's Macey isn't it, from number 11?" he asked.

"Who's asking?" I said, confused, removing an earphone to pause my music.

"My bad. I'm Tom. I live just there!" he smiled, pointing to the house opposite ours. "We're students too. We've been trying to convince Ruby and the others to come around for a party for a while now. We noticed that you were new too, I've been meaning to introduce myself."

"Oh, hi. Yeah, I'm Macey. Sorry, I have seen you around. I'm in a rush right now though, I have to get to my train," I replied politely.

"We're having another party next weekend if you fancy it?

Friday night. Let the others know and get back to us," he rushed. "It'll be nice of you all to join us, especially you Macey. That way I can properly introduce myself!" he beamed, flashing me a friendly grin.

"Cool. I'll let you know ASAP. Thanks Tom." I wasn't a huge partier so the likeliness of me actually attending one of their shindigs was low. I smiled anyway, being polite, and he smiled back, before heading into his house. I waved, popped my earphone back in, and finally got back on my way. As I was walking, I opened up the group WhatsApp we have for all us housemates, plus Anna, as she spends so much time with us.

Macey: Just spoken to Tom from across the road. He stopped me on the way to the station. Asked if we'd go to one of his house parties next week. I said I'd speak to you guys?

Ruby: Aw Tom's lovely! I've met him a few times because of Issac, they are pretty good friends, and Tom's mentioned before about having us girls round his for a party when I told him we lived across from him.

Charlotte: Is Tom fit?

Ruby: You've met him @Charlotte. Don't you remember that party at Issac's last semester? You were pretty drunk, lol. We could go to Tom's party, It's only over the road after all

Libby: What day?

Macey: Friday night @Libby

Charlotte: You didn't answer my question @Ruby

To which no one replied. I think we all assumed that Charlotte would totally go, if it meant there would be an opportunity to meet someone. I got to the station at 10:25am, in just enough time to dash to the platform and board the train. It was eerily quiet, which worked out in my favour, as I got first dibs of all the seats. I sat by the window, of course, at a seat with a table attached. I always appreciated having the extra space and being able to watch the world go by was a must. I brought a notebook to scribble ideas into, so I placed it on the table, along with my water bottle and granola bar, ready for me to tuck into later. I still had two hours to kill on the journey, so I better make it last.

By the time we had pulled into Bristol Temple Meads, I was panicking about being late to the event. The Waterstones where it was being held was a 20-minute walk from the station, according to Google Maps. It was 12:40pm when the doors flew open and I jumped off the train step. I shuffled quickly through the platform traffic, before hurriedly leaving the station. I wasn't sure of the way; I had only been to Bristol a few times. It was the closest major city to Plymouth, meaning it was the place all us university students headed for big live music events, or book signings, if you were like me. I navigated my way to Waterstones using online navigation, arriving promptly at one o'clock and searching my bag for my ticket to get in.

The room where the meet and greet was taking place was already pretty full when I got inside. There were chairs all lined up, in rows, with a small table at the front where I could see Isla was due to be sitting. She wasn't there yet, but there was a buzz in the room already. There was quite the mix of people, mostly females, as I expected. Some younger, like myself, and a few older women, I'd say who were at least 60. They huddled in groups, chatting just as excitedly as the younger girls were.

I wish I had someone to share my book love with, it's typical that all my friends preferred movies. I theorised that the older women may be a part of a book club, one where they read young love stories and reminisced about the good old days, the early stages of their relationships with their spouses they'd been with since they were 16. Most of us youngens probably hadn't experienced that yet, it would be interesting to hear the more experienced women's perspectives, if they were willing to shed some light on their own fairy tales.

I went and found a seat towards the back and popped myself down next to an older woman who seemed as if she was alone too. I smiled at her, in an attempt to initiate conversation, but she continued looking forward and didn't acknowledge me. I nodded, acknowledging her lack of acknowledgment, and slumped down further into my chair. The room suddenly fell silent, as a lady marched up to the microphone that was in place, ready for Isla to use.

"If everyone could get settled in their chairs, we're just about to start!"

It was her assistant. I recognised her from Isla's Instagram account. I think her name is Beth. She's a bit younger than Isla, a bit shorter too. Looks a little like Charlotte, very bouncy and enthusiastic.

I checked my phone quickly, to see I had a text from Sam. It was a picture of a dish with "Tofu Sukiyaki!" as the caption.

I miss your mums cooking!

I made it myself Macey!!!

I shot him the surprised emoji back, before he responded again.

Mum's family are flying in from Japan this weekend and she said that I should really be seen to be helping her with meal prep, or they'll be disappointed that I haven't learned how to cook. Which is why I have started to learn. A week before they arrive. I'm a computer programmer. I don't belong in the kitchen.

LOL. It looks good anyway Sam. You can cook for me when I'm home next. Phone's going on silent now though, the meet and greet I told you that I was going to is about to start. TTYL xx

TTYLY! He replied, as he usually does. Talk to you later, love you. Sam is known for abbreviating things that haven't been abbreviated before. It's just one of his many character traits.

"Hello everybody!" Isla said as she graced the platform. "It's so good to see you all here!" she added, in her gentle, yet excitable tone. I was used to hearing her voice, after watching countless interviews and videos of hers that she's published on social media. She has this way of speaking; it just relaxes me. I shot her a smile, even though I knew she probably couldn't see my face in the busy crowd. She went on to talk for about another half an hour, discussing all things *Bold and Bright*. Most of which I already knew, thanks to me being a fan and reading all of the tweets Isla puts out. She often shares behind the scenes information and fun easter eggs on her Twitter, which I am obsessed with going through and checking to see if I noticed them myself in her novels. She then spoke a little bit about her upcoming projects, one of which sounded super exciting. It was going to be different for Isla, as it was a romance set in the past. All of her work thus far is more contemporary, but this was going to be a historical fiction, which surprisingly, I was so looking forward to.

"Does anyone have any questions before I sign copies for all of you lovely people?" she pondered, scanning the audience for any eager arms shooting up. I was desperate to ask something, but too afraid to have all the eyes on me. I shuffled about awkwardly in my seat, which Beth, the assistant, mistook for me wanting to ask Isla something. A microphone appeared in front of my face and I felt as if I had no other choice.

"Hi! What's your name?" Isla asked, looking directly at me.

"Macey," I managed to squeak out.

"Hi Macey! What's your question?" she asked, smiling gently.

"What is your motivation for writing so many picture-perfect love stories?"

Isla laughed.

"Great question, Macey, thank you. The answer is, escapism. We all need a world full of happily ever afters to escape into every now and then."

I nodded, laughing too. "Thanks Isla. I think we can all relate to that." I was so nervous, public speaking was not my forte. I could never imagine being Isla, up there, addressing the audience with so much confidence and the perfect presence.

———

"THANK you again for your question, Macey."

She remembered who I was. It was only a few minutes ago that I was speaking to her from the audience, but I thought that she might have potentially forgotten about me whilst I was in the queue. I was much more settled now that we were one on one, and my ability to string a sentence together was much stronger.

"No, thank you!" I said happily. "I really loved hearing your answer. My own work is my escape too."

"You're a writer?" she asked, kindly.

"Aspiring," I corrected.

"No such thing. If you write, you're a writer," she declared, signing her name on my book as she spoke.

I blushed. "Thank you," I said, taking the book from her and placing it in my tote. "Is it okay if we get a photo?"

"Of course!" she replied cheerfully. I passed my phone to Beth who snapped a shot, before thanking Isla once again. Not only for the photo, but for igniting my love for reading, all those years ago. I guess she was partially to thank for the course change too. It was a series of fortunate events that led me to switch, wanting to be a writer because of Isla, finally deciding to follow my own passions, and meeting Ted. He was the cherry on top of the cake, the tip of the iceberg as such. Fate is a funny old thing.

"You're more than welcome Macey. I hope to see your name pop up in the author world soon! What was your surname so I can keep an eye out?" Isla queried.

"Banks. Macey Banks." I said, realising I just unintentionally sounded like James Bond.

"I'll be watching out for you Macey Banks," Isla said with a wink. "Bye!" she called out as I was swiftly moved on by the security.

That's the thing with these events, you don't get to spend as much time with the authors that I'd like to. It's understandable, of course, they have a lot of people to see. There's just so much more I'd like to say to Isla, and so many more questions I'd like to ask. I was thankful I got to meet her however, and pulling up the selfie on my phone just made me smile even more. I quickly sent it to my Dad, letting him know that it had gone well, as he had pestered me to update him. Not only about this, but about my life as a whole after my return to university. He told me he'd miss me when I went back, and he wanted to be "in the know" even if I wasn't living at home anymore. I don't think he was ever "in the know", but I do what I can to please. He was being really supportive at the moment, and I know my Mum was trying too. I sent my Mum the photo also, along with a photo of the signed book I had just got, showcasing Isla's personalised message to me. It read:

To Macey, keep on writing, keep on being you. Enjoy the books too!
    All my love, Isla Stewart.

I typed "Just finished at the meet and greet I told you about yesterday, with the author that I bang on about all the time. She was so lovely! Look what she wrote in my book!" to accompany the photos, before pressing send and shoving my phone back into my bag.

As I approached the door, I could see it had started to drizzle, so I got my umbrella out of my tote and opened it up as I got outside. I stood around for a few seconds, pondering what to do. I hadn't bought a return train ticket, as I wasn't sure what time the meet and greet would finish. I wasn't in a rush to get back to Plymouth, but now the weather had turned bad, I wasn't sure that I fancied walking around aimlessly in the rain. I usually enjoyed a stroll round the shops, but not when the weather is like this. I was still standing under my umbrella, debating my next move, when a car pulled up in front of me. The window rolled down and a head appeared, their eyes catching mine straight away.

"Macey?" a voice spoke, confusion apparent in their tone.

CHAPTER 8 - ISLA

"That went well," I said as I leaned back against the train seat.

"Yes, it did," Beth agreed. "I just about laughed out loud at your answer to that darling girl who asked about your motivation for writing picture perfect love stories."

"Why would you laugh? I wasn't lying!" I said indignantly, but smiled to show I was amused. I knew exactly where Beth was going, this was familiar ground for us.

"No, you weren't lying, but really Isla. You write books about love and claim escapism as your motivation, and yet you run from every chance of love yourself. One broken heart shouldn't make you a spinster for life."

"Hey, don't knock the 'hashtag-spinsterlife' until you try it. I'm redefining spinsterhood, thank you very much," I said with a laugh. Beth rolled her eyes.

We were on the train back to Bath from Bristol. It had been a great day, but I was exhausted and grateful for the company. The meet and greet had lasted a few hours and then there was stuff to take care of with the book store staff, so it was early evening by the time we finally got on the train to go home. Beth and I each had a hot chocolate from the cafe at the train station, and a pastry. We didn't travel much for business, so when we did, this was our little treat for ourselves.

The meet and greet had been a huge success, there were a bunch of people who showed up. They were really receptive to my talk and then we had a great Q & A session. They then all stayed to have me sign their copies of my newest book. I was thrilled with the reception *Bold and Bright* had received, even though it was only recently released. A lot of the attendees had already read it and had lovely things to say as they had their copies signed.

"So, what are you going to do tomorrow?" Beth's question cut into my thoughts from the day.

"Sleep," I said simply. I was knackered.

Beth laughed. "Just sleep? The whole day?"

"Oh, you know me. I'll sleep in, then go see my parents. I'll probably read a bit. I finished that one book I'd been sent for a review, but I saw you'd put another one on the pile."

"Yeah, soz about that. It just came in, an urgent request from your publisher. It's a new author and they wanted to have your review for the marketing."

"Ahh, new competition?" I asked, raising an eyebrow.

"Ha! Doubtful, you're too beloved Isla."

"No one is ever too beloved to not have younger, fresher competition," I said firmly.

"Whatever," Beth said, rolling her eyes. "But really, it's a new author, and yes, she is in the same genre, but just flipping through she's got a totally different style, so I think your status is safe."

"For now," I replied with a grin, as I took a sip of my hot chocolate.

Beth and I joked about it, but I knew eventually someone would take my spot as one of the top selling romance authors. In some ways I almost welcomed that day, it might take some of the pressure off.

———

THE NEXT WEEK started off fine, I was making slow progress on my latest manuscript. I couldn't quite figure out why this project was giving me so much trouble. It wasn't just the multiple time periods and points of view, I was struggling to connect with it in general. I normally don't struggle with writer's block, but I was now and it was very frustrating.

Wednesday rolled around and it was time for my next lunch with Henry. He'd texted to confirm and we were meeting at another little cafe, near the Abbey. I was looking forward to seeing him, and looking forward to taking a break from writing. I'd been working at home all morning and by late morning I was ready to beat my head against the keyboard. By the time I had to leave to meet Henry, I couldn't get out the door fast enough.

I dashed down the road and enjoyed getting some fresh air and tried to clear my mind. All the problems with my writing were crashing around my head and it was about to do me in. The air was crisp and there had been a slight frost on the ground this morning when I woke up. My mum had already started complaining about the cold when I was over on Sunday, but I was loving it. I had on my favorite camel coat and a luxurious blanket scarf from this little knitwear shop in town that I loved. It had been a splurge, made from cashmere and super soft, but it was my favourite.

Henry was standing outside the cafe waiting for me, rubbing his hands together to keep them warm. He looked up and smiled when he saw me approaching. And wow, his smile really was the most incredible one I'd ever seen, especially when I was the one he was smiling at.

"You know, they make these things called gloves, and I hear they do a really good job of keeping your hands warm," I said, smiling at him in return.

Henry laughed, "I know, I know. Please don't tell my mum or I'll never hear the end of it. I keep forgetting it's getting cold and I left them at home."

I laughed, "I promise, I won't say a word to her. You should have waited inside for me though."

"No, I wanted to make sure you saw me and didn't think I wasn't here yet or something." He was so sincere, it was touching.

We walked inside, ordered our food and then got a seat. The cafe was busy, but not terribly crowded. The majority of tourists were gone now, especially during the weekdays. So we were able to get a table near the window and we settled in to enjoy another nice conversation. Henry was easy to talk to, since we already knew each other. Sure, we were getting reacquainted and catching up on years of being apart, but he wasn't a stranger and I found it easier to let my guard down with him.

"So, I finished *A Courageous Beginning*, and now I'm on to *Courageous With You*. You really are an excellent writer Isla!"

"Thank you," I said, blushing slightly.

"You probably hear that all the time. I just, well, I can't remember the last time I felt so emotionally connected to a book."

"Thank you," I said again. "That's always a lovely compliment to hear. And one I especially need today," I said with a laugh.

"Why today?" Henry asked curiously, taking a bite out of the sandwich that had just arrived at the table.

I played with the food on my plate a little, thinking of how to answer. "I don't know, I'm just struggling with what I'm writing at the moment, and feeling disconnected emotionally from the project. It's different from what I usually write, not a straight forward romance."

"What's it about?"

"Well, I can't give you too many details," I said with a grin. "But basically it's a family drama, spread across three generations with three points of view. There's romance in it, in each of the three intersecting stories, but the romance isn't the driving force of the book. It's about the three women and the journeys their lives took them on and how their stories are connected."

"Sounds fascinating. So what's the struggle?"

"I don't know, I'm probably putting too much pressure on myself, it wouldn't be the first time. I first had this idea years ago, but my publisher wanted the typical romance so this idea got put on the shelf for a while. I've been waiting ages to finally be able to work this idea but now that I'm writing it, I'm struggling. I'm worried it will be too different, a step too far for the readers."

"If they like your writing, it shouldn't really matter what the story is. I mean, I'll be the first to admit that *A Courageous Beginning* isn't my normal type of book, and I got a few raised eyebrows from the blokes at work."

I laughed, "I'm not surprised."

"But it was incredible and I'm totally sold on your writing. I'm sure I'm not the only reader of yours who would be interested in reading anything you write, regardless of the genre."

"Tell that to my publisher!" I exclaimed, taking a bite of one of my crisps. "They're concerned but trying to stay optimistic. *Bold and Bright* is slightly less of a romance, a bit heavier on the self-discovery aspects for the main character and so far it's selling similarly to my other works during their initial launch periods, and getting good reviews, so it's making my publishers think this next project might work. But they love to remind me that this is a leap for them."

"So why are you struggling to connect with it? Is it just because it's a different genre?" Henry seemed genuinely curious about my writing.

"I think it's just worries over whether people will like it or not. Historical women's fiction is not what my other books are about. It's a big departure. And I usually only release one book a year, so if this flops, it could have a big impact on my career. Every week there are new authors published, there's always new competition. And that's good, I'm not greedy with my readers, I want them to read other authors. I guess I just feel like it's been this amazing wave of success over the last several years and I keep feeling like eventually that wave will fizzle out."

"I'm sure that's a normal feeling. But you can't let that stop you from writing stories you believe in. What was the inspiration for this story?"

I paused, "It's personal, loosely based around my family history.

I've always found the stories of my grandparents so interesting. I grew up here in Bath but the rest of the family is in Edinburgh where my dad is from or Portland, Oregon, in the States, where my mum is from."

"That must have been fun having family in two different countries, did you visit the States often?"

"Twice every year," I said with a laugh. "We'd go every summer and then we alternated Christmases with each family, so we either went to Portland for Christmas or for New Year. It was pretty great. Most of my grandparents have passed, my parents are older. My Gram in Scotland is 97, we're lucky she's still with us. To be honest, she could outlive us all."

Henry smiled. "So what family stories got you so fascinated in their history?"

"Mum's side of the family is originally from Scotland as well. So, my dad's side stayed in Scotland but my mum's side left and created a new life in America, in the 1890s. The stories I was told about my great-great-grandparents who immigrated and their descendants, down to my mum, compared to the stories of my great-great-grandparents and their descendants on my dad's side, the parallel lives, the idea of is the grass greener on the other side of the Atlantic, and all that. Then Mum choosing to study in the UK and meeting Dad, it felt like this full circle moment. The two families weren't from the same village or anything, but they were nearby and they did have things in common. The reasons for my mum's ancestors to immigrate were the same factors that were impacting my dad's ancestors. So, the same issues, but one family left Scotland and one family stayed."

"Wow," Henry said quietly. "Sounds like a pretty cool story."

"It makes for the great basis of an intergenerational story, that's for sure. But it's a lot. So many different pieces to the puzzle. Timelines and characters to keep track of. And I need to make sure that it's not too based on my family. I'm writing a novel, not a family history or memoir. It's a delicate balance. The personal connection is what gives it some depth, at least I think it does. But what if it's all too much? What if it's too different? Or my readers don't like the multiple points of view or the older characters from the previous time periods? It needs to feel modern even with the historical plot lines. What if it all comes across as self-serving, like I'm telling the story I want to tell even if it's not what readers are going to want to read?" I sighed, feeling the frustration bubbling up inside me again.

Henry paused for a moment then raised an eyebrow, smiled and said, "You're really good at coming up with lots of what ifs, aren't you?"

I gave a small laugh, "I mean, it kind of goes with being a writer. Asking questions and imagining different outcomes."

Henry laughed. "Good point."

"I know I need to just let go and write the story. A lot of these worries will be addressed in the editing process. I just want to feel confident about the first draft I send to my editor. I don't want her to panic that it's all too different and then have her freak out my publishers. I just feel like all the professional worries are getting muddled up in my brain and I struggle to write the story."

"Well, that makes sense. I think you need to give yourself a break, don't be too hard on yourself. You'll figure out the writing eventually. I wish I could give better advice, but I know nothing about writing novels," Henry replied, grinning sheepishly.

"Honestly, just being able to talk about it helps, so thanks. I haven't really spoken out loud about this to someone."

"I'm always happy to listen."

We enjoyed the rest of our lunch, talking about whatever crossed our minds. After lunch he had to get back to work, and I felt a little better about trying to write again.

———

THAT WEEKEND, Georgie begged me to go on a viewing with her. The place she'd mentioned at our picnic had already sold, but she found a new one and she was insistent that I consider it. I agreed to meet with her, more to just spend time with my friend, than because I was seriously thinking of buying a flat. Of course, I should have known better. Georgie knows me too well, and she found a perfect place for me.

I arrived at the address she'd texted me. It was on a little mews street not far from the Royal Crescent. Every house was different and eclectically decorated with random potted and hanging plants by every door or hanging from every balcony. There were a couple trees that filtered dappled sunlight onto the cobbled street.

Georgie was waiting for me in front. The mews house had two levels, with a balcony overhanging the front door. It was made from the same golden limestone that my house was made from, and it glowed in the afternoon light. There were lace curtains in the windows and flower pots by the front door. Suddenly I was imagining roses and peonies in the flower pots in the summer.

My feelings must have been visible on my face because as soon as Georgie saw me she said, "I knew you'd love it."

"Georgie, I really don't need another house," I said pleadingly.

"No, but you could use an investment. It needs some work inside but if you can provide the funds, I can arrange the work and manage the project. I think it needs about twenty grand invested in it but it would add nearly eighty grand to the overall value. You could rent it out, which I could also help manage through my office, and the rental would more than pay the mortgage on the property. Then, down the road, if you decide to sell it, it would probably go for double what you'd pay for it now. It's a total win Isla."

"Well you've thought it all through. Okay, fine, show me the house and talk me through your plan."

Georgie smiled brightly and linked her arm through mine before leading us into the house.

Going through the property I could immediately see what she was talking about. The house was perfect. Smaller than my own, it was two bedrooms and one bathroom upstairs, with a small kitchen and living room on the ground floor. There was a tiny patio in the back, off the kitchen. Lots of historical character and charm.

Listening to Georgie's plans it was hard not to get swept up by her excitement. It would be a great rental property, either for a long term lease or as a vacation rental. The numbers definitely made sense, and were very tempting.

When we finished touring the house, Georgie looked at me and knew she'd convinced me.

"Come on, let's go get some coffee and we'll talk about putting in an offer. I also want to hear about your dates with Henry."

"For the millionth time, they aren't dates," I said with a groan.

We walked to the nearest coffee shop and settled in at a booth in the back. I told her about my two lunches with Henry and our first dinner at his mum's place.

"It's been nice, connecting with him again. But as I keep trying to tell you, we're just friends, for now. That's it. And we're both happy that way. At least for now. Don't pressure me Georgie," I said with a grin. "You know I do things in my own time, you can't rush me."

"You know I'd be more inclined to believe that if you'd had even one decent relationship since Evil Edwin. You're not *that* happy being single, you just feel safer. It's understandable, but I'm not going to let you act like you're making the choice to be single out of a clear informed decision and not out of fear. You had one really serious relationship that went terribly wrong, and you've been single ever since. You've convinced yourself you're happier as you are, but you've never been in a solid relationship with someone who truly loves and respects you and gives you the freedom to be who you really are with them."

"Georgie, we can't all be you and Grant," I said softly, looking down at my coffee.

She reached out and put her hand over mine, "Isla, you know my past. You know I've been through my own difficulties but I still found Grant. It wasn't always easy for us, but we found a way and were willing to give each other a chance. And before you give me your usual excuse of being busy with your career, I was the busiest I've ever been with my career when I met Grant."

She was right. She was in the middle of growing her business, having just gone independent and opening her own agency and property management office. It was before she could afford to hire any staff and she was doing the work of at least three people by herself.

"I'm not you Georgie."

"It's not about being me, it's about being yourself. Unapologetically and fearlessly yourself."

"You make it sound so simple."

"It's not, it's bloody hard. But what's harder is denying who you are and what you want, and I don't think you actually want to be single forever. You have so much to give. Edwin never appreciated that. He used it and took advantage of it. He bled you dry, until you thought that's what love was, giving endlessly and getting nothing in return. But that's the opposite of what real love is."

"Look, you're right, ok? But I *am* busy, and I have a lot going on with the new book. Henry and I are enjoying getting to know each other again and are happy to be friends for now. The future will take care of itself."

Georgie held up her hands in surrender. "Alright, I'll back off. For now. I'm just saying, Henry's cool, I always liked him back in school, he was a good guy. I'm glad you're spending time with him, you already seem loads happier," she said with a self-satisfied smile.

I smiled and rolled my eyes. We finished our coffees and said goodbye, but not before Georgie made me promise to consider putting in an offer on the mews house. I was seriously considering it. The numbers all added up and I'd never have a better opportunity than being able to put up the money but have Georgie and her team do all the work.

I slowly walked home, thinking over everything Georgie and I talked about, and my recent lunches with Henry. I really was enjoying spending time with him. I felt happier and lighter in his presence than I have with any other man I've met in recent years.

Our shared history made it easier to open up to him. But I also didn't want to rush into things and start feeling something for Henry that he might not feel for me. He'd never seemed seriously interested in me in school. He'd never tried to stay in touch with me after school. Even when he found out I was living next to his mum, I never heard a word from him. So if he'd ever felt for me what I felt for him, surely I would have heard something from him before he moved back to Bath. Right? I kicked a rock down the path in front of me.

"Ugh," I said out loud in frustration. A pigeon cooed beside me. "I need to get home," I muttered under my breath.

CHAPTER 9 - MACEY

"Ted?" I said, as dazed as he was. "What are you doing here?"

"Don't worry, I'm not stalking you–"

"I didn't think you were, radio silence and all," I said pointedly.

He sighed, "Yeah, about that—"

"It's okay," I interrupted again. I guess I was making a habit of that now. "Why are you here?" I continued. The wind had picked up and the drizzle had now become a downpour. I was getting soaked, despite clutching onto my umbrella, which Ted noticed.

"Get in the car, you look freezing. I'll explain. I'm going back to Plymouth now, if you're headed that way, I can give you a lift?"

I was still as dazed as ever, so I agreed, walking around to the passenger side and trying my best to elegantly lower myself down into the seat. I turned to look at Ted, at this point, fully aware that I must look like a drowned rat.

"Hi," I said.

"Hi," he replied, laughing. Looking at him close up, he was even more handsome than I remembered. His chiselled cheeks looked so fine as he pursed his lips to speak. His hair was slightly damp, looking far better than mine though. He pulled off that look, whereas I just looked like I'd taken a shower and forgotten to undress. He leant over to me, not changing his fixed gaze.

"Your mascara has run," he said, before wiping my under eyes with his sleeve.

"Thanks," I stuttered, a bit bewildered by him and his confidence once more.

"I came to pick my sister up. She was coming to a meet and greet for Isla Stewart. I actually thought," he took a breath, "and hoped, that you'd be here. Not that I imagined you actually would!" he laughed incredulously. "I've been meaning to text but I got so busy with uni work, though I haven't stopped thinking about our chat over coffee the other week. We should do that again sometime."

I sighed, "Sure."

"My sister text just before I saw you, to say that she no longer needed a lift. I nipped home last night, to Exeter, and she was banging on about having to get the train here today. I said I'd bring her, hang around in Bristol for a bit and then head back to Plymouth after I'd dropped her back home. I have a mate up here, so I called in to see him," he explained. "I was just deciding on my next move when I saw you across the way. I was surprised to say the least. I recognised you, in that dress, instantly."

"I see."

"Not talkative today?" Ted quizzed.

"I'm not going to lie to you Ted, I was a bit annoyed when you didn't text after you said you would. I'd rather just be upfront about it."

"Hey! You didn't text me either."

"You have a point, to be fair. I didn't know if I should. I was letting you take the lead. It was you who wanted to arrange another date after all," I argued.

"I'm sorry. I should have. I really wanted to know how you got on in your first week of term too. I guess you can tell me all about it now."

I flashed him a small smile.

"Let's start over, with this mini road trip. We can get to know each other properly over the next two and a bit hours. *When Harry Met Sally* style."

"You've seen that movie?" I asked.

"It's one of my favourites," he shrugged.

"Same!" I said, turning to him and accepting his offer to start over. He passed me the aux and by doing so, we called a truce. I was always happy to control the music. I pulled up my trusty "ROADTRIPS!" playlist, the first song to come on was "Fast Car" by Tracy Chapman.

"Phenomenal choice," he declared, before reaching to turn the volume up. In doing so, his hand brushed my knee.

I smiled, turning to hide my pleased expression. *"Pull it together Macey!"* I said over and over to myself, in my head.

I wasn't sure what it was about this guy, but for some reason, he had the ability to give me butterflies on our second ever meeting, and that must mean something. I swore that only crystal-clear glasses would be worn this time, and I am still planning on sticking by that. He might have perfect cheekbones and an exceptional jawline, with equally as mesmerising eyes and that cute, yet captivating smile, but I barely know him! It's not been long since our first date at all, so maybe it's crazy of me to accept a lift off him anyway. I keep getting swept up in his charm without even noticing—but maybe he is right. Maybe this road trip will be an ideal way to get to know him. Unconventional? Yes. Borderline creepy? Maybe.

I'm hoping he's telling the truth, that he wasn't stalking me. I'm sure he wasn't. He's just a guy who is kind enough to drive a girl two hours home. I trusted him, despite hardly knowing him. I had a positive gut feeling—yet I started to feel a bit uneasy. The nervousness began to creep in, feeling similarly to how I felt after Owen and I broke up. The unfamiliarity, a sense of the unknown. I'm struggling to work out whether the butterflies are an enemy. A swarm who've launched a vicious attack, to let me know that something bad is about to happen. Or, if as a matter of fact, they are just nudging me, gently, so that yes, I'm on guard, but I should be excited, more than anything. Maybe I'm not scared of Ted, maybe I'm scared of the fluttering feeling, and getting confused about what it means. Maybe it's just that I do like him, cheekbones, literature knowledge, and all.

"What animal would you be reincarnated as?" Ted asked, out of the blue.

"That's random," I said, shaking my head at him.

He nodded. "It is. However, asking the most random questions is the best way to get to know someone."

"Is that a scientifically proven statement? Or one you've just made up?" I stared at him.

"Just answer the question Macey, I'm dying to know!"

"I did one of those quizzes once that tells you what animal you're most similar to. I got a bear, so I guess that?" I revealed.

"A bear? What does that say about you then? Should I be worried?" Ted said, with a fake concerned look on his face. He frowned his brows and shot me a glare. "I'm being serious!!!" he protested. "Bears are scary."

"I didn't know you were a wimp!" I joked. "Nothing to worry about, I don't think. It just said that bears are strong and courageous. Oh, and something about being in touch with the earth. But I'd say that's because I'm a Taurus. Earth sign and all that."

Ted raised his eyebrows. "Astrology?"

"Big fan," I added.

"Interesting. I don't know much about it, other than that I'm an Aquarius, which I know isn't a Water sign, despite what people say. It's an Air sign," he announced proudly.

I giggled, "You're right. It is an Air sign. Aquarius' are great."

"Phew!" Ted shouted, taking an exaggerated sigh of relief. "You can ask me a question now if you like?"

I internally debated what I was going to ask him for a second. "If we're recreating *When Harry Met Sally* right now, does that mean we're not going to see each other for years after this?" I questioned.

"We're not recreating it," Ted said sternly. "We're rewriting it."

"We are?"

"Yeah. Harry and Sally never went to a Starbucks drive-through, did they?" he said, steering the car towards a motorway exit. "What do you want?"

I cackled. "Smooth. Is this our second coffee date?"

"It is Macey. I bet you didn't expect that. Perfect timing or divine intervention? Now, what do you want?"

"Grande latte with oat milk and a shot of hazelnut please," I told the speaker, waiting to be mocked by Ted for my ultra-specific order.

"Make that two," he called out instead. He turned to me, "It sounded good. I hope it's not disappointing, or I will be blaming you, M."

After a minute, we were driving away, drinks in hand. I looked over as he took a sip.

"You like?" I was eager to find out what he thought, and of course know if I had disappointed him.

"Delicious! The hazelnut is a great addition. You can't even taste the difference with it having oat milk too, I'll probably get it moving forward now, I just had never tried it before," he exclaimed.

"Here," I said, reaching over to wipe some froth off his upper lip, returning his favour from earlier.

"Thanks. But I was saving that for later!" Ted teased. "Are you named after anyone?" he asked, starting the next round of 21 questions.

"First name wise, apparently not. My parents just said they have always liked the name Macey and naming me so had nothing to do with the fact that *I Try* was released approximately seven months before I was born."

"Ah, I had wondered whether they were just big Macy Gray fans. But yours is spelt differently right?"

"Yeah, it has an E thrown in there. Not sure why they did that."

"Maybe to hide the fact that you are actually named after Macy Gray?"

"Probably. It doesn't help that my middle name starts with G too," I laughed.

"What is it?"

"Genevieve. After my great-aunt. My mum and her were really close when Mum was younger apparently. She died just before I was born, when Mum was pregnant. Mum took it really hard. She still talks a lot about Aunt Genevieve. Even more than my Grandma!" I laughed.

"Macey Genevieve Banks. What a name."

"Do you have a middle name?"

"Well Macey, I should probably admit this now. My actual name is Edward, if you hadn't guessed already. Though I have always gone by Ted. My mother only ever calls me Edward when she's angry. My middle name is Jack."

I laughed. "Edward. Edward Jack Leakes, who'd have thought?"

"Quit with the Edward. It makes me feel like I'm in trouble."

"I'll bear that in mind," I smirked. "I like M though, you can keep calling me that if you like. No one has before."

"Really? It's a pretty obvious nickname," Ted joked.

"My dad calls me his strawberry lace. I guess we're more about the less obvious nicknames in my household." I proceeded to tell Ted the story of how the name came about, and he couldn't help but laugh.

"Being named after his favourite confectionary is pretty sweet— pardon the pun!" he sighed, dismayed at his poor attempt at humour.

"Funny," I insulted, before grabbing my phone, opening Spotify and shuffling the song.

Suddenly, Ted broke into song and belted the lyrics of *I Try* at the top of his lungs. "I don't know why your parents wouldn't admit they named you after Macy Gray. She's legendary."

I burst out laughing. "You have a great singing voice, Ted."

"I was in the school choir, I know. The teachers loved it."

I joked, "If that's what they told you."

"Rude!" Ted exclaimed, turning to look at me. "I love your hair, by the way Macey. It's striking. It's what got my attention when I first saw you in that bookstore. I just had to say."

"Thank you," I blushed. "It's kind of you to say. I've had grief throughout my life about it. You know, being ginger and all."

"I never understood why people don't like ginger hair. I think it's the best, most interesting hair colour there is," he smiled. "I bet they were all just jealous."

"You sound like my Dad," I laughed.

"I'll keep the compliments to myself in the future then?" Ted jokingly sulked.

"No, it's okay. Keep 'em coming," I protested.

"Well, I also like your eyes Macey, green is gorgeous."

"You can tell? A lot of the time they look brown." I actually did wonder how he could tell, as you have to look at them for a while to notice.

Ted blushed himself this time. "Yeah I noticed," he replied shyly.

The next few hours were spent karaoking to timeless indie love songs (according to Ted, that's the best genre of music) and telling stories of our past, and present too. I told him all about my parents and their work, I told him about Sam, and mentioned a little bit about Owen. I didn't go into too much detail as Ted wasn't giving up too much about any exes of his own, despite how many hints I dropped to get him to open up, as I was curious and did kind of want to know. He did gush about his family a lot however, which I thought was very sweet.

"My mum is an engineer and my Dad works in the police force," Ted told me. "I do have a younger sister, as you know, she's called Evie. I also have an older brother, Joseph, or Joey as we call him. Evie is 18 and Joey is 26. Joey graduated a few years back and is a playwright in London. He lives with his fiancé Anton there. I stayed with them when I did my placement year. Evie is doing her A-Levels at the moment. She's doing English Lan, English Lit, History and Sociology. She wants to do Journalism at uni next year;

I think she'll end up staying at home and going to Exeter. She's a bit of a home bird, wants to stay close to her friends and boyfriend. Young love, eh!" he continued. "So yeah, all us kids are writers, one way or another. Funny how we turned out like that, when our parents do nothing of the sort. That's kind of the same for you, isn't it?"

"Yeah. I don't know where I got my love for writing from," I said, absorbing everything he just told me. "Your family sounds great; I love that you're all so close."

"Most of the time," he laughed, "I couldn't imagine being an only child though."

I paused, twiddling my thumbs for a second, before deciding to go for the easiest answer. "It's strange, but at the same time, it's all I've ever known. I couldn't imagine having siblings, it seems like so much fun. Every time we look at photos of me in the hospital with my mum after I was born, she always tells me that my birth was so traumatic, she'd never do it again. So that was that. I guess it was my fault," I laughed. "Anyway. What do you like about Plymouth so much?"

"It reminds me of being a kid actually. Having spent a lot of time there when I was younger, it was an obvious move for university. My grand-parents live nearby too, hence why we were always there growing up," Ted explained.

"That's lovely. You must love it, considering you chose to stay on to do a Masters."

"In the second year of my undergraduate degree, I really got interested in creative writing, kind of wishing I'd specified in that. So I joined the Creative Writing Society, which I am now President of, and decided that I had to stay on for as long as possible," he smirked. "You should join, M. You'd love it. We're a friendly bunch."

"I'd love to."

———

As we pulled up to my front door, Ted turned to look at me.

"I really enjoyed that Macey. Thanks for being unexpected, great company."

"You didn't expect me to be great company?" I teased.

"No, I didn't expect to have any company at all!" he replied. "On the two occasions that I've spent time with you, you've been great company, M."

I smiled. "Glad to be of assistance. This time and the previous."

"I may need your assistance again sometime, if that's okay?" he said, with a shy smile of his own.

"If you remember to text me, I may consider it," I jibed.

"I won't forget this time. I promise. I'm taking full responsibility to organise being in your great company again."

"Sounds like a plan," I said, collecting my belongings and opening the car door. "See you soon then, Ted."

"Bye Macey," he sang, as I walked up the steps to my front door.

I turned back to look at him, hoping he wouldn't notice me gazing. He was still sitting there, smiling. He hadn't started the car back up again yet, instead he looked as if he was deep in thought. He ran his hand through his hair and threw his head back, taking a breath. His eyes were closed, so he was definitely oblivious to the fact that I was watching him. He looked so calm, yet as if there was energy trapped inside of him, waiting to be let out. I smiled to myself, secretly hoping that he was thinking about me.

I searched in my tote to find my key, hearing the car finally starting up behind me. He honked his horn, so I turned around to wave again, noticing him waving as he began to navigate the over-crowded street that we lived on. I laughed to myself thinking of how frustrated people get when they attempt to drive up the hill, worried that a car will come and block their already narrow path.

"I'm home!" I called out, as I wandered into the porch. Bending down to unlace my Docs, I noticed Ruby was sitting on a step near the top of the staircase. She had her head in her hands, and I could hear a small, muffled whimper.

"Ruby?! What's wrong?" I had never seen her visibly upset before, let alone cry. She came across as tough as nails, so this sudden show of emotion had taken me aback slightly.

"Uni," she sobbed.

"What's going on?" I pondered.

"I am SO stressed. I have work coming out of my ears and I just don't feel good enough, at all."

"Imposter syndrome. I get it." I sighed.

"I forget that you used to do Psychology."

We both laughed. "But surely you know, that you are more than good enough? You got onto this degree programme, you smashed your first year, your art is amazing?!" I questioned, whilst comforting her.

She sniffled. "Thanks Macey, but I just don't feel it much of the time despite what people say, and it's making me not enjoy what I do anymore."

"We often struggle to see our own worth but that doesn't mean it's not there. We just need to be reminded of it every so often, until we can see it again on our own."

"You're right. I don't know why I let it get to me so much."

"Hey, that doesn't mean you can't feel what needs feeling, and have a cry about it if you need to. Crying is cathartic and way better than holding it all in," I replied.

"I know you love doing Creative Writing and English, and you were obviously born to do it, but you would have made good counsellor had you done Psychology, just to let you know."

I smiled. "Thanks Ruby. Always know that I am here for you, if you need to rant or chat about it, or anything else for that matter."

"Thanks Mace," she said softly, giving me a hug.

"Remember why you're doing what you're doing and you'll find your love for art again. Sometimes the pressures of university can take away the passion."

She agreed. "Thank you again, for listening."

CHAPTER 10 - ISLA

The following Wednesday, I found myself meeting Henry again. Somehow we'd fallen into a pattern of lunch on Wednesdays. It worked. It was a day I was usually writing at home and not in meetings or working with Beth. But when I told her I was meeting him again for lunch her reaction was not surprising.

"Should I just block out every Wednesday for your lunch dates?" she said, raising an eyebrow.

"You can block out Wednesday for me to spend as I like, as you've always done," I said with a laugh and a smile. "I just happen to be seeing Henry again, because it just happens to be a time we're both free." Beth just smiled and nodded satisfactorily as if I'd conceded some great point in her favour. I knew everyone meant well, but I kind of wished people would just back off from asking about Henry. I felt like a teenager when everyone teases you about your first boyfriend and you just want everyone to be chill about it.

I knew Mrs. Russell knew I'm seeing Henry each week as well, she keeps giving me these looks but then deliberately asks me about other things. And somehow my mum has found out, I blame

Georgie. She, Beth, Mum, and Mrs. R would have Henry and I down the aisle by spring if they had their way. I'd stop seeing Henry so often to get them to chill out, but I enjoyed talking to him so much.

I made my way to the pub Henry suggested we meet at. It's an old favourite of mine, but for some reason I haven't been in ages. He wasn't standing outside like usual, so I went in and found him by the bar. It was warm and cosy inside, there was a fire going in the log burner in the corner.

"Decided what you want to eat?" I asked him as I approached, seeing him looking at the menu.

Henry looked up and smiled at me. "I'm trying to decide, shepherd's pie or the potato soup."

I looked over his arm at the menu, "Ooh, I was hoping the potato soup was still on the menu, it's been over a year since I've been here but that was always my favourite at this time of year."

"Potato soup it is then," Henry decided.

Standing so close to him, I couldn't help notice how good he smelled. Like cedar and sandalwood and spice. I took a step back slightly to put a bit of distance between us.

The guy behind the bar came up to us to take our order when Henry signaled he'd made his decision.

"Oh hey Isla! It's been ages! How're things?"

I looked up and realised the guy behind the bar was an old friend from school.

"Percy!? Oh my gosh, I didn't know you worked here. I haven't seen you in ages."

"I don't just work here, I took ownership of the place about five months ago. I was general manager under the old owner but he was ready to retire and I was ready to take it on. I'm just filling in behind the bar today, one of our usual lunchtime staff is out sick. Good to see you."

"Percy that's fantastic. Good to see you too," I said smiling.

"So is this your fiancé? I heard you were living in London?"

My face froze, "Umm, no. The engagement was broken off.

Years ago. I've been back in Bath since. I'm a writer now. Umm, this is my friend. Henry. He's newly moved back to Bath." I was trying to speak in complete sentences but failing. I turned to Henry, "Henry, this is Percy. Wait, do you two remember each other? Percy was a couple years below us in school."

Henry was looking at me, kind of funny, but he rearranged his features into a pleasant smile and turned to Percy. "Nice to see you Percy. You have a brother named Fred don't you?"

"Yeah! Did you know Fred?" Percy looked a bit shocked.

"We were in lessons together. Didn't hang out much after school since he did football, but I remember him talking about his younger brother Percy a lot."

"Oh—" I started, then stopped and cast a quick look at Percy.

Percy's face went a bit sad, "Wow, thanks mate, it's nice to hear that. Fred passed on five years back. Car accident on a stormy night. We still talk about him loads in the family of course, but I don't run into people very much anymore who talk about him."

Henry looked stricken, "I'm so sorry Percy. That's tragic. Fred and I weren't great mates, but he was a good guy, always knew how to keep us entertained during English. And he really did talk about you loads. Always said you were the brains of the family and were going to grow up to do great things."

Percy wiped his eyes with the back of his hand, "Thanks Henry, truly. It means a lot to hear that. I know Fred would have been proud when I bought this place. He would have been sitting at the end of the bar every evening asking for a free pint."

We all stood in silence for a bit, each thinking about Percy's brother.

"Well, what can I get you two? On the house, as old friends."

We tried to insist on paying but Percy wouldn't hear it. We ordered our soup and indulged in a pint of cider, even though it was still a work day. We settled in at a table by the log burner.

"Wow, I had no idea about Fred," Henry said sadly, leaning back in his chair.

"I know. I forgot you would have known him."

"Everyone knew Fred," Henry said nostalgically.

He was right, Fred was the golden boy of our school. Tall, handsome, great with the football. A friend to every guy and every girl wanted to date him. His popularity could have gone to his head, but he was unfailingly nice to everyone.

"Do you still see anyone else from school?" Henry asked.

"Not very many. Most of the people from our old group moved away. But I'm still very close to Georgie. You remember Georgianna Gilbert? She's Harrison now, married to a great guy named Grant. But she was my best friend in school."

Henry's eyes went wide and a bunch of expressions flashed on his face at once.

"Wait, hold on. Yes, I remember Georgianna Gilbert, the two of you were inseparable."

"We still are," I said with a laugh.

"But go back a bit, you said Georgie is married to Grant Harrison?"

"Yes, do you know him? He's not from here, they met at the uni, then after they graduated he stayed. They talked about leaving Bath for London or somewhere like that, but ended up staying here and both of them have built businesses."

"I know," Henry said. "Grant's startup is one of the first businesses that hired me when I set up my firm. He's mentioned his wife Georgie but I never put it together that it might be Georgie Gilbert."

I laughed. "It's a small world, isn't it?"

"It is," Henry smiled.

Our soup arrived, with giant hunks of fresh bread, and we tucked in. We ate in silence for a few minutes before Henry spoke up.

"So, there was a fiancé?" He was trying to be casual but there was curiosity written all over his face.

"Ugh, I was hoping you'd missed Percy saying that," I said rolling my eyes.

"Nope," he grinned. "If you don't want to talk about it, you don't have to. Mum hasn't said anything to me. Does she know the story?"

"Of course, your mum knows everything about me," I laughed. "But it's a credit to her character that she hasn't shared all my private stories, even to her own son."

"Mum would never tell other people's tales. She has definite views on that sort of thing," Henry chuckled.

"Well, I'm not telling you the whole story. It's too embarrassing. But I left Bath to go to uni. First a sociology degree in the States, at Oregon State University. I liked Oregon and wanted to study in the States and my family in Portland were fairly close by but not so close I felt pressure to see them all the time. A couple of my cousins were going to be at OSU at the same time, so it seemed like a good plan. Then I got accepted to do a Masters and then a PhD in public policy at Cambridge, where my parents went, and where they met. I was more interested in the theory and academics of public policy, so I thought I'd be an academic like my dad, rather than actually do public policy like my mum. But, as you do, I met a guy half way through my PhD. I fell hard and fast. We got engaged, and then when he graduated, he got a great job in London, while I was still finishing my degree. We decided to move to London, and I hoped I'd find something after I graduated. There are plenty of universities in London where I could've tried to teach. Anyway, my career didn't work out the way I thought and neither did the relationship. We never made it down the aisle. I left him and London behind and came back to Bath. Kind of started over from scratch."

Henry had been listening with interest, "I'm sorry it didn't work out."

"I'm not," I said definitively. "I'm better off. The end was inevitable and if we'd been married, getting out of it would have been a bigger nightmare than it already was."

"I can relate to that."

"Okay then, spill. I told you my sad love story, your turn," I said with a crooked smile.

"Don't think I didn't notice that most of your story was about where you went to uni, which was very interesting by the way, I always wanted to study in the States but couldn't afford it."

"Perks of having an American passport and family in the area. My dual citizenship meant I didn't count as an international student and I took my gap year to establish residency in the area so I could pay in-state tuition. It ended up being only a little more than doing my undergrad here would have been."

"Lucky you!" Henry exclaimed. "Well, my story is similar, I did my undergrad at LSE, but that led to an MBA at Oxford—"

"Are we going to have problems?" I asked with a small giggle.

"No, I can be a gentleman and overlook the fact you went to the inferior uni."

"Ha! Inferior. You would think that."

"Hush, I'm telling you my story."

"You're right, forgive me. Carry on," I said, waving a piece of bread before dipping it into my soup.

"I met a woman who was also in the MBA program. I'd been keeping a low profile, any business program can be competitive, but when you're at the level of Oxford, doing an MBA, well, the competition is fierce. But she noticed me and cornered me one day and told me to ask her out for a drink."

"Bold!"

"Very. Not usually my type, her boldness or her appearance. She looked like a supermodel and it was a bit intimidating. I had no clue what she saw in me."

"Well, have you had a full body replacement since Oxford? Because I'm pretty sure any woman with eyes can see what she saw in you Henry," I said simply.

"Are you saying I'm handsome Isla?"

"No comment. Continue your story."

Henry smiled. "All the guys in our program were after her, but I was the only one she had interest in. I asked her out and we ended up dating for over a year. As graduation approached we were both applying for jobs. She was applying for all the top finance companies, in London, New York, Hong Kong, nothing was too out of reach, she wanted the top. It was admirable, her drive, her focus. She didn't settle for anything less than perfect."

"Admirable, but also a bit unrealistic, don't you think? I mean, not to speak badly of her, but she sounds like one of those people that makes the rest of us feel like crap about our choices," I said laughing.

"Exactly," Henry agreed with a wry smile. "And here we arrive at the turn in the story. I was totally supportive, and would have moved wherever she got a job and made something work for me. I knew that long term I really wanted to start my own business, so I was more interested in getting a job with any company in the consulting area where I could see how a business worked on the inside. But she had all these expectations that we'd both be these high flyers in the upper stratosphere of the business world."

"Yikes," I said with a grimace.

"I loved her, but it became increasingly clear I wasn't good enough. She didn't want a partner who was supportive and let her put her career first. She saw it as a personal failing on my part. The funny thing is, she'd probably love the business I've grown, but my plan and my timeline for accomplishing things didn't meet her standard."

"So who broke up with who in the end?" I asked as I took a sip of my cider.

"She did. I fought to the bitter end to try to make it work. I thought we could work through it, if she could just understand my perspective and how my wanting to take things slow and get to know different aspects of my industry didn't mean I wasn't taking things seriously or being an underachiever. And it definitely didn't mean I was less worthy as a partner."

He looked down and swirled his spoon around his soup. "I don't know. Maybe I should have ended it sooner. The writing was certainly on the wall, as they say. I didn't like her constant passive aggressive—and sometimes just outright aggressive—comments about me and my career choices. And I definitely didn't appreciate the way she constantly put me down and made me feel less worthy but then spun any criticism of her actions or defense of myself as me not appreciating that she's a strong woman or saying that I just wanted her to be meek and mild. Literally nothing I said or did was right and there was no middle ground for us."

"Wow, nothing like being gaslit and made to feel like you are the only problem in the relationship. I hope you know now that you were right to call her out on her behaviour?"

"I do. Now. I didn't recognise the gaslighting or the psychological manipulation at the time. I guess I was blinded by love," he laughed bitterly. "When she left me though, it was a huge wake up call. I know I did everything I could to make it work. It wasn't my fault. But I couldn't stand staying in London. She got a job with a big bank there. If she'd moved to Hong Kong or something, I might have stayed, but London suddenly felt too small. We were in different fields but our paths might have still crossed. So that's when I moved to San Fransisco. I found a great job with a consultancy firm out there, got in at ground level when they were still small and worked my way up as the firm grew, until I was national director for them."

"Wow," I said, impressed. "And you walked away from that to start your own firm? That must have been daunting."

"It was, but I had a great boss, who totally backed me up. Didn't make me feel like I was making the wrong decision. He just made me promise that I wouldn't become their competition," Henry said with a laugh. "My company has a different focus and different type of client we market to, so thankfully my old colleagues were safe."

I laughed. The more I got to know Henry, the more fascinating he became. And our pasts were more similar than I'd realised.

"I feel bad now," I said with a small laugh. "I downplayed my previous relationship but you really opened up about yours. Thank you for trusting me."

"Of course I trust you," he said simply. "Plus, my mum trusts you, and I trust her completely."

I smiled. "She's an excellent judge of character. I'm honoured she chose to be friends with me. And now that I know more of your story, I can tell why she thinks we'd be a good match."

Henry grinned bashfully, "I'm sorry about that. She really does have the best intentions. But sometimes she gets ahead of herself."

"I get it. She just wants both of us to be happy."

"Mum was just so totally and completely happy with Dad," Henry said with a sad smile. "She always says that she wants that for me, to find someone who makes me feel as good as she and my dad felt together."

"I know losing him was very hard for her, we've talked about it a few times. By all accounts, what they had was the rarest form of true love. Not everyone gets so lucky."

Henry looked thoughtful, and started to say something, then paused and seemed to switch ideas before saying, "So what about your parents?"

"Definitely true love. They were meant to be. They've been through so much. But they've stuck with their marriage and have always done the daily work to keep it strong. Honestly, they're one of the reasons I knew my old relationship wasn't working. But like you, I thought I could make it work. If I fought hard enough. If I was good enough..." my voice faded.

"You don't have to talk about it," Henry said gently. "We can change the subject completely."

"No, it's fine," I said quietly. "I really don't want to go into details, but it was pretty similar to your story. I was never good enough for him. He was constantly nit-picking about me. He didn't like that I wasn't finding the right job, he said someone with my education should have a better job than the ones I was getting interviewed for. He thought my writing was frivolous and would tease me mercilessly any time he caught me writing. In the beginning the criticisms were more general, about jobs or career stuff. But eventually it got really personal. The flat wasn't immaculate when he got home from work. My outfit for his work party wasn't stylish enough. He hated my hair, one day he made an appointment for me at a salon and told them exactly what he wanted done to it. Like, full colour and cut."

Henry's face grew stormy, "He did what?!"

"I know! But I was young and I thought I loved him."

"Please tell me you didn't go through with the salon appointment."

I cringed, "To my everlasting shame and horror, I unfortunately did. I don't really care about my hair, so I thought, fine, if it will make him happy, let the stylist do what he wants."

I paused and looked down at my hands, which had started subconsciously twisting the napkin in my lap. "I didn't recognise myself. My long auburn hair was gone. They dyed it honey blonde and cropped it to my jaw line in an angled bob. It's not that it looked terrible, it was very stylish and sleek. But it wasn't me. And I could never style it the way they did. It took ages for it to grow out to a point I could manage it on my own again. And worst of all, he hated it. Booked me back in immediately to have them dye it back to my natural colour. Which of course didn't totally work, you can't do that much processing and dying. They tried their best. And that's just one story of many. So yeah, I understand trying to make a bad relationship work, and I relate to the gaslighting and emotional manipulation. Been there, done that, got the t-shirt."

"Wait, there were t-shirts? Now I really feel cheated," Henry said with a crooked smile, trying to inject some humour into the intense conversation.

I laughed. "Maybe I only imagined the t-shirt. It was all pretty hazy at the end."

"You don't have to give more details, but that was when you moved back to Bath?"

I sighed inwardly, relieved that the conversation was changing directions. I already couldn't believe how much I'd confided in Henry about my past. "Yes, like you, I couldn't stay in London after the relationship ended. Now, I only go when I have to for book stuff. I had a couple suitcases and a few boxes. Georgie and Grant showed up in his car, loaded me and my things in the back and drove back to Bath. They'd only been dating a couple months then, but Grant dropped everything to help me just because I was Georgie's best friend."

"When did you start writing? I mean, you mentioned you'd tried writing before, but when did you decide to try it as a career?"

"I had degrees in public policy but I had no motivation to work in that field and I'd waited too long after graduation to try to get an academic position. I hadn't been publishing or presenting at conferences, I was a failed academic. I felt like a failure in general. I'd moved back in with my parents, into the room I grew up in. They were great, super supportive, but it was still embarrassing. Mum started having me do copywriting for one of the charities she worked for. That led to more copywriting and blog work. A lot of it had a creative spin to it and I really enjoyed it. Mum and Georgie both encouraged me to stick with writing. I had an idea for a novel, *A Courageous Beginning*, I guess because I wanted to write a story about someone in a similar position to me but who manages to overcome her past and find happiness. I thought it was just a therapeutic exercise, a bit of catharsis really. I never thought anything would happen with it. But the uni put on an event for the Creative Writing students that was open to the public. A panel discussion with an editor, a literary agent, a publisher, and a couple writers. It was great. Somehow I mustered up the nerve to go up to the agent at the end and chat to her for a bit."

"Don't tell me, she loved your book and signed you immediately?"

I laughed, "Ha! No, that would have been a good story. No, but she gave me great advice and after I gave her the pitch for my story, she gave me the names of a few agents who I should send query letters to. I sent three letters out, the first two sent back almost immediate rejection letters. I didn't hear from the third one for ages. But after a couple months, and after giving up on her, I got a phone call saying she was going to be in Bath and could we meet up."

"Wow!"

"Yeah, so it turned out there'd been a shuffle with my manuscript and it got set aside and forgotten about for a bit in the mailroom before it finally ended up on her desk, just a few days before she called me. As soon as she saw it she knew she wanted to represent me. She came out to Bath just to try to win me over in person. The rest is history."

"That's amazing," Henry said excitedly.

"I know, it's pretty crazy. She moved fast too, she got me a great book deal with my publisher within a few months and they loved it so much they sped up the process to publication. I already had a complete manuscript. So within a year it was on bookshelves."

"And you were an instant success?" He had a glimmer in his eye as he smiled.

"Hardly!" I laughed. "It was a slow start. I just managed to make back my advance in the first year, plus a modest profit for the publisher. They agreed to let me publish the sequel. When the second book came out, both books did a lot better and it's been better with every book since. It took a while to establish my author platform and build a following, and even now I'm not a crazy best-selling author. I mean, I do pretty well, especially for my genre. I'm a best seller for my publisher. And my readers are really engaged and consistent. They buy my books and they show up, both online and in person at book events."

"Pretty sure I saw your latest book climbing a best seller list in the paper, " Henry said with a grin.

"Okay, I'm doing really well," I admitted. "I'm not crazy rich, but I have a lovely house in a beautiful city and if Georgie has her way I'm about to buy my first investment property. I can't complain. It's a far cry from where my life was several years ago when I first returned to Bath. I'm lucky."

"Well, you've also worked your socks off from the sound of it."

"Yeah, it was intense the first few years, then a bit easier but mostly because it felt more fun once I was engaging with my readers more. Then, the last few years or so, I feel like I've found my rhythm. I enjoy the whole process more, not just the writing but working with everyone involved and interacting with the readers. I feel more in control and less like I'm doing what I'm being told to do. I have more power with my publisher now, because the books sell well and I'm their top selling and most consistent author." I said with a smile. "Or I was, before I started having trouble with my latest book. I'm not sure how things are going to work out."

"Still struggling to connect with it?" Henry asked with concern.

"A bit. I'm sure I'll get past it, but it's annoying."

"Well I'm happy to listen and talk through anything with you if you need a sounding board."

"You're a star. Thanks. But you need to get back to work and I need to get back to writing."

"Well, maybe we could meet again soon, for dinner or something, when we'd have more time and not be rushed to get back to work."

He said it so casually, and with a friendly tone. But something in his eyes made me pause. Lunch felt safe. Just two friends having lunch. But dinner? And what the heck is "something"?

As if reading my mind, Henry gave a small smile, "I promise, just friends. Two people who are happy being single but who also need to eat dinner and socialise from time to time."

I breathed a small sigh of relief, but I don't think I was imagining Henry's smile flickering just a little in response.

"Dinner would be great, I'll look at my schedule and get back to you."

We said goodbye and I walked home. Along the way I replayed my previous lunches with Henry. He's always been friendly, just friendly. There's never really been any flirting, just friendly chat. But maybe he's just been giving us space to get to know each other again?

Why did friendship have to feel so complicated?

CHAPTER 11 - MACEY

"Could I borrow your highlighter Macey?" Libby asked, shuffling across the floor to sit next to me.

"Of course," I replied, passing her the compact. "You only need a little bit, it's so pigmented!"

"Thank you!" she said, picking up her brush to apply it.

It was now Friday and Libby, Anna, Charlotte, Ruby and I were getting ready for Tom's party, which was due to start in about an hour. We were sprawled across Charlotte's bedroom floor, surrounded by our individual make-up bags and outfit choices that we had disregarded. I was currently curling my hair, after applying my makeup already. I'd gone for a slightly heavier look than usual, a brown smokey eye paired with winged liner and a pair of dramatic lashes.

It was only a house party, but I didn't have many opportunities to dress up, so I thought I'd go all out and have some fun with it. It was nice getting ready with all the girls, we were all helping each other whilst doing so, which I really appreciated. I had Ruby checking the back of my head to make sure each strand was curled, and Charlotte straightening out the back of my dress each time I got up to avoid it creasing.

"Who wants another drink?" I called out, as I was leaving the room.

"Is that even a question?" Charlotte cackled, initiating a shared laughter that filled the room.

I laughed along. "I take that as everyone?" To which they all nodded in unison.

I left to go to the kitchen, which was only next door. Charlotte had actually taken the lounge as her bedroom, claiming the acoustics were better there for when she had to practise her singing. Our house was pretty spacious, her having the downstairs room just meant we used one of the upstairs bedrooms as our shared space, the one with the terrace. It worked out pretty well all in all, the bedrooms being split across three floors actually meant that noise was never an issue.

I was on the top floor, and rarely heard Charlotte singing, unless she was wandering around the house doing it. Which she did do, sometimes. It had been decided that Charlotte's bedroom would be the designated "getting ready" space for any social events, seeing as it was closest to the kitchen, making it easy to get drinks. Charlotte emphasised the importance of pre-drinking, and of course we all obeyed. I grabbed us all a canned cocktail, a favourite of ours, before setting them down on the kitchen side to check my phone.

Still nothing.

It had now been almost another week since I last saw Ted, and subsequently, last heard from him. He promised he would text, to make plans for our next date, and that I needn't worry about him not getting in touch. I sighed. I thought that now it was Friday, he might text, if his week at university was busy or something similar, and with it now being the weekend, he was finally free. I didn't think that excused him however, seeing as it literally takes two seconds to message, but it is what it is. I collected the cans up once more and strolled back into Charlotte's room to distribute them.

"Why the glum face?" Ruby asked, as I was passing them out.

"I still haven't heard from Ted. That's weird, right?" I questioned.

"After your road-trip shindig the other day, that is weird," Charlotte responded.

After I had gotten back last Saturday, I caught them up on the events of the day over dinner. They were all dumbfounded, shocked that we had bumped into each other, by chance, outside of Plymouth.

"He seemed so keen!" Libby added, for moral support.

Charlotte turned to me. "All the conversations you had, they sounded so sincere and genuine. I was holding out hope for him," she sighed. "Maybe he just isn't the dating type, like Ruby said. Try not to think about him too much, I suppose. It isn't fair of him to just ghost you though. He should at least tell you how he's feeling."

"I guess so," I said, the disappointment somewhat apparent in my tone, though I was trying to pretend that I didn't care too much.

"Maybe you'll meet someone at the party tonight," Ruby said jokingly. "Tom will have loads of friends there, plenty of eligible bachelors who are actually willing to date!" she laughed. "You and Charlotte can wing woman each other; I know she's on the prowl too."

I giggled, "That could be a laugh. I don't know if I trust Charlotte to choose men for me though!" To which everyone, except Charlotte, laughed at.

"Hey!" she exclaimed. "I'm offended."

"I'm joking. I'll go on the pull with you, if you like. I'll probably do less pulling though, more scoping out potential guys for you. I'm not that bothered, honestly."

"If you say so," Charlotte teased.

"I swear. I might just hang out with Ruby, Libby and Anna. The ones who are in committed relationships. It seems more like my vibe," I scoffed.

"I'm not in a committed relationship..." Ruby huffed, to which we all rolled our eyes.

Charlotte glared at me, "You're not in a committed relationship though Macey. Now is your chance!"

"I am committed to my writing," I said, laughing.

She continued to glare, jokingly of course. "I'm not accepting that. I am setting you up tonight. I know deep down that you want a man in your life, so I am determined to find you one!"

———

HERE GOES NOTHING. I thought to myself as I knocked on the door. I smoothed out my dress with my cold hands, ensuring there were no creases before the door was opened. I was wearing a long sleeve, all black body con. I didn't usually wear dresses that were so figuring hugging, but this one seemed to cling in all the right places, showing off my curves nicely. Not being a huge partier, I didn't have many suitable dresses, so when I saw this one on Depop, I had to snap it up.

These sorts of social gatherings make me feel slightly uneasy, and I could feel the nervousness begin to creep in. I was excited nonetheless, to dance the night away and forget about my worries. Forget about uni stress, my parents, and of course, Ted. Not only did I just have to make it through the night without embarrassing myself, I now had the pressure of finding a man, either for Charlotte, or reluctantly, myself, hanging over my head.

"Come in!" Tom chimed in as he opened the door. All five of us shuffling in, Ruby passing Tom a crate of cider as she entered last. "Cheers!" he exclaimed. "I'll pop it in the fridge," he paused for a quick second, before looking directly at me. "Hey Macey," he added, before introducing us all to his friend from home, who was visiting for the weekend. "This is Nick." We all introduced ourselves, hugging the lads one by one, with Nick lingering for an extra moment whilst his arms were around me.

Ruby smiled. "I think Nick has the hots for you Mace!" she said, laughing, as he walked away. I quietly laughed, realising his random show of affection did not go unnoticed.

"Right. So Macey and I wing woman-ing each other is no longer happening then!" Charlotte said in a huff.

I just laughed, looking over at Nick who was organising the

drinks in the fridge with Tom. He was tall, but not too tall. About five foot nine. He had dark brown hair and dark brown eyebrows, which were prominent on his face. He was stocky, of a big build. *He seemed nice enough*, I thought to myself, exiting the hallway to follow the rest of my group. The living room had been organised so that there was plenty of floor space. All sofas and chairs were pushed to the edges, giving everyone enough space to move about. There was a big speaker set up at the far side of the room, with a guy manning it whilst chatting to some of the other attendees.

Ruby tapped me on the shoulder. "There's Issac."

I smiled in response and my mind drifted to thoughts of Ted and our meetings. I grabbed a drink off Nick when he came in to help forget.

———

ABOUT AN HOUR LATER, drinks were flowing, and the music had gotten louder. It was pumping within the four walls of the lounge, and beyond. I was secretly worried about the neighbours, concerned that they'd make a complaint and the party would get shut down. Not that I wouldn't welcome an excuse to leave.

I was looking for an opportunity to slip out of the front door when a drunk Nick wandered over to me.

"Planning your escape?" he asked, as I hovered by the exit.

"Um no," I said, nervous all of a sudden. "I'm just wanting some fresh air." The door was swung open as people were coming in and out, and the crisp evening breeze was refreshing as it was getting hotter inside.

"Fair enough," Nick said, smiling at me. "So Macey," he continued. "Are you single?"

"Yep," I answered, shuffling about. I scanned around, searching for one of the girls. I couldn't see any of them, and I was starting to feel uncomfortable in Nick's disorderly presence. He was edging closer to me, the stench of whisky escaping on his breath every time he opened his mouth to speak. He drew closer, disregarding personal space completely.

"Looking?" he said, placing one hand against the wall and another by his side.

"Erm, no, not really," I replied, desperately trying to escape his increasingly more intimidating grasp.

He slid his free hand from where it was hovering next to my face, toward my hip. He slowly started reaching for my arse, forcing me to exhale suddenly.

"Nick. No," I stuttered, in an attempt to get him to lay off.

"Hey. You can give me a kiss, Macey. Come on, just kiss me." He got closer, not moving his hand from my behind.

"No," I said, more sternly this time. I felt like he was closing in on me, leaving me with few options as to where to go. His hands were crawling all over me at this point, trapping me in a corner of the hallway, just out of eye's way.

"You know you want to." His slimy hands wiggling their way upwards, whilst his eyes were scanning my body, looking me up and down, as if he was a lion, about to pounce on his prey.

"No," I winced again, as he began to cup my face.

Suddenly, a voice bellowed from down the hall. "She said no," it roared, scaring Nick who abruptly removed me from his grasp.

"Woah, mate!" Nick begged, as he was being charged at. Before I could do anything, an arm grabbed me and pulled me away.

"We were just having a laugh!" Nick protested. "No need to cock-block me!"

"She isn't interested pal. That's obvious."

Suddenly, I was sitting on the stairs, completely unaware as to what was going on. I'd stumbled around and found a place to sit and catch my breath. I could hear more shouting next to me, some sort of confrontation. Everything had all happened so fast, in a blur, that I hadn't even seen who my apparent knight in shining armour was, nor could I clearly hear what was now being said.

I shakily got up, turning back towards Nick, to see what was going on, only to get lost in the crowd that had begun to form around me. I was being pushed aside. I could no longer see Nick, or who he was arguing with, for that matter.

"You wanna take this outside?" Nick yelled.

"Not particularly, no," the other voice replied.

"You wanna settle it here then, grandpa? What are you gonna do in your sweater and loafers?" Nick jeered again.

It was at this point I realised who it was. I thrust my way through the onlookers and shouted for them to stop.

Ted spun around, after hearing my voice. "Macey, it's fine. I've got this!" he said, looking directly at me. I grabbed him by the arm, to pull him away, and as I did, he toppled onto me.

"What the fuck Nick?" I cried, realising he'd punched Ted. Nick stepped back, almost in shock at his own actions. Everyone swiftly cleared my way as I guided Ted through the front door, propping him on the step.

"I'm fine!" he said, grimacing as he muttered the two words.

"I don't think you are," I said worriedly, attempting to use my sleeve to wipe off some of the blood and assess the damage. "We should go to hospital."

"No need." Ted winced. "It's just a punch. I may be a grandpa, but I can take a punch," he added, with a slight smile.

I sighed in relief. "If you're sure. What are you even doing here?"

"I was going to ask you the same question M."

"Tom invited all the girls last week, Nick is a friend of his from home, I'd never seen him before this."

"Tom works at the shop I used to work at. I trained him. We became pals and he invited me. I didn't know it'd end up like this. I should have stuck to my word when I said my uni partying days ended with the undergraduate degree." He looked towards me. "This wasn't how I planned on seeing you again Macey. I'm sorry."

"For what? You saved my butt up there," I whispered.

"I'm sorry for not texting,"

"I think you just made up for that. Come on, let's go over the road to mine and get you cleaned up," I said, whilst helping him up off the step.

————

"I'm not a violent person, you know." Ted said as I wiped the remaining blood off his face. I'd found a cloth in the cupboard after we'd arrived back at the house and doused it in some antiseptic that Charlotte had for emergencies.

The girls had heard the carfuffle and found me and Ted just as we were leaving. I told them to stay at the party, help clean up, and I'd see them when they were done. Most of the house had been cleared out, Nick had seemingly disappeared, I guess to avoid everyone after what he had done quickly became common knowledge. Tom also found Ted and I as we were leaving, apologising profusely for what had happened and on behalf of his friend. I was more worried about Ted, more than what had happened to me, so I swiftly accepted Tom's well wishes and took Ted to the safety of my home. I pushed what had gone down with Nick to the back of my mind and focused on making sure Ted was okay.

"Does it hurt?" I pondered aloud.

"The antiseptic stings a bit when it gets in the wound. My nose feels sore, but I can touch it and breathe ok so I don't think it's broken."

"Should we go to the hospital just in case?"

"There's not much they could do, so there's no point."

"Fair enough. Just let me know if it continues to sting. It should ease up a bit after I've finished." I continued, "I know you're not violent Ted. You literally did nothing of the sort. Many people would have hit back. You didn't. You just confronted him, and put him in his place in doing so. That's pretty legendary. I'm sorry he hit you though. I know it's my fault,"

Ted interrupted, "It was not your fault at all Macey, I wish you hadn't said that. He's obviously just a dick who is used to getting what he wants. Which is pathetic, and no excuse for what he did to you. Speaking of which, are you okay? You've been so stressed, making sure I'm alright, when you're the real victim here."

"I'm fine," I shrugged. "He was just a bit slimy. Let's just say, it's a good job you got there when you did." I was glad we were sitting at the table and Ted couldn't see my shaking legs. I was shook up, and didn't want to admit it. Being in Ted's company was certainly reassuring, but I couldn't shake the overwhelming desire to cry. It had just been a lot.

"The universe keeps pushing us together in the strangest ways, doesn't it?"

I laughed. "It seems like it."

"Thank you for looking after me, M. I think we both took a bit of a knock tonight, eh?"

I nodded.

"It's not even 10pm yet," he continued.

"Fancy a walk?" I asked, smiling. Ted agreed so I ran upstairs to get us both a fleece, texting the girls on route to let them know we were going for a stroll and I wouldn't be home too late.

————

"I LIKE YOUR GRANDPA SWEATERS, you know. Very edgy."

"Thanks," Ted laughed and turned to look at me as we made it to the sea.

"It's so cold!" I said, shivering.

"The walk was your idea," Ted joked, as we wandered down the shoreline.

"I know, I just thought it would be a good time to finally take you up on your beach walk offer. I forgot that it's now October and consequently freezing."

Ted smirked, "Well I'm glad we finally got our beach walk, even if the circumstances haven't been ideal."

I bit my lip, thinking back to the evening's events. "Yeah. Not the best, but it is nice to see you. Thank you again for what you did back there, I was starting to panic a little. Usually I can hold my ground in those sorts of situations, normally finding a way to get away. But he was being really forceful." I paused. "Like I said earlier, I don't know what I would have done if you hadn't arrived when you did."

"Hey, it's okay M. I guess my protective instincts kicked in," he said, coyly. "I know you don't need protecting, you're a fierce one, I can tell. But I saw he was being pushy and once I heard you say no, I knew I had to help. I hated seeing you like that," Ted said, lowering his voice as he said the last part. "I wish I had texted you, because then at least we could have arranged to go to the party together. I had no idea you'd be there."

"Third time meeting is the charm, eh?" I laughed, in an attempt to lighten the conversation. "I don't think I'll be going to any more parties, any time soon though."

Ted paused, awkwardly shuffling his weight from one leg to the other. "I know we've only met three times now Macey, but I do really think you're great. I've thought that since the day we met, and each one of our conversations since has only confirmed that."

"Then why didn't you text me?" I teased.

Ted looked as if he was concentrating, focused on what he wanted to say. He sat down on some rocks that we'd arrived at and I joined him.

"I was nervous Macey, worried I was going to fuck it up," he said, turning to face me. "I just needed time to figure it out. I don't really date. I haven't done for ages. I wasn't planning on it either. But then I met you, spent time with you. You haven't left my mind. You're absolutely gorgeous, yet I can see that you have a heart of gold also. I knew I had to see you again, see if you were interested in me, too. I was spiralling, I still am, I should probably shut up. This might seem like a lot, so I apologise. I'm not usually this forward. I will say this though," he paused. "I never believed in fate, or anything of the sort. Until now. I feel as if some external force is mocking my fear of messaging you, and to make up for my incompetence, they're guiding me to you, in rather unconventional ways. The first time we met, I shouldn't even have been at the bookstore! I was only there because the book I had ordered didn't turn up that morning as it should have, and I was panicking I wouldn't have it in time for Evie's birthday. The second time, after I hadn't messaged, I was only hanging around outside because Evie was messing me around with whether she needed a lift or not. The third, tonight, I wasn't planning on going to the party at all, hence why I turned up late. I was hounded with texts off Tom, wondering where I was, so I thought I'd dip in and show my face, that's all."

I was flattered, floored even, by everything that he had said. Yet, I was struggling to process his sudden outburst of affection. Instead of saying anything of real value, I replied without much thought.

"So what you're saying is, we really have Evie to thank for everything?"

"I guess," he laughed. "Is that all you're going to say?"

I shrugged. "I'm a woman of few words when I'm taken aback Ted." Contemplating my next move, I shuffled around awkwardly myself.

The wind was picking up and Ted's hair was blowing all over. Luckily, my trusty bobble had been on my wrist, so I was able to tie my hair up when we'd left the house. I giggled, extending my arm out to brush the hairs away from his face, our eyes locking when his were finally uncovered. I slid my hand down the back of his head, resting it on his neck, before pulling his face close to mine.

Taking a breath, I went on to whisper, "I like you too." My heart was pounding, and the adrenaline began to kick in. I'd never had the confidence to do anything like this before, but being this close to Ted, it just felt right.

He smiled, raising his own hand up to rest on mine, as I was cupping his face. I could tell he was patiently waiting, allowing me to take the lead. What felt like hours passed, although in reality it was only a few seconds. I leant in, pressing my lips against his, and the kiss slowly intensified. He moved his arms down and placed them on my hips, bringing my body closer to his. I could feel his warmth upon me, it was no longer a cold October evening. It was the warmest day of the year.

CHAPTER 12 - ISLA

The next day I ended up back at the mews house that Georgie wants me to buy for a second viewing with her. I followed her around as she pointed out more of the features and discussed what she wanted to do in the property, but I struggled to stay focused.

"I was thinking, we could knock down this wall, to create more of an open plan kitchen/diner here, that would flow nicely into the living room. Then, we can open up the space a tiny bit more too, if we put in a nice banister along the stairs, instead of this wall," she said, gesturing wildly with all of her plans.

"Mmm-hmm," I murmured noncommittally.

"Hey," Georgie snapped her fingers in front of my face.

I startled and took a step back.

"Are you paying attention? Where are you right now?" she asked, looking worried.

"Yeah, soz. I'm paying attention. Knock down that wall to open up the kitchen," I said pointing. "And replace that wall with an open bannister. It's a good idea. A bannister would look pretty at Christmas with some evergreen garlands."

Georgie narrowed her eyes at me, trying to read my expression. She knows me too well, it's a bit frightening sometimes.

"What is going on? I can tell the difference between when that brain of yours is actually paying attention and when it's split off in a million directions thinking of too many things at once. Is it Henry?"

"Oh for flips sake, no, it's not about Henry," I said with frustration. "Or, oh I don't know, I guess it is about Henry." I tugged my scarf off my neck. It was suddenly feeling overly warm in this place.

"I'm just asking, as your friend, what the bloomin' heck is wrong with you? You have not been acting yourself all day. I know you had lunch with Henry yesterday, so that's why I asked if your mental distraction today has anything to do with him."

I just looked at Georgie, I didn't know what to say.

Looking worried, "Isla, talk to me."

"I will, but can we finish here? I promise I was listening, talk me through the rest of your plans and then we can go get coffee."

"Okay," Georgie said, giving me a sideways glance to make sure I was listening, "I'll be quick. There's just a couple things I wanted to discuss with you about the upstairs."

We got through the rest of the viewing and then went to one of our favorite cafes. I ordered a large latte and a muffin. I was ready to drown my frustrations in caffeine, foam, and carbs.

"Alright, spill," Georgie demanded.

"Bearing in mind that I was listening to you the other day, you know, regarding giving a relationship a chance and being brave enough to try to fall in love again, blah blah blah, it's just not that simple. At least not for me. But between you and Beth and my mum and Mrs. R, I feel like I'm getting pressure from all sides to give Henry a chance but I don't even know if he's interested in me in that way. I think he is, but I haven't been in this situation in ages. And how do I know if it's worth risking my heart again if I don't even know if the guy likes me or not? He and I talked yesterday at lunch about our pasts and it got kind of heavy. We both know what it's like to be in a relationship with the wrong person. To give and give and give and not get anything back except a kick in the teeth. On paper Henry is great. In so many ways. And we're so alike too. And we have history, it's not like he's a complete stranger. But we both have said we're happy being single and doing our own thing."

"Don't you think," Georgie said softly, "that maybe you're over-thinking this just a little bit?"

I opened my mouth to reply but she held her hand up and silenced me.

"No, I mean it. We both know that's what you do. I'm the impulsive one and you're the one who will worry over a problem or a question for days, agonising over different possibilities before finally deciding how to move forward. It's not a bad thing overall, but every now and then, and I think this is such a time, it freezes you and prevents you from just letting things progress naturally."

I looked down at my latte, "We saw Percy yesterday, he owns the pub now, the one you and I used to go to all the time."

"Percy? Gosh, I haven't seen him since his wedding. Good for him though, I remember him talking about wanting to buy that place when the owner was ready to retire." Georgie sighed, and popped her chin down on her hand. "I miss the old group. I hope Grant and I can meet you and Henry for dinner some time, just so I can catch up with him too. If he even remembers me," she said with a laugh.

"He remembered you," I said laughing as well. "Who could forget you?" I winked at her and Georgie blushed. "He also knows Grant. Grant's company hired Henry's to do some consulting work."

"Well I'll be damned," Georgie exclaimed. "What a small world! Grant mentioned he'd hired a consultant but he hadn't told me their name."

"Anyway, since yesterday I haven't been able to stop thinking about lunch. Particularly about Percy's brother Fred. He had his whole life ahead of him and then he didn't anymore. I truly am happy right now, I know no one wants to believe that, but I am. But could I be happier? Maybe. Could I be happier if I was in a relationship? I don't know. Possibly? Or I could be miserable. It wasn't just Edwin. I know there weren't a ton of guys before him but there were a few and none of them were that great either. Maybe I'm just not meant to be in a relationship. There's nothing wrong with that. It's fairy tales and romance novels that convince us we have to be in a relationship to be happy." I noticed Georgie start to say something and put my hand up. "And I say that realising that I write some of those romance novels that contribute to these false ideals. So yeah, call me a hypocrite."

Georgie frowned, "I was not going to call you a hypocrite. I was going to point out that you're right. Some people are genuinely happier being single and independent. And if I honestly thought you were thriving the way you are now, I'd tell you to just keep Henry as a friend. But I don't think you are as happy as you could be. And when it comes to your novels, the thing that makes them special, the thing that makes people love them even when they claim they don't usually like romances, is that your books aren't traditional romances. We don't read and love your books because we're waiting to see what guy the girl is going to fall for."

I nervously picked at the crumbs of my muffin, Georgie and I so rarely talked about my books, I always felt awkward when she brought them up. "Then why do you read them?"

Georgie rolled her eyes, "I can't believe I have to explain your own novels to you. We read them," she said slowly, as if explaining something to a child, "because we're watching to see how the heroine is going to work through her fears and insecurities and create the life she wants and deserves, and in the process open herself up to finding lasting love. It's not love that makes her happy in the end. She creates her own happiness first."

"It's easy to create your own happiness when it's fiction Georgie. No one is going to buy books where the main character is just as messed up and confused at the end as she is in the beginning."

"Isla, cut the excuses. You keep writing a narrative where the character goes through great struggles and comes through stronger in the end. Your characters do the work to figure out who they really are and what they really want. But you're not. When you moved back home from London, after Evil Edwin, you were a shell of a person. I haven't forgotten the state you were in Isla. You've moved on, but only to a certain point. You're entirely focused on your career."

"So are you!"

"Yes, but I also have Grant and you know we're trying to have a baby. I'm working hard now so that if I do finally get pregnant, I can slow down then."

"So because I'm not married and trying to get pregnant there's something wrong with me?"

"You know damn well that's not what I'm saying," Georgie said crossly.

"I know, I'm sorry," I said sincerely, immediately regretting my previous tone. I was acting like a petulant teenager and all Georgie was trying to do was help. I didn't know what was wrong with me today. Georgie had been trying so hard to get pregnant, for years now. She and Grant were on their third round of IVF. Georgie had already had to come to terms with the idea that if she never got pregnant it didn't mean there was something wrong with her, but it had been a long road to get to that point.

Georgie sighed, "Isla, you have your writing and your readers, and that's great. But I know you, you rarely make time for things other than work. Something just for you. You don't even travel."

"I travel! I just went to Bristol."

Rolling her eyes, "I mean for something other than work. I know you love travelling to author events, but when was the last time you went somewhere just to get away? When was the last time you left your writing behind for a bit and just relaxed?"

"You know, sometimes I hate how well you know me," I said, giving Georgie a crooked smile.

"You love it and you know it," Georgie laughed. "Just know that I see you. I'm your best friend and I've known you the longest.

I see how tired and sad you look when you think no one's watching. You're not happy Isla and when you talk about Henry, I see something different in you. A glimmer of something. A little sparkle in your eye. That's why I'm encouraging your friendship with him. Do you like him? I know you did back in school. What's holding you back? What is going to make you finally get past what happened with Edwin?"

I sighed, "I don't know."

Georgie reached out and grabbed my hand. "We all love you and support you. We just want you to be happy."

"I know," I said quietly. "Maybe I should get away for a bit. I can't stop writing, I'm on a deadline, but I'm struggling so much with this book." I put my head in my hands, leaning on the table.

"Maybe getting away would help you focus on whatever is blocking you?"

"Possibly. I feel like I just need to think about everything you're saying and about the book."

"What's bothering you about the book?" Georgie asked with concern.

"I was so excited about this book idea and now I feel like it was a mistake. Everyone's going to hate it."

"Well, that wouldn't be the worst thing."

"Hey!" I said with a half laugh.

"I'm just saying, you can't be the perfect author who always gets it right all the time. I keep waiting for you to write a dud," Georgie said with a grin.

"Thanks, at least I'll be living up to someone's expectations if my next novel is a total failure. You always know how to make me feel better."

"Any time babe," Georgie said, winking.

"A trip away somewhere would be nice though, you're right, I haven't been anywhere that wasn't work related in ages. I'll have to have a think about where, I kind of feel like it should be somewhere I haven't been."

"Okay, so before I let you go, what do you think about the house?"

"You know what? Draft up the paperwork, I'll buy it."

"Really?!" Georgie squealed and waved her hands in front of her face. "Don't say that just to make me happy, if you want to keep looking we can."

"No, it's perfect Georgie, really. It would be a great holiday let, and if that doesn't work we can also rent it out as a short or long term residence. But a holiday let might be great for while you're doing work on it. I've looked at the financials, I can afford it. So put it all together and let's put in an offer."

"Oh my gosh, this is so exciting! And don't worry, I'll handle everything, like I promised."

"I'm counting on that," I said with a laugh. "Remember, I'm the money, you're the rest."

"Don't you worry. I'll get everything drafted up, please don't leave town until you sign the paperwork."

"Alright, I won't leave town until then, I promise. So how are you? I know I've been a mess lately, but how's the IVF going? I feel like you always talk about houses you want me to buy. I haven't wanted to pry, but are you alright?"

"Yeah, I'm good," Georgie said quietly. "Honestly I think it's harder on Grant. Like, I'm doing everything I'm supposed to be doing, but otherwise it's just a lot of waiting and hoping. We're trying to make our relationship a priority and support each other. So many couples who do IVF end up divorced before they have a baby. We made a promise that if treatments ever came between us and our marriage we'd stop." Georgie looked down at her coffee, "But we have decided this is the last round. So if it doesn't work, we'll move forward with adoption."

"And Grant is on board with that?"

"Absolutely, he agrees that ultimately we just want a family. We're fortunate that we are in a position to be able to afford IVF, so we wanted to try it, but we're 40 now, I'm not afraid of being an older parent, but I don't want to keep spending time going down this path if it's not going to work. So, either it will be third time lucky or three strikes and we're out," Georgie said with a laugh.

I laughed with her, "Well, you know I support you, no matter what path you take to parenthood, and I can't wait to be an auntie. Georgie, you're going to be a great mum, and I know it's going to happen for you, one way or another."

Georgie smiled. "I should let you get going, I've taken up a fair amount of your day."

"Yeah, I need to get back to writing. And now apparently also try to book a mini break somewhere," I said with a wink.

"Okay, so I'll get all the paperwork for the offer put together so you can sign before you leave, then you'll take off and think things through and get your head on straight, then you'll come home, marry Henry, and have babies and raise your kids to be best friends with my kids. Sound good?"

I laughed out loud at Georgie's silly expression, "Yes to the first two things, no comment or promises on the rest."

"I had to try," Georgie said with an exaggerated sigh.

We got up and I gave her a big hug, "You really are the best friend. I might never be a mum myself, but I know I'm going to be an aunt very soon and I can't wait."

Georgie hugged me back, "Take care of yourself Isla."

We said goodbye and I walked home, shuffling through fallen leaves along the way. I wasn't looking forward to getting back to writing, which I didn't like. I normally really enjoyed writing, so maybe Georgie was on to something in regards to a getaway. I could go on a bit of a writer's retreat, hole up somewhere on the coast and just focus on writing.

As I walked up to my house I saw Henry coming out of Mrs. Russell's house.

"Isla, hi! How's things?" He greeted me as I walked up and met him at the front gate.

"Hiya! Good to see you, is your mum alright?"

"Yeah, she's fine, I just had a rare break in my schedule and thought I'd come have a cuppa with her."

"Oh that's nice, I bet she enjoyed that."

"We both did. It's definitely the perk of moving back to Bath. I missed being able to just drop in for a chat and some tea when I was living in the States. Where are you coming back from?"

"I had a second house viewing with Georgie and then we got coffee."

"Are you going to put in an offer?"

"I am actually. She's putting all the paperwork together. It's a good investment."

"That's great, we'll have to celebrate once everything gets accepted."

"Yeah, that would be fun. It would be nice to have everyone over to see the place."

"So, about that invitation for dinner, have you had a chance to look at your schedule?"

"Umm, my schedule is kind of up in the air right now. I think I'm going to leave town for a little bit."

"Leave town? Another work trip? Where are you going?" Henry asked with an interested smile.

"Not for work, or at least not for a reader event. I think I just need to get away. I'm still struggling with the book, nothing is helping. I think I need to just go hide away somewhere for a bit and focus on just writing. Too many distractions here in Bath," I said, shifting from one foot to the other.

"I hope I haven't been a distraction," Henry said with a worried expression. "I've really enjoyed our lunches."

"No, it's not you. I need to eat. And I've enjoyed our lunches too," I said, trying to laugh.

He didn't look like he totally believed me, but he smiled just the same.

"Well, when you get back then. Dinner? Or just our usual lunch if that's more convenient."

"Yeah, sure, either one. I'll let you know once I decide where and when I'm going and when I'll be back. It won't be for longer than a long weekend. Beth would panic if I left for more than four days," I said with a casual laugh.

Henry smiled. "Okay then, I look forward to hearing from you. See ya." He turned and started walking away.

I started walking to my front gate when I noticed him turn back around to come back to me.

"Isla, hey. So, maybe I'm reading this situation wrong, it wouldn't be the first time, but are you sure you're alright? I've been thinking about you after our last conversation."

I sighed, and tried to smile. "I'm sorry, yeah, I'm fine. I'm just up against a huge deadline and I'm so behind and nothing is working. I really do just need to focus on my book until I have a complete draft. I can't edit and fix something that hasn't even been written and my editor is going to kill me if I don't deliver this first draft on time."

"I know you have a lot on your plate, so I'm grateful you give me any time at all," Henry said sheepishly. "Just know that I want to be here for you if I can, any time you need to talk."

"Thanks Henry, I really appreciate that. Lunch with you has been the highlight of my week these last few weeks," I said with a shy smile. He gave me a smile in return. "I promise, as soon as I'm back and can get a break from the writing we'll meet up again."

"Okay, good. I look forward to it." He said, smiling wider now. "Alright, I won't keep you, I need to get back to work, and I know you do too. Safe travels to wherever you decide to go."

"Thanks Henry."

He nodded and turned to walk quickly away, his hands still buried in his pockets and his head down. He'd left me feeling more confused than ever.

CHAPTER 13 - MACEY

"Morning campers," I called out, as Charlotte and Ruby filed into the kitchen.

They were dressed similarly, in hoodies and pyjama bottoms, with the same tired expression etched across their faces.

"Sleep well then?" I teased, them both collapsing at the dining table where I was sitting.

All that left their mouths were grunts, inhuman like sounds that I struggled to translate into something meaningful.

"Are you going to tell me what happened last night, to get you into this state? The party finished before 10pm, what did you do after?" I laughed, taking a sip of my coffee.

"I'm really, really hungover," Charlotte moaned.

"I can see that, but that doesn't answer my question," I said.

"Issac and Tom came over for more drinks here when we'd finished cleaning up," Ruby explained. "We would have invited you and Ted, but we saw your text saying that you were out together. We didn't hear you get back either."

"I got back at around midnight I think, alone, and went to bed. Where were you? I didn't see you downstairs."

"We were on the terrace," Charlotte added, yawning as she spoke each word. "By the way Macey, are you okay after last night? We didn't see what happened, as all us girls were in the garden at the time. We tried to catch you when you left Tom's but you were making a swift exit, understandably of course. Tom filled us in when he came over,"

"Tom, Tom, Tom!" Ruby interrupted.

"Shut up Ruby. This is about Macey," Charlotte protested.

"It did shake me up. I'm feeling better today though, I'm just lucky that Ted got there when he did. I feel so bad that he got hit. I can't believe Nick started on him!" I paused, fiddling with my hair nervously. "The night ended on a high however."

"It did?" Charlotte's eyes widened as she caught on to what I was insinuating. "Spill the tea!" she giggled excitedly.

"So Ted and I went on a walk, as you know. We went to the beach. We were walking and chatting for ages and then we sat down on some rocks and chatted some more."

"Go on!" Charlotte chimed in, bouncing in her seat with anticipation.

"Calm down," Ruby said, rolling her eyes at Charlotte's eagerness.

"I kissed him. And he kissed me back. Ted and I kissed," I announced, waiting for Charlotte to spontaneously combust from the news of me having such an encounter with the male species. She was acting like I'd never been near a man before, regardless of the fact I'd told her all about Owen.

"Oh. My. God!" she squealed, practically jumping out of her seat. She began pacing around the kitchen, before breaking into some sort of interpretive dance.

"What is up with her today?" I said, turning to Ruby for some sort of answer.

"Tom, Tom, Tom," Ruby reiterated, as Charlotte continued dancing with joy. "She spent three hours with him last night and is now in love."

"I am not in love. Yet," Charlotte said, laughing as she said the last part. "Tom is so lovely though Macey, nothing like Nick, he kept reassuring us of that. He was really worried about you actually, but Ruby and I said that Ted would be looking after you."

I smiled, thinking back to last night.

"Anyway. I'm just excited because if you and Ted get together, and Tom and I do… and Ruby and Issac are going steady… eeeek!" She couldn't even string a sentence together. She was so hyper, which was a drastic change to how she was a mere ten minutes ago, slumped over the table in hungover agony.

"So what happened after you kissed?" Ruby asked, looking back at me.

"We just sat there for a while, with each other. It was nice." I smiled at the memory once again. "He had his arms around me, trying to shield me from the arctic temperatures. He asked if I'd go on an actual, proper date with him, later today. Of course, I agreed. I really like him already," I said, blushing.

"Dreamy!" Ruby responded, whilst Charlotte was still gawking over the news.

"He walked me back, a little while later, and kissed me again when I let myself into the house. I'm getting all giddy thinking about it again, which isn't like me," I joked.

"Just enjoy it," Ruby urged kindly, before continuing. "I remember what you said about your ex, Owen wasn't it? He didn't sound great, but don't let that affect how you feel about Ted. Allow yourself to run with it and be giddy. He's a lovely guy and you're a lovely girl Macey, a top match really."

Charlotte nodded. "Yeah, even Tom said last night that you'd make a perfect couple."

"Tom doesn't know me," I laughed.

"Charlotte wouldn't shut up about you. Tom was telling her about Ted, and she was firing facts about you back at him. They were basically comparing notes, consequently concluding that you should just get married, immediately."

"On what grounds?" I pondered, looking at both Ruby and Charlotte.

"I don't quite remember now," Charlotte sighed. "Something about books, reading, writing, that sort of thing."

"Yeah, we are similar in that sense."

"Oh, and how you both haven't stopped banging on about each other since you met!" she confirmed.

I raised my eyebrows in response. "I haven't mentioned him that much," I objected, looking at Ruby for back up.

Instead, she smirked into her cup of coffee.

"He's spoken about me though?" I asked.

"Apparently so," Ruby yawned. "I didn't drink as much as Charlotte last night, so I remember the details. Issac and Tom both said that when they caught up with Ted in the pub last week, he kept going on about a girl he'd met. They tried to get him to message you but he was majorly overthinking it and chickened out. Kinda sweet if you ask me."

I nodded. "It is."

It was strange to think that Ted of all people was nervous. I suspected that there must have been some sort of explanation for his silence but he always appeared so confident.

———

"CHARLOTTE!!!" I screamed from the top of the stairs. "Have you seen my blush knitted jumper?"

"It's in the wash!" she screeched back.

Great, I thought. It was now Saturday evening and I wasn't feeling the most body confident tonight, so the idea of wearing something comfy (and relatively oversized) sounded ideal. Nothing else that I'd tried on looked quite right, and when I'd flicked through my camera roll for outfit inspiration, the blush pink number seemed perfect. I collapsed on my bed, once again looking through my photos in the hope it would push me to make a decision. Suddenly, Charlotte appeared at my door.

"Fashion crisis?" she questioned, looking over at me. I was on my bed, practically drowning in the garments that I had decided weren't going to work.

"The first two times I met Ted; I was wearing the same dress," I exhaled. "So that's definitely off the cards."

She giggled. "That red dress is super cute though!"

I smiled. "What do you wear for a first date?" I questioned aloud. "I haven't been on many."

"Just wear what you feel good in," Charlotte reassured.

———

"I'M REALLY SORRY. I'm going to have to cancel tonight," the text from Ted read. I slowly sat down on my bed and re-read the message I'd just received from Ted. A million and one thoughts went through my head, starting off with the classic, "is it me?" I called out to Charlotte to come back to my room and she appeared at the door again moments later. Already having read my expression, she immediately came and sat next to me on the bed. "What's going on?" she asked, inquisitively.

"He's cancelled." I replied, looking as glum as I felt.

"What do you mean he's cancelled? He was kissing you last night, and now he's cancelled?"

I passed her the phone so she could read the text for herself.

"He might have a good reason!" I said, automatically defending him without even realising.

"He best have a bloody good reason or I am having a word! Screw that. I am having a word! I will reply," she said, tapping away on my phone.

"No Charlotte," I said, taking the phone from her. "I can fight my own battles, or at least compose my own texts."

She sighed. "I know you can. But what is he playing at? You said he was being so dreamy last night, you said you'd finally felt like he was going to show up, instead of leaving you hanging like he did prior. And then you get this? That's the opposite of showing up!"

"I know," I whimpered quietly, feeling a tear escape from the corner of my eye.

"Hey," Charlotte said gently. "Come here," she said, embracing me. "He doesn't deserve someone like you. I can tell you must like him a lot, but he's not worth getting upset about if he's going to act like this. You are worth so much more and I know you know that!"

I sniffled. "I do know that, I do."

"Come on then." Charlotte said, grabbing my hand and leading me out of the room. "Seeing as you're already dressed and ready, we may as well go out!"

I groaned. "I'm not in the mood now!"

"Just to the pub down the road. Just us two, for a girly drink and a heart to heart. Macey, when have you ever refused a glass of rosé? Don't start now."

I laughed. "Fair enough. Just one. I really just want to get into bed and sulk."

"One glass, one chat, and you'll remember how much of a girl boss you really are."

————

I BOUNDED my way downstairs and quickly pulled on my Doc Martens. I was wearing a navy corduroy skirt, paired with a cream roll neck jumper and some gold accessories. My hair was down for once, I'd allowed my natural curls out to play, each one falling down my back in an effortless manner. I never usually had a good hair day, so I was enjoying it whilst it lasted. I checked myself one last time in the mirror and opened the front door, to immediately be greeted by Ted.

It had been two days since he had cancelled on me, and after spending yesterday moping, I received a text from him last night, apologising profusely and asking for a chance to explain, and to see me too. He asked if he could pick me up today, and take me on the date he originally had planned. I was reluctant at first, I didn't want to seem like a pushover, and Charlotte had insisted that I needed to stand my ground too. But I couldn't help but feel like there was more to it, and I needed to offer my ear to listen and know what Ted had to say.

He was stood at the bottom of the steps, a huge grin slapped across his face. I guess he was happy that I had finally agreed, under the condition that all I was doing was hearing him out, and I wasn't making any promises. He was wearing black jeans and an open blue shirt with a grey t-shirt underneath. His hair was how he usually had it, floppy and messy but in a cute way. He was holding a huge bunch of sunflowers, wrapped up in the most stunning bow.

"I thought I best do this whole first date thing properly," he said, nervously. "And they are also to say sorry, for you know, everything."

I couldn't help but beam as I stared them down in awe. "Ted, those are so pretty, are they really for me?"

"Who else would they be for?" he laughed, handing them over. "I thought I'd give them to you now so you can run inside and pop them in some water."

"Good idea. Give me two seconds," I responded. "Thank you so much for them, sunflowers are my favourite. How did you know?"

He looked at me. "They're my favourite too." he said simply, winking at me.

I dashed back inside, stunned at his kind gesture, shouting for Ruby who was in the kitchen.

"Rubes! Do we have a vase?" I called out as I walked down the hallway.

"For what?" she said, coming to the door. She stopped as soon as she saw the huge bouquet. "Man did gooooood!"

I laughed. "He certainly did."

———

"POSITANO. MY FAVOURITE ITALIAN PLACE," Ted explained as we approached the restaurant. Despite living in Plymouth the whole of last year, I'd never been, much to Ted's dismay. "I love Italian food so much!" Ted continued. "The owners of this place are so lovely as well. I think you'll really enjoy the vibe. Oh, and I checked already, they have vegan options!" he said with a smile. I blushed at his thoughtfulness as he opened the door for me.

"Welcome!" a friendly face announced as we shuffled inside. "Ted! I thought it would be you!" the man exclaimed as Ted went to hug him. "I recognised your surname on the booking and Alfie said that he had spoken with you earlier. Now, who is this lovely lady in your company?"

"Mario, this is Macey," Ted said proudly, whilst winking at the gentleman.

"Got it," Mario said with a small smile.

"Hi Mario," I said, introducing myself. I was not quite sure how Ted was on a first name basis with literally everyone we encounter, but it was sweet to see, nonetheless.

Mario began walking through the restaurant, walking straight past all of the tables and towards the kitchen. We followed, and I looked at Ted, obviously confused. He grinned, and ushered me towards the back door. Right on cue, Mario opened the wooden doors which revealed a small terrace. It was surrounded by fairy lights and had one small table in the middle. The table had been neatly decorated with a few candles and tall wine glasses, as well as necessary cutlery and napkins. There were blankets thrown over the chairs and soft Italian opera coming from a small radio in the corner.

I gasped. "Is this... for us?" I said with a stutter. Mario swiftly left and Ted led me over to the table.

"Macey, again, who else would it be for?"

I was in shock. Ted had seemingly gone to a lot of effort for our first date. I took my place at the table and thanked him yet again. I noted how I'd never been on a date like this, whether that be on a first date or years in.

"Alfie is Mario's grandson. Mario is the owner and Alfie, his dad and his siblings all work here too. I have been coming here since I was a kid, when I used to come to Plymouth and visit my grandparents. Alfie is my age and we used to play together, out on this terrace actually. He'd be here whilst his family worked, and I'd slip out of our family meals to see him. I called him this morning and he helped set all of this up, albeit so last minute. I wanted it to be special."

Still in disbelief, I impulsively grabbed his hand that was on the table and looked him in the eye. Caught off guard, he bowed his head slightly, before squeezing my hand to let me know that it was okay. "Thank you, really."

"You're more than welcome," he replied, rubbing his thumb against my hand as he held it for a little while longer. "But I should really be thanking you. Thanks for giving me another chance to take you out."

I took a breath. "Why did you cancel in the first place? Was it me?"

"Of course not Macey. It was, well, me. I was incredibly nervous. Like to the point where I could see no other alternative than to cancel. I know I should have just told you the truth, on that message, but I couldn't bring myself to do it. I know that you think of me as this super confident guy, but that's not the truth, well, not all the time at least. I am pretty confident, day to day, but when it comes to big, important stuff, I lose my nerve more often than not. I was putting a lot of pressure on myself, throughout all of this, with you, and I was then beating myself up further for feeling so incapable."

I sat back in shock. "Wow Ted. I wish you'd told me all of this sooner."

"I wish I had too Macey because I knew you would have understood, but the nerves got the better of me and I just couldn't admit it. To you, or myself. I also don't want my nervousness to put you off, and I don't want you to see this as me pressuring you. I'm just being honest with my feelings as I feel like that's the best thing to do."

"Certainly. Communication is key. I do understand and I do

wish you'd opened up sooner but I also understand why you didn't. Thank you for telling me now though. But I still don't get why you were so nervous." I paused. "After our first meeting, I told the girls about you, and Ruby realised who you were. She described you as the most eligible bachelor, yet, someone who never seemed to date. Until now, I guess," I laughed. "Have you dated? Or had any serious relationships for that matter? I told you about Owen on the way back from Bristol, but you didn't seem to give anything up. I just wondered—"

Before I could continue, Ted sighed. "Most eligible bachelor? Wow!" he laughed. "This being my fourth year at Plymouth, I guess I've built up a reputation then. For never dating."

I smiled, patiently waiting for him to elaborate further. He caught on. I could tell he was apprehensive, he was shuffling around in his seat and fiddling with any loose strands of hair that fell onto his face. Seeing him so vulnerable was different.

"I never wanted to be that guy. That guy who dated a lot, slept around, you know. I think that's what people always expect me to be for some reason? I don't know if it's because I come across quite confident, and people often mistake that for being cocky? I am not cocky; I just know my worth. And I also know how good it feels to be in a healthy, stable relationship. I'd rather have that, with someone I think is worth it, than throw myself at people just because society tells me too."

I smiled.

"I had a serious relationship before uni," he continued. "We were together from when we were in our last year of secondary school, all throughout sixth form, and we broke up just before coming to uni. The split was amicable. We had, and still do have, so much respect for one other. We just felt like our time had come to an end, we were moving so far apart, literally the other ends of the UK. She just graduated from Edinburgh. We loved each other enough to let each other go. We've now totally moved on, she's with an awesome guy, Jake. She's called Lily by the way. I'm still friends with her, and I'm friends with him now too. I see them, along with other people from school, when I go home sometimes. You know, for BBQ's or nights out. There are no negative feelings. We ran our course, and that's it. I chose to wait until I found something like that again, instead of jumping into just anything. I like my own company. I am happy alone. I wanted to wait until I found someone that enriched my life, rather than took from it, if that makes sense?"

He exhaled, before meeting my eyes once again.

"Totally, I respect that completely. All of it. Everyone should live their lives how they want to, not in the ways that society suggests. Is it weird to say that your ex sounds lovely?" I said, laughing.

"Not weird at all. I'm glad you think that way. I'd love for you to meet all my friends one day, including Lily and Jake, if you'd want to. I know this is just our first date, technically," he took a breath. "Though, I'd really like things to go further, if you've forgiven me for the rocky start. I started to panic a few days ago because I was finding myself catching feelings for you, and I was hoping they were reciprocated. I hadn't met someone that I wished to immediately sacrifice the happiness I'd found from being alone for, until I met you."

I couldn't find the eloquent words to express how I felt.

"I just know you'll enrich my life Macey, and I hope you'll give me the opportunity to enrich yours too."

I nodded, visibly taken aback. I grabbed Ted's hand again, squeezing it once more, to let him know that I would very much like my life enriched, by him, from here on out.

———

"WHAT WOULD YOU LIKE TO ORDER?" a young waitress asked as she placed down some water on the table. She was short and petite, she only looked around 17. She had long, dark brown, almost black hair that was tied back in a ponytail and thick, luscious eyelashes. She smiled at me, before looking at Ted.

"This is Melissa. Alfie's sister," Ted said, acknowledging her.

I smiled. "Hey! Could I get the Penne All'Arrabbiata please? And I'm good with just the water to drink!"

"Good choice!" she replied.

"I'll have the same," Ted chirped, as Melissa jotted the details down before leaving the terrace.

"You don't always have to copy what I get," I said to Ted, laughing.

"I like to," he smiled. "Helps me, get to know you."

He was still holding my hand at this point, he hadn't let it go since I grabbed his earlier.

"How am I meant to get to know you though if you always get the same as me?" I joked.

"I am sure you'll figure out a way," he laughed, before continuing. "But first, I have a question for you, I'm really interested to know, what made you become vegan?"

"I was raised vegetarian since birth, both my parents were veggies. I tried meat a few times growing up, but was never really fussed anyway. A few years ago I started hearing more about veganism, and at the same time, my parents were co-writing a research paper into the link between diet and someone's psychological state. In doing that, they realised there were a lot of the benefits of eating plant-based on someone's mental well-being. I was already interested in veganism from my own research, so when they told me about what they had found, it just swayed me even further. We all went vegan after that. That was about four years ago now."

"That's really cool." Ted responded. "I've tried some of the meat alternatives recently and they're really good. Me ordering what you do, not only allows me to get to know you better, but it also saves the planet and some animals, and now apparently my mental health as well. It's a win-win really!" he winked.

I laughed. "Oh, so that's the real reason is it? I'm just helping you to make better choices?"

"I think just taking you on a proper date Macey, was the best choice I've made in a while," he paused. "So yeah, you are."

"Smooth!" I managed to muster out. I felt my knees go weak, so it was a good job we were sat down. I had never caught feelings for someone this quick before. Everything felt like it was going at 100 miles per hour, but at the same time, it felt like the perfect pace for Ted and me. We were so comfortable in each other's company already; silences were not awkward, and I still felt so at ease in his presence. I felt like there was no need for any pretence from me, still, even though the pressure was mounting, and things were picking up between us two. Thinking back to how casual our first coffee "date" was, I felt as if I was getting to know him in the best way possible, even if he gives little away.

Before I could say anything else, Melissa arrived with our meals.

"Penne All'Arrabbiata, twice!" she said, placing the dishes down in front of us.

I smiled at Ted, acknowledging his last comment, before turning to Melissa. "Thank you so much, these look delicious!"

"You are welcome. If you need anything, just give me a shout."

"Thanks Mel!" Ted added as she left.

———

"THANKS FOR A GREAT DATE," Ted said as I went to open the passenger door.

I paused, before turning to him and sitting for a moment longer. I was thinking back to the evening we'd just shared. It truly was a great date, probably the best I'd ever been on, which is a big title for a first date. The company was lovely, and the pasta was delicious. It had been followed by a delightful sorbet for dessert too, despite the bitter weather. Thankfully, we wrapped up in the blankets that Positano had provided and played footsie under the table to keep warm. Ted had insisted that I chose dessert as well, and as sorbet was the only vegan option, we went for that. He swore he didn't mind, even if he was grimacing when the iciness tickled his self-proclaimed "sensitive" teeth. I couldn't help but laugh at his goofiness, whilst also admiring his dedication to the cause. I wanted to tell him so many times that he didn't have to try so hard to impress me, as I was pretty much already won over.

"I'd like to do it again, soon," he said, continuing.

"Same," I smiled. "I'm not the best with words, and stuff."

Ted looked up and smiled. "You don't need to be with me. Though, I'd recommend working on it, considering you're doing a writing degree."

"Oi!" I joked. "I can write the write, but can't talk the talk."

"Write the write?" Ted raised his brow.

"You know what I mean! I get, I guess, shy?" I sighed.

"You were pretty confident the other night, M."

"Hey, I don't know what came over me then. Must have been the adrenaline." I laughed.

"To be fair, I guess it's my turn," he said, before tucking my hair behind my ear and leaning closer to me. "I really do like you, a lot."

At this point, Ted was inches away from my lips. His recently recognisable scent brushed against me, as his body etched closer to mine. He smelt of autumn. A crisp yet bright day. One where I'd wander through a park, meandering through trees, looking for conkers on leaf-covered paths. Intermittent breezes disturbed laying leaves, wafting earthy aromas towards me. He smelt like that, combined with the smell of a fresh batch of cinnamon buns. He smelt like home after a cold day. The perfect mixture of sweet and sexy. A fragrance that brought me comfort, but made me excited. I wanted him even closer, I wanted to feel that warmth yet again.

I rested my hand on his shoulder as I snapped back to reality after losing myself in his spirit. I pursed my lips and paused, waiting for him to take his turn as he'd so eagerly promised. My whole body tingled with anticipation. This wasn't about to be any ordinary kiss. It wasn't like any of the others I'd had, with Ted or anyone else. The one's we'd shared the other night after the beach walk felt spontaneous, fun, little to no strings were attached. Now, there was pressure. I could feel it bubbling up inside me, as well as feeling the tension mount from Ted.

As soon as those words had left his lips, his whole manner had changed. He was now anxious again, scared. Reduced self-confidence and timid eyes were now his main features, I could tell how much this meant to him. My fingers trailed to his side, in the hope that my actions would indicate for him to proceed. I could feel the heat radiating from his body, even though my hand was firmly above his clothes. I tugged at the hem of his shirt, encouraging him even more, before I finally found some words to fill the silence.

"Good."

He laughed. I could tell he wanted to say something. I could tell he wanted to make a joke, like he usually does. I could tell he wanted to wind me up, tease me for being a writer who struggled to articulate herself in real life. But he did none of the above. He just smiled, before finally kissing me. Open mouthed, yet soft. With each breath, the kiss got deeper and more meaningful. His eyes remained shut as I peeked to gaze over him. He was grinning into the kiss, obviously content, which made me beam. I think if this was a movie, literal sparks would be flying right now. I think that's why I feel so warm when I am with Ted, our chemistry is evidently electric. He continued to kiss me, intensely, but so considerately, before pulling his face away from mine. He rested his thumb underneath my lower lip and stared me down.

"Good?" he questioned. "Is that it?"

"I really do like you, a lot, too," I said sheepishly.

"Good," he replied, placing one final kiss on my forehead. "I can't say car kissing and having to lean over is the most comfortable, yet that still managed to be the best kiss of my life," he exhaled, crashing back into his seat.

"Good!" I said, and we both burst out laughing.

"I guess we both missed out on the literacy lessons where they taught us 100 other words for good."

"We must have!" I jibed, poking his shoulder in play. I turned to open the door once again and Ted grabbed my hand.

"Night M," he said, clutching onto me for a moment longer.

"Night Ted," I echoed, before making my exit and wandering up the steps to my front door. I wanted to turn around so bad, but I didn't want it to be too cheesy. I fiddled to find my keys, and I still hadn't heard Ted's car start up. He had an old, or as he liked to say, "vintage" one, and it usually liked to roar when the ignition was turned. It felt like that evening all over again, the one where Ted dropped me off after the meet and greet with Isla Stewart. I remember feeling so optimistic, hoping that when I saw him trapped in his daze, he was thinking about me. Despite everything that has happened in-between, I felt the same. I was positive that he was worth it all.

I decided to turn around again, to see if it was a classic case of déjà vu. However, this time, it was different. Not only had so much changed since that evening, Ted was now looking at me, directly. His eyes were wide, and his smile matched that. He signalled to his phone, indicating that he was going to text me. I forgot about my keys for a second and rummaged for my phone instead. A text notification appeared from Ted and it read:

Though she be but little, she is fierce ;)

I glanced back at him, laughing. I quickly punched out a reply.

You can't take credit for that one, I know it's Shakespeare.

I felt my phone vibrate in my palm, once again he'd text.

:D Fierce and beautiful.

He began to start up the car and I waved, blushing at the words that were staring at me from my phone. I let myself into the house, hung up my jacket and walked down the hall. Ruby was still in the kitchen, working on an assignment.

"Good night?" she said, peering up at me over the stacks of papers that were surrounding her.

"Yeah. It was really good." I winked, before exiting the kitchen.

A wave of happiness engulfed me as I strolled upstairs. I, Macey Genevieve Banks, was smitten with Plymouth's most eligible bachelor. And I could confidently say, he was smitten with me, too.

CHAPTER 14 - ISLA

"You want to what!?" Beth looked at me incredulously.

"I want to go away for a bit. I need you to look up some kind of cute cottage I can rent for a long weekend. I was thinking, I'd leave on a Thursday and come back by Monday morning?"

"But you don't have any free long weekends for months. You have appointments or meetings every Thursday, Friday, and Monday for the next," she paused and looked at my calendar on her computer, counting under her breath, "Eleven weeks! There's no way you can run off next weekend or something like that."

I sat down across from her at the desk and smiled at her, "We both know you can find a way. I need three full days to focus on writing. More if possible, now that I think about it. If I can't deliver this manuscript you're going to be the one fielding all the persistent emails from my editor. I'm causing a headache for you now, to save you stress later." I smiled at her sweetly.

"Either way I'm still stressed," Beth grumbled, but I could see the ghost of a smile on her face.

"I know, I'm sorry, but I really need this. If I fail to deliver this next book and I disappoint everyone and lose my contract and everyone stops buying my books, where do you think your paychecks are going to come from?" I teased with a smile. Technically I was the boss, but Beth and I both knew who ran this show ninety percent of the time.

"God you're so dramatic when you want something," Beth said laughing, taking off her reading glasses and rubbing the bridge of her nose. It's something she does when she's really exasperated with me. It's endearing really. I know she loves me.

"Please Beth. I need this. Writing here at home or in coffeeshops around Bath isn't working. There's too many distractions between you, Georgie, my parents, Mrs. R—"

"—And Henry?" Beth interrupted.

"Look, I just need to get away from everyone and go somewhere where the book is the only thing I have to focus on. I can agree to calling you for an hour each day to go over administrative stuff, but surely none of the meetings you have me scheduled for in the next couple weeks are that important. We've rescheduled things before. I'm not asking to go away for a month, just a few days, just to get over whatever this block is."

"Alright, leave it with me. I'll work on clearing the schedule and then I'll look up places you can stay. Do you have a preference for where this magical cottage you're escaping to is located?"

"Nope. Just somewhere away from Bath, where I have to travel for at least a couple hours to get to it."

"Trading your Jane Austen locations for something more Brontë?"

I laughed, "Maybe not quite so tragic and moody, but yes, something different from here. And somewhere fairly private, not with a bunch of tourists around."

"Okay, I'll get it sorted. Now please go upstairs and let me get back to work. If you can't focus on your writing, there's a bunch of emails I moved to your folder that need your attention."

"Yes boss," I said with a wink and then left the office before Beth could change her mind. I went upstairs and went through the emails Beth had mentioned, they ended up being a good distraction.

A little while later, Georgie called, to let me know that the paperwork was just about ready. She asked if she could come over this evening to sign everything.

"I know it's last minute, but I'll bring a Chinese takeaway for dinner?"

"Deal, you know I'm not going to turn down free food."

Georgie laughed, "Okay, I'll see you later."

We hung up and I took my laptop to sit in the chair by the bay window in my bedroom. I scrolled aimlessly through what I'd already written and through my notes, before making a few more notes. I tried some freewriting and character building exercises, realising I must be getting desperate if I was resorting to basic creative writing invention techniques to try and jumpstart my writing. I looked back at what I'd noted down for one of my main characters, the female lead from the present day POV and plot line, and realised that I'd basically spent the past hour describing myself. This book was not supposed to be quite that personal.

"Ugh," I moaned, leaning my head against the back of my chair.

My hand hovered over the delete button on the keyboard, ready to just erase everything, but something stopped myself from pressing it. Instead I quickly opened a new file on my computer and cut and pasted everything over to that. I'm not much of a reflective journaler, but seeing my past and my thoughts laid out like that made me think that it might be worth looking at again in the future. I thought back to what Georgie had said about readers wanting to see characters achieve their own happiness outside of a relationship and that I keep running from doing that work in my own life.

I sighed and I started over, trying to think more consciously about this particular character. I didn't want to write a fictionalised version of me. I didn't want to feel disappointed when this character got her life sorted out while mine would confuse me long after the book was published.

I did wonder why my past was coming up so much now. I honestly felt like I was over it. It happened. It's done. I was in a really good place with it these days.

Eventually, I heard Beth call up from downstairs, "Georgie's here!"

"Saved by the bell," I muttered to myself, grateful for an excuse to put my writing to the side.

I went downstairs and found Georgie and Beth in the kitchen. They were unpacking a ridiculous amount of yummy smelling Chinese takeaway from our favourite place.

"You don't mind if Beth stays right? I figured she'd still be here so I brought extra food," Georgie said, waving her hand over the array of dishes, rice, spring rolls and prawn toast.

"Of course I don't mind. Beth, you're always welcome to stay for dinner. But Georgie, my goodness, this is enough to feed ten people!"

"I'll take some of the leftovers with me, but I figured you and Beth probably wouldn't mind some as well."

"I never turn down extra food from this place, it's the best," Beth said happily.

We sat down to eat and Georgie and I told Beth about the house I was buying and we all talked excitedly about interiors and home furnishings. After dinner I signed the paperwork so that Georgie could move forward with the buying process. Beth then brought out her tablet and showed us her top three options for my getaway.

"I'm so glad you're actually going to go somewhere!" Georgie exclaimed.

"Well it was a bit of a nightmare to rearrange her schedule, but next weekend you'll be off, Thursday to Monday," Beth said as she gave me a stern look. I felt like Cinderella being told she had to be home from the ball by midnight. "But you can't leave until after eleven o'clock on Thursday morning. You had a noon meeting that couldn't be cancelled, but I got it moved up to ten o'clock and it's scheduled to last for an hour. We'll get you on the next train after eleven."

"So where should I go?" I asked, starting to feel excited.

"I found three cottages that are available next weekend at reasonable rates. It's kind of off-season for most of them at this point in the year."

Beth placed her tablet on the table and started talking through the options. The first two were lovely. One was in the Peak District and one was just outside York, so I'd be able to go into the city if I wanted. Both were good options, but Beth had definitely saved the best for last.

"It's not north, but it is away from Bath," she said as she pulled up the last place and I gasped.

"I knew you'd like this one," she said with a satisfied grin.

It was perfect. The cottage was in Warwickshire, nestled among farmland and rolling hills, with lots of trees. The listing indicated it was a five minute walk to the nearest village with a store, tea room, pub, and a few other businesses. It also had access to miles of country walks. It was near Warwick Castle, which could be fun to explore one day, I've always wanted to visit but hadn't got around to it yet. The cottage was small but had everything I would need and was on the same property of the family who ran it as a holiday let, so I wouldn't be completely isolated. It looked like something out of a fairy tale and I couldn't wait.

"Book it," I said firmly.

Beth nodded and took the tablet back. "I called them earlier to confirm it was still available and told them I needed to talk to you first. They're holding it for another hour, so I'll go call them quickly."

Beth walked out of the kitchen and Georgie and I looked at each other excitedly.

"I wish I could come with you now! That place looks amazing."

"It looks perfect," I agreed. "Just what I need." I leaned back in my chair and groaned, "This week is going to go so slow! I just want to get there already."

"There, there," Georgie said, petting my hand sarcastically. "I'm sure you'll survive. And look on the bright side, this will give you one more time to see Henry for your Wednesday lunch before you leave."

I looked down at my hands in my lap.

"Isla, I know that look. What did you do?"

"Nothing," I said dramatically, well aware I sounded like a teenager.

Georgie glared at me from her seat.

"Ugh," I sighed. "Fine. I ran into Henry yesterday as I was coming home and he was leaving his mum's next door. We talked and it was fine but I kind of told him I needed some time to work on my book."

Georgie's eyes narrowed, "You told him you needed time? I don't believe you. You're just determined to push good things away aren't you."

"Oh stop it," I said laughing. "I'm going on this getaway, just like you suggested, at great hassle to Beth for rearranging my schedule. I told Henry I'd see him when I got back."

Georgie's expression softened, "Okay, as long as you didn't end things with him."

"No, I didn't end things, I wouldn't do that. Georgie, I can't explain it. The thought of a relationship terrifies me but there's something about him. I mean, he's not any guy. He's Henry. I'm really enjoying the friendship we're rekindling. But he's not the same guy I had a crush on in school and I'm not the same girl that he was unfailingly kind to all the time. I just wish people would let things unfold naturally. It's like none of you trust me."

"Of course we trust you," Beth's voice came over my shoulder as she came back into the kitchen. "We just also know your tendency for self-sabotage." She said that last bit with a kindness in her voice and facial expression. "You have a laser focus when it comes to your work, but your personal life...well, you give new meaning to overthinking things. But it's understandable given your past."

I laughed. I knew she was right. Beth was one of the few people outside my family who knew the full story of my past relationship.

And she'd been through the wars with a couple nasty exes of her own in the past as well, it was one of the things we bonded over early on in our working relationship.

"As your friend, I want you to be open to new people and experiences. None of us are getting any younger and you deserve a hot guy like Henry. Who by the sound of things, is also funny and charming and successful. But as your employee who basically runs your life and has to put out fires when you get behind deadlines, I want you to give yourself space from whatever is bothering you, Henry included, and get this book finished."

We all laughed.

"Message understood Beth. Believe me, I want to get it done too. It's going to drive me insane soon if I don't start making significant progress."

Georgie poured us all some more drinks. G&Ts for Beth and I and a mocktail for herself. We enjoyed talking about anything and everything but Henry or my book for the rest of the evening and it was nice to just be with some friends and relax.

———

THE NEXT DAY I woke up early and couldn't get back to sleep. It was a bitterly cold morning and there was frost in the front garden when I looked out the window. I bundled up in my snuggliest clothes, wrapping my favorite thick cardigan tightly around my body as I went downstairs to make some tea. I loved the cold. Any excuse to throw some logs in the fire and wear cosy jumpers just made me happy. These kinds of mornings were my favourite.

I took my tea and read by the fire I'd just made in the front room for a while, until I saw Mrs. Russell out the window adjusting some of the protective sheets she'd placed over her plants.

I rushed to the front door and stepped out onto my front step.

"Mrs. Russell, you shouldn't be out in this cold!"

"Oh, Isla dear! I just wanted to make sure these plants were covered properly."

She looked a little distracted. I stepped out of my slippers and into my boots by the door and put the door on the latch to go outside.

"Here, let me help you."

I entered her garden and helped secure all the coverings, everything looked fine to me, so I wasn't sure what she had been worried about. I looked over at her and she was wearing just a cardigan, not even as thick as mine.

"Mrs. Russell, it's freezing out here, you really should be inside."

"It is a bit chilly isn't it? I should probably make a fire."

"I tell you what, why don't you come over to mine, I already have a fire going. I'll make you a cuppa and we'll get you all warm and toasty in no time."

"That sounds lovely dear."

We finished in her garden and then I wrapped my arm around her and we walked up my front path and into the living room. I settled her in the chair closest to the fire and grabbed a blanket from the basket nearby and tucked it around her.

"You're such a dear, Isla, this is lovely."

"Just you wait. I'll go put the kettle on and be right back."

"Take your time dear, I'm plenty comfy now."

I bustled into the kitchen and went about filling the kettle and getting everything out for tea. One thing Mrs. R and I had bonded over early on was that we're both very much into our teas. We enjoy a good cup of PG Tips if we want, but we do love the premium stuff as well. I was just looking through the selection in my cupboard when I heard Mrs. R call out.

"Do you have any more of the breakfast tea from Fortnums? I've run out."

"You bet I do!" I called back, and reached for the blue tin. I took down my white and gold patterned tea set, placing the strainer in the pot and putting the cups onto the saucers. Mrs. R hadn't been over for tea in a while so I decided to do the full display. Once the tea was ready I carried it through to the living room on a tray and set it on the table by Mrs. R.

"Oh Isla, this looks lovely. I have always admired this set of yours."

"Having you over is always a good excuse to use it," I said, handing her a cup and saucer before taking one of my own and sitting down on the sofa.

"Now what were you really doing outside this morning in this bitter weather, because we both know those coverings were fine."

Mrs. R sighed. "I just couldn't sit still, I've been tidying and pottering around the house all morning."

"Is something wrong?" I asked worriedly.

"Not really. Nothing I want to bother you about."

"Mrs. Russell, bother me. Please. You should know by now there's nothing you can't talk to me about."

She sighed. "I'm just worried about Henry," she said looking down at her tea.

"Is something wrong with him? He seemed fine when we had lunch earlier this week."

She smiled, "Oh he really enjoys having lunch with you Isla. Thank you for making time for him, it's been so nice for him to get out of the office and reconnect with an old friend."

"I'm happy to meet him for lunch, it's been nice getting to know him again," I said warmly. "But he hasn't hinted that anything is wrong, what is it you're worried about?"

"Oh I'm probably just worrying over nothing," she said with a small smile.

"You wouldn't be the first mum in the history of mums to worry over a bit of nothing," I said with a kind laugh.

"You're right about that," she said, laughing too. "I don't want you to feel any pressure, Henry has told me that the two of you are enjoying your friendship and I don't want to interfere. But I really wish he'd..." Her voice trailed off and she turned to look at the fire dancing in the fireplace. "Well, let's just say that while I don't want to interfere, I wish you both weren't so stubborn. I think you're a better match for each other than either of you will admit. Honestly, I worry about both of you. Neither of you deserves to be single for the rest of your lives."

I could hear the tone in her voice, I imagine it's what she used on her former pupils when she tried to impart some stern wisdom.

Her voice softened, "I know I have no business telling you how to live your life, but you and Henry are so alike, in so many ways. As someone who knows you both very well, I just know you'd each bring something special to a relationship. You compliment each other with your differences and balance each other with your similarities. But I know you both have been through a lot. Henry's ex was truly awful. I never liked that woman, but I was kind to her out of love for Henry. I hate how much she hurt Henry, but even more I hate how she made him doubt himself."

"I can definitely relate to that," I said quietly.

"I know you can. It's just one of the reasons I feel like you two understand each other. You both have experienced great pain because you've been open to letting yourself love."

I started to speak, then paused, not quite sure how to phrase what I wanted to say. Finally I said, "Mrs. Russell, you know I adore you. And Henry is a wonderful man…"

She looked at me and put up a hand to stop me, "Isla please, don't worry yourself. Your relationship with Henry will be what it will be. I'm glad you've found each other again, but I'll stop meddling. I know the two of you would be good together, but whether you and Henry take that step is up to the two of you."

I looked down at my own tea, thinking about what she was saying. Eventually I looked up. "Thank you, I appreciate you letting us make our own decision about this. I do really like Henry, I always have. But my past aside, things are really stressful right now with my next book. I feel like I'm not able to make decisions about anything right now. But I do enjoy spending time with him, and I don't plan on stopping seeing him," I said with a smile.

Mrs. Russell smiled back, "Good. I'm glad. He feels the same."

CHAPTER 15 - MACEY

"So, are you guys official yet?" Libby asked me as she placed her drink down on the table.

It was now Saturday, November 14th, and Libby, Anna, Ruby, Charlotte and I were out for cocktails. We'd barely spent any time together recently and had decided last week that this Saturday evening would be dedicated to the girls. Ruby had been spending all of her time with Issac, as was Charlotte with Tom, and well, I had been spending all of my time with Ted. And boy, had it been a dream.

After our first "proper" date, we had been seeing each other non stop over the past month. Most days we'd meet after morning lectures and meander around town for a coffee and cake, other days we'd go food shopping together, before cooking in the evening, either at his place or mine. We'd have tapas nights on the terrace, often joined by the other couples too. Weekends were spent lounging in bed, reading together, in silence, just enjoying each other's company. I even got Ted to read one of my other favourite Isla Stewart novels, *Where the Path Ends*, and despite his initial protest, he thoroughly enjoyed it.

On the days we were at Ted's flat, we'd cosy up in front of the fireplace and read our favourite poems to each other, drinking hot chocolate and listening to the playlists we'd created ourselves. They were filled with songs that reminded us of one another, many of them from our first road trip back to Plymouth from Bristol, when we accidentally had bumped into each other and he drove me home. On the days we were at my flat, we'd play board games with the gang and order Chinese takeaway to see us into the evening. We loved a good Sunday walk, often venturing out into Plymouth's surrounding countryside, though sometimes we stayed closer to home and just skipped down to the pier.

Luckily, my freelance writing work had begun to pick up, and two publications were now paying me to write for them regularly, meaning I didn't have to work an out-of-home job. I could spend time with Ted whilst I wrote, he would work on uni projects whilst lying next to me, often playing with my hair or scratching my back, much to my joy.

Last weekend we decided to have an art filled weekend. It started off with painting together at home on Friday night, in which I learnt that Ted not only writes a cracking poem, he can paint amazingly too. I, on the other hand, lack in the painting department, and because of that, I got bored rather quickly. What was meant to be an art session, quickly turned into play fighting with the water colours, which then transpired into a make out session, covered in paint and all. The next day, Saturday, we took a private pottery class, and jokingly re-enacted the very smutty scene from *Ghost*. "Unchained Melody" was immediately added to our playlist, and we died from laughter when we sang it in the car on the way home.

Of course, some days I'd spend studying, Ted helping me with my notes and testing me for upcoming exams. Ted was the best study partner; his words of positive encouragement constantly rang in my ears. If he wasn't there with me physically, he was sending me motivation via text, to keep me going. He was so supportive, especially when it came to my writing work. He was the first one to read each article when they got posted online, and he'd almost instantly send me his thoughts, wherever he happened to be.

My favourite evenings with him were spent on the beach, watching the wintery sunsets and eating oversized New York style pizzas from the local parlour. Whenever we go down to the shore at dusk, he gives me one of his hoodies to wear, and most of the time, I don't give them back. They are like having a hug from him, even when he's not around, and I savour each cuddle from Ted, as they are the best. We did spend a lot of time down at the beach. If we weren't chilling on the rocks, we'd be playing in the arcades. Ted set me a challenge to beat him on the racing car simulator, which I still haven't managed to do.

In the past few weeks, I also joined the Creative Writing Society, which has been so much fun. Of course, it's been fabulous to spend time with more like-minded people, but it's been another way to spend time with Ted too, with him being the President. I've attended all the meetings and gotten to know more of Ted's friends too who are on the board, and I am so happy to be involved in something I truly feel so passionate about.

"Not official, yet," I said, fiddling with my straw. "I've only known him a month and a half. No offence, Charlotte. I know you're very loved up."

"None taken," Charlotte chimed in. "Tom and I are officially boyfriend and girlfriend, as of yesterday. He asked me in bed, just after we'd had sex. It was actually quite romantic!" she confessed, grinning. "I know it's only been a month," she continued. "But I think he's the one!"

I smiled. I wondered if Charlotte and Tom's relationship was indeed going fast, or whether mine and Ted's was going slow. I felt like it was going at the appropriate pace, but I couldn't help comparing myself and my *situationship* to the other girls. Ruby and Issac were finally officially together too, but they had been in the talking/seeing each other stage for almost a year at the point where they put a label on it. I guess everyone's relationships just go at different rates, and that's okay.

I can't even remember how long it took Owen and I to get together, it just kind of happened. We were so young, it started at school. I think he only asked me out because his friends pressured him too, and that was that. We just never broke up after it, for a very long time at least, before I realised that I deserve way more than an immature, narcissistic man-boy who stays with a girl because in his words, "choices were limited at school".

Being with Ted is so refreshing, as for one, he doesn't think going to the gym and smoking cheap cigarettes are personality traits. And two, I am more like him than anyone else I've ever encountered. I want us to be official, just so I can scream how perfect he is from the rooftops, and upload cutesy Instagram photos. But I also don't want to rush things, and it's not like I am super eager to introduce my family to him anyway.

"What did your Mum and Dad say when you told them you were seeing someone?" Ruby wondered aloud.

"I haven't told them yet," I confessed, still fiddling with my straw. "After Owen and I broke up, they were so relieved. Although it was serious, with how long we were together, I think they both knew it wasn't going to last much past sixth form. I think it surprised them when we stayed together for as long as we did, but looking back, I think part of the reason I dragged it out that long was to spite them. Things would have been easier if I'd ended it sooner, and I think they would have trusted me more to make better decisions when it comes to guys." I took a breath. "Everything with Ted is so great right now, I don't want anything to ruin it."

All the girls looked at me sympathetically.

"It's so obvious how perfect you are for each other, it's only a matter of time before you can change your relationship status on Facebook!" Charlotte insisted.

We all laughed. "I guess so," I said, looking down at the remnants of my Sex on the Beach.

"Tonight's for the girls anyway, you'll be seeing Ted soon enough, and I am sure you'll feel so much better once you're in his company again. Don't let any anxious thoughts you're having ruin your evening!" Ruby reassured, hugging me as she spoke.

She was right. I was due to see Ted on Monday after not seeing him for three days, and although it didn't sound like a long time apart, I was desperate to see him once again.

"You guys are a match made in heaven, really," Charlotte added. "Like one of those couples out of those books you read, by Isla."

I laughed. "You remembered the author's name at least!"

"Yeah, I know her." Charlotte said. "As in, know *know* her!" she clarified.

"Wait, how'd you mean?" I said blankly.

"Beth, my cousin, is Isla's personal assistant."

"Charlotte. Your cousin is Isla Stewart's PA and you are only just telling me this, now?"

"LOL. I forgot. Isla's lovely. I've met her a few times over the years!" she said with her signature ditziness.

I stared at her, still confused. "I've brought up Isla and her books on several occasions now, how has this not been revealed already?"

Charlotte bit her lip. "I guess I wasn't paying complete attention…"

"She's always too busy thinking about boys, there can't be much room for anything else up there," Ruby said jokingly, pointing at Charlotte's head.

"I must have just missed the part where you mentioned Isla's name. I remember you talking about the books you like to read but not necessarily the author of them. I switch off, often."

"Thanks. I didn't realise I was so boring."

"It's not that…" Charlotte continued.

I laughed. "I'll let you off Charlotte. You just best promise to tell me if you switch off mid another one of our conversations." I wasn't actually offended that Charlotte had admitted to not fully listening to the stories I had told her that often revolved around reading, I was just more concerned that her ears were not working properly.

"How's Beth anyway?" Libby asked. "I know you don't get to see her very often."

"I spoke with her on video call the other day. I try and get to Bath sometimes, but we still don't get to see each other as often as we'd both like. I probably see her less now than when I was growing up and she lived in a different country."

"How so?" I asked, curious. Charlotte hadn't mentioned much about her family and life back home.

She continued. "I lived in Guernsey. She lived in Bath. My dad is her mum's brother. We would go over to England for Dad's work every other month or something like that. I lived in Guernsey with both my mum and dad until I was 16, and then my parents divorced. My dad moved to Bath to be closer to his parents and work. My mum's from Guernsey so I think he only lived there for so long because of her. Mum and I stayed in Guernsey, until I moved over for Uni at 18. Mum's still in Guernsey, with the rest of the family over there. So I kinda have 3 homes. Plymouth, Bath and Guernsey. Beth is 15 years older than me. I'm the youngest grand-child, which is a bit boring. Everyone either flew the Guernsey nest before me or they were already living on the mainland. Being an only child too, I did wish I had my cousins around when I was little. So that's why I cling onto them more now. Beth has a twin brother, Rob, and two younger brothers, Elliot and Daniel, who are in their late twenties. We're all dotted around the UK now, but I love them dearly."

I smiled. "I wish I had cousins! I literally don't have any. My mum and dad both don't have siblings, and neither do I. I think that wins at the most boring." I sighed. "I do wish I had a bigger family. I love hearing everyone's stories about theirs. I think that's why I am so excited to meet Ted's family eventually. I'm nervous too, don't get me wrong, but I can't wait to meet them nonetheless."

"They'll love you Macey. You have nothing to worry about," Ruby added in reassurance.

I secretly, definitely, hoped so.

"Could you possibly do me a favour Charlotte?" I asked eagerly. She stared at me, waiting for me to elaborate before she committed to anything. "Now I know that you have this link to Isla, it would be great to use that to the Creative Writing Society's advantage. They are holding an author talk soon and Ted is stressing out over the guest speaker, or lack thereof. The person they had booked has had to cancel, and there's a big meeting on Monday where he has to tell the rest of the committee. The society is struggling for money at the moment, and if the event falls flat, it will have a huge impact on their overall standing. I was going to try and help, and maybe relieve some of his stress."

Charlotte's eyes went wide.

"Get your head out of the gutter," I laughed. "Not like that." The others giggled. "I meant like, find someone else to do the talk, so he doesn't have to worry about that side of it. Do you think Isla would do it? Could you maybe, please, put me in touch with her? It would seem a bit random if I were to try and contact her myself, out of the blue, but I think if you could give her a heads up, and I could mention that I know you, it could really help. What do you think?" I rambled, politely.

"Sure," Charlotte shrugged. "It's no skin off my nose and I'm pretty sure Isla would love to partake. I'll drop Beth a text tomorrow with your contact details and get the ball rolling."

"You're an angel Charlotte!" I said, reaching over to hug her.

"I know!" she responded, flicking her hair before hugging me back.

"Morning champ!" Ted said jokingly as I got in his car. It was Monday morning and we were finally reunited, after what felt like the longest four days apart. Ted had been staying with his grand-parents, and I wasn't used to him being away.

"What's this in aid of?" I questioned, eyeing up the bunch of flowers he had placed on the passenger seat before I got in.

"We've got a long, busy, and stressful day ahead, filled with potentially boring meetings. I wanted to make you smile before you hate me for putting you through it all."

I placed a kiss on his cheek before thanking him for the gesture. "I am sure it won't be too rough!" I continued, maintaining some level of optimism.

"Macey. You've never been to a financial planning meeting for a university society that is under money-related pressure. Let me tell you, it is rough!" he said, emphasising the last part. "I am not quite sure why you were so adamant on coming."

"Because I wanted to support you," I murmured, shyly.

"Well, I appreciate that. And your commitment to the society overall. You've been a great new member," he admitted, whilst starting up the car. He moved his hand over to rest it on my thigh and stroked my leg in thanks. I smiled, moments like these were my favourite.

———

WE WANDERED into the on-campus room that we'd hired out for the meeting and took our seats along with some other members of the board. Even though I wasn't technically on the committee, Ted allowed me to come to these meetings as I was super eager to support him and be involved. Ted sat next to the Vice-President, Rosa, and I sat on the other side of him. Rosa was stunning. A short, slim, doe-eyed girl with brunette waves and a killer smile. She flashed me one as I sat down and immediately greeted me.

"Hey Macey! So good to see you again!"

"It's so lovely to see you too, Rosa. How's your novel going?" Ted had told me that Rosa was writing a fantasy novel, set in the

Victorian era. It sounded really unusual and I was very much looking forward to reading it.

"It's going well! Thank you! Well done on all your recent publications, I caught up on them yesterday. Ted can't stop talking about them, and you. He seems so proud!"

I felt my face flush a crimson colour as I turned to speak to the other members who'd just arrived. Arjun, the secretary, sat next to me, and Yang, the treasurer, sat next to Rosa. A few other members of the society who were heavily involved in the logistics were there too. The society had quite the mix of people, all from different courses and different backgrounds. Ted and Rosa did their undergraduate degree together, both having studied Literature. They were both now doing their Masters in Creative Writing. Arjun was a third year English and Creative Writing student, my course, so he was always there to offer me advice when I needed it. Yang was a second year Accounting and Finance student, who just loved writing in her spare time. She also loved that she was really the only one who was knowledgeable on money matters, and we needed that greatly right now.

Ted took a swig of his water and began. "I think the first issue we need to address is the lack of a notable guest speaker at our *What It Takes to Be an Author* event next week. The author we had lined up has had to drop out for personal reasons, which is extremely unfortunate, seeing as this is meant to be a huge fundraiser for us. I just don't think we'll get the ticket sales without a big name on the line up."

"I'm on that," I interjected.

"You are?" Ted and Rosa replied in unison.

"Yes, I am waiting for a call back, I should hear in the next hour. Whilst we're still here actually." I smiled.

Ted placed his hand on my shoulder before quickly moving it away.

"Thanks Macey!" he said smartly, in an attempt to remain professional.

"If we sell out the event, we'll have enough cash to see us

through the end of the year. The end of semester Creative Writing Society Ball in December is the next big event, and the money from that will hopefully set us up nicely for the new term come January," Yang announced, still fixated on her binder of notes.

She carried the binder everywhere with her, we had nicknamed it the financial bible. In it were all the ins and outs of the society and our spending. I was so glad that we had Yang, as without her, we'd struggle. We then spent the next hour trawling through Yang's notes, discussing how we can boost our funds and put us in a better position overall.

As Yang was finishing up, I began to feel my phone vibrate in my pocket, so I swiftly exited the room.

"Hello?"

"Hi, is this Macey?"

"Yes, it is!'

"Hi Macey, I'm Beth, Isla's assistant. I got a text with your number on from my cousin Charlotte, regarding the talk your society is hosting, and I discussed it with Isla. She'd be more than happy to take part! Charlotte mentioned that society was worried about money, so just to clarify, no, we don't take fees for this sort of thing. She can't wait to meet you!"

"Wow! Amazing news, thank you so much. I can't wait."

"Would you be able to drop me an email with all of the finer details and I'll get it popped in Isla's diary?" Beth pondered.

"Of course, I'll have that over to you by this afternoon."

"Thank you so much Macey, talk to you soon!" she said, before giving me her email address.

"Bye!" I sang as she hung up the phone.

I can't believe I had managed to pull this off, with a little help from Charlotte too of course. Isla Stewart, the greatest romance novelist of our generation was coming to speak at a university event I was helping organise. I just couldn't wait to tell Ted. I got up from where I was sitting and walked back in the room. The group were having a break and Ted was over in the corner speaking to Rosa in a rather hushed tone. I didn't want to intrude so I took my seat again, waiting for everyone to be back and ready to start the second half of the meeting. When Ted sat down next to me, he held my hand under the table, softly squeezing it like he usually does.

"How'd the call go?" he whispered in my ear.

I just smiled at him, before breaking away from his grasp to stand and address the room.

"Sorry for standing. I'm just quite small and find it easier to make eye contact with you all this way," I laughed, which encouraged the others to as well.

"I just got off the call, and long story cut short, Isla Stewart, author of *A Courageous Beginning*, *Lost in Love*, *Time Will Tell*, to name a few, will be the main guest speaker at our event next week. That's all," I announced before sitting down.

Ted turned to me with a shocked expression plastered across his face.

"You did what?!" he couldn't help but beam.

Before I could reply, Rosa spoke up. "Isla Stewart?! As in THE Isla Stewart? How on earth did you manage that?"

"I have my ways," I managed to muster as everyone else remained silent in surprise.

Yang was so excited; she could barely stay in her seat. "This is great!" she shouted. "Not only do I get to hear Isla Stewart talk, and potentially meet her, this will be incredible for sales! I think Macey has just saved the day."

I giggled, "Thanks Yang."

Ted put his arm on the back of my chair. I so desperately wanted to hug him. I knew he had been so worried about the event, and the society as a whole, and as much as I wanted to hear Isla talk like Yang, and meet her again, I wanted to help the society more than anything else.

Ted rose from his seat a moment later, and I laughed, knowing he was doing that in solidarity with my short self. "The second issue we need to address is the absence of Matty. Sadly, he has decided to leave his position as Social Secretary to focus on his studies. I was panicking about this earlier, but after speaking with Rosa and hearing recent news, I think I have a solution. Macey," he paused and turned to look at me. Ted was so tall, that when he was standing and I was sitting, he totally hovered over me. "Will you take on the position of Social Secretary, aka all around event wizard slash genius?"

"I feel like I'm being proposed to," I said, smiling. "But yes, of course, I'd love to."

"Welcome aboard, Macey!" he said, shaking my hand.

BY SEVEN O'CLOCK, we were back at Ted's flat. We'd ordered a Greek takeaway to celebrate a successful day of meetings, and me joining the committee too. We popped open a bottle of fizz to accompany the mezze we'd ordered, and sat cross legged on the living room floor. As usual, we'd ordered way too much for just two people, meaning we were currently surrounded by hummus, pita and falafel. Ted had lit a candle on the coffee table for "ambiance" and had our go-to playlist playing in the background. I loved these low-key date nights with Ted. Food, a good drink and of course good company was the ideal combination in my opinion. As we finished up eating, Ted pulled me onto the sofa for a cuddle. I was laid on top of him, and he was fiddling with my ponytail.

"I know I asked you a pretty important question today," he said timidly, referring to my new position as Social Secretary. "But I wondered if it would be okay to ask you another? Or would that be too much?"

"Go ahead!" I said impatiently, wondering what it could be that he wanted to ask.

I could feel his body tense up below mine and I started to worry that something was seriously up.

"Will you be my girlfriend?" he blurted out. "You know, like, officially?"

I could feel tears beginning to form in my eyes. I sat up to look directly at Ted, who suddenly looked very overcome with emotion too.

"Look at us!" I laughed. "What a soppy pair," I mumbled, in-between sobs. "Of course I will."

"Good!" Ted laughed, wiping away his own tears. "You just mean a lot to me, Macey Genevieve, and I was scared you would say no."

"Why would I ever say no? You are the best thing that's ever happened to me, and I don't care whether it's too soon to say that. You really are my best friend, and now smoking hot boyfriend all rolled into one."

He laughed some more before pulling me closer to him. He placed a soft kiss on my forehead before hugging me tight.

"My girlfriend, Macey," He hummed into my hair. "I like it. It's got a nice ring to it."

CHAPTER 16 - ISLA

My time away was brilliant, just what I needed. The cottage was delightful, full of history and charm and gorgeous views from nearly every window. On Thursday, I arrived by early afternoon and after getting settled at the cottage I just walked, from one village to another and through the countryside and woodland. I had a notebook and pen with me and would stop every now and then to write down thoughts that would pop up and things that I wanted to research further for the book or dive deeper into.

That night I stopped at a pub in the village nearest the cottage for dinner. It was a beautiful old pub with a thatched roof and lots of cosy nooks to sit in. I had the most delicious meal and sat enjoying my drink whilst I wrote more notes and thought about everything I'd jotted down earlier in the day. Eventually I put the notebook aside and took advantage of the spot where I was sitting, tucked out of the way but still able to see the majority of the people in the pub, to do some people watching. Pretty quickly I figured out who the locals were, chatting and laughing and looking up every time someone new walked into the pub to see if they knew them. There were friendly waves and smiles and hellos whenever another villager walked in. There were a lot of locals, but there were also a few other visitors like me, sitting along the edges of the pub like I was, not getting into the middle of the conversations about village life.

Eventually I spotted a couple, sitting across the room from me. They'd had their meal and were enjoying their drinks like I was. They seemed completely lost in their own world, heads together, hands clasped, laughing at private jokes and sharing knowing smiles. I didn't see any rings on either of their fingers, but they looked to be a little older, not quite my age but not in their twenties anymore either.

I tried not to, but every now and then, especially when I saw a couple like this, I would wonder what my life would be like now if I'd stayed with Edwin. It was a completely pointless exercise, because several years later, if I'd still been with Edwin, I'd be a shadow of myself by now. I was lucky to get free of him when I did. But now my thoughts were different looking at this couple. I found myself thinking of what it would be like if Henry was on this trip with me. And I really didn't know what to think about that. My lunches with him had been fun and exciting so far. He's a great guy, we'd fallen back into an easy rhythm. And I already knew he'd never hurt me like Edwin did.

As I sat there and watched the couple, I started to feel like I hadn't really thought much about what I really wanted. Am I resisting a relationship because I'm as happy as I claim? Or because I'm scared? I never liked feeling like I was making a decision based on fear. But I also never wanted to be hurt again as badly as I was before. There was something about the couple in the pub that made me feel like I was missing out and I never felt that before in all the years since Edwin left me. Was it just a fluke? Or was it because I'd finally met someone and found something in Henry that made me think a relationship was possible? These were all the questions I didn't want to think about this weekend, so I finished my drink and left the pub to go and try to sleep.

On Friday, my first morning at the cottage, I enjoyed a nice breakfast and then sat down to write and finally, the words came. The new environment was definitely working. That first morning at the cottage the words were flowing. My characters were speaking to me at last and I could get into their heads without getting distracted by my own thoughts. It was just what I had hoped for. I spent most of that day just trying to clean up the mess I'd made of the draft over the previous weeks and then Saturday at the cottage I started making progress with writing more of the manuscript. I wasn't going to finish the first draft while at the cottage but I made a really good dent in what remained of it. Sunday was another day of writing and I wished I could have extended my trip, I wasn't ready to go back the next day. I had written nearly five full chapters in just two days and I was buzzing with how good it felt to be writing.

Monday arrived and I had one last writing session in the morning before my taxi came to pick me up and take me back to the train station to go back to Bath. Thankfully I had a seat in the quiet car on the train so I got some more writing done.

When I arrived back in Bath, I found Beth waiting for me at the station.

"How'd it go?" she asked hesitantly.

"Great!" I exclaimed breathlessly. "I have to do that more often, it was amazing. I'm not quite caught back up but I'm getting there. I got nearly five chapters written at the cottage and then finished the fifth chapter and started writing a sixth chapter on the train."

Beth's eyes flew wide, "Six chapters?! That's faster than you've written anything for this whole book so far!"

"I know," I said, as we walked out to her car. "It feels great. I'm now almost halfway through the first draft. I still have a lot to do but my outline for the second half is a lot stronger than it was before I left, I just kept getting ideas! I feel cautiously optimistic that I'll get it done on time."

"Good, well, if there's anything I can do to make it easier. Maybe we need to lighten your schedule a little bit. If one weekend away led to so much writing, maybe we need to cut back on your meetings and interviews a bit, at least until this draft is done."

"That might actually be a good idea. I hate to say it, but I do think that just getting away from all the calls and meetings and interviews made a big difference."

"I'll have a look at your schedule and see what I can do about what's already on it and then I'll start spacing things out more going forward."

We got into her car and made the short drive to my house. Once we got there she helped me carry my things inside. I knew there were a few things she needed me to go over with her for my publishers before I could get back to writing.

"Oh, I also confirmed for you to speak at the Creative Writing Society event at Plymouth University. Macey, the Social Secretary, sounded excited. I get the impression they were really looking to fill the speaker role for their event, at least that's what my cousin hinted at," Beth said with a kind laugh.

"Well I'm happy to help, you know I love talking to students. And if she's a friend of Charlotte's, even better. I'm looking forward to it."

We moved on to other topics and then when we finished, I made us some tea and we took a break before we both got back to work.

"So..." she started cautiously. "Have you thought more about Henry?"

I paused, then said, "Not really. While I was away I focused entirely on my book." There was no way I was going to tell her the truth.

We finished tea and I got back to work. I still had a lot of catching up to do.

———

I SPENT the remainder of the week writing. I was finally feeling like my deadline was possible and I would be able to meet it.

There were a few texts from Henry, asking how my trip went and if we could meet up. I made an excuse to miss our Wednesday lunch, saying I was staying home to write and eating at my desk. It was true to a certain extent. I avoided the city centre in case I would bump into him on his lunch break or after work. If I left my house it was to go write at Mum and Dad's or to go to the uni library to do some research or use their quiet rooms for a change of location. I went for long walks and just tried to think of my book and nothing else.

That weekend I was coming home from a walk when I saw Henry leaving Mrs. Russell's house. I froze, trying to decide if I should turn and walk back the way I came until he left, but before I could decide, he turned and saw me.

"Don't run away Isla," he said with a small laugh, but there was a sadness in his eyes. "It's good to see you. I just had lunch with Mum, she wanted to invite you but I told her you seemed to be either very busy or trying to avoid me."

My heart constricted, "I'm sorry Henry. I'm not avoiding you, not really. I'm finally making progress on the book and I just can't afford to be distracted."

"And I'm a distraction."

"My feelings for you are a distraction," I said, the words slipping out before I could stop them.

Henry's eyes widened, and the sadness I'd seen was replaced with something else, something like hope. "Feelings for me? That's encouraging. But also confusing, because this whole time I thought I was the only one investing any feelings in this, which would have been entirely my fault since we both said from the beginning that we were just interested in friendship right now."

"You have feelings for me?" I asked hesitantly.

"Of course I do!" Henry laughed kindly, taking a few steps towards me.

I laughed. "So much for the whole 'just friendship' thing. This has all gotten complicated."

"Does it have to be complicated?" he asked kindly, reaching out to take my hand.

"Henry..." I started slowly. "We haven't seen each other in years. It's been a lifetime. Literally. We both have gone off and had completely separate lives for over two decades. I'm not the same shy girl who admired you from a distance, and despite the ready smile and easygoing nature, I can tell your past has changed you too. We're still getting to know each other as we are now. I can't just get swept up in how I used to feel about you and confuse that with how I feel about you now. But you're so easy to be around. I find myself letting my guard down around you. Which terrifies me."

His brow furrowed, trying to keep up with what I was saying. "Why does it terrify you? I never want you to feel scared or uncomfortable around me."

"It's not *you* that I feel scared around, it's all the things you make me feel, the life I've been starting to imagine. You're making me feel things that I haven't felt in over a decade. You're making me want things I never thought I'd be brave enough to want again after how bad it went last time."

"Edwin," he said quietly.

"Yeah, Edwin. Or Evil Edwin as Georgie always refers to him as," I said with a bitter laugh. "When you've been nearly destroyed by a relationship, you're far less willing to risk it again."

"I can understand that."

"You're the first guy I've met who I think actually might be able to understand."

"So, can we talk? Can you tell me the whole story?"

I hesitated, frozen on the path, figuratively and literally, it really was freezing outside. Finally I said, "I suppose. Why don't you come in, I'll make us some tea. It's a long story if you're trying to fully understand it. And trying to understand me."

"Okay," Henry said. "I do want to understand."

I awkwardly indicated for him to follow me. I let us into my house and suddenly felt very aware that there was a man in my space. Henry had never been over to my place. Only my father and

Grant had ever been in here. When the whole social group got together it was usually at Georgie and Grant's house. She was so much better at entertaining large groups than I was, and I was always more protective over my personal space, which now felt like it was being invaded.

We took off our coats and I made us tea and we sat down in the living room. Henry had been happy to make a fire while I made tea so it was feeling very cosy in the living room by the time I brought the tea in.

I tried to make myself comfortable and I could tell Henry was waiting patiently for me to be ready to dive into it. Finally I took a breath and started.

"It started slowly at first. When Edwin and I first met he was charming, as most sociopaths are. Funny, outgoing, intelligent, handsome, and he had such a magnetic and disarming smile. We met in a club at Cambridge. We were on different courses but were both PhD students. He was friendly with everyone but he also had this thing where he decided if he wanted to let you into his circle. It felt very exclusive to be noticed by him. That should have been my first sign to run a mile in the opposite direction but when he started paying attention to me I couldn't help but feel flattered and intrigued.

"At first it was fine, great even. He was very attentive and interested in my research. He asked the right questions and complimented my work. He was unlike any other guy I'd dated, so when he asked me to be exclusive and be his girlfriend, I said yes immediately. I mean, the fact that he asked felt so old-fashioned and sweet. He gave me a beautiful necklace, a diamond pendant. He said he'd hoped I'd wear it every day. That was sign number two. Eventually that damned necklace started to feel like a collar with a tag that said, 'I belong to Edwin Johnson.' But it felt so romantic and thoughtful at the time. All my uni friends were jealous and it wasn't long before everyone within even the wider edges of Edwin's social circle knew I was his. That's when things really started getting weird.

"It was slow and really subtle, like certain guys just stopped talking to me, or if they did it was only about school stuff. And afterwards, when I looked back I realised that around that same time there were girlfriends of mine who I stopped seeing. I always thought we all just got too busy, but later I learned that he'd been casually telling them that I didn't have time for them anymore. With close friends like Georgie or with my parents, he was always the model boyfriend. So I never felt, at least not in the beginning, that I was being controlled or cut off from my social circle. I think he knew that would be too obvious.

"While we were still at Cambridge it wasn't too bad. Graduation was when it started to get hard, but we'd been together for two years by then. He was a year ahead of me, so he graduated first. He got a job in London. He did a PhD in history, with a focus on medieval British history. He got a job at a museum in London. We didn't even discuss it. He just accepted it. I was still writing my thesis, I didn't have to stay in Cambridge all the time, I could commute for the few times a month I needed to meet with an advisor. But I didn't even have a choice, he literally just told me I could move to London with him or we could break up. He wasn't willing to do long distance, even just between London and Cambridge. This should have been a major red flag but by this point I loved him too much, so I moved to London.

"I couldn't afford it though, he never expected to split the bills equally, but he would always make comments about how much he was supporting me, how much he was carrying the both of us financially. If dinner wasn't made when he got home, if the flat wasn't clean, if the food shop hadn't been done or his dry cleaning hadn't been picked up, I'd get a lecture on how I wasn't doing my part. He was working full time to pay for everything, and chores were how I could contribute since I couldn't do so financially. The thing was, it wasn't like I wasn't doing anything all day. I was still doing my research and doing interviews and internships and meetings. We'd always split chores and errands when we lived together in Cambridge, because we were both students. But now, because he was working, he wanted me to do everything. And because I loved him, I did. I bent over backwards to get everything done, meet his expectations and get my PhD work done. By graduation I was ready to collapse. I'd lost a lot of weight from stress, which he praised. He wouldn't stop complimenting my thinner body in front of our friends."

I noticed Henry tense in his chair, I could tell he wanted to say something, but he stopped himself and just nodded at me to continue.

"I eventually got a job in public policy in London but I'd always wanted a teaching and research position. I'd interviewed with a few smaller universities around London, but he dismissed all of them. If I wasn't going to be a professor at Cambridge or Oxford or LSE or somewhere equally impressive, what was the point? And he would have never moved to Oxford or back to Cambridge and he was so critical of me commuting. It was a lose-lose situation.

"I think he could tell I was unhappy and that he needed to try to control the situation. The diamond necklace went missing and I was frantic. I was honestly terrified of telling him it was gone and that I'd lost it, but I always put it on the dish beside the bed at night and put it on first thing in the morning. A few days later, he surprised me with a romantic dinner and an excuse about how his bad attitude had been due to stress at work, even though his bad attitude had been grating on me for a year by that point. He then proposed, with a ring made from the diamond from the necklace. At the time I thought it was romantic. But later it bothered me. He never asked me, never told me, it was another reminder that everything he gave me, he could take away. It was another way he could control me.

"I foolishly said yes, thinking that if we were married things would be better. But I was in my mid-twenties when we met and only 27 when we ended, I was so young. I didn't see all the signs along the way, it was only looking back that I could see the ocean of red flags behind me. Years of emotional abuse, financial abuse, gaslighting, lying. Feeling like every problem with our relationship was my fault, like I was never good enough.

"A few months after the engagement, he broke it off. He was terrible. He just decided he didn't want me anymore. He'd met someone else, someone he felt fit his life better. He was tired of trying to make me good enough. Clearly, no hair appointment or new wardrobe would make me appropriate for the social group he was trying to claw his way into. His new girlfriend was in the right social circles and was connected to the aristocracy. So I was out and she was in. I literally had three days to move out, his orders. He was going away with her on a city break to Lisbon and I was supposed to be gone when he got back. I was just dismissed.

"I felt so powerless. I hated that after years of torture the relationship was ending on his terms, but, after the fact, I slowly realised I dodged a bullet. It still has taken a long time for me to come to terms with everything, honestly I don't know if I'll ever understand how I could allow that to happen to me. I felt like I was slowly getting boiled alive. I didn't realise how hot the water had gotten until it was almost too late.

"So after years of working on my education and trying to start a career, I'd ended up living in London, working a job I hated, engaged then heartbroken. No, not just heartbroken, completely broken...physically, mentally, emotionally. I was destroyed. Georgie and Grant came to pick me up. I told you that part. What I didn't tell you was that I was so weak from not eating and all the weight loss from stress that Grant had to carry me downstairs to the car once all my things were loaded in. My parents took me straight to the GP when I got back to Bath. I was bed bound for two weeks after moving home. I was 27 and had almost nothing to show for my life, other than my university degrees. I'd lost all my friends except Georgie, I had no career, no money, I'd quit my job to move home but Edwin had always controlled the money.

"Even when I was making money, he'd come up with new bills or fees I needed to help pay. There was never anything left. All the savings were in his name. I was literally left with nothing. That's why my career means so much to me now. It's mine. I built it. I own this beautiful house, which was not a cheap property to buy. I've now bought a second property. I eat out at nice restaurants. I can buy nice things if I see something I like.

"People tease me for my independence but when you've been so completely controlled, independence is like air or water. I need it to live now. It's not as easy as people think, to just give a relationship a try and see what happens. I did that once and it nearly destroyed me."

The air was heavy between us, the fire crackling was the only sound. I could see my story weighing on Henry's mind, I could almost hear his brain spinning trying to think of what to say in response. I just looked at him and waited.

He started, slowly, "Isla... I knew your story had to be difficult, and just from the small bit that you had shared before, I knew that your hesitation to pursue a relationship wasn't the result of some small action. I understand pain and trauma, gaslighting and manipulation. But even my own past relationship issues are nothing compared to what you had to deal with, though my past does help give me perspective that other men might not have."

I nodded. "From what you've told me about your ex, and from the few things your mum has let slip, I know you do have a different perspective on this, I think that's why I've been able to tell you everything. I've tried dating again. Years ago now. When I turned 30, Georgie was determined to get me dating again, she didn't want me to waste my whole life—her words, not mine. Anyway, it never worked out. They always wanted more than I could give, and the couple that stuck around long enough to try to understand me, freaked out as soon as I tried to explain my past." I frowned into my tea thinking about it. "Baggage. That's what they called it. They didn't want to deal with baggage from my previous relationship."

"Well that's just a load of nonsense. Anyone older than 20 has baggage. We all get our hearts broken at least once or twice, we all go through some kind of personal trauma at some point in our life, even if it's not relationship related."

"I know. These guys acted like they were above it all. Good vibes and positivity and all that. God, their so-called positivity was so toxic. They used my so-called baggage as a stick to beat me with. They all just felt like a different version of Edwin. So I gave up. By 30, I had my book deal and two books to my name with a third on the way. I focused on my career and my friendships. I tried to stay open, but I think over time I just got used to how things were and resigned myself to being single. I focused on the positives of that, rather than the negatives. I honestly don't think that maybe I'm missing out on anything until I talk to Georgie or my mum or your mum," I said with a small laugh.

Henry smiled. "I feel the same. My life in San Francisco was great. I had good friends and a great job, a nice flat, I enjoyed the city and traveling around the US and Canada when I could get away. I didn't feel like I was missing out, until I'd talk to Mum and she'd ask if I'd met anyone yet," he said laughing.

I laughed, "Mums. They always make us think about things we'd rather not think about."

Henry went quiet for a moment. "The thing I'm trying to understand Isla, is we've spent a fair bit of time together now, getting reacquainted. You've known me for years, and yes there was a long gap where we weren't in touch, but I'm still me. You have to know I'd never treat you the way Edwin did. So, why the hesitation? Why suddenly start avoiding me?"

"First of all, I wasn't consciously avoiding you, not the way you think. I really have been under a lot of pressure about the book. That wasn't just an excuse I made up to get out of seeing you. But, on a subconscious level, it's just moving so fast. Everyone's asking me about how things are going with us. Is there anything new to report? How do I feel? Are we becoming more serious? I don't have answers to these questions Henry. And even though you don't pressure me, I can tell that you're asking these questions as well. I'm more trouble than I'm worth Henry, believe me."

"Now that's just not fair, to you or to me," Henry said firmly. He paused and then in a more gentle tone he continued. "You're not trouble Isla. You're human. You've been through something very traumatic and you've never had to trust someone again like you trusted him. Why not give me a chance? You used to trust me, and so far, you've trusted me enough to be friends, can't we at least try for something more?"

"Like it's so easy," I said bitterly. I could feel the tears start to prick at my eyes.

"No, it's not easy. Do you think it's easy for me? I'm terrified of being hurt again."

"Henry, it wasn't just my heart that was broken or my pride that was wounded," I said quietly. I wanted to make sure he really understood. "It took months for me to physically recover and regain the weight I'd lost, for my hair to grow back after stress made it start falling out, for my stomach to not get sick because it was finally getting food and it didn't know how to deal with that."

"You have scars Isla," Henry said softly. "I understand that. I'm not saying we have to rush anything. I'm saying we both deserve happiness and I think we might be able to make something work here. I haven't felt like this for anyone in years and it's not just rose coloured memories of our past selves. You're right, you're not the same shy girl you used to be. You're strong, confident, funny, and intelligent. Even if we didn't have our past connection I think I'd be well on my way to falling for you."

I could feel my heart start to race and the walls closing in. Talking about relationships and dating in the abstract hypotheticals was one thing, but having a man in my living room actually hearing my story and saying he wants to date me anyway was more than I could process.

"I can't do this right now," I said shakily.

"Okay," he said, frowning, realising how I was feeling. "I'm sorry, the last thing I wanted was to come into your home and make you feel uncomfortable. You were willing to share your story and I wanted to listen, to understand. But I won't push you."

I paused, unsure what to say next. Finally, "I'm sorry Henry. I'm sorry I need more time."

Henry hesitated for a moment, I could tell he was trying to think of the right way to say what he wanted to say. "Isla, I don't want to be one more person in your life pushing you to make a decision before you feel ready. I think you deserve to live a full life again and not be trapped by the past. But I also know better than others that you have to be ready to make that decision for yourself, no one can make it for you. It took me years and even then, it wasn't until I saw you in the bookshop after so long that I realised I really was over my past and ready to move on. No other woman has made me feel that way since my ex broke my heart. So I'll wait. We can stay in 'friends for now' mode for as long as you need. I enjoy spending time with you, I don't want to lose that."

"I don't want to lose that either," I said quietly, feeling the tears start to spill over.

"Oh Isla," Henry said, his voice barely more than a whisper. He stood up from his chair opposite mine and moved to the couch, gesturing for me to join him. I hesitated but then moved to sit next to him.

"Can I hug you?" he asked kindly. "I don't want to push my luck here," he laughed gently. "But I hate seeing people I...care about cry."

I nodded and leant into his side. He lifted his arm and wrapped it around me and rested his chin on the top of my head. I couldn't remember the last time I felt physical affection from a man other than my father. The tears came faster and Henry just held me as we watched the fire dance in the grate.

"Isla," Henry said softly. "I just want you to know that you're not more trouble than you're worth, like you think. You're not trouble at all, but even if you were, you'd be worth all the trouble in the world if it meant having you in my life for good. I'm not going anywhere."

CHAPTER 17 - MACEY

The intensifying hum of my alarm woke me just before day broke. I turned over to face Ted, who'd been cuddling me in the same position for most of the night. I shook him gently before whispering in his ear. "Rise and shine babe, rise and shine!" I murmured, eager for him to stir.

"Why so early?" he said, in his groggy yet cute morning tone.

"Today's the big day!" I announced, the excitement evident in my voice as I sat up and stretched. I was hoping Ted would match my enthusiasm, but instead he grabbed my pillow and placed it over his head. I thought I hated mornings, but then I met Ted. He cannot physically function before nine in the morning, and that's on a good day.

"Come on!" I shouted, prodding him. "We have so much to do."

"Why's today a big day?" he asked, confused. "Are we getting married?"

"Nope, that's not today," I giggled.

"Oh yes, I haven't asked your dad for your hand in marriage yet," he teased, pulling me down next to him to cuddle for a while longer. "Do people still do that?"

"I guess so, even if it is pretty old fashioned. But hold your horses, I need to tell him you exist first."

"You still haven't told your parents about us?" Ted questioned, upset apparent in his tone. He rubbed his eyes before finally sitting up himself. "M?" he probed, after he got no response.

"I just don't know how they're going to react Ted. I've sprung quite a few big things on them recently and I don't feel like they trust me to make big, thought out decisions. They think I rush into things already and I am not in the mood to be judged by them."

"You switched courses, yeah, but what were the other big things?"

"Owen and I's breakup for one. As relieved as they were that it was over, afterwards they kind of decided that I was incapable of finding someone decent, regardless of the fact that everything shitty that happened in that relationship was down to Owen. They put me through a lot of therapy after the split and I think they would deem it was a waste of time if I jumped into another relationship. I thought it was horrendously ironic, considering."

"Considering what?"

"You know, the situation with my parents."

"Thing is Macey, I don't. You have barely spoken about your parents. I've tried to ask but you've shut the conversation down every time."

"I'm sorry, I'm just not as close to them as I know you are with yours. My parents aren't actually together anymore."

"Since when?" Ted asked, surprised.

"A while now. It was about two years ago I think?"

"But you've spoken about them being at home?"

"Yeah, they still live together. They're just not, together *together* anymore."

"I wish you'd told me about this M. I bang on about my parents all the time. That must have come across pretty inconsiderate of me, even though I genuinely had no idea."

"No, it's fine. You didn't know, and I love hearing about your parents anyway. They seem so lovely and so happy together, still. I wish my parents were like that."

"They are great, and they can't wait to meet you. When I told them about you the other week, they were so excited. They were actually trying to persuade me to ask you something, but I've been holding back."

"What's that?"

"Well, on Thursday it's Thanksgiving, and as you know, my mum is American. We celebrate it in our house and I always go home for it. I know I mentioned I was going home this weekend, but I haven't asked you to come with me yet. So, I know it's short notice, but will you? Will you come and meet my parents and do the whole Thanksgiving shindig?"

I laughed. "Of course I will! Though I do wish you'd have given me more notice, so you know, I can freak out for even longer about how I will act when I meet your parents!"

"Hey, you're perfect just the way you are. No need to freak out, no need to act in any other way. Marie and Trevor are going to love you, as will Evie and Joey and Anton too. I can't wait for you to meet Evie especially; you can chat about Isla's books."

"Speaking of which, we NEED to get ready!" I said, hitting Ted with the pillow. "Isla is going to be arriving on campus at eleven and we need to get set up beforehand."

Ted got up from the bed and got undressed, ready for the shower. "Don't think you've avoided talking about your parents M, we shall be revisiting this later."

"Whatever you say Champ." I replied, happy that I'd managed to put off the talk for a little while longer.

———

WE STROLLED through town to campus, Ted holding one hand and a Greggs vegan sausage roll clutched in the other. I was feeling more than content, I had my stellar boyfriend and the perfect breakfast in my company. However, memories of the morning conversation we'd had were hanging over me. We'd passed by Plymouth Guild-hall and the Sundial before I had finally plucked up the courage to revisit our earlier chat.

"Why were you holding back from asking me to come to Thanksgiving?" I blabbed.

"I was worried that you'd think it was too soon to meet my family. I know we've only been official for a week and I thought that me asking you could potentially scare you off." He squeezed my hand in reassurance before adding. "I don't think it's too soon. I feel like I've known you forever M."

"Yeah, I agree. It isn't too soon, it feels right. I've been so excited to meet them. You need to stop worrying that you're scaring me off!" I replied, hesitance still lingering in my voice.

"Is there something else?" Ted kindly asked. I loved how sweet he was when it came to how I felt, he never disregarded my emotions or belittled how I felt. It had taken some getting used to, seeing as I knew exactly how it felt to have someone constantly invalidate you and your feelings.

"I know I should really tell my parents. I was pushing it to the back of my mind as well as my to-do list. But now I can't stop thinking about it. I feel like the longer I leave it, the worse I'm going to feel, and the angrier they will be." I paused. "All the stuff with Owen…"

"You and Owen broke up a while ago now though. You'd hope they are past thinking about him."

"It's not that simple unfortunately. Owen was a big part of my life. And my parents are complicated." I stopped walking for a second and looked around, trying to stop myself from becoming upset.

"Hey, hey!" Ted said, embracing me in a comforting side hug. "What's brought all of this on?"

"I feel like it's been building up for a while. I'm so stressed about my parents, and their looming divorce. I'm stressed about telling them about you, I'm stressed about something, me, fucking this up."

"Nothing is going to fuck this up Macey. I won't let it. I promise," Ted said calmly, wiping away my tears before they could even form properly. "Now, we've got an event to host. Let's figure that out first and then we'll speak to your parents later."

"Sounds like a plan," I agreed, slotting my hand back into Ted's and continuing on our way to uni.

———

"Hey lovebirds!" Rosa called out as we entered the lecture hall where the talk with Isla was to be held. Confused, I just laughed in response as Ted did as well. Ted and I were waiting to post anything online about us becoming official, until we had told my parents. Neither of them were big social media users, but it didn't feel right to post about it yet anyway, whilst they were still none the wiser. I assumed Ted must have mentioned it to her in class, and began distributing the information packs I'd had printed for the event around the room. As I did, Rosa wandered over to me.

"These look great Macey!" she said, flicking through one of the booklets that I'd just placed down. "There's some super resources in there for aspiring writers, as well as all the relevant contact information for our guest speaker. Fab job! Wasn't it so kind of Isla to offer up an email address so that people could get in touch with her if they needed any more advice?"

"Yeah, so kind," I mumbled, taking the book from her and arranging it neatly on the remaining table.

"Is everything okay?" Rosa asked, her eyes wide with concern.

"I'm just stressed. I have a lot on my plate at the moment."

"Is it anything to do with Ted? I thought you guys were super happy, especially now that you're official!"

"Yeah, about that. I still haven't told my parents, that's probably the biggest reason as to why I'm so stressed, as well as hoping that the event will run smoothly. Ted and I were keeping things on the down-low for a while, just until I'd told my family. It's just I'm not sure how my parents will react, and my ex, well, I haven't expressed this to Ted, but I'm scared of him finding out too. Owen, my ex-boyfriend, is a bit… much?" I said, struggling to find the words to describe him. As much as the breakup was Owen's doing, he was a super jealous person and I knew he would struggle seeing me with someone else.

"Oh right. I'm sorry Macey. Ted just texted me after it happened. He was so excited and proud of himself I guess," she laughed. "It was really sweet."

I gushed at the thought of him being so proud that he had to tell someone immediately. "That is really sweet," I said, smiling. "I'm meeting his parents this weekend, which is just another thing to be stressed about. I know it seems like I'm panicking so much over very little, but I can't help it. Sorry for bombarding you with this!" I added whilst biting my lip.

"Hey, if you're stressed about it, you're stressed about it. And know, you can always talk to me if you need to. Though I'd say you just need to figure everything out, one at a time. Start with calling your parents, now, before the event starts. You've got enough time, and you don't want to be thinking about it whilst Isla's here."

"Thanks Rosa. I will call them now; I'll grab Ted as well. You're coming for coffee with Isla after the talk too, right?"

"I sure am, I wouldn't miss that for the world!"

———

"THE SMOKING AREA?" Ted laughed as I dragged him outside.

"I couldn't think of where else to go and I need fresh air!" I exclaimed, jumping on the wall.

"I don't think the air is very fresh out here babe, but anything for you!" he said, joining me.

"We've got twenty minutes until Isla arrives. It's Monday, which is both my parents' days off. Hopefully they'll be at home, together, so I can kill two birds with one stone."

I pulled up my dad's contact number and pressed "call". He

answered almost immediately. I selected speakerphone so Ted could hear what was said too.

"Hi Macey. Is everything ok?" he said, sounding almost shocked that I had rang. I usually text, I think the last time we spoke on the phone was when I told him and Mum about the course change. I guess he was used to me delivering bad news whilst on call, therefore expecting it now.

"Hi Dad. I just needed to talk to you and Mum about something, quickly. I don't have a lot of time. Is she there?"

"Yeah, I'll get her."

A few moments passed before I heard Mum enter the room. Ted squeezed my leg in support as he felt my body tense up.

"Hi Macey," she said hurriedly, as if she was in a rush.

"I won't keep you long," I announced. "I just had to get something off my chest."

"You're not changing courses, again, are you? We have only just come to terms with the last switch," Dad joked. I felt more comfortable talking to him, my mum was who I was more worried about.

"There's been a lot going on in my life recently and I haven't had a chance to fill you in. I joined the Creative Writing Society, where I became Social Secretary for one."

"That's really cool M! Well done," Dad said.

"Well done Macey!" Mum added.

"I also met someone. Who is now my boyfriend. We actually met at the end of September, but just became official last week. He's called—"

Mum interrupted me. "You have a boyfriend?"

"That's what she said," Dad exhaled. "Who's the lucky guy?" he added, slightly sarcastically.

"He's called Ted. He's 22 and doing a Master's degree in Creative Writing here at Plymouth. He's really cool, I think you'd like him."

"I'm sure he is a great guy, Macey. But don't you think it's a little soon to be getting into a relationship? After what happened with Owen?"

I rolled my eyes, before noticing that Ted looked a little uncomfortable.

"Dad, it's different. I'm different now too, I'm in a really good place and Ted is perfect for me." I said, in an attempt to reassure Ted that everything was okay.

"As long as I'm not going to have to pick you up off any floors again..." Dad paused. "I'm happy for you Macey, I'd like to meet the fella. Make sure he's as perfect as you claim him to be."

I smiled. I knew Dad would be the more understanding of the two.

"Not so fast Simon. I warned you after last time Macey. I do not want to be close to getting another restraining order." Ted's eyes widened and I contemplated taking the phone off speaker mode.

"Look, that will not be necessary," I protested in a hush tone. "Ted's a good guy. You'll like him. I'm happy, he's happy, you'll be happy. I have to go but we'll speak about this more soon!" I added in a hurry. "Bye!" I hung up before they could say anything else. "I know we've got time before Isla comes, but I can't be bothered to talk to them for any longer," I said to Ted, nervously laughing.

"What was all that about?" Ted questioned as I remained on the wall. He'd jumped off mid call and was pacing in front of me. He stopped, turning to me with a concerned look on his face. "A restraining order?"

I sighed. "After Owen broke up with me, I guess you could say he regretted his decision. He was borderline stalking me for a while, before Mum threatened him with a restraining order. He backed off after that. I don't know why he was so persistent, after what he would say—"

"What do you mean? What did he say?"

"He would always say things like I was easily replaceable. I think he was just trying to assert control. One minute he'd be all over me, the next, the opposite. I never knew if I was coming or going with him. It was very up and down. The last argument, and subsequent final breakup, was the final straw for me. How he made me feel, was so bad. I swore I couldn't go back there, and he wasn't used to that. So when he tried to contact me, and get me back under his spell, and I didn't engage with it, he flipped. Calling me all hours of the day, showing up at work, things like that. Like I said though, he stopped when my mum threatened him with the order."

"Wow," Ted took a breath. "I wish you'd told me all of this sooner."

"It's fine, I haven't heard from him in months now. He finally got the message I believe, luckily. That's why I was scared to tell my parents, and why their reaction was as I thought it would be."

"Yeah… what was that about your dad picking you up off the floor?"

I paused, realising I hadn't thought about what had actually happened that day for a while now. Ted noticed my apprehension and rested his hand on my thigh.

"You don't have to tell me if you don't want to, if you're not ready."

"It's okay," I said aloud, whilst internally reassuring myself that I can get through this story without crying. It's been over a year now; I can do this.

"The day we broke up, I was at Owen's house. We were arguing, and it had gotten to the point where he was shouting, rather loud, and I felt really intimidated, as usual. I was hiding in a corner of his bedroom, trying to process what was happening. I was trying to get my breath, but I was struggling. I remember my back began to slide further and further down the wall and eventually, I was on the floor. Owen had gotten up from where he was sitting and walked toward me. I can still remember the heat of his body as he looked down at me. He asked me why I was being so pathetic, that I'd never been like this before.

"I remember my heart was racing and my breathing was so disturbed. I tried to explain to him how I was feeling, but I couldn't get the words out. Every time I tried to open my mouth to speak, only whimpers escaped. He told me he didn't want to be with me anymore. I felt like my whole world was crumbling as he said those words. Though I knew it was for the best, I couldn't help but feel so helpless. He was the only constant in my life back then, and I didn't feel ready to lose him. I remember shouting at him, saying that he's said it before, and didn't mean it. At this point, he was sneering at me from the end of his bed again. He emphasised that this time he did in fact mean it, and it was for good.

"He then went on to ask why I was making such a big deal out of it, because a few weeks prior I'd texted Sam saying I didn't want to be with him anymore. I remember that part so vividly. It shocked me that he had snooped through my phone. I told him that I thought we'd work things out. I did think things were different this time around. I knew he was reading my messages, but I didn't want to believe it. I remember begging at this point, asking him repeatedly whether he loved me. I was so desperate. He said he didn't love me. He said I was disposable and always had been. He said he was just waiting for someone better to come around.

"After he dropped that bomb, I curled further up into a ball and sobbed. It wasn't until my parents arrived half an hour later, my dad scooping myself and all of my broken pieces off the floor, that I opened my eyes. Dad told me that this had to be the last time. He had whispered it in my ear as he carried me down the stairs. He told me that I can't keep doing this to myself. He was right. I so wanted to believe that I would stop, going back to him. But I felt like I just couldn't. I remember telling my dad that he'll come around, because he always did.

"It was hard to speak after I felt like all my energy had been drained out of me, but I said it loud enough for my mum to hear. I turned to look at her, still in my dad's arms, and she rolled her eyes as she opened the front door. She simply shouted no at me, physically putting her foot down. She told me that I will see, maybe in a week, or a month. Or even a year. That him ending things today, was the best thing that could ever happen to me."

I paused for a moment. "I then remember her slagging off Owen's house, to which Ms. Shay, Owen's mum shouted from the kitchen. 'You've never been welcome here,' she said."

"I don't care," my mum had replied. "Sort your son out and we wouldn't have to be around, yet again."

"Under normal circumstances, I would have cringed at our parents' dislike of one another, but none of my emotions were functioning. In the car on the way home, Dad turned around to look at me. I was sunken in the back seat. Hood up, eyes red and sore."

"This really does need to stop. You can't keep going back to him, he is terrible, for you, but outright, just terrible. And you will realise that, I promise," he said, passing me a can of Coke. "For the shock," he told me. "Panic attacks are nasty."

"I hadn't even realised that I'd had a panic attack. But it was a huge one. I'd never really experienced any form of anxiety before that, but now I do every so often. I guess I have Owen to thank for that."

"That's...a lot." Ted was visibly upset. He stood awkwardly for a second before pulling me off the wall and into a hug. He stroked the back of my head and held me close for a few seconds, before speaking once again.

"I am so sorry you had to go through that. How he could hurt you like that...it's beyond me."

I struggled to say much more. I hugged him back tightly. I felt safe with him. He kissed me on the forehead and squeezed me a little tighter.

"I love you," Ted whispered.

I broke the embrace and stepped back. I looked at him, dumbfounded. Did he really just tell me he loved me?

He continued, "I know it's a bit soon but—"

My brain was going a million miles per hour. My palms were sweaty, and I felt that overwhelming, dizzy feeling again. But this time, it was in the best possible way. "I love you too." I interrupted.

"You do?"

"Of course," I replied, blushing.

"Hearing all of that, what he did to you, how he treated you, just made me realise even more, how in love with you I am. I never want anyone else to hurt you like that again. I for one, will never hurt you, I can promise that. I am sorry I had to tell you all of this in the smoking area, of all places. It isn't very romantic."

'It's perfect Ted, you needn't worry about that. I am so happy that fate brought us together. And that you got over the insecurities that were initially holding you back."

He slipped his fingers through my hand and led me back towards the door. "I'm sure Isla's waiting for us now. Maybe we could suggest a novel idea where the two main characters profess their love for each other whilst surrounded by the stench of tobacco?"

"Where'd you get that idea from? Very creative," I laughed.

"Oh you know, it would only be the greatest love story of all time."

————

"MACEY! HI!" Isla called out as I entered the lecture hall where the event was being held. As always, she looked gorgeous. Her dark auburn hair was curled, with the two front strands pinned back with a silver clip. She was wearing a pair of burgundy trousers, along with a thin black jumper and black kitten heels. It wasn't too dissimilar to the outfit I was wearing, a pair of wide legged checked trousers, with an oversized beige sweater tucked in. I was wearing trainers though, of course, and my hair was up in my apparently signature bun. I wanted to look cool, yet professional.

"I love your outfit!" Isla added as I approached. *Nailed it*, I thought to myself.

"Hey Isla! Thank you. And thank you also for joining us today. Everyone is so excited!"

"I've been really looking forward to this too. When Beth saw the email, she knew it'd be right up my street! I love talking to young people about being an author, and telling them all the things I'd wish I'd heard at your age!"

I smiled, taking it all in. I still couldn't believe I was on a first name basis with Isla Stewart.

"People should be arriving in the next ten minutes," I told Isla, cautious of the fact that the event we've been frantically planning is about to start. I was nervous, I wanted everything to go according to plan. For Isla, for Ted, for the society, and for me too. "I'm just going to check a few things with Ted before they do," I added, turning around to locate him. I was still on a high from the events that unfolded earlier, and I wanted to speak to him again before we got swept up in all the chaos.

"Everything good?" Ted asked as I wandered over to the stall he was manning. He had set up a station to be based at with Rosa, a place where students could submit any questions they had for Isla, for the Q&A part of the event. They'd decided to go traditional and have guests write questions down and post them in a box, rather than have them submitted online. I also had suggested that people may not feel comfortable with asking questions live on a microphone, so this seemed to be the ideal situation. Ted and Rosa could also veto any that weren't appropriate this way as well.

"Everything's very good." I said smiling. Ted walked around the desk and pulled me in for another hug, before breaking away and getting his phone out of his pocket. "Hey Rosa, could you take a picture of Macey and I please?"

"Of course!" Rosa said enthusiastically. I beamed, even before the photo had been taken.

"What was that in aid of?" I asked, after Ted had sat back down.

"Do I need a reason to take a photo with my beautiful girlfriend? Though, I did really want to remember today."

"You big softie," I giggled, poking fun at him. I wasn't used to someone being quite this affectionate with me, and although I brushed it off often, I really, really enjoyed it. I wandered over to find my seat in the auditorium when my phone pinged in my pocket. It pinged again, and again. I pulled it out to see what the irregular stream of notifications were about.

Instagram: poet_ted tagged you in a post.

Facebook: Ted Leakes said he was with you in Plymouth, England.

Facebook: Ted Leakes sent you a relationship request.

I quickly unlocked my phone to see what he had written. The caption was the same on both the Instagram and Facebook posts, it accompanied the photo we had just taken.

Proud of my gorgeous girlfriend today. Smashing it as always x

I smiled to myself and liked both posts, commenting on each of them as well. Other comments were starting to come in, including ones from his friends.

Happy for you mate!

What a good-looking couple.

A great pair! :)

The third was from Rosa. The other two names I didn't recognise, but the compliments felt lovely all the same. I accepted his relationship request, glancing over at him to see if he'd seen. He was looking at his phone, smiling when the notification pinged. I felt fuzzy inside, happy that we were now Facebook official, because according to Charlotte, that was important.

CHAPTER 18 - ISLA

I stood at the front of the room where the talk would be given, talking to a couple members of the Creative Writing Society as the rest of the guests filtered in and took their seats. Macey has been a sweetheart, she seemed so excited to have me there, and the Society President, Ted, seemed like a nice guy. I was pretty sure they were dating, it certainly looked that way based on the looks they kept giving each other. Like they were the only people in the room who mattered. Why was it that everywhere I looked I seemed to see happy couples? They made me think about Henry. Our talk had been intense the other night, and we hadn't seen each other since. But I was looking forward to seeing him again. It was like a dam had broken and I felt less hesitant to move forward with him.

I sighed quietly and tried to focus on my notes. And when it was time, I took a seat while I waited for Ted to introduce me.

The talk went well. I mostly focused on sharing my journey to being a published writer, how I published my first book and how my career grew. I also talked about my writing process and my advice for young writers just starting off. All the students were really engaged and very interested. The Q&A portion at the end of the talk went great, the students asked fantastic questions that the society had collected and read out for me. These were my favourite kinds of events, it made me feel like I was having some impact on young people.

The event ran a little long, since I wanted to answer as many of the questions as possible. After it finished, I went for coffee with the committee that ran the society. Ted very kindly took my order and told me to sit down with Macey.

"I hope I lived up to everyone's expectations," I said with a nervous laugh.

"You were amazing!" Macey exclaimed. "You exceeded everyone's expectations. Thank you so much for coming."

"It was my pleasure. Beth was really excited for me to do this. I think you're housemates with her cousin Charlotte?"

"Yeah, Charlotte's the best. I'm so grateful that you came to support the society."

"I'm always happy to help with student organisations. It's really important to me to connect with young writers," I said sincerely.

Macey and I chatted for a bit, while we waited for our drinks and for the rest of the committee to arrive, since we'd all walked over separately. Macey was a lovely young woman, very thoughtful and quiet, but when she talked to Ted, she seemed very sure of herself. There was something about her that I recognised.

"Macey, have we met before? You seem so familiar to me for some reason," I finally asked her while Ted was talking to someone else.

Macey beamed, "Yes! I came to your *Bold and Bright* event in Bristol! I asked a question and then later we chatted for a moment when you signed my book. I told you I wanted to be a writer."

"Ah yes, I remember you now, you asked in the Q&A what made me write stories with happy endings."

Her smile grew bigger as she realised I really did remember her from the event. "It was such an honour to get to meet you. And an even bigger honour that you're here today. I really appreciate it and it's been so much fun getting to talk to you again."

"I agree," I said smiling. "So, are you and Ted dating? You seemed very close earlier."

Macey blushed, "Yeah, it's still new, but he's great."

"How did you meet?" I asked, genuinely curious.

Macey smiled, "We met in a bookshop, we were both reaching for the last copy of your book, *A Courageous Beginning*. I wanted to buy a fresh copy and he wanted it for his sister."

"A fresh copy?" I asked, trying not to giggle, but Macey saw my face and we both burst into laughter.

"I've read my copy so many times, I just felt like getting a new one. But he made a convincing case for why he deserved the last copy. We just kind of kept talking from there."

"Well I have to say, that is not only one of the best 'how we met' stories, it's also one of the best stories I've heard involving one of my books. I'm very grateful for readers like you Macey," I said.

"Your books are my favourite. They just make me believe in love and happy endings. I didn't really know if it could happen, but then I met Ted."

"Well you're very lucky, love doesn't come around for everyone."

"With your books, you must see love in your life all the time."

"Like I told you when I answered your question in Bristol, my books are escapism. They're fantasy. True love doesn't come around very often, so when it does, you have to hold on to it."

Once again I thought of Henry. Love seemed so much easier and more natural when I was Macey's age, it got scarier when you got older. We enjoyed the rest of our coffee and conversation and I got to talk a little bit more with all of the members of the committee and we had a great time. They were all so smart and so much farther ahead than I was at that age. It was great to see so many young people who are brave enough to go straight for what they want, rather than go the long way around like I feel I did.

I left Macey and Ted at the coffee shop and headed for the train station. I wasn't looking forward to the train ride back to Bath. I'd spent the whole train ride to Plymouth thinking about Henry. We'd texted a few times but I hadn't seen him in over a week. I think he was giving me time to get my head around what we'd talked about. I really wanted to give him a chance, give us a chance. But it wasn't something I could just dive right into.

I had been so absorbed in the activities of the day I hadn't checked my phone since my final instructions from Beth this morning, so I pulled it out of my bag, making a mental note to text Macey later for some pictures from the day. Beth would be cross with me for not getting any pictures to post to my social media.

When I turned on my phone I saw a bunch of missed calls and messages, from Henry and from Beth. Missed calls from both him and Beth seemed like a bad sign. I randomly tapped a text from Beth and when I saw, it stopped me in my tracks.

Call Henry ASAP. Mrs R in hospital. Then call me. I'll meet you at Bath Spa when your train arrives and take you to hospital. Call him!!!

I felt someone brush roughly past me and tut loudly under their breath. Then soon after someone else said, "Out of the way luv," before swerving around me. I quickly stepped to the side and scanned the other messages before checking my watch. I had to hurry or I'd miss my train. I stepped back into the rush on the pavement and speed walked to the station. Once I was on the plat-form waiting for the train to arrive I stepped away from the crowd. With shaking fingers, I tapped through Henry's texts to call him. He picked up almost instantly.

"Isla, I don't know if you heard from Beth first—"

I interrupted him, "—I'm on my way. I'm in Plymouth, but I'm on the platform waiting for my train and Beth will meet me at Bath Spa and bring me to the hospital. I'm on my way," I repeated. I took a shaky breath and then asked what I was afraid to ask, "How bad is it?"

Henry paused on the other end, "…It's…it's bad Isla."

I heard his voice break and I knew he was trying not to cry. "Oh God, Henry, please say she's…" I couldn't finish.

"She's alive, Isla. She's alive. But it's bad." His voice was quiet and cracked.

"What happened Henry? I saw her just the other day, she seemed tired but no more than usual. Is it like last time? Did she collapse?" I asked, thinking of when I had to take her to the hospital last year when she had a funny turn.

"No, it's not like last time. She…Isla…" His voice dropped to a whisper, "She was hit by a car. It's really bad. Please just come. We're in A&E. They've taken her back for tests, I'm in the waiting room right now. If they let me go in to sit with her I won't be able to answer my mobile but I can text. Just…please just come."

I saw my train pulling into the station. I moved towards the edge of the platform and said, "My train is arriving now. I'll be there as soon as I can, but it's more than a two-hour journey. Text me updates please."

"I will. Thank you Isla," he said, sounding so hollow.

I hung up and began tapping my foot impatiently on the platform while the train came to a stop in front of me and people began getting off. Finally, I was able to get on and get a seat. I immediately called Beth.

As soon as I heard the call connect I spoke in a rush, "I talked to Henry. Oh my God, Beth, it's terrible."

"I know Isla. How much was he able to tell you?"

"Just that she was hit by a car! How on earth? And that she's been taken back for tests and that it's really bad. But that's all I know."

Beth went quiet.

"Beth?"

"It was really bad Isla. Terrifying," her voice was trembling and I could hear her swallow a sob.

"Beth, what happened?"

"We were in the city centre…"

"You were with her!?"

"She came round to your place while I was there working, she didn't know you were away. She needed to run an errand to the library and was hoping you'd walk over with her. I didn't think she should walk by herself in the cold so I offered to drive her over. We had just parked and were walking to the library, chatting happily, and this car just came out of nowhere. I could hear it speeding, it didn't sound right. I still can't picture exactly what happened. I was still walking but Mrs. Russell had stopped to check something in her handbag, we were only a few feet apart but she was near the edge of the pavement. I heard the brakes lock and the tyres squeal, I looked back and I didn't see her."

I could hear Beth crying on the other end and my heart ached. Of all the days for me to be away from Bath.

"Beth, it's okay, it wasn't your fault if that's what you're thinking."

"I should have—"

"—You couldn't have changed anything. You couldn't have known a random car was going to be speeding down the road. What happened next?"

Beth took a deep breath, "I realised the car hit her. I saw her lying on the ground. I looked at the car, where it had stopped, only for it to suddenly reverse and then drive away."

"It was a hit and run?!"

"Yeah, they're still looking for the driver. Another witness got the number plate. A small group of bystanders immediately went into action. Someone called 999, another person on the scene was an off-duty nurse so she started providing first aid. I felt so hopeless, all I could do was call Henry. Thank goodness I had his number. I was allowed to ride in the ambulance with her. But when we got to the hospital they made me wait for Henry in the A&E waiting room. An emergency doctor had been with the ambulance crew so they started working on her there, on the scene and were able to get her stabilised. Isla…"

I knew what came next wasn't going to be good.

"Her heart stopped for a minute."

I burst into tears. The young woman sitting across the aisle from me looked over with a worried look on her face.

"They got it started again on the scene and it stayed steady the whole drive to the A&E. I don't know what happened, or how she was, after they took her in, but Henry will."

"Beth, are you okay? Were you hurt at all?"

"No, the car missed me completely, I'm shaken up, but physically I'm fine. The one good thing is that she wasn't hit straight on. One of the witnesses said the car just kind of clipped her on the corner. They said it seemed like she realised what was happening a second before the impact and turned to move away. That probably saved her life. They think her hip is broken from where it connected with the car, but the head trauma was from how hard she hit the pavement when she fell."

"Oh my God. Beth…"

"I know. It's bad. Are you going to be alright on the train? I can stay on the phone with you if you want."

"I'll be fine. I should hang up. It feels weird being on the phone. But I'll see you when I arrive?"

"I'll be there, and then I'll drive us straight to the hospital."

"Okay, see you in a couple hours or so."

I finally hung up and just put my hands up to my face. A moment later I felt a hand on my shoulder. Through my tears I looked up and saw it was the woman from across the aisle, she was holding out a tissue.

"I don't know what you just heard on that phone call, but I know how it feels to get devastating news, alone on a train, with at least a few stops before you can get off and get to the people you're trying to get back to. I can sit with you if you want."

I rarely talked to strangers on a train. But it was a kindness I desperately needed.

"I'd really appreciate that."

She smiled and sat down next to me. I started crying again and she reached out and held my hand. I cried for a bit, but eventually I was able to explain the main points of the news I'd received.

"It's hard, but there's still a lot you don't know. The waiting is the hardest part, but by tomorrow you should know a lot more," she said reassuringly.

"I really hope so," I said quietly.

The train arrived and I got up shakily. The kind stranger helped me get off the train and onto the platform even though she was continuing on.

As she reboarded the train, she turned around and said, "Stay strong. It's going to be alright."

"Thank you, for everything."

She smiled and walked back into the train. I walked a few feet and then quickly turned around.

"Wait!—" I stopped, she was gone, I couldn't see her.

I never got her name.

The train pulled away and I needed to get to Beth. It was late afternoon and the autumn sun was already starting to set. I rushed out to the front of the train station and saw Beth standing by her car, shifting from one foot to the next. I ran straight into her arms and gave her a hug. Then stepped back to look at her. Satisfied that she really was physically unharmed, I said, "Let's get to the hospital."

On the way, I texted Henry to let him know I was off the train and on my way to see him.

The drive was short and Beth drove me straight up to the entrance.

"I'll drop you off here while I go find a place to park and I'll meet you inside."

I dashed inside, texting Henry again.

I practically flew into the A&E waiting room and skidded to a stop when I saw Henry sitting in the corner. There were a few other people, sitting in small groups and talking quietly. But looking at Henry, all alone, my heart broke. He looked distraught, his face was pale and drawn and his eyes were red, he'd clearly been crying.

I walked up to him and knelt in front of his chair, putting my hands on his knees.

"Henry?"

He looked at me and what I saw wasn't a grown man, but a little boy, desperately afraid he was losing his mother, the only parent he had left.

"Isla..." he said, his voice rough. He reached out and wrapped his arms around me into a crushing hug. Then we both burst into tears.

Beth found us, still holding each other and crying. I didn't know how long it had been. She hovered while we waited, like an angel standing guard. It seemed like forever, but eventually a nurse came out to bring Henry back to a private room to talk to the doctor.

"Come with me, Isla? Whatever they are going to say, I don't want to hear it alone."

"Of course I will."

We walked down the hall and into a room that felt like it had delivered bad news to countless families before.

"The doctor will be in soon," the nurse said, not revealing anything with her expression.

Another few minutes passed, each one felt like an eternity. Then an older woman, with grey hair, wearing scrubs and a white coat came in.

"I'm Dr. Varma. You're Jacqueline's son Henry?"

"Yes, and this is her friend, Isla."

She smiled at both of us, and I held my breath.

"Is my mum alright?"

"She's stable."

Henry let out a huge breath and started taking in gulps of air. Dr. Varma gave him a minute to catch his breath.

"She's suffered a lot of physical trauma. Her pelvis was broken, so we have to take her for surgery to repair it. Now she's stable, we can take her soon. There was so much head trauma too, so we're monitoring that, but the swelling isn't as bad as we thought. And thankfully, even though her heart stopped on the scene, it seems to be strong enough now and her brain function seems ok as well.

We'll know more when she wakes up. Right now the broken pelvis is our biggest concern."

"When can I see her?" Henry asked, his voice was rough.

"I can take you both to her right now, but you can only stay for a minute. You can hold her hand. Tell her you love her. We don't know if patients can hear when they're unconscious, but I've always been of the mind that it can't hurt, it can only help. But then we have to take her to the operating theatre."

"Okay," Henry said quietly.

"Stay here, and I'll have a nurse come and take you. I'll see you again after the operation."

Dr. Varma left and a moment later a nurse, a different one from the one who brought us back here, came to take us into the treatment area. I wasn't sure if they would let me come since I wasn't family, but no one asked and Henry was holding my hand so tightly I don't think I could have left him, even if I wanted to. And I didn't want to.

We came to the area where they were treating Mrs. Russell. She was laying on the bed and looked so tiny on it, covered in wires and monitors. There was visible bruising but it looked like they'd cleaned her of any blood from the accident. I felt Henry stiffen when he saw her.

"I'll be back in a minute," the nurse said, before leaving us.

Henry was frozen, just staring at his mum. I wanted to let him have a second to process things, so I disentangled my hand from his and walked up to her bedside. I gently took her hand and leaned down closer to her.

"Henry and I are here, we're sending you all of our love. I know you're a fighter and you're going to get better. You need to wake up soon so we can have a cuppa and a good natter," I leaned down and kissed her hand.

I looked up and reached out a hand to Henry. "Come talk to her Henry. Let her hear your voice. It's okay," I said gently.

He reached up and roughly brushed tears away from his eyes and walked towards me. I traded places with him so he could be closer and then stepped back a few steps to give him some privacy. He leaned down and said something I couldn't hear, before he kissed her hand. The nurse came back to get her ready and another nurse walked us out and gave us directions to a separate waiting room for the operating theatre. It was a quieter waiting room than A&E, which I was grateful for. There were a few other groups and families waiting to hear about their loved ones in surgery. I texted Beth and told her where we were at so she could join us.

After a moment, Henry excused himself and walked back into the corridor. I waited for a minute but something felt wrong, so I went after him. He wasn't in the corridor anymore so I walked down and around the corner, where I found him crouched on the floor, sobbing quietly, his face buried in his hands.

"Oh Henry," I said softly, going to him and wrapping my arms around him.

"I can't lose her Isla, I can't. Not yet, she's still so young. I can't lose her. Not so close to my Dad passing, I just can't…"

"I know Henry, I know. It's going to be okay, you have to stay positive. Dr. Varma seemed optimistic. We just have to wait."

He gulped and nodded.

I looked up and saw Beth at the end of the corridor. She looked concerned.

"Henry, let's go sit down properly, I don't like you sitting on the floor of the corridor. You need to take care of yourself."

He nodded again and I stood up and helped him stand.

"Please stay," he said.

"I won't leave you. I promise."

We waited for several hours in that little waiting room. Long into the late night hours. I refused to leave Henry and Beth wouldn't leave me. Beth went and got us coffee and snacks. Henry wouldn't let go of my hand. He looked haunted and hollow. I was as worried for him as I was for Mrs. Russell. He wouldn't sleep but he did close his eyes from time to time. Beth and I took turns trying to nap but it was hard in the hospital chairs.

Finally, sometime in the early morning hours, a nurse came out to say they were done in surgery and moving her to ICU, but that the doctor would be out soon to speak to us. We were taken back to another private room and Dr. Varma came in again, looking tired but smiling kindly.

"She did well," Dr. Varma said.

Henry breathed out a sigh of relief.

"She has a long road to recovery, she'll need physiotherapy for her hips and she'll need at-home care after we release her, but she'll be here in hospital for a while. We need to keep her in ICU for at least a few days to monitor her, then she'll need to be admitted to a regular ward for at least a week, probably longer. You'll have time to arrange at home care. She'll need to sleep on a ground floor, no stairs."

"She can stay with me, there's a lift in my building, she wouldn't have to deal with stairs at all," Henry said, sounding stronger now that there seemed to be a task he could work on, some way he could help.

"That would be good."

We talked with Dr. Varma for a little bit longer and then she left, giving us instructions to report to the ICU waiting room in a couple hours, as Mrs. Russell wouldn't be moved up there right away. We found Beth and she made us go out for a walk around the hospital for fresh air and then to get breakfast from a cafe nearby before going back to the hospital. The sun wasn't up yet but the cafe across the street opened early for breakfast and after missing dinner and eating crisps all night, a proper breakfast was just what we all needed.

Henry was quiet the whole time, but his breathing seemed more regular and he managed to eat. We got back to the hospital and checked in at the ICU waiting room and waited until a nurse came back to bring Henry back to see his mum. Once again, he took my hand and brought me with him.

She still looked frail, as she had looked in A&E before the surgery, but there was a little more colour in her face now, despite the bruising. She didn't look as pale as she had. She was still sleeping, the nurse said she probably wouldn't regain full consciousness until later in the day, especially with all the pain medication they had her on after the surgery. We sat with her awhile, until finally she did wake up briefly. She was worn out and still hazy from the drugs they had her on. But she recognised Henry and told us she loved us before falling back to sleep.

We sat by her side the rest of the day, taking turns to go for a walk around the hospital or get food from the cafeteria downstairs, until finally a nurse came by in the evening to say visiting hours were ending and we needed to leave. I think she might have just been trying to get Henry to go home for a bit, he looked done in.

We found Beth again, and walked out together.

"Do you remember where you parked yesterday Henry?"

"I came here in such a rush, but yeah, I think I know where my car is," he said with a slight laugh. His face clouded over.

"Henry?"

"I...I don't think I can go home. I wish they'd let me stay here with her." He looked helplessly over his shoulder back at the hospital.

"You need a proper night's sleep in a decent bed, not a chair at her bedside," I said gently.

"Still, I don't think I can be alone."

"Then you don't have to be. Go pack some of your things, and come over to mine." Turning to Beth, "Beth, you should come too, stay over if you like, but we can all have dinner together. Neither of you should have to be alone tonight after what you went through yesterday, and I'd quite like the company myself."

So we made a plan, Henry would get some things from his flat, and the keys to his mum's house, and then come over to mine. Beth drove the two of us back to my house. It felt weird knowing that Mrs. Russell wasn't next door. Beth called and ordered a couple pizzas for us and I got out some bottles of cider I had in the fridge. Henry arrived with a small duffle bag and there was an awkward moment where we stood in the entryway, both clearly thinking about the last time he was in my house.

Beth quickly dispelled the awkwardness and when the pizza arrived we all sat down in the kitchen. Beth decided to go home to sleep, but said she'd check in with us the next day and come to the hospital if needed. I made sure the guest room was set up and that Henry would have everything he needed and we said goodnight.

It felt weird sleeping in my bed, knowing Henry was just down the hall. Part of me wanted to be with him instead.

CHAPTER 19 - MACEY

I took the opportunity of some alone time to take a leisurely walk home from the coffee shop where we had just been chatting with Isla. Normally, Ted and I would spend most evenings together, but today was different, which was slightly disappointing. I was hoping to have dinner with him, to celebrate the saying of the big L-word, and of course to also celebrate the talk being successful too, but he had to go and help his grandfather with a few things, which of course I understood.

Ted wanted to drop me off at my place before he had to head to his grandparents' house, but I insisted that it really was okay and that the fresh air would certainly do me good, after a long day inside. I began the walk home, taking a detour as usual, to walk by the sea. I walked past numerous ice-cream kiosks that were closed, and sweet summer memories came flooding back to me. I was excited for the weather to get warmer again, whilst not wanting to wish away winter and the upcoming festivities.

Whilst I was down by the shore, I noticed a somewhat familiar figure across the street. For a split second I stayed still, considering what to do next, but before much thought, I started running. I cut through Hoe Park before making it to my front door a mere ten minutes later, without looking back the whole time. I fumbled around in my bag frantically, my breathing getting deeper and my hands starting to shake. I managed to find my key, so I hastily unlocked the door and threw myself inside. I leant against the hallway wall, trying to steady my breathing, when a voice cut through my distressed state.

"Macey? Are you okay?" Libby asked curiously as she appeared from the kitchen.

I struggled, trying to find the words to explain what just happened. "I...I thought I saw...saw him."

"Who?" Libby quizzed, making sense of what I was trying to say.

"Nick," I managed to get out in one breath. "I thought I saw him down by the shore. There was a guy who looked like him and without thinking, I ran home," I said trembling.

"It won't have been him, he lives in Ireland," Libby replied.

"I know," I responded, feeling silly. "It just looked like him, and I guess flight or fight kicked in, and I just ran," I managed to explain once I had composed myself slightly. "I felt really scared," I added, confused.

"Hey, it's okay," Libby said reassuringly. "He can't hurt you, he's not here. You're safe now. I didn't realise it had affected you so much. You haven't really mentioned him, or what happened, since."

"I didn't think it had impacted me like this. Of course, I've been a bit reluctant about going to any big social events, but it's not like I frequent them anyway. I pushed it to the back of my mind for the most part, though I did mention it to my therapist. I think just seeing someone who looked like him, unlocked everything in my brain that I had been suppressing."

"I get you. Look, let me make you a hot drink. Go and sit down on the sofa and I'll text Ted to come over," she said, getting her phone out to do it that instant.

"He's busy!" I interjected, worried that I would be bothering him.

"I think he'd want to be with you Macey, and I think you need to be with him. There's only so much I can do, and getting you a coffee is one of them!" she laughed, guiding me upstairs to the living room and passing me a blanket to snuggle under. "Rest," she continued. "I'll be back up in a minute."

I laid there for around fifteen minutes, Libby still hadn't come back up, but I could hear faint voices downstairs. I knew Charlotte and Ruby were out, so I assumed it was Libby talking to Anna. I had finally stopped shaking, and my breathing was definitely much steadier now. I sat up for a moment, pondering whether to go back downstairs, before deciding to just lay back down, and try to take a nap. I needed it, the adrenaline rush had taken it out of me for sure. Just as I closed my eyes, there was a knock at the door.

"Come in," I said timidly, not sure as to who it was.

"Only me," Ted replied, pushing open the door. I breathed a sigh of relief when he came around the corner, carrying a mug filled with coffee. He placed it down on the side table next to the sofa I was laying on and perched down next to me.

"Thank you," I said, extending my arm out from underneath the blanket to hold his. He kissed my hand before brushing the hairs away from my face.

"Libby made the coffee. I just brought it up. She explained to me what happened. I came as quickly as I could. I'm sorry."

"I meant thank you for coming. But thanks for bringing up the coffee too," I sniffled.

"Are you okay? I didn't realise what happened with Nick had been affecting you like this."

"It hasn't," I reiterated. "But thinking I saw him, even just for a split second, was so scary. I was feeling fine about the whole situation, I've been talking it through with my therapist, it's been ok. Him not being around, had made it easier. I just panicked. Irrationally."

"I understand," Ted responded softly. "You're shaken up."

I sighed. "Yeah, I know. Can I have a hug?"

"Of course. I didn't want to come too close, in case you weren't feeling up for that after everything."

My eyes began to well up and I fought to hold back the tears, but before I knew it, I was sobbing.

"Hey, hey!" Ted said, sitting back up from where he was laid next to me. "Did I do something wrong?"

"No! I'm crying because you do everything right Ted. I'm so lucky to have you. Overwhelmed, but so lucky," I sniffled.

He smiled. "You will always, always, be safe with me."

———

ON TUESDAY the girls and I were having veggie fajitas and catching up. Seeing as I was going to be out of town this weekend visiting Ted's family, I wanted to fill the girls in on recent developments before I left on Thursday.

"Ted told me he loved me yesterday." I announced to the girls over dinner.

Charlotte gasped, "He did what?!"

"I know, it took me by surprise too. Not that I don't love him, but we'd only been official for literally a week when he said it. I felt like the timing was right though."

"What were you talking about for it to come up?" Ruby questioned whilst attempting to reconstruct an overstuffed fajita that had sadly fallen apart.

"I was telling him about Owen and I's breakup. How badly he hurt me, not just that day, but some of the other times too. We had just told my parents that we were together and of course they weren't overly enthusiastic. I felt like I needed to do a bit of explaining to him, about why they seemed less than impressed."

"Did you say it back?" she said.

"Of course," I said, blushing. "I do love him. I've never felt this way about anyone before."

"Well it sounds as if you had an exciting day Macey. I saw Ted's social media posts a few hours after they were uploaded and I actually aww'd out loud. He's a cutie," Charlotte chimed in. Libby looked over at me, as if she was waiting for me to explain to the girls what else had happened yesterday.

"I also had a really bad panic attack last night."

"What?" Charlotte said, shocked.

"I thought I saw Nick. Of course, it wasn't him," I replied, picking at my food. "It was down by the shore and I ran all the way home afterwards. Libby was here though and really helped me. She texted Ted and he came over as soon as he could as well. I was in shock, it really caught me off guard."

"Do you think you could benefit from talking to someone Macey? Like a professional about it?"

"I already do, I have a therapist that I've been seeing for years. Having parents that are psychologists, it's kind of expected that you will see one long term. They know better than anyone the benefits it has. I don't see her as regularly when things are okay, but she's always on hand to speak to. I've mentioned what happened with Nick to her a few times now, but when I next speak to her, I'll tell her about what happened last night too."

Ruby smiled. "You've got this Mace, and we're all here to help you as much as we can too." The other girls nodded in unison.

"I really appreciate that. I know I have such a strong support network now, and I am so thankful for it. Between you all and Ted, I've got more than any girl could ever want or need. I really am so lucky. Maybe one day you'll be able to drag me to a party again. But for now, fajita night is where I want to be." I said laughing, to which the girls laughed at too.

———

THURSDAY ROLLED AROUND before I could say the word Thanksgiving. It was eleven o'clock and I was frantically trying to get organised, rather last minute, after a busy few days of university work and writing commissions.

"Are you ready yet M?" Ted impatiently, yet lovingly, called up the stairs.

Charlotte had let him in, seeing as I was doing a mad dash around the house, trying to figure out what I could have possibly forgotten.

"I can't remember what I've forgotten!" I cried in a panic, flustered with both expectations and anticipation.

"You just need to bring yourself, honestly," Ted shouted.

"I think I need clothes and such too!" I said as I looked down the stairs at him, holdall over my shoulder and rucksack on my back.

"I see you packed the kitchen sink?" Ted jibed as he went to take the holdall off me.

"Ha, ha, ha," I jeered, emphasising each fake laugh. "I needed outfit options, just in case."

"In case of what? We're probably going to be spending most of the weekend in hoodies on the sofa or swimwear in the pool. You've got a bikini, right?"

"Shit. That was it. Two minutes." I quickly spun around and ran back up the stairs. I flung open my bedroom door and rifled through my drawers until I found the red two-piece that rarely sees the light of day. I am not a big swimmer, or bikini wearer for that matter. I hurried back downstairs, bikini in hand, to find Ted outside and waiting by the car.

"Good choice!" he called out as I fled down the steps by the front door. "I can't wait to see you in that." Smirking, he held his hand out in front of him as I approached. I grabbed it, and he pulled me into a hug.

"I have been waiting for this weekend Macey. I am so excited. I can't wait for you to be introduced to my family. They are going to love you, as much as I do. I know you'll just fit right in."

I exhaled in relief, rubbing my head against his rising chest. He placed a kiss on my head before pulling away. I looked up at him, grinning. "Good."

He laughed, his own smile stretching across the span of his rosy cheeks. His eyes were bright as usual, and he genuinely looked as excited as he claimed. Like a puppy when they seek a treat or a child on Christmas morning. The way he looked at me, made me feel like that too.

"Come on now M, we need to leave!"

"Can we not just stand and hug, curb-side, forever? I really enjoyed that," I giggled.

"Okay, okay, I am sure we can arrange that for our next date night!" he said sarcastically.

"I'm not joking," I whispered, opening the passenger side door. "I'd say I'm easily pleased, but being in your arms is truly the best feeling, and my favourite place to be."

Ted turned to me, us both now in the car. "You feeling okay M? You're being very mushy."

"Hey! You're my boyfriend and I love you, am I not allowed to be mushy?"

"You certainly are. It just doesn't happen very often. You know, you've said it yourself, you can't always talk the talk!" he laughed, saying the last part in air quotations.

"Well I guess the words are flowing freely today. Enjoy it whilst it lasts."

———

"MACEY! Come in! And you too Ted!" Marie bellowed as she opened the front door.

"Thanks Mother!" Ted laughed as he went in to hug her. I stood awkwardly behind him for a second, waiting for my cue to say something.

"Aren't you gorgeous?" Marie said to me as she broke the hug with Ted off. I smiled. She was short, like me, with a greying brunette bob, welcoming brown eyes and a cheery smile to boot. "Thank you." I replied sincerely, as she went on to embrace me. "It's so lovely to meet you!" I added over her shoulder.

"We've been counting down the days!" Marie said enthusiastically, before calling out for her husband. "Trevor!" she shouted, her previously sweet and soft tone escalating into something sterner. "Trevor! The kids are here!"

A moment or so later, Trevor appeared. He introduced himself to me, his thick West Country accent a stark contrast to Marie's jolly American one.

"How'd you do?" Trevor asked me, before extending his arm for a handshake. I shook his hand and introduced myself once more, mesmerised by his voice as he murmured something about Ted picking "a good 'un".

He was shorter than Ted but slightly taller than Marie. I made a mental note to ask Ted where he got his height from later on, as I was half expecting his parents to be six foot-plus too. Trevor had greying light brown hair, with a matching beard. He looked kind of like Ted, just older, which made me even more intrigued to meet Ted's siblings and see who they took after. Trevor took the bags off Ted and I, as Marie began to show us up the stairs to our room. I smiled at Ted as he grabbed my hand and squeezed it, our universal sign of reassurance.

"I know where my bedroom is," Ted joked as we got to the landing, rolling his eyes at his eager parents.

"We know," Marie replied. "I just wanted to point out the bathrooms and such to Macey."

"Do you think I am incapable of giving her a tour?" Ted jokingly prodded his mother before pulling her in for a side hug.

Marie laughed, "Yes, I do. And you wouldn't know what I am about to say!"

Ted's eyes widened, and without saying anything, I could tell he was praying that his Mum wasn't about to reveal anything embarrassing.

"I've put together a little welcome box for you Macey. It has towels in for you, as well as some pamper products and some snacks as well. It's here," she said, reaching down by the bed before presenting me with a crate style hamper.

I gasped, "This is too much!"

"Not at all sweetie. We want you to feel at home here!"

Overcome with emotion at her hospitality, I went to hug Marie again as a show of thanks. I wanted to cry, with happiness of course, but I was determined to not turn into a blubbering mess the first time I met Ted's family.

"Joey and Anton should be arriving soon. Their ETA according to Anton's latest text message is 13:57pm. I am assuming they have used satellite navigation for that, and it isn't just a number plucked from thin air!" Trevor announced from the doorway. "Evie is on her way back from sixth form right now. I am not sure of her ETA."

Ted laughed as Trevor and Marie made their way downstairs, to give us some time to "settle in" as Marie put it. "My dad is very particular," Ted explained, grabbing my waist after he closed his door. "You'll get used to this wacky family of mine!" he added whilst playing with my hair.

"I love them already!" I said. "Just as I knew I would. They are so welcoming Ted. I can see where you get your kindness from."

He blushed. "I love you Macey. I really do. I am so thankful for you."

"I love you too. But aren't we meant to be saving the thanks for dinner?"

"That's usually how it goes, but I didn't want to get too soppy in front of my parents. Plus, I knew that after my big thank you speech, by the way, that was it, that I'd want to kiss you a lot, and again, I don't know if I'd want to do that in front of my parents."

Before I could reply, he'd pulled me down onto his tartan duvet clad bed and was placing gentle kisses on my neck. I giggled, pulling him closer to me, his warm breath escaping and inviting goosebumps to crawl over my exposed skin. I've shared moments like this and more since meeting Ted, yet each time feels even more special. He tugged at the bottom of my grey t-shirt, after fiddling with the waistband of my flares for a while. I giggled again, as much as I was enjoying this, I didn't think it was particularly a good time to be engaging in such activities with my boyfriend.

As if induced by my intuition, there was a knock at the door.

Ted rolled over, groaned in dismay under his breath, before shouting "one minute!" to the visitor. He smoothed his hair as I sat up and tightened my suddenly loose ponytail too. He went to open the door and I perched where I was for a moment.

"Hey Eves!" Ted said happily as he squeezed his sister for a moment. I got up off the bed and wandered over to be next to Ted.

"Hey!" I added, nervous to meet another of the leading ladies in Ted's life.

"Hey," Evie responded shyly. I think she was nervous too, for some reason, which ultimately made me feel better. I wasn't sure as to why she was apprehensive about meeting me, I thought I'd be the only anxious one. She was slightly taller than me, and looked like a younger version of her mum. She has medium length, deep brown hair, a similar colour to her mother's, apart from the two blonde strands she had obviously dyed at the front. She was fair skinned and had freckles, bushy eyebrows and long eyelashes. She was so pretty. She had a cool look about her, definitely more edgy and hip than me. Just thinking that made me feel like a grand-mother. Her eyes were lined softly with black kohl and she was wearing a small nose ring too.

"The parents have asked if we can go and help them with dinner prep, if that's okay?" Evie asked.

"Of course!" Ted and I said in union, both laughing at our synchronicity.

Evie laughed as she left to head downstairs. As I went to follow, Ted noticed that I was shivering.

"Cold?" he questioned as he hovered behind me.

"Yeah…" I said, pausing.

"Let me grab you a jumper, one second. The house is an old one, built hundreds of years ago. I forget how chilly it can get; we are pretty much all used to it by now."

He bent down to search under his bed for a jumper, eventually pulling out a navy sweater with the words "Leakes and Associates" across the front.

"Grandad's business. Had the jumper for years."

I laughed, taking the sweater and pulling it over my head.

"It looks great on you," Ted said, kissing me on the forehead whilst simultaneously pushing me through the door in a hurry. "I don't want to keep the chefs waiting. They get antsy when there's Thanksgiving dinner to be prepared."

———

"EVENING SWIM?!" Ted cocked his head around the door as I was laid out across his bed, reading a book. "Or are you too busy reading?"

"No, I'm down for that," I said smiling, closing the book and popping it on the bedside table. "Let me get changed," I added whilst jumping off the bed to grab my bikini.

"Meet you down there," Ted whispered as he swiftly left again. He'd been busy helping his dad with a DIY project, and had left me alone to read for most of the afternoon. It was now Friday, the day after Thanksgiving. Evie had been out at sixth form all day; Marie had been working and Joey and Anton had to leave early this morning to head back to London for work over the weekend. It was nice meeting them, albeit briefly. Joey was a carbon copy of his dad. It seemed as if Evie took after her mum, Joey his dad, and Ted was somewhere in the middle, a little bit of both. Ted did tell me that he gets his height from his Grandad, and that he wants me to meet his grandparents once we're back in Plymouth.

The Thanksgiving meal was delicious, Marie had kindly cooked me a vegan turkey alternative, so I could still experience the tradition as authentically as possible. Ted actually had the "furkey" too —a term his dad coined whilst we were eating, that we all found hilarious.

We spent the evening after dinner telling each other what we were thankful for, as well as sharing stories of the Leakes' family Thanksgiving past and I also shared some stories of Christmas' growing up too, though they weren't nearly as entertaining, being an only child and all. I loved hearing about what Ted was like as a child, as well as the funny anecdotes that all the siblings shared. Joey and Anton also discussed details of their wedding that they are organising, and it was so lovely to hear of the intricate plans they had been working on. It made me dream of the day that I get to marry Ted—hopefully, anyway.

I know we haven't been together for too long in the grand scheme of things, but I couldn't imagine spending my life with anyone else. We haven't even argued thus far. I know that some people claim that couples that don't argue don't exist, or they do in fact argue and just hide it, but Ted and I just don't. He gets me more than anyone else has ever, boyfriends, friends, or family. He's all three of those things rolled into one. Spending time with Ted's family only solidified this, and although it did make me miss my family, I knew it wouldn't be long before I saw them again.

The rest of the evening after all the fun conversations was filled with games and snacks, until Marie and Trevor went to bed and left all the kids to watch *Die Hard*–apparently, it's an annual Thanksgiving tradition in their family. Marie had to be up for work on Friday, and Trevor was keen to "make the most of" the Friday he had off, a rarity according to him. His work as a Superintendent kept him busy, and he was glad to be able to take a long weekend off to spend with the family. Marie worked the usual 9-5 schedule in her role as the site manager and lead engineer for a local firm, so she'd be around this weekend too. We were planning to go on a country walk at some point over the next few days, and of course do lots of relaxing too as Ted had implied.

I grabbed another one of the towels from the hamper that Marie had prepared for me, and wrapped it around myself to head downstairs in. I slipped on Ted's sliders that were by the door and grimaced as the cold air engulfed me. I wandered down to the pool area, it was at the far end of the garden, and spotted Ted doing lengths whilst music was coming from the speaker that he had set up.

"Hey pretty lady in red," Ted shouted as he came up for air. "Get in here!"

It was seven o'clock and a typical winter evening, both chilly and dark, so I was glad for the heated water and the outdoor lights that were dotted around the pool.

I sat on the edge, towel still wrapped around me, toes dipped in the tepid water below. Ted swam over to me and placed each of his arms either side of my body.

"Get in!" he exclaimed excitedly.

"I am getting acclimatised!" I replied adamantly. Before I could say more, Ted had pulled the towel from around me and thrown it toward the lawn. I laughed, and then sighed. "That's not helping. I am now colder!"

"Here then," he said, grabbing my waist as I squealed anxiously. He lifted me up from the side and brought me close to his body, my legs straddling his waist as he began to float through the water. "How's that?"

"The body heat helps actually!" I stated, placing a kiss on his head.

"It's a heated pool Macey. It shouldn't feel cold anyway."

I faked a shiver for maximum effect.

Ted rolled his eyes. "I'm surprised you didn't go into acting, considering you can give a performance like that. What's up?"

I laughed nervously, whilst still clinging onto Ted like a monkey around a tree. As my grip got firmer, he pressed on. "Macey, what's wrong?"

"I just don't like being in my swimwear in front of you. I feel really self-conscious," I said quietly.

"What? How's it different to when you wear that really pretty floral underwear set in bed? Or when you discard that really pretty floral underwear set, and it ends up on the floor?"

I cackled. "It just is. Though, I do often feel self-conscious then too."

"Really?" he asked, eyebrows raised in typical Ted fashion.

"Yeah," I murmured under my breath.

"M. You are insanely beautiful. Every day, I thank my lucky stars that I am with you, not just on Thanksgiving. To be honest, I am very surprised that someone as utterly gorgeous as you has settled with someone just relatively handsome like me." He smirked. "From the day I met you, I've been mesmerised by not just that face of yours, but by your soul too. You're a special one. And red's my favourite colour on you anyway. So wear it more."

"Is it actually?"

"Yeah. It reminds me of the day we met. You were wearing that flowery red dress. I guess it also reminds me of when we met, again, after Isla's meet and greet. Seeing as you're an outfit repeater!"

"Hey!" I exclaimed, jokingly donning an angry face.

"That's what you said to me too, on that first day we met. When I tried to grab the last copy of A Courageous Beginning and you shouted HEY at me," Ted said laughing. "It was from that moment on, that I knew we were meant to be."

"I can't tell if you're joking or not." I teased, waiting to be proved either way.

"Of course I am not joking Macey. I've never felt an instant connection with anyone but you. I just sucked at first as there was so much pressure. I knew I couldn't mess this one up."

I blushed. "I love you so much." It was all I could think to say in the moment. I placed my hands around Ted's neck and brought his face even closer to mine than it already was. Our lips met for a few moments, the kiss intensifying as time went on. As it got more passionate, Ted's hands found their way to my bikini bottoms, and I felt him gently pull at the tie that was keeping them on. "Yeah?" He questioned coyly, and I nodded. I pulled us toward the edge of the pool, resting my back against the ledge. He pressed his body up against mine and took his turn of placing kisses across my collarbone, and all the way down my chest, until he disappeared under the water for a few seconds, returning moments later for air. We stayed there for a few more moments, enjoying each other's company as such, before Ted stopped in his tracks.

"Shall we, let's say, finish in the summer house?" He whispered in my ear.

I nodded, allowing him to scoop me up and carry me bridal style out of the water. We both looked at each other, as I was laid in his arms, and burst out laughing. It was difficult to be serious with Ted, but it was moments like these that I knew I would never forget.

———

"Knock knock!" I said aloud as I patiently waited outside of Evie's bedroom door.

Sunday had rolled around and I was preparing to head back to Plymouth after a dreamy weekend in Exeter with Ted's family. Friday night was incredible, and Saturday, yesterday, was bliss. We all went for a long family walk, followed by lunch in the pub and decorating for Christmas, yes, Christmas, in the afternoon. Marie was adamant that they don't usually put their decorations up so early, but she wanted to this year, seeing as Ted and I were there.

It was so special getting in the spirit with Ted and his family. It felt so cosy, and definitely made me so excited for the season ahead. My mum and dad never went hard at Christmas, so experiencing the Leakes' going all out was so enjoyable. We put the tree up, along with a wreath on each and every door and enough fairy lights to light the whole of the South West.

"Come in!" Evie called out from the other side of the door.

"Hey, is it okay if I sit?" I asked.

"Of course!" she replied, joining me on the bed. She sat at one end, cross legged, and I sat at the other.

"Ted's just packing up the car, we'll be making a move soon. I just wanted to have a chat before we did."

Evie smiled. "It's been lovely meeting you this weekend."

"Ditto."

"Ted seems really happy with you, it's great to see," Evie said, still smiling.

"Your mum mentioned that you had a boyfriend, Toby isn't it? Maybe next time I'm here, I can meet him too?"

Evie's smile faded as she shuffled about awkwardly. "Maybe," she replied quietly. I noticed her body language changed, she tensed up like I used to do whenever I spoke about Owen.

"Forgive me for asking Evie, you don't have to tell me, but is everything okay with him? You haven't said much about him and I don't want to intrude but—"

Before I could finish, she interrupted me.

"—It's fine, I know that Ted has probably said something."

"He hasn't really. Nothing other than that you had a boyfriend that he was yet to meet, and that you rarely brought up. I think he's just a little worried as he seems to think you've changed a lot since dating him. I just thought I'd ask as I've been in a similar position before."

Evie looked at me blankly.

"I was in a relationship that I wasn't happy in. And I never wanted to speak about him. I shut myself off from people because I was ashamed of it. He didn't treat me very well and after it finished, I realised that it was actually him that made me become so distant from other people. He was actually pretty abusive. I'm not saying Toby is—"

"—No, I get it. Toby's not like that, but I'm not happy. I just feel really trapped, and I don't want to feel more trapped, which I think introducing him to the family would do. I'm thinking about ending things, I'm just not happy with him, but he does treat me well. It's all that is consuming my thoughts at the moment. I can't stop thinking about it."

"I get it," I replied gently. "If I'm honest with you, it will be that way for a while. I still think about Owen too. Like, a lot. It's hard not to."

Evie sighed. "I understand. Thank you for this, you've made me realise I've got some talking to do, rather than just thinking. It's pretty fun having a new, big sister!"

I grinned. "It's pretty fun having a new, little sister! I'm always here if you need a chat."

A voice called from outside. "Can I come in?"

I got up to open it and saw Ted loitering, bags in one hand and car keys in the other.

"Everything ok?" he asked.

"Girl talk!" I said, jokingly ushering him away from the entrance.

Ted nodded, not saying much. I turned around to give Evie a hug and said a proper goodbye, before following Ted downstairs with the rest of our belongings.

"I'll see you soon!" I called upstairs to Evie, once we were by the front door. She appeared on the top step and waved to me, as I was hugging Marie and Trevor goodbye too. "Thank you so much for having me!" I said, almost bursting with gratitude. This weekend was exactly what I needed. Ted nodded in acknowledgement, again, not saying a huge ton. I assumed he was tired, and probably dreading the long drive ahead.

"Are you okay?" I asked, as we walked down the drive. He was a few steps in front of me, which he never did. He always stays by my side, joking that he has to slow down and match my pace as I have "little legs".

"Yeah. Just tired," he replied, confirming my theory. I hopped into the passenger seat and did my belt up, before resting my hand on his thigh.

"I really loved this weekend Ted. Your family are as amazing as I expected."

He responded with a smile, and with that, we enjoyed the rest of the journey in mostly comfortable, yet occasionally awkward, silence.

CHAPTER 20 - ISLA

The next week passed by in a blur of visits to the hospital and Henry staying over at mine. We both lived the same distance from the hospital but it just developed as a pattern that he'd drive us to visit with his mum during the day and then come back to mine in the evening. Beth did my food shopping for me and Henry would make us a late dinner at my house when we got home after visiting hours ended.

Mrs. Russell had stayed in ICU for three days before they moved her to the general ward. Thankfully she regained full consciousness the next afternoon when we went back to be with her. She didn't say much, but she was able to tell both Henry and I that she loved us before she fell asleep again. Henry looked so relieved. She was doing better and talking more when they moved her out of ICU, which was a good sign. Henry still didn't seem to want me to leave him at the hospital, but I needed to get some work done so I promised I'd meet him there in the afternoon.

I wrote as much as I could in the morning after he left for the hospital and then took a break and met Georgie for coffee at a nearby cafe. She'd been worried about me and Mrs. Russell and I'd been trying to keep her updated via text, but after a very emotional week and trying to hold myself together for Henry, I really needed to see a friend.

She was waiting for me at the cafe, and had already ordered a latte for me. I noticed she just had some mint tea. We chatted for a bit and I caught her up on the latest with Mrs. Russell's recovery.

"She'll need to stay in the hospital for at least the next week, but they're hoping that perhaps next Friday she'll be able to be released. She'll be in a wheelchair and will need help. I'm going to go to Henry's flat with him and see what we need to do to convert his guest room into a room for her."

"Oh I can help with that," Georgie said quickly. She seemed to want something to do to help. "If you can get a spare key for me, and tell me what you need, I'll make all the arrangements for everything."

"That would be brilliant Georgie, thank you. I'll talk to Henry." I looked at her and noticed her eyes seemed a little puffy and she had dark circles. "I've been talking all about me and everything going on. But how are you?"

"I'm just so exhausted," Georgie said, rubbing her eyes.

"I can tell, are you okay?"

"Yeah, I'm fine."

"If you're so tired, why did you just get mint tea? You should have a latte or something. You clearly need the caffeine."

"I'm trying to cut it out," she said quickly, fidgeting with the napkin on the table.

I knew she was already avoiding alcohol since they didn't know if or when she'd get pregnant, but she still drank the occasional coffee. Unless…

"Oh my God. Georgie, are you—"

"—I don't want to say anything," she interrupted in a rush.

"Georgie!" I exclaimed with a smile, but my smile dropped as soon as I saw her pained expression.

"Isla, I really can't talk about it. It's too soon. I'm only about four weeks. Of course we knew almost right away since we've been tracking everything, but a million things could still go wrong. I just can't get excited, I can't talk about it. I don't want to jinx it. Not this soon."

My heart felt like it would burst. I was so excited for Georgie and Grant but I totally understood her worries. Four weeks was really early, even women without Georgie's complications could have issues that early.

"Georgie I'm thinking so many positive thoughts for you. It's going to be alright. I just know it," I said, reaching out to take her hand.

She squeezed it tightly. "Thanks Isla. We need it. Grant is excited but we're both so scared."

"That's natural, but it's going to be okay. We should go to that spa you love and just have a relaxing girl's Saturday or something like that soon. After Mrs. Russell is released and settled at Henry's. I'll take a break and you and I can have a girl's day."

"That would be amazing Isla, I'd love to do that," she said with a relieved smile.

We finished our coffee and I rushed to the hospital, knowing if I was any later, Henry would start to worry. Things had changed between us. It was hard to describe. The accident had definitely brought us closer. But seeing him so vulnerable shifted something in me. I'd never seen Edwin like that. I'd never had a man need me before. Want me, desire me even, but never *need* me. Edwin always pushed me away if he wasn't feeling well or was having a bad day. I always felt like I just made things worse for him.

But Henry didn't like to let me out of his sight, especially in those first few days. He was starting to adjust to the routine that he and Mrs. Russell were going to be living with for a while, but it was hard for him handling all the hospital stuff on his own. It seemed to bring up bad memories of losing his father, and every time I saw him, when he thought I wasn't looking, he just looked like a lost little boy.

I walked into Mrs. Russell's room, she was in the bed at the end of the room, thankfully there were only a few other patients sharing the room with her. Henry had the curtain partially drawn around them, but I looked through and saw him sitting with her quietly while she slept.

He looked up when he heard me approach and relief came over his face. He stood up and met me at the curtain.

"She's sleeping. Let's walk down the hall," he said.

He slipped my arm through his and we walked to the sitting area at the end of the hall and we sat down in a couple of the arm chairs. He took a deep breath and leaned back in the chair while running his hand through his hair. He hadn't shaved since the day of the accident. There were dark circles under his eyes and I knew he wasn't eating enough.

"Have you had anything for breakfast today? Or lunch?" I asked with concern.

Henry waved his hand dismissively.

"Henry!" I exclaimed, sighing exasperatedly. "Your mum is going to lecture me six ways from Sunday for letting you get into such a state. You look terrible."

"Thanks," he said with a laugh.

"I mean it. You need to eat a proper meal. Why don't you let me sit with her while you go get some food?"

"She just got another dose of her pain medication, why don't you come with me, then you can make sure I actually eat."

"Fair point. Okay, let's go. I'm not letting you back up to her room until you've eaten a full meal and had at least one bottle of water. I doubt you're drinking enough either."

Henry rubbed his face as we stood up and started walking downstairs to the cafeteria. "It's hard Isla. I just hate leaving her, but I think if I sit in there for much longer the nurses are going to kick me out. They've been saying the same thing as you."

"Because we're all noticing that you're not taking care of yourself, and your mum needs you to be taking care of yourself Henry. You'll be no use to her if you collapse from exhaustion by time she gets released. I can help take care of her but I can't be taking care of both of you."

Henry stopped in the middle of the corridor and took my hand,

"You have been taking care of both of us Isla, it hasn't gone unnoticed. Thank you."

"Henry, your mum is like a second mum to me. She's more than just my neighbour, she's family. That makes you important too. I wouldn't let either of you go through this alone."

Henry nodded and swallowed hard. I could see he was on the verge of tears again. He has been so strong through this, but so openly vulnerable and emotional as well.

I squeezed his hand and started walking again.

Downstairs we got some food, not the greatest, but what you expect at a hospital. I knew I was pushing my luck getting him to leave Mrs. Russell's room, there was no way I was getting him to leave the hospital to go to a restaurant or pub nearby. But he had some protein, carbs and vegetables, so I was happy.

"The doctor says Mum might be able to come home later next week, or early the week after. She's been making good progress, so they're optimistic about releasing her sooner rather than later."

"That's great news," I said smiling.

"But now I have to get everything at my flat ready. I'm going to need some medical assistance devices for the bathroom and for her bed, and I need to get some things from her place to make her room at mine feel more homely for her. She's going to be with me for a while before she'll be well enough to be on her own. I don't want her to feel like a guest, I want her to feel at home."

"I spoke with Georgie, she says she can help with all of that."

"Really?" Henry looked both relieved and grateful.

"Yes, she says just get her a key and a list of anything needed, and she and her team will make sure that your flat is ready for when your mum is released. And I have a key to your mum's so give me a list of things you want me to get from her place and I'll pack it all up for Georgie to take over. We'll get all that sorted, you don't need to worry about it."

Henry sighed with relief. "Isla, that would be amazing, and such a huge help."

"We'll take care of it. What else can we do? Do you need

someone to organise a carer? Or at least research options for you? Beth was starting to look some up but she didn't want to overstep."

"Actually, that would be great. I have some information the hospital has given me, along with the list of everything that I need for the flat, but I haven't had a chance to look into any of it."

"I'll get all that from you before I leave tonight and I'll get it to Georgie and Beth, we'll sort it all out. All you need to worry about is being here for your mum. I know it helps her to see you when she's awake. Is there anything you think she'd like me to bring from home for her while she's still here?"

"I was meaning to go to her place but I just haven't gotten around to it yet. She'd probably like to have her own dressing gown and slippers, and I should get her phone, she didn't have it on her when they brought her here, so she probably left it at home. She's probably got a million missed calls and texts by now, I haven't been able to tell too many people..." His voice drifted off, getting lost in the mental list he was calculating.

I grabbed a notebook and pen out of my handbag. "Here, write it down. I'll run home and get it and bring it back before visiting hours end for the day, and then I'll take you out for dinner to make sure you eat more than just this," I said, gesturing at the meager meal provided by the hospital cafeteria.

"That would be great, but...don't leave me just yet. It's nice to be with you."

"I'll stay with you for an hour, it won't take me long to go to your mum's and get back here."

He reached across the table and took my hand again, I gave it a squeeze and smiled at him.

"It's really going to be okay," I said.

———

ANOTHER WEEK PASSED AND GEORGIE, Beth and I focused on getting everything ready for Mrs. Russell to be released and sent home to Henry's flat. Georgie handled all the furniture and assistance needs,

Beth took care of arranging the schedule for the visiting carers and organising the various notes the doctors had given Henry. I picked up the things Mrs. Russell would need in the hospital and brought those back to Henry and then spent the next week choosing personal items as well as necessities from Mrs. Russell's house that she would want and need for her time living with Henry. By the time she came home to Henry's, the girls and I had created a lovely room for her to stay in while she recovered.

Henry's building was newer and had a large lift and wide corridors and doorways, so it would be easy getting her up to the flat in a wheelchair. His flat was spacious with a generous open floor plan and large windows that looked out over Bath. It was the complete opposite to my house, where mine was cosy and historic, his was sleek and modern. It had all the newest features and amenities, including an indoor swimming pool downstairs which the physiotherapist we had contacted for later in Mrs. Russell's recovery said would be great for her treatment plan. There was also a large garden and some paved walking paths, so we could take Mrs. Russell for a walk in her wheelchair until she was strong enough to walk on her own.

The day finally arrived, and Beth and Georgie were waiting at Henry's flat when Henry and I brought Mrs. Russell home. Henry had wanted me to be at the hospital. Mrs. Russell was doing so well, and it had only been a couple of weeks since the accident and the surgery. They still hadn't found the driver. They found the car, which turned out to be stolen. The CCTV footage from when the car was taken, didn't show a clear shot of the driver's face. We were all frustrated, but were grateful that at least Mrs. Russell would make a full recovery eventually. The festive season was in full swing and I don't think any of us could have dealt with spending Christmas without her.

Henry had seen most of the changes we'd made to his flat in preparation for his mum coming home, but the girls and I still had one surprise up our sleeve.

As soon as we walked in, Henry came to a standstill, and Mrs. Russell's hands flew to her face in surprise.

"Oh my goodness!" she exclaimed, a bright smile filling her face.

"Surprise!" Beth and Georgie shouted, standing on either side of the gorgeous Christmas tree we'd put up just that morning, after Henry left for the hospital.

Henry turned and looked at me, a huge smile on his face. "Did you know about this?"

"Of course I did," I said smugly. "It was Georgie's idea, but I would have thought about it anyway. Your mum always does the best tree each year, we didn't want you to miss out." I crouched down to be at eye level with Mrs. Russell in her wheelchair, and gently took her hand. "And don't you worry, we left plenty of ornaments for you and Henry to put on the tree. I've brought over all your boxes of ornaments from your attic. The ones that seemed like they'd have sentimental value we left for you to put up."

"Thank you dear," she said, getting a little teary eyed. "It's just so lovely, and so thoughtful. I was worried we wouldn't be able to do much of a Christmas this year."

"Well we couldn't have that," I said, leaning over to give her a kiss on her cheek as she squeezed my hand.

We got her settled in a plush armchair beside the tree and she told us which ornaments to put where as we finished decorating the tree. Georgie had non-alcoholic spiced cider for her and Mrs. Russell, and mulled wine for the rest of us and we all smiled and laughed more than we'd smiled and laughed in the last two weeks.

It was fun having the girls there with us, but I also couldn't help thinking that this is what Christmas would be like if I was with Henry. Doing his mum's tree with him each year. The thought hit me out of nowhere and I didn't know what to do with it. I tried to busy myself with the ornaments and refilling drinks for everyone.

Henry and I had settled back into friend mode after that night at my house when I told him about Edwin. And that was fine. Henry made sure everything felt normal and didn't make things awkward after our conversation, we had just slipped back into our easy friendship.

But then his mum had the accident and I needed to be there for her as much as for him. All the time I spent at the hospital was changing a lot of things for me where Henry was concerned.

The night nurse came to make sure that everything had gone well with arriving home and to go over her night medications. Georgie and Beth had gone home, but I stayed to help Henry make sense of everything the nurse was saying and make notes.

Finally it was just me and Henry in the living room after Mrs. Russell had gone to bed and the nurse had left. We were on the couch in front of the fireplace and the sparkling Christmas tree. The light from the fire and the fairy lights glittered and glowed in the reflections in the windows. We each had another glass of mulled wine and my head was feeling light, both from exhaustion from the long day and from the wine.

Henry looked at me, "Thank you Isla. For everything you've done the last two weeks but also everything you've done here to get the flat ready. You and Beth and Georgie outdid yourselves, this place is even better than I could have imagined, let alone organised myself. Especially the Christmas decorations."

"I know how important Christmas is to your mum, and I imagine it's important to you as well. We didn't want you to miss out or be stressed trying to organise this yourself. We wanted you to come home and have everything be as it should."

"It's perfect Isla, really."

"Good, I'm happy you and your mum love it so much. She looked so happy earlier," I sighed, feeling content.

"She was, that's the best I've seen her since all of this started."

"I thought the same. It was good to see her smiling and laughing. I just hope we didn't wear her out."

"She'll sleep well tonight, and I'll make sure she rests tomorrow. But she'll love being able to sit by the tree tomorrow."

I smiled, and without thinking, I leaned my head down on Henry's shoulder, sighing happily. Henry leaned his head down to rest gently on mine. It was such a natural thing, but I could feel the uncertainty start to rise in me.

Henry lifted his head and chuckled.

I looked up at him, "What?"

He just shook his head. "You let your guard down for a second. It felt nice. Then I could feel you tense up when you realised it."

I sighed.

"It's fine, we can just forget it happened." He smiled but I could see in his eyes he didn't want to forget it.

"I'm sorry Henry. I do want this…I want you. I just don't know how to move forward from friendship to something more. No one has tried to get close to me for years Henry. I'm out of my depth. I write about this stuff in my novels but I don't live it."

He looked at me, not speaking but allowing me to go on.

"I don't know exactly how I feel, but I know it's different from how I felt that night we spoke. Your mum's accident has changed a lot of things."

Henry took a deep breath, "You went through something horrible with your past relationship. Your ex treated you in a way that no person deserves to ever be treated. And when you eventually tried to start dating again, it didn't go well, so you retreated again. It makes sense that you would try to protect yourself. But you have to know that I would never hurt you in that way. Ever."

He looked so sincere.

"I know you would never hurt me the way that Edwin did. But you could hurt me in a different way. I could give my heart again only to have it broken again. Maybe not in the same way, maybe not as bad, but it's still scary to think about. Staying single and being on my own has always felt safer."

Henry began to speak but I put a hand up.

I continued, "If these last two weeks have taught me anything it's that we really don't know what is going to happen next. I never would have imagined that a simple trip into town for Beth and your mum would have resulted in such a catastrophe. Thank God your mum is going to be okay, but she has months of hard work in her recovery ahead of her. The fact is, no one is ever safe. If anything had happened to your mum, I would have been more devastated by that than I was after Edwin. My heart could always get broken, by anyone, not just a man." I sighed, and tucked my hair behind my ear.

"Isla, you're exhausted, not just with all the stuff with mum, but in general. We don't have to talk about this tonight."

"No, I want to talk about it. I might chicken out later."

Henry looked at me intensely. "What are you saying Isla?"

"You said that night that you thought we could make something work, did you mean that?"

"Of course I did. It's been years since school, but I still think you're incredible. I know I never made a move then, and later I thought I'd missed my chance. I'm not missing it again. I've never met a woman as incredible or as maddening as you Isla Stewart," he said with a laugh. "I know it's a lot to ask. To trust me, to trust yourself. But I also said the other night that we didn't have to rush anything. We can take this slow."

I looked down and picked at some fluff on my jeans. "I just worry that I'll still need to go slower than you want."

Henry reached out and took my hand gently in his. "Isla, I'm fine with that. I mean it when I say we can take things slowly. We can sit and watch the glaciers pass us by."

I laughed. "Okay, I might not need to take things that slowly."

"Even if you did, I'd wait. You're worth it. I'm just saying, I want an honest chance. I want you to let your guard down, not treat me like an old school friend or like your neighbour's son who you just happen to make time for once a week for lunch."

"Oh Henry, I'm sorry if I've made you feel that way!" I exclaimed. I felt horrid at the thought that that's how he felt.

"It's okay, I knew there was more to your story. I was going to be patient. Once you told me your story it all made sense, and trust me, I totally empathise with your past and would never want to pressure you. But I also don't think it's fair to yourself to never let yourself try to fall in love again. You've been incredible these last two weeks, I don't know what I would have done if you hadn't come to the hospital or been there for me and mum at this time. We both have needed you and have been grateful for your care."

"There's nowhere else I would have been," I said, squeezing his hand. Somehow, this man wound his way into my life again and was starting to creep his way into my heart once more. It wasn't just that I wanted to support him during this crisis. Beyond the first couple days I could have left him with the various family members who came to check on him and Mrs. Russell. But the thought of leaving either of them to deal with this on their own was unthinkable. Henry and I needed each other as we tried to help Mrs. Russell.

"Henry, I'm a mess. More so than usual right now because of the book," I started. "And then there's everything with your mum and you're going to have your hands full helping her through her recovery. Obviously I want to help with that too, I don't want you to have to do it by yourself. But I'm just trying to be realistic. I don't want to disappoint you."

"You could never disappoint me Isla. All I want is a chance. And time to get to know each other more and let this progress naturally. I'd also like to support you with your writing, even if all I can do is bring you coffee and croissants."

"Coffee and croissants are integral parts of the writing process," I said giggling.

"We'll both be there for Mum, she needs you as much as she needs me. She thinks of you as a daughter you know. She loves you so much. And even in just the short time I've spent getting to know you again, I can see why she loves you. I don't think it's much of a stretch to think that one day I'll love you as well. I'd be lying if I said I wasn't already falling for you, despite you pushing me away so much."

"I think I'm finally at a point where hearing you say that, doesn't completely freak me out."

"Like I said, all I want is a chance. Do you think we can do this?" he asked, giving me a cautious smile.

I smiled back nervously, "I think we can."

"Am I pushing my luck if I ask if I can kiss you?"

My heart skipped a beat. "You're not pushing your luck, but I haven't kissed anyone in over a decade," I said nervously.

"Well that sounds like something I'd be very happy to help you with if you'd like to change that status." He looked so sexy when he smiled at me.

I nodded, too nervous to speak. I needed him to kiss me before I bolted from the couch.

He leaned in and gently pressed his lips to mine as he put his hand around the back of my head and drew me closer. I was overwhelmed by the closeness of him, the scent of his cologne, the nearness of his body, his lips against mine. But I let myself go and melted into the kiss. He sensed me relax into him and he deepened the kiss, instinct took over and I kissed him back. It was magic.

CHAPTER 21 - MACEY

"Ted, please could you pass me that bag?" I shouted, pointing to a bag near him. I didn't get a response, so I repeated myself, realising that the Christmas music that Rosa had put on shuffle was drowning my voice out. Ted was at the other side of the room, wrapping fairy lights around a bannister with help from Arjun and Yang. We were getting set up for the Creative Writing Society's Christmas Ball. It was tonight, and we were hoping it would raise us enough money to see us into the next semester and beyond. Thankfully, Isla's talk at the event in November really boosted our funds, so we were in a pretty good financial position. Ted wandered over to me and passed me the bin liner full of multicoloured tinsel, before swiftly walking away.

"Hey. Are you okay?" I called out after him.

He stopped in his tracks and pivoted around to face me. "Yeah, fine."

That was all I was getting out of Ted at the moment. Since we got home from Exeter a week and a half ago, he's been acting really out of character. Granted, we've both been super busy, not only organising the final details for the ball, but cramming for upcoming uni exams and finishing this semester's coursework. I hadn't thought too much of it, and just put it down to stress, but he's hardly spoken to me all day today, which is a rarity, especially when we're around other people. To be fair, we hadn't spent too much time together over the past week or so, seeing as we have both been so busy, so it hasn't been too noticeable, but now, it is, and it's playing on my mind.

"Can we talk?' I said, desperation probably a little too apparent in my tone. I needed to get to the bottom of this before it ate away at me. I'd got better at controlling my anxious thoughts and feelings since meeting Ted, but occasionally I did still spiral.

"Busy day," he paused, contemplation apparent on his face. "Give me ten minutes?" He asked, smiling with that half smile he normally does. I couldn't tell whether it was the cute side smirk, or a forced grimace.

"Okay," I replied, whilst stringing tinsel from the ceiling. Ted walked away briskly just as I was about to shout "I love you" after him.

———

"THE LAST TIME we were out here, you told me you loved me for the first time. It feels like a lifetime ago, but it was really only a few weeks back."

Ted smiled, whilst awkwardly shuffling from one foot to another. We were standing in the smoking area outside uni, as the ball was being held in one of the event spaces inside. Only this time, the air hung heavy, and it wasn't down to lingering tobacco stench.

"What's wrong?" I continued, determined for Ted to open up.

"I heard what you said in Exeter, to Evie. It's been playing on my mind all week and I know I should have said something sooner, but I was scared. You know how I feel about you, and how I feel about the possibility of, well, losing you. I couldn't even face bringing it up—"

"—What are you talking about?" I interrupted, oblivious as to what he was referring to. "What did I supposedly say?"

"When you were talking to Evie, just before we left Exeter, you said you still think about Owen all the time—"

"—I meant him, and his toxic ways still play on my mind! That I get worried that my past will affect my relationship with you. Not that I long for him or anything like that! I would have thought you'd have known that," I interrupted once again.

"Yes, I should have. But at the time, I didn't hear it like that. I got so worried that you were still in love with him, however stupid that might sound. I am really kicking myself now Macey. Knowing what he did to you, I am so sorry that I would ever think you'd go back there. Those words just rang in my ears, it was like my greatest nightmare was being confirmed."

"Hey, it's okay. But you have to trust that I would never go back to him. You know how terrible he was to me, and I'd like to think that you think more of me than someone who would crawl back to their controlling ex when they have the most perfect boyfriend in the world."

Ted visibly relaxed before gently grabbing my waist and pulling me in for a hug. He stroked my head as I nestled into his chest.

"I'm sorry," he said simply, exhaling. "I do trust you, and I trust that you wouldn't ever go back there. I know I'm not perfect, my insecurities and all, but I'm so thankful that you understand and are willing to stick around."

"Hey, you're not the only one with insecurities and such. Don't act like I haven't given you a hard time of it too!" I said, half laughing.

"We've all got baggage Macey, I'm just fortunate that I've got someone who's willing to unpack it with me."

————

"ZIP ME UP?" I asked Charlotte as she loitered in my room. She was already ready, and impatiently waiting for Tom to arrive. I'd roped in all the housemates and their significant others into coming to the ball, and I was really excited to spend the night together as a big group. "What's Tom's ETA?" I pondered aloud as Charlotte came over to help me into the dress.

I'd opted for a red silk number, with thin spaghetti straps and a body con fit. It was ruched in the middle which meant it was super flattering, and it made my bum look great if I do say so myself. I'd ordered it online, especially after how complementary Ted is whenever I wear red. And of course, it was super festive.

"He's about fifteen minutes away, according to his last text, which was five minutes ago. He's booked a minivan from here to take us all."

"Fab!" I replied, whilst wiggling about in an attempt to make the dress fit. "It's a little tight," I said, concerned.

"It's fine Macey. Stop stressing. It's a good tight fit. Slinky. Sexy!" She laughed. "Is Ted far away?"

"I'm not sure, let me check my phone!" I released my hair from my grasp and ruffled it over my shoulder. I'd curled it, and naturally it had gone huge. I'd opted for a red lip too, to match the dress, and simple, but effective, winged eyeliner. My shoes were a pair of nude heels with a clear strap. I headed over to my desk where my phone lay, and unlocked it to reveal the notification from Ted.

I'll be 5 minutes x

"He'll be 5 minutes," I said out loud.

"Great. Did you speak to him earlier, about you know, whatever was going on with him?" Charlotte questioned.

"Yeah. He had misconstrued something I'd said in Exeter, to Evie, his sister. He thought he'd heard me saying I missed my ex Owen, but really I was explaining to Evie how even though we ended a long time ago now, his controlling behaviour still affects me, and I often worry if that affects my relationship with Ted."

"Ah. A classic case of miscommunication then." Charlotte

concluded. "So is everything okay now? Now that you've talked it out?"

"Yeah, we're good. Ted just worries a lot, and I think he keeps it to himself, because that's what men are told to do. He tries not to succumb to societal pressure, as you know, he has a very strong sense of self and isn't bothered by the idea of masculinity, but sometimes, he is affected by it."

"Of course. It's a hard one to navigate. I've started to get Tom involved with my meditations. I'm hoping it will get him more in touch with his emotions. Failing that, we do have pretty good pillow talk."

I laughed. "As long as they are talking about their feelings, that's good."

As Charlotte and I finished talking, there was a knock at the door. Assuming it was Ted, I bolted down the stairs giddily, happy that things were once again, back on track. I opened the door, and there he was, standing suited and booted on my doorstep, with his arms behind his back.

"What are you hiding?" I said jokingly, waiting for him to reveal whatever he was holding. He whipped out a bunch of mistletoe and dangled it above my head.

"I was going to bring you flowers, but I thought this was more seasonally appropriate."

I laughed, looking up at the small posie that was tied neatly with some hessian. I edged forward, closer to Ted, and placed a delicate kiss on his lips, before breaking away and grinning.

"I love you."

"I love you too."

————

WE HAD PLANNED on getting there earlier than the other attendees to make sure everything was in check before the ball was about to start. After Charlotte insisted on taking one thousand group photos, we were running behind schedule. When we eventually got to uni, Ted and I broke off from the rest of the group and went to find other members of the society committee, to ensure that we were good to go, as guests had already started to filter in.

"Hey," we both said to Rosa as we found her at the bar, before I asked her to take a photo of Ted and I.

"Of course!" she replied as I passed her my phone. "Smile!"

Ted wrapped his arm around my waist and pulled me closer to his side.

"I'm so proud of you," I said to Ted as Rosa handed me my phone back. "Half way through your Masters and smashing it."

Ted blushed. "And I am so proud of you Macey. For everything you are doing," he said, whilst tucking a strand of hair behind my ear. "How about we grab another drink, mingle a little bit, and then make a swift exit? I know we should be here, being the President and Social Secretary, but you and I both are not huge party goers and I think our time could be used better elsewhere."

"How so?" I questioned.

"I have a brand-new copy of *Wuthering Heights* that we could read?"

"Now you're speaking my language!" I laughed, ushering Ted back to the bar to grab me a drink.

"What are you having?" he whispered into my ear.

"Just a lemonade, please," I said, still holding his hand. Ted leant over the bar and ordered my drink and his too, him opting for a lemonade as well, when a voice behind us shouted above the music.

"I'll have what he's got."

I froze. I instantly recognised who it was, and before I could say anything, everything went black.

———

"M? M? Are you okay?"

An arm grabbed my shoulder and I flinched.

"Hey, it's me, Ted, what happened?"

I opened my eyes. I was sitting on a stool, steps away from the bar.

"I think it was just another panic attack. Often when they happen, I can't see anything. I just have to find some space and wait for my brain to recalibrate almost. Shutdown mode," my words stumbled out as I tried to get my breath.

Ted rubbed my thigh and moved my hair from where it had found itself, all over my face.

"Did you see him?"

"See who?" Ted questioned, looking concerned.

Before I could reply, he reappeared, staring directly at Ted and I.

A sharp intake of breath indicated to Ted that the person standing in front of us, was in fact the one who had induced my earlier frenzy.

"Can I help you?" Ted asked him, to which he just got laughter as a response. I went to explain, but the words failed to leave my mouth. Instead, my breathing just got more erratic, and I started to feel the tight feeling in my chest return.

"Macey. Calm the fuck down. Why do you always act like this? You can really be so pathetic."

I could feel Ted tense up as he heard each word.

"Who are you and why the fuck are you talking to my girlfriend like that?" Ted shouted, getting more agitated as each moment passed. He was met with more laughter, which only forced Ted up from his seat and toward the source of my anguish.

"Owen, nice to meet you finally!" Owen said, extending his hand out to Ted.

Ted's jaw visibly dropped.

"I heard you were the one keeping an eye on my girl for me whilst she's down here. Cheers mate!" Owen continued, hands back in his pockets and a smug look on his face. He'd obviously had a drink, or two. I'd never seen him like this before.

I turned to look at Ted, who was so visibly speechless. I got up from where I was and approached Owen.

"How did you find me?" I managed to sputter out.

"Well, it wasn't actually as difficult as you would think Macey. Obviously, I knew you were at university in Plymouth, so I had a look at your socials and saw that you were involved in the Creative Writing Society. I then had a look at what events they were hosting, and boom, as if by luck, there was one today, on my day off. It must have been fate!"

"You drove five hours to come here, for what?" I replied, still in shock.

"For you Macey. I know things have been strained between us recently, but I know you're who I'm meant to be with," Owen replied, drawing nearer to me.

"Is that right?" Ted said, stepping between us both and shielding me from Owen. "I think it's time for you to leave," he added, edging even closer to Owen, mere inches away from his face.

"It's okay Macey. I'm here now," Owen said, completely disregarding Ted.

"She doesn't fucking want you to be here Owen. I know exactly what you did, and the kind of person you still so evidently are." Ted replied. "I'm sorry to speak on your behalf Macey," he added, turning to me.

"No, you're right Ted. Owen, please leave. I haven't wanted to see you since the day we broke up. I was done with you then and I am even more so done with you now. You've only shown up because you've caught wind of the fact I have finally moved on and I'm now with Ted." I said, having finally found my voice.

Owen laughed. "He'll get sick of you eventually Mace. He'll abandon you. Just like your parents abandoned your sister..."

I froze once again. This time my eyes quickly went to Ted. I could see him mentally processing what Owen had just said.

"Your...sister?" Ted sputtered out. "You have a sister?"

Owen cackled. "Seems like you've been hiding a lot from this lover boy of yours."

Ted stared at me blankly, waiting for me to explain.

"I don't know her...my parents...they gave her up for adoption a long time before I was born. They were super young when they had her and had no other choice…they don't know where she is now and neither do I…I wish I did though…" I said hurriedly, feeling the need to quickly explain. I could see disappointment beginning to crawl over Ted's face and I was desperate for him to hear what I had to say.

"Why didn't you tell me?" Ted replied sadly, no anger in his tone, just confusion and hurt.

I could hear Owen sneering to the side of me.

"You had no right." I said, turning to him. He looked around, avoiding eye contact with me. "You had no right to come here," I repeated, the anger inside of me rising. "And meddle in Ted and I's relationship like that. I would have told him, in time. It's not some crazy big secret I've purposely hidden from him, it's something that I've been trying to come to terms with for years, and something that I don't have to share, but would when it felt right. You stole that opportunity from me, and made it seem like me not telling Ted was some malicious act. You had no right."

"Macey," Ted said, reaching for my lower back and edging himself nearer to me once again. "He's not worth it."

Owen turned to walk away and in doing so, he disappeared into the crowd without giving me a second look.

———

"Let's get you home," Ted said, guiding me through the venue and out of the doors. "I'll call a taxi now."

I stood beside him, trembling, as the blustery winds entangled my hair and sent a shiver down my spine. Noticing me shivering, Ted pulled me into him and rested his head on mine. I began to feel tears form at the back of my eyes and before I knew it, I was sobbing.

"Hey, Macey, you're safe, okay? He's gone, I'm here."

Struggling to find the words to respond with, I snuggled further into him and stayed like that until the taxi arrived.

"I'm sorry," I managed to finally muster out whilst we were on the way home.

"What are you apologising for?" Ted asked curiously.

"Everything. I feel like I've brought so much chaos into your life. So much drama! Firstly with Nick, and now Owen…"

"Let me stop you there," Ted replied, his hand grazing my knee. He turned to me, as we were sitting in the back seats together, and took a deep breath. "Nothing that has happened, has been your fault? So how could I possibly be angry at you, and subsequently warrant an apology, for things that were completely out of your control? Come on Macey, you know me, and you know that I'd never expect such thing."

"I know. I just feel bad. And I guess I just needed reassurance from you that I was indeed worth sacrificing your singlehood for."

"You will forever be worth it Macey G, no matter what."

———

"MERRY CHRISTMAS!" Dad sang as I opened the living room door on Christmas morning. He was sitting next to Mum, on the sofa, in front of the crackling fire.

I smiled. Christmas was one of two days of the year where my parents pretended to be happy in each other's company, the other being my birthday. Christmas songs played softly in the background and a collection of presents, labelled as mine, were scattered around the Christmas tree. Ted followed shortly afterwards with coffees for us all on a kitchen tray, my mum smiling up at him happily as he placed one in her awaiting hands. I knelt down next to the tree, fiddling with some loose paper on one of the presents and thought back over the last few weeks.

After the Christmas Ball shenanigans, the semester ended and Ted and I travelled up to Glossop together. He'd finally been able to meet my parents. A lot had happened since my run in with Owen, and I was glad Ted had been here to support me through it all. Mum had been adamant on following through on her threat of a restraining order against Owen and we had enough grounds to go to the police. Because of the past, it got granted pretty quickly. So now, he legally can't talk to me, let alone come near me. It was relief, considering him showing up at the ball was seemingly out of nowhere. Having the order in place hopefully prevents something else happening in the future.

We had also spoken a lot about my big sister, Ted, Mum, Dad and I. They explained their story to Ted and it was really great to see Mum and Dad bond with him, whilst speaking so candidly about their life stories. Ted was genuinely fascinated too.

"Sounds like you were just destined to be together!" Ted had exclaimed, before suddenly biting his tongue, worried that he'd offended my separated parents. "I'm sorry, I forgot for a moment," he went on to say.

"It certainly felt like that!" Dad had said, reassuring him. Mum and Dad exchanged a small smile, as did Ted and I.

After a lengthy conversation, we decided we were going to begin the process of looking for her. We decided now was the time because my parents finally felt ready. It had been hard for them, knowing that she was out there all of these years, but they also were so scared of being rejected, and they didn't want to disrupt the happiness their daughter may have found with her new family. I've always wanted to know her, but I wanted to respect my parents' wishes first and foremost. Now that we were finally beginning the process, I was so excited.

I explained to Ted after we'd spoken to my parents that I had wanted to tell him, but it was a part of my life I kept secret for so long, and barely anyone knows. Not the housemates, not him. It's painful, knowing that there is a member of your family out there that you have no contact with. I spent many hours imagining what she was like when I was growing up, and I guess a part of me didn't want to be disappointed if we ever finally met either. I'd built her up so much in my mind, and our meeting, that I felt if I told anyone about her, they might be the first to squash my dreams and shut me down. She was a part of my life I could just cling onto, a story I wasn't sure I wanted to know the ending to. I also felt envy when I was around Ted and his siblings, not in a malicious way, but rather a deep desire to have bonds like that of my own. I told him of how on Thanksgiving, seeing him with Evie and Joey made me wish I was surrounded by brothers and sisters growing up, and now too.

"I know it's not the same," Ted said, resting his hand on my thigh in comfort. "But Evie and Joey do love you, you all got along so well at Thanksgiving. Think of them as your honorary siblings for now."

"For now?" I questioned worriedly.

"Yeah, for now. Because in a few years they'll officially be your sister-in-law and brother-in-law," he replied smiling.

It had been a few days and nights of emotional conversations, but now Christmas had arrived, it was time to enjoy it as a family.

"Open it then!" Dad said excitedly, whilst Mum sipped on her coffee and Ted watched on. I tore gently at the paper, trying hard to not ruin the pretty wrapping completely.

"Collector's edition," Dad eagerly explained and I stroked the cover.

It was an older looking version of *Pride and Prejudice*, a book I mentioned that I had wanted to read a while back. It was lovely that he'd remembered. I went on to open the rest of the gifts, which ranged from more books to gift cards for clothes shops. There were also some edible gifts of course, including the obligatory selection box, only a vegan version. I gave Mum and Dad their presents, before waiting eagerly to receive mine from Ted.

I love giving gifts of course, but Ted had been hyping up my gift, and I was desperate to find out what it was. We had decided to just give each other one small gift this year, as we wanted to save up and go on a trip together sometime next year instead. He handed me a wrapped box and I hurriedly tore off the paper. *Sense and Sensibility.*

"Collector's edition," Ted laughed. My Dad peered over, laughing too. "Great minds son!"

"Oh Ted, I love it! Thank you! I now have Austen's best works, both collectors editions. The perfect gifts, thank you both, again." I said, looking over at Dad before giving Ted a big hug. I then gave Ted his gift, which was in a rather large box.

"I thought we said small presents!" He protested, before tearing off the paper. The nondescript wrapping wasn't giving anything away, so he quickly ripped the box open. After getting a glance at what was inside, he audibly gasped.

"Macey..." He said whilst slowly lifting the gift out of its box. "I thought we said small presents," he repeated, aghast.

"I wanted to get you something special, and this was truly a great find, if I say so myself. I got it from that little antiques shop we often walk past in Plymouth."

Ted's face lit up as he remembered which one I was referring to.

"It's a vintage, 1940's one, from the brand Oliver, in the shade matte black. They don't make typewriters like it anymore!"

"It's absolutely stunning," he said kindly, before placing a gentle kiss on my forehead. "I can't wait to use it, and write you lots and lots of love letters."

"I'm sure you will," I said laughing.

"Roasties, Simon! Roasties!" Mum interrupted in a panic. "They need to go in now!"

"I'm on it!" Dad replied, abruptly getting up and dashing into the kitchen with Mum. As much as they tried to be civil on Christmas Day, the occasional bicker did still happen.

———

OUR CHRISTMAS LUNCH was served early, as usual, so that Mum could go out on her annual Christmas Day walk, alone, and Dad could have his annual Christmas Day nap. I was used to spending most of the day alone, usually reading a book or watching re-runs of my favourite festive TV shows, but this year was different, as Ted was here. We lounged on the sofa for most of the afternoon, reading my new books together and cuddling.

"Thank you again for my present Macey. I love it. I'm so grate-ful. But truly, all I could ever want for Christmas, is you."

I burst out laughing. "You're welcome, but did you mean to rip off Mariah Carey for that Ted-ism?" I said, giggling, whilst playing with Ted's hair.

"Ted-isms?" Ted looked at me, confused.

"Your quotes that you make up, That I used to think were from the internet or something. I guess this one you did steal!" I couldn't stop laughing.

Ted jokingly glared at me. "Can you stop laughing, and just kiss me instead, please?"

"Since you asked so nicely," I replied, but before I could, Ted pulled me into him, locking his lips against mine. When the kiss finally broke off, he whispered in my ear.

"Let's go for a drive!"

"A drive?! Now?!"

"Yes, now! If we leave this minute, we'll catch the sunset at that place you told me about."

"Winnats pass?!" I asked excitedly.

"That's the one."

———

WE PULLED up close to Winnats Pass about thirty minutes later. Ted had brought his laptop, and we'd put the back seats down before we'd left, so we could lay across them whilst watching a movie in the back. I bought a few duvets too from home, so we could snuggle up in them and not catch frostbite seeing as the boot would be open.

I got out of the car to take a photo of the sunset and after doing so, I turned back around to look at the set up. It looked incredibly cosy. Ted had strung fairy lights around the edges of the car, but was yet to turn them on. When he did, the twinkling effect made it look so inviting. There were cushions, and a throw too, as well as a tote bag laid in the middle. "What's in the bag?" I shouted back to Ted, who was adjusting the fairy lights once again.

"Snacks of course! Your selection box from your parents, and some vegan snacks I had in the boot that I'd been saving for you," he shouted back. "Shall we watch *Love Actually*?" he added.

I stared back at Ted, words failing me. As much as things have been difficult recently, I couldn't help but feel like I was exactly where I was meant to be right now. Being young, and in love, comes with its challenges. It's hard to not get caught up in old drama or get distracted by new people. But as the old saying goes, when you know, you know. And that's what it was like with Ted. I knew from the moment I met him, and I keep getting reminded of that. Every so often he'll do something that just reminds me how much I know; how much I am sure that he is the one.

People will say that when you're young, you don't have a clue about love. Some people even say that you can't ever know for sure. But I've never been so sure of something in my life. There will be hiccups, bumps in the road. Nothing is ever perfect.

I've always said, I want a partner to want in on my life, rather than me want out of mine. I used to date people to distract myself from what was going on in my life, whereas now, I want to make my life so good that I don't wish to use guys as a way of escaping anymore. It was naive of me to think that no one would want to be a part of the life I am building and also that no one would want me. I am worthy of so much more than I used to believe.

Whilst Ted completes me, he also has made me realise that I am more than enough, just me. He's shown me how to love myself, by loving me, and to me, that's true love.

CHAPTER 22 - ISLA

C hristmas drew near and we settled into an easy rhythm. I spent half the day working at my house, and then in the afternoons I would go over to Henry's to be with Mrs. Russell, while Henry went into his office for a few hours to do work he couldn't do at home. I'd write while Mrs. Russell rested or read a book. Sometimes Beth would meet me at Henry's and we'd work together there. I think Mrs. Russell appreciated having the female company.

In the evenings, Henry would cook, or bring home takeaway on his way back from the office. We'd have a nice meal and then Henry and I would spend the evening talking, after his mum went to sleep. He always called for a taxi to take me home, he never let me go home alone. I think he would have liked me to stay over, a few times he offered to sleep on the couch and let me have his bed. He was a gentleman, but it still felt like a step too far this early on.

But it was nice spending time together and getting closer. You'd think dating in your 40s would be harder, but in some ways it was easier. It was clear we were only interested in each other, I didn't have to worry about whether Henry wanted to keep his options open, he was very clear in that regard. There were no mind games or tricks. I was learning to trust that Henry was exactly as he appeared and behaved, and he was learning not to take my caution or hesitation as disinterest.

As far as the physical side of the relationship went, we were obviously taking things slow. I liked the idea of becoming more intimate, but I just wasn't there yet. Some old wounds would take longer to fully heal than others. Edwin had messed with my head and while I had tried to forget a lot of the damage he'd done, now that I was attempting a new relationship, old insecurities needed to be worked through finally. But Henry was patient and kind. And we were kissing a lot. Kissing Henry was the best thing in the world. Some days I felt like I lived my life from one kiss to the next.

Things were going well with Mrs. Russell's recovery. She would stay at Henry's until well into the new year, so in the meantime I was keeping an eye on her house and on her garden. The physiotherapist had started coming to work with her, but they were starting really cautiously and were mostly doing a lot of range of motion exercises, nothing weight bearing yet. They'd start the pool exercises after the new year, and gradually increase from there. She was in good spirits, and I think the festive season was helping. Beth and I would bring things from town to cheer her up. Treats from the shops and new books. She was reading a lot, which seemed a good sign in terms of her cognitive function. We'd been so worried about any lasting head trauma but so far all seemed good.

I was also frantically getting ready for Christmas. I was doing all my own shopping, plus both Henry and Mrs. Russell had asked for help doing theirs. I was buying all of Henry's gifts for his mum, and all of Mrs. Russell's gifts for Henry. I felt like Santa Claus! Bath was beautifully decorated for Christmas and all the shops were full of tempting gifts to give—and to hope to receive. I'd managed to find everything that Mrs. Russell and Henry had on their lists for each other, plus my own gifts for each of them, though I was still trying to find something special for Henry, but what do you give the man in your life who you're still trying to get used to the idea of him being your boyfriend?

I had all the gifts for my parents and Georgie and Grant sorted. I said a small prayer when I passed by the children's section of Marks & Spencer, hoping that by this time next year I'd be buying gifts for Georgie and Grant's baby. I was dropping everything by my house after a shopping trip in the city centre when I noticed my mum parked outside.

"Mum!" I called, as I got out of the taxi with all my bags. "What brings you by?"

"Hi sweetheart, I just thought I'd pop by and see if you were in, I was on my way home."

"I hope you haven't been waiting long."

"Not at all," she said as she leaned in to give me a kiss on the cheek. "You look like you've had a productive trip in town."

"I found lots of gifts for people. Come inside, I'll make us some tea."

I put all the gifts upstairs in my office where I'd wrap them later, and then came back downstairs to the kitchen. Mum was already making herself at home and putting the kettle on.

"Sit down," she said. "It's my turn to make tea for you, you're always so good at making it for Dad and I when you come over."

"Mum, what's going on?" I asked curiously.

"Does something need to be going on for me to come over and make my lovely daughter some tea?"

"Well, considering this is the first time you've done it in I can't remember how long, yes. It's a bit suspicious," I said with a laugh. My smile dropped suddenly, "There's nothing wrong with you or Dad, is there?"

"No Isla, nothing's wrong. Just sit down. We'll talk when I get the tea finished."

I played with a pen that had been left on the table while I waited. I had no idea what this was about. Mum seemed so casual, but if it wasn't a big deal she'd say something already. Finally she brought the two mugs over and joined me.

"I just wanted to chat," Mum said kindly.

"About?" I asked.

Mum smiled. "About Henry. You two seem to be getting close? I remember you used to talk about him all the time when you were in school. And I was thrilled when I heard you were getting to know each other again now that he's moved back to Bath."

I smiled. "Yeah, it's been great getting to know him again. And yes, we are getting close."

"How do you feel about that?" Mum asked slowly.

I paused. Mum always knew me so well. "I don't know. We're taking things slow, but Mrs. Russell's accident really changed things. For both Henry and I. Life can change so fast. And I'm not getting any younger."

"Isla, you shouldn't make a decision because you think you're getting old."

"It's not that," I said quickly. Then stopped.

"What is it?" Mum asked, a knowing look in her eyes.

"I...it's...I..." My voice drifted off.

"Honey?"

I took a deep breath. "Life can change so fast Mum. Henry has come back into my life and he's amazing and he really cares about me. I think he might even love me Mum. I know he's falling in love with me and I think...I'm falling in love with him and it terrifies me but I think I'm more scared of living without him. Every day he shows me in a million little ways that he's there for me and that he wants me. And he's so open and vulnerable with me. He's so easy to be around and I feel like I can be myself and that I'm enough... I'm enough Mum." I burst into tears and put my head in my hands.

"Oh sweetheart," she said, moving her chair closer to mine and wrapping her arms around me. "Of course you're enough! You're amazing! And I hate that that bastard Edwin ever made you think otherwise. All your dad and I want for you is that you feel satisfied and happy with yourself and your life. We are so proud of everything you've accomplished honey."

"Mum, I'm so tired. I'm tired of running. Of hiding from love. For so long I've been hanging on to the idea that if I'd just been enough for Edwin, things would have been different. Since coming back to Bath, I've come to understand logically how messed up I was to think any of it was my fault, or that I somehow deserved how he treated me, but emotionally I think I've still been hanging on to it," I gulped back a sob and tried to take a breath. Mum was gripping my hand and watching me silently.

"Since Henry came back into my life, I've started feeling like I don't want to be on my own forever. I do deserve love, the kind of love that builds you up, not the twisted thing I thought was love, that nearly destroyed me."

"And do you think Henry can be that positive kind of love?" Mum asked gently.

I paused, thinking about it and trying to arrange all the mix of emotions and thoughts that have been swirling in my mind lately. "Yes Mum, I think he can. But not because I'm scared of losing him the way we almost lost Mrs. Russell, but because I'm ready to let go of the past and embrace the future. And I want a future with Henry."

"Oh Isla," Mum said, smiling widely.

We both laughed and I felt a million times lighter. I knew things would still feel awkward and uncertain, real life doesn't feature immediate happy ever afters like my novels do. You have to work at it. But I wasn't scared of going in that direction anymore. I knew I deserved to have a life with someone as amazing as Henry.

———

CHRISTMAS DAY WAS perfect and magical. I spent the morning at my parents house and we did our usual Christmas gift exchange and Christmas lunch and then we all went over to Henry's to spend the rest of the day with him and his mum and enjoy some mulled wine and cider and some sweet treats. Our parents chatted as Henry and I curled up on the couch. We talked about our Christmas mornings and what gifts we'd been given and just generally enjoyed being together and listening to our parents talk and laugh. It was a cosy, festive evening.

Eventually my parents headed home and Mrs. Russell said goodnight. I waited while Henry helped her get ready for bed and then he joined me back out on the couch, with fresh glasses of champagne for each of us.

"I've been waiting all day to give you your Christmas gifts."

I laughed, "Me too."

"Thanks again for doing all the shopping for Mum. She was so happy watching me open the gifts she'd asked you to get for me. And you found such perfect gifts for me to give to her. You've really saved Christmas for us Isla."

"I was happy to help," I said with a smile. "Your mum's been through so much, and so have you. You both deserved a special Christmas this year."

He sat down in front of the Christmas tree and I moved down from the couch to join him.

"Open mine first," I said, smiling like a little kid. I really hadn't been sure what to get him. I knew I needed something special. I found some nice practical gifts, a beautiful cobalt blue scarf that I knew would go well with his blue eyes, a leather folio and notepad he could use for work, and a novel I'd heard him mention he wanted to read. But the big gift was thanks to a tip off from his mum.

Mrs. Russell had told me that Henry loved botany and horticulture. I'd noticed a few coffee table books at his flat on various plant related topics and had thought about finding one to add to his collection, but then just a few days before Christmas, and just by chance, I'd been walking past a secondhand bookstore and had an impulse to go in. I wandered the shelves and in the back, in the antique book section, I found a 1940s book on flora and fauna of southern England with large watercolour illustrations. Something about it just had Henry's name jumping off the pages at me.

I watched as he carefully unwrapped the book. It was large, with a thick leather cover and decorative spine.

"Isla...this is magnificent!" Henry exclaimed breathlessly, immediately beginning to carefully flip through the pages.

"Do you like it?" I asked hopefully. "I noticed you had a lot of books about plants and your mum said you had an interest. I know your flat is very modern but when I saw this book I just thought of you."

"Isla, it's perfect, truly. You know Mum is a keen gardener, but so was Dad. Our old house, where I grew up, had a huge vegetable patch in the back of the house. There was nothing Dad couldn't grow. He would have recognised every plant and animal in this book."

I smiled, relieved I'd made the right choice. When he looked up at me, I could see the joy in his eyes and it made me fall just a little bit more for him. Any man who could get that excited over a book about plants, was definitely the right sort of man for me.

He set the book down and nervously ran his hand through his hair.

"Alright, your turn," he said with a shaky laugh.

He'd found a few simple gifts for me as well. A knitted hat with matching mittens, in gorgeous plum coloured cashmere. And a set of luxury soaps that his mum must have told him were one of my favorite brands. Once those were open, he reached for a small box that had been tucked away under the tree.

"I had no idea what to get you for Christmas as your main gift, the others were easy but this one was a challenge," he said with a chuckle. "I wanted to get you something special but I didn't want to freak you out."

I laughed. "I'm sorry, I certainly didn't mean to make you anxious over what to give me. I'd be happy with anything."

"But you don't deserve just anything. I wanted to find something that would be meaningful but not feel too intimate since we're still taking things slow."

"A wise decision," I nodded with mock sageness.

Henry laughed. "If you don't like it, we can take it back and you can pick something, but I was wandering through an antique shop near the Royal Crescent and I stumbled on this."

He held out a small rectangular box, wrapped in red paper with an emerald green bow. I took it from him and opened it carefully. Inside was a beautiful and intricately carved wood box.

"Henry, this is lovely!" I exclaimed.

"Keep opening it," he prompted me gently.

I lifted the wood box out of the gift wrap and found a brass clasp on the side. I gently opened the box to find the most beautiful fountain pen, nestled in sapphire blue velvet. It had a gold nib and the body of the pen had a stunning blue and white floral pattern on it, with a band of gold around the middle where the pen twisted to open to insert the ink.

"It's from around the 1920s, according to the gentleman who sold it to me, and the engraving on the bottom of the box."

I flipped the wooden box upside down and saw carved in the corner what looked like a name and the year 1923.

"Apparently the boxes were made in the same company that did the pens, so the date of the box is the date the pen was made," Henry explained. "It still works, and I have some extra cartridges of ink to give you. You can get more from the shop I bought the pen in."

"It's too beautiful to use!" I half whispered.

"Beautiful things are meant to be enjoyed. Perhaps this won't be the pen you chuck in your bag to take into town," he said laughing.

"Perish the thought!"

"But I thought it could live on your desk and when you're working there during the day, you might think of me, at least a little."

"I'll think of you every time I look at it! And use it. I promise I will. It will be my special pen. Goodness knows what kind of history this pen has. We writers can get very attached to pens."

"I had a feeling that would be the case," he replied smiling.

I gathered up my gifts to take home and then Henry and I sat back down on the couch, I leaned up against him and he put his arm around me as we sat and watched the fire dance.

"You've seemed different the last few days," Henry said quietly.

"Are things going better with the writing? You just seem, I don't know. Happier? Lighter?"

"I am," I said, smiling. I took a sip of my champagne. "Mum came over to talk to me and we had a good chat. I finally realised some things and I don't know, I just feel better about stuff. As horrible as your mum's accident was, it really shifted my perspective on things. I think we've all had a reminder that we shouldn't take things for granted."

He hugged me tighter to his side. "I agree. I want you to always know how important you are to me."

I twisted to face him, "I do know that Henry. And I want you to know how important you are to me. I know I've been hesitant, resistant even, but I'm all in now. We both have been through so much. I've had a crush on you since school. When you came back into my life all these years later, it just felt so easy. We're so different from how we were in school, but we still get along so well and have so much in common."

"I agree," Henry said smiling.

I took a deep breath. "Henry, I don't want to waste time. I don't think I want to go so slow. I want to be with you. I know you're the right person for me. I used to be afraid of falling in love again. But I'm not afraid anymore."

"Isla," Henry said breathlessly. "What...what exactly are you saying?"

"I'm saying I love you Henry. I think I've been falling in love with you since that day in the bookshop, but I was too scared to admit it. But I'm not scared anymore."

Henry reached out and pulled me into a kiss. Everything we wanted to say but didn't know how to express was shared in that kiss. When he finally gently pulled away we both had to catch our breath. His eyes were sparkling from the fireplace and the Christmas lights. But there was also something more in his eyes. Desire and hope.

"Isla," he started slowly. "Hearing that is the best gift you could have given me today. Just knowing that we want the same things. I love you too Isla. I know I told you I was falling in love with you but that's because I was afraid if I told you I loved you, it would scare you away. But I love you. Without any reservation or worry. I'm all in. You're the only woman I will ever want."

"I feel the same Henry."

He looked around for a moment, like he was trying to decide what to say next. Finally he got up from the couch.

"Wait here for a second," he said distractedly and walked out of the room. He came back a moment later and sat back on the couch. I noticed he had something in his hand and my heart started to beat faster.

"Isla, I love you. That will never change. And I will tell you every day how much I love you so that you never forget and never doubt my love. I wasn't going to give this to you today, I was going to wait longer because I didn't want to scare you. But I saw this while shopping for your Christmas gifts and I knew it was meant for you. There's no rush. And if you don't want to accept it today that's okay. But I need you to know how sure I am of what we have."

I realised it was a small box in his hand and he opened it to reveal the most perfect ring I've ever seen. It was clearly vintage, with a silver filigree band. It had a large round cut sapphire center stone that was flanked by two pear cut diamonds.

"I want to marry you one day. I'd marry you tomorrow if I could. I don't want to waste time either. We've finally found each other and I know you are the one I want to be with. If you're not ready for this—"

I cut him off with a kiss. When I pulled back he looked dazed. "Yes Henry. I will marry you."

"You will?" he asked, seeming unable to believe it.

"Yes, I will. But...umm...maybe not tomorrow?" I said with a laugh.

Henry chuckled.

I continued, "But only because I never thought I'd be engaged again and I want to enjoy it. I want to enjoy every day of being your fiancée before I spend the rest of my life as your wife."

Henry smiled so brightly it outshone all the lights around us. He lifted up the ring, "May I?"

I nodded, smiling, as he slipped the ring on my finger. It fit perfectly.

He kissed me again. "So, day after tomorrow?" Henry joked.

I burst out laughing. "How about next Christmas? It seems fitting somehow."

"Next Christmas it is."

We sat together on the couch, just enjoying being in our little bubble of happiness.

After a while I had a thought. "Henry, I have a confession."

"Uh-oh," Henry replied, but grinning.

I smiled. "No, I just had a thought. You…you're the hero I always write about. You're the happy ever after I'm always searching for in my novels. I feel like I have to pinch myself."

"How about I kiss you instead?"

"That sounds good to me," I said smiling, leaning up to meet his lips.

———

THE NEXT FEW months went by in a blur of writing. Finally, in April I was able to deliver my completed novel to my publishers, on time thankfully, and I began working on it with my editor. My agent and the people in the publishing office made me nervous sometimes but I adored working with my editor. She's been with me from the first book and always helps me make the books better than I imagined they could be. Editing was going well and I felt like my career was getting back into a steady place. I was no longer afraid I wouldn't be able to deliver. *Bold and Bright* was also doing well, and was still hanging around in the Top 10 charts, even if it was closer to #10 than it was to #1.

Mrs. Russell was doing much better, she flirted up a storm with her physiotherapists and wanted to make plans to move back into her house, though Henry and I have tried to convince her that won't be for a little while longer. But she has been able to get out more in her wheelchair with me or with Henry. Between the two of us, we tried to get her out of the flat at least once a day for an hour or so. Beth and my mum have been helping, and Henry's clients have been great about allowing him to do more work at home.

Georgie was glowing! The pregnancy was progressing nicely and in a surprise twist that was like something out of one of my novels, she and Grant were expecting twins! She still had moments of worry and fear that something would happen with the pregnancy but her doctors told her all was well and to enjoy it. She wasn't yet preparing the nursery but I was already buying cute baby things when I found something while out shopping. I couldn't wait to be an auntie to those babies!

The progress on the mews house was going well. I think having that project helped Georgie distract herself from her worries. I made sure she let her team do all the heavy lifting and the renovations and decorating were nearly done. We were going to put it up as a holiday let throughout the summer and autumn and then evaluate what we wanted to do in the long term. It might not get much use as a holiday let during the winter, but I kind of liked the idea of having it for family to stay in when we didn't have paying guests.

Henry and I have fallen into a nice pattern and wedding planning was underway for the coming December. Once I admitted to myself, and to Henry, that I was in love with him, everything just felt so natural. I was no longer second guessing myself. If anything, I felt like more myself with Henry than I ever felt before. He saw all my quirks and personality traits and appreciated them. He accepted me just as I was and while I already knew I was good enough, it somehow felt validating to have someone else, someone who didn't have to love me, tell me they accepted me and I was good enough, just as I was. I couldn't wait to spend the rest of my life with him.

CHAPTER 23 - MACEY

"Wake up Birthday Girl!" Ted said excitedly as my head was still squashed into my pillow.

"It isn't my birthday yet!" I groaned, turning over to ignore him.

"HEY!" he exclaimed, dismayed at the fact I was pretty unresponsive today. "I'm usually the grumpy one in the morning, and you're usually the one begging ME to get up!"

"I know, I know," I sighed, stirring. "I'm just tired!"

"Aren't you excited?" he said, laying down next to me and grabbing my waist. I giggled as his cold hands tickled the skin under my nightshirt.

"I am," I protested, sitting up to face him.

My birthday is next week but today, this weekend, we're headed up to Glossop to begin the celebrations, along with all of the housemates and their significant others. My mum and dad are throwing a large party to celebrate, with all of my friends from university, some of my school friends, including Sam, and some family members too. It was nice of them to let my university friends stay, we do have the room thankfully, and it'll be good to have a full house for once.

"We need to pack." I added, reluctantly getting up to begin organising. "The minivan that Tom hired will be arriving at ten, which gives us approximately two hours."

"Who's the designated driver?"

"Tom apparently. He's taken out the insurance for it. According to Charlotte, he's a good driver. I'd hope so, having eight of us on board."

"I've never been in a car with him but I'm sure he is. Stop fretting," Ted said, coming over to me for a cuddle.

"No time," I said bluntly, dipping out of his hold. "I love you, but we have things to do," I told him, leaving him hanging with his arms mid-air, before I left through my bedroom door to use the bathroom.

"No fair!" he shouted after me. On my way to the bathroom, I bumped into Charlotte, who also appeared to be stressing out.

"Everything okay?" I asked her, knowing the feeling.

"My dress, the one I ordered for tonight, hasn't arrived yet. What am I going to do?" she said, frantically.

"Wear something else?" I suggested, which I didn't intend to sound so sarcastic.

Charlotte moaned. "I don't have anything."

"I'm sure you do Charlotte. I don't mind what you wear, new or old, just as long as you're there! I'm so happy that everyone could make it."

"I can't believe how quickly it's come around!" she responded. "It feels like our New Year's party was only a few weeks ago, but it's actually been over five months now."

"I know, me too. It's gone so quick," I said, before dashing into the bathroom.

As I got ready, I thought about the past five months. They had flown by. Christmas and New Year's Eve were both so magical, Ted and I's first ones together and we spent every waking minute in each other's company. After the most perfect Christmas Day, we had an equally amazing Boxing Day / another Christmas Day with his family, back down south. My parents were sad to see us go so quick, but we did promise to visit regularly after New Year, which we have stuck to. We spent the few days between Christmas and New Year with Ted's family in Exeter, before heading back to Plymouth for New Years with everyone. It was so much fun. I've always dreamt of a New Year's Eve like that with my friends, and it made me so happy when it finally happened.

The start of semester two was smooth, and I settled back into uni life after the long winter break just fine. Weekends were filled with ice skating and snowball fights with the gang on the odd weekend when it snowed, and we spent windy evenings at the beach as usual, wrapped up in scarfs and a million blankets to keep us toasty. My relationship with my parents has been great too, our regular visits up north have certainly helped, but also, everyone seems to be getting along just fine at the moment. My parents love Ted, which didn't surprise me of course, and they are constantly begging for us to visit even more.

The five-hour drive is long, but getting to show Ted my home has been so lovely. We've been exploring the Peak District, and he's got to spend time with Sam too, which is a dream come true. On each visit we've spoken more and more about my sister with my parents, and we're hoping that we will find her soon. I feel like we're getting close, but only time will tell. I've met more of Ted's friends as well, on our equally as frequent trips to Exeter, including Lily and Jake. We've been on double dates with them, which to my surprise, was not awkward at all.

"Who's in here?" A voice sang from behind the door.

"Just me," I said, opening it, to which Ruby stumbled in from outside.

"Sorry," she said, laughing. "I had my face pressed up against the door."

I cackled. "I'm ready now. For the journey at least. I'm going to get ready for the party properly later, when we get to Glossop. For now, comfy clothes and no make-up it is."

"You're not wearing any make-up?" Charlotte called from the bottom of the stairs.

"No Charlotte. I'm going bare faced!"

"Well I don't want to look too glamorous if you're all going casual!" she shouted back.

Ruby and I laughed.

"I'm going for the messy bun and sweatpants look!" I replied.

"Oh damn, should I have worn makeup?!" Tom said, appearing at the door.

"Oh hey!" Ruby and I said in unison.

"When did you sneak in?" I continued.

"Oh I've been downstairs for a while, listening to Charlotte stressing about outfits or some such matter. I came up to use the bathroom if that's okay?" he said, gesturing towards us.

We shuffled out of Tom's way and onto the landing. I headed back to my bedroom where Ted was waiting with his suitcase in hand. "Ready, already?" I asked, stopping in my tracks.

"I'll start packing up the car," he said, smiling.

"What are you smiling at?" I teased, leaning against the door frame.

"You," he replied. "Messy buns and sweatpants, it's my favourite look of yours."

———

"Mum? Dad?" I shouted, pushing the door open with one hand, the other carrying three bags. "You home? We're here!"

We'd finally made it to Glossop after the long drive, and I was desperate to relax for a while before I needed to do my hair and makeup for the party. I started showing everyone around downstairs when both my parents came down and greeted us all. They introduced themselves to everyone, before showing them where they were all going to sleep. We had two spare bedrooms for two of the couples and Dad had agreed to sleep on the sofa and give up his room for the remaining pair, whilst Ted and I were in my bedroom. We all fit comfortably enough.

"What time have you told people to arrive again?" I asked Dad as we gathered some drinks for everyone as they retreated to the lounge.

"Six, I think!" he laughed. "You're best off checking with your mum. But you've got time. Just chill out for a while with your mates, your mum and I will start setting everything up, and then get ready. It's your birthday weekend Macey. Take it easy."

I smiled. "Thanks Dad. I can't wait. And thanks again for letting everyone stay. It's so special having everyone I care so much about here."

"Anything for you, my strawberry lace. Now, go and be with your friends. I'll bring the drinks through."

———

"You look incredible." Ted said as I posed next to my large "21" balloons. My parents had gone all out, filling the house with various decorations, including ribbons and garlands, and embarrassing baby pictures of me too. When I questioned them on the latter, they insisted they were necessary, seeing as I am turning the "big twenty-one". I stood in front of said decorations, as Ted snapped some photos of me on my phone.

"I really am so lucky!" he said from behind the lens.

Blushing, I walked over and took the phone from him, handing it to Libby. "Please could you take a photo of Ted and I, together?"

"Of course!" she replied eagerly. "You are such a power couple!" she added as she took the photo.

We both burst out laughing, which actually made for a rather cute, candid shot. I immediately uploaded the photo to Instagram; it was too good not to. I tagged Ted and captioned it with "let the celebrations begin! #twentyone" along with some party emojis before closing my phone off and leaving it on the table. I was adamant that I didn't want to touch it for the rest of the evening, and instead live in the present, as they say. Ted had bought a few disposable cameras for us to capture the evening on, which I already couldn't wait to use and subsequently develop. Dad was controlling the music from his desktop computer in the study, so I didn't have to worry about that either. It was connected to a few speakers around the house, meaning it would be loud enough. Luckily, our house was detached, so we didn't have to worry about upsetting any neighbours. Our nearest neighbours were invited anyway, eradicating that possible cause for concern.

———

"Dad. What on earth is this song?" I said a little while later as the drinks were flowing, and our downstairs living space was starting to get overpopulated. I hadn't even realised that I knew this many people, but it was lovely to see lots of old faces and catch up with them.

Dad huffed. "A 60's classic Macey. I thought I'd brought you up better than that!"

"I'm changing the playlist!" I laughed, heading off to the study to do so. I wandered over to the computer and grabbed the mouse to find a new playlist, one that had songs that "us kids" would actually know, and be able to dance to. Just as I had pressed shuffle on the new playlist, the window behind the music player tab caught my eye. It was my dad's emails, and a new one had just come through.

Normally I wouldn't be one to snoop, but a certain word in the preview caught my eye, "Adoption". I felt a rush of emotions, could this be the email we've been waiting for? When the email opened up, I sat down at the desk chair to read it, as my eyes were struggling to see the small print on the screen when I was stood up. The body of the email didn't say much, something about there being some information attached. I clicked on the attachment and when it opened, I saw it was a letter. I immediately scanned the document in search for a name or some other hint of who my sister could be.

I couldn't believe what I had just read. My mind was going a million miles per hour and my heart was beating just as fast to keep up. Isla…Isla Stewart, as in my favourite author in the world, as in the woman I've met a few times now, on different occasions, was my sister?! The sister I've known about my whole life, yet never met, but actually have met? I tried to calm myself down, breathing in for eight and out for eight, just like my therapist had taught me to do. It wasn't helping. I was still hyperventilating. Before I could think what to do next, Ted came into the room.

"M, you've been in here ages, you're missing your own birthday party!" he said, kissing me on the head from behind as I was still sitting down. I couldn't think of a reply. I just stayed silent. "M. What's wrong?" he said jokingly, spinning the chair around so that I was facing him. I stared at him blankly. He persisted. "M. Seriously. What's up?"

"I—I—" I stuttered, then chose to just point to the computer, directing him to read the document that was open on the screen. A few minutes of silence passed. When he finished reading, he bent down next to me. I got up, brushing past him, and began pacing up and down the room.

"That was sent to your Dad?"

I nodded.

"Isla's your sister? And she's agreed to make contact with you all?" He continued, looking as confused as I was a moment ago.

Without much thought, I strode towards the door. Ted followed me as if he'd read my mind and grabbed my arm hastily. I flinched. "Shit. Sorry M. I didn't mean to grab you like that. I just think you should wait it out a little, don't say anything to your parents now."

"Why?" I asked. "This is what we've been waiting for Ted! We've found my sister! And it's Isla!" Suddenly, the shock had dissipated and it started to feel real. "Isla-freaking-Stewart is my sister. Wow."

"It's your party. Your special day. Maybe just wait it out, until tomorrow at least? Your dad is bound to see the email then anyway. You don't want him to be mad at you for snooping!"

"Ted, he can't possibly be mad at me right now," I said, rather excitedly. "I think he'll be made up."

"I think it'll be a shock to your mum and dad both. That their daughter is a famous author, one their other daughter has unknowingly admired for years as just that, a famous author. Not a blood relative."

"Come on. You're being a party pooper now. This is what we've been working toward! Are you not excited? You love Isla!"

"Of course I am babe. Just right now, your house is flooded with people and you and your parents are all a little tipsy."

"I couldn't possibly hold this in Ted, even until just tomorrow," and with that, I left the room, adamant on finding my parents and sharing the news.

————

I HESITATED behind the kitchen door where I knew my parents were. Ted was right. I couldn't bombard them with such big news in front of a rather large crowd. I needed to tell them when there weren't so many people around, so tomorrow would have to do.

I was overly excited at first, but thinking rationally now, I know telling them tomorrow would be for the best. I turned around and headed back to the study to find Ted, feeling slightly dizzy from both the news and the vodka shots I'd been doing fifteen minutes prior.

"Are you feeling alright?" he said as I stumbled into the room.

"I didn't realise how much I'd had to drink," I replied, laughing. "You were right, I'll tell Dad to check his emails tomorrow."

"Can I get you some water?" Ted said kindly, getting up from where he was sitting.

"That would be perfect," I said, sitting down on the couch that was in the study. I laid down and stared up at the ceiling, attempting to process what I had just found out. But before long, and even before Ted had a chance to return with the water, I was fast asleep.

————

"TED AND I are going to stay in Glossop for a few more days, so feel free to leave whenever and don't wait for us." I said as I entered the spare bedroom where all of the housemates and their partners had gathered. "Does anyone want any breakfast?"

"I'm too hungover for breakfast," Charlotte said groggily, whilst the others nodded in agreement.

"Is everything okay Macey? How are you going to get back?" Tom chimed in, a concerned look on his face.

"Oh yeah, everything's fine. Mum or Dad will probably drive us halfway and then we'll get a train for the remainder of the journey."

Ted hugged me from behind as he'd followed me in.

"Where did you disappear to last night Macey? We couldn't find you!" Issac said whilst passing Ruby a bottle of water. She was hidden under a blanket, apparently it was a heavy night for her too.

"I passed out in the study quite early," I said laughing. "It was you lads' fault!" I added, directing my mock anger at Tom and Issac. "Encouraging me to do 21 shots for my 21st, I think I managed three before I ended up asleep in the study."

"I went to get her some water and she was asleep by the time I got back to her," Ted explained, whilst the others laughed at my inability to "hack it".

I smiled. I knew today would be an emotional one, once I'd finally spoken to my parents about what I saw on Dad's computer yesterday. I was ready however, although it did take me a few minutes this morning to realise what had happened last night wasn't a dream.

"Will you be back in Plymouth for your birthday?" Charlotte asked suddenly.

"Of course!" I responded, reassuring her that our plans still stood. "I wouldn't miss my actual birthday, with you all, for the world."

———

ONCE ALL THE housemates and their significant others had left, I cleaned myself up, got dressed and called Mum, Dad and Ted into the study. Mum and Dad looked confused, as to why I'd called a family meeting in a room that's barely used by anyone other than Dad. I perched on the couch with Ted whilst my parents hovered near the computer.

"Are you alright Macey? Did you have fun last night?" Dad said worriedly.

"I had a lot of fun, thank you both. My friends really enjoyed it too. I really appreciate all of the effort that everyone went to. It was certainly a night I won't forget!"

"Are you looking forward to your birthday in Plymouth? Why have you delayed going back? Not that we don't want you here of course," Mum questioned.

"No no, I can't wait, we'll be back down south before then. I just needed a bit more time to speak with the both of you," I hesitated. "Dad. Have you checked your emails yet?"

Dad raised an eyebrow. "No, I never do on the weekends, why?"

"Last night when I was changing the music in here, I saw an email come in on your computer. I shouldn't have opened it. But I did. I'm sorry for that. However, you should really check it now. It's about your daughter...my sister..."

Mum's eyes widened. "They've found her?"

I nodded. Dad sat down at his desk and pulled up the email in question. Mum hovered behind him and read the attached document over his shoulder.

"Her name... is Isla. Isla Stewart." Dad announced, whilst getting choked up.

"Why does that sound familiar? Mum said, curiously.

Before I could reply, I witnessed Dad's light bulb moment.

"The author! The author Macey likes! The one who spoke at her university recently."

"Oh, my, gosh," Mum managed to muster out as tears began to fall down my face. Ted clutched my side and pulled me in for a hug as Mum and Dad wandered over towards me. I stood up to hug them both, standing there with them for a moment, as the realisation began to set in for everyone.

"So you've met her! You've met your sister!" Dad said after a little while.

"Yep. Of course I had no idea. It's crazy to think back on now, the fact I've met her on several occasions. I always felt an odd attachment to her, even before I'd met her, but I put that down to the fact I've loved her work for years."

"Well, I'm glad she got to be a part of your life in a way," Mum said smiling.

She was right. I hadn't thought of that until just now. That even though she wasn't in my life as my sister, she was still involved in it somehow. I'm lucky that I found her books, it certainly feels like fate now.

———

THE REST of May came and went pretty uneventfully. My birthday at the start of May, back down in Plymouth, was lovely with all of my friends. We celebrated with quiet drinks at home, nothing as crazy as the party a few days prior. We ate fast food, laughed a lot and I got some really special gifts. Ted certainly spoiled me, he got me a personalised book page holder with our favourite quote from *Wuthering Heights*.

"Whatever our souls are made of, his and mine are the same." He read as I grazed my finger over the intricate embossing.

It made me smile from ear to ear. I'd read that quote over and over before meeting Ted, yet I'd never really, truly, understood it until I felt the connection that I have with him. He also got me a ring with my birthstone and a pair of earrings to match. I might have shed a tear or two at his generosity. The girls clubbed together and got me a Polaroid camera, something I've wanted for a long time. They must have guessed, and I was as thankful to them too.

The rest of May saw uni begin to draw to a close. We all had a few exams here and there, but assignments were being handed in and we were all eagerly making plans for the summer ahead. The group, as in Ted and I and the housemates and their partners, had decided to rent out a villa in Italy for a few weeks come July, and we were excitedly mapping out the trip as it drew closer. I'm sure that the rest of the summer was going to be spent between Plymouth with everyone, Exeter with Ted's family and up North with mine. We wanted to fit as much in as possible before I headed into 3rd year. Ted had already secured a full time graduate position for a year in Plymouth after his Masters, and after that, well who knows! I'll be finished with university by then, so fingers crossed I'll have a better idea of what I want to do, or at least, where I want the world to take me.

Before summer started, there was one very special meeting due to take place, and I still couldn't believe that it was happening. It had only been a month since I found out that Isla Stewart was my sister, but I had honestly been waiting for the day forever. I've always known of "big sis", but I would have never expected it to be Isla herself. Tomorrow is the big day, and as much as I am excited, I'm kind of nervous too. She doesn't actually know that it's me yet, the girl she's met before. Mum and Dad thought it would be best for her to find out tomorrow. They are going to meet her first, and I'll go in a while afterward. We're staying over in Bath tonight, where Isla lives, and I've brought Ted with me for moral support.

"How are you feeling?" Ted asked gently, whilst stroking my leg. We were lounging on the huge hotel bed, my parents were in the room next door. We were devouring a novel together, of course, but I couldn't seem to concentrate.

"I'm okay. Apprehensive," I paused. "It's going to be a lot for Isla. I can't help but think about how she must be feeling!"

"It's a lot for you too Mace. You're meeting your sister for the first time!"

"Well, not the first time," I laughed.

"You know what I mean. The first time where you know that you're related to each other. How are you feeling, really?"

"I am really excited you know. I could never have dreamed of my sister being my biggest idol. It still feels surreal."

"I bet she'll be as excited when she finds out about you. And I bet she'll be even more excited tomorrow when she realises who you are. You two got along so well. She'll be well chuffed."

I giggled.

"What?" Ted said inquisitively.

"You said chuffed. I like that you're picking up Northern slang!"

"Oh gi or!" Ted said, in the brashest, fakest, Northern accent I've ever heard.

CHAPTER 24 - ISLA

Henry and I were walking down the road in Bath city centre, heading for the coffee shop where I would be meeting my birth parents. I still couldn't believe it. I felt like I was in a day dream. I was gripping Henry's hand and he kept looking down at me to check I was ok. The last few weeks had been a blur of discussions and email exchanges but it felt like yesterday I got the email that drastically changed my life.

In late April, on a beautiful sunny day, Henry and I were enjoying a lazy spring picnic together while Mrs. Russell was at an appointment and then would be going out with some of her friends. Henry and I found ourselves with a rare afternoon away from responsibilities. He'd finished up some projects at work and I was done with the latest batch of edits and was waiting to hear from my editor with her next round of feedback.

I leant back in the sun and tilted my face up, I lifted my hand to shield my eyes and saw the sun glint off my ring. It had been months since we got engaged and I still got a shiver of excitement when I saw the ring on my hand. It was a reminder I hadn't imagined that whole night. The worrier side of my brain wondered if the doubt would creep in the closer we got to the wedding, but it hadn't. If anything, everyday we got closer to the wedding, I got more certain of my decision.

We'd picked a venue and I think I'd found a dress. Georgie, Beth, Mum, and Mrs. Russell are going with me for a second try-on later in the week. Henry and I had appointments with a few caterers coming up and I'd selected a baker for the cake so we just needed to go for a tasting to pick the flavour. Mrs. Russell and Mum are helping me pick a florist. It's a lot but it's exciting and feels so right. I looked over at Henry and he's also enjoying the sun, with a satisfied smile on his face.

As we sat on the picnic blanket, enjoying some brie and crackers, I heard my phone go off with an email notification.

"Damn, I thought I'd silenced that," I said.

"Do you need to check it?"

"Well I don't *need* to…"

"But you're going to?" Henry laughed.

"Sorry, I just want to make sure it's nothing from my editor. Two seconds."

I opened up the email and immediately froze.

"What is it?" Henry asked me, looking concerned.

"It's…" I said slowly. "It's from the agency that handled my adoption."

"Your adoption?"

I looked at Henry. "I told you I was adopted. Everyone at school knew. I've always known about it."

"No, I know, I'm just trying to keep up with the conversation," Henry said, laughing slightly. "I remember from school. That horrible girl tried to tease you about it once and you set her straight. That was the best day."

I smiled at the memory. "Yeah. Still can't quite figure out how she thought it was going to make me feel bad, being brought up in a family spread between three countries, having two passports, getting trips to Disney because we would fly into LA before flying up to Oregon, and being made to feel like a miracle child after all the miscarriages Mum suffered."

"That girl was just jealous," Henry said, leaning over to kiss me. "So why is the adoption agency emailing you?"

I was brought back to the words staring up at me from the email on my phone. "Umm, they were contacted by my birth parents. They want to know if I want to be connected with them."

Henry's eyes went wide. "You've found your birth parents?"

"Well, technically I think they've found me," I said incredulously. "We never knew much about them, just that my birth mum was only 15 or 16 years old when I was born. I think they were from up north? But maybe that's just something I made up, I can't remember. My parents never hid the adoption from me. They were so happy to have a child finally and the whole family knew how much trouble they'd had trying to conceive." I looked at the email again.

"So do you want to make contact? I mean, is ignoring this even an option?" Henry asked.

I thought about it, but I knew the answer. "No. It's not an option. Not for me. I need to talk to Mum and Dad before I respond, but I'm not going to run from my past ever again, and my adoption is part of my past. I always thought I was fine not knowing. I've had a great life and amazing parents, but now that this door has cracked open...how do I not walk through it Henry? Maybe I'll never have a relationship with these people, but I owe it to myself to at least hear their side of the story."

Henry squeezed my hand. "You know I'll support you, no matter what. I think the fact that they're the ones reaching out is a good sign."

"Yeah...yes, I suppose it is. Sorry, I'm probably overthinking this," I said, shaking my head, trying to clear my mind.

Henry squeezed my hand again. "You're not overthinking, you're overwhelmed. And that's to be expected. Give yourself some time. Let this sink in a bit."

"You're probably right."

"Take a breath Isla."

"Yeah, waiting a little while won't hurt," I agreed.

"No," Henry laughed softly. "I mean, literally, take a deep breath. Your breathing is really shallow right now. You look like you're going to faint."

I burst out laughing, a little hysterically, and then calmed myself down and took a deep breath like Henry suggested.

As much as I felt I should let myself wait, I wanted to talk to my parents as soon as possible, so instead of going back to Henry's place for dinner, we went over to my parents. I told them about the email and they were as surprised as I was, but ultimately we all agreed that I needed to reply to the agency and make contact with my birth parents.

Simon and Valerie. Those were their names. The names of my birth parents. It was weird to think about. When I responded to the email from the adoption agency, I asked the agency to forward a letter I wrote to my birth parents, and agreed to be put in contact. We exchanged a few messages and arranged to meet. We haven't shared much yet, it seemed easier to wait until we could speak in person.

Today was the day. They were coming to meet me in Bath. Simon and Valerie. My birth parents. It felt weird thinking that. Mum and Dad will always be my parents, the ones who raised me and loved me and shared a family with me. But Simon and Valerie and I shared blood and DNA and while that didn't necessarily make for a stronger bond, it was still something and I was really curious to meet them.

Henry and I arrived at the coffee shop we had agreed to meet at, and I was shaking so much I felt like I was going to pass out. I was so nervous. Henry came with me but agreed to sit in the corner unless I called him over.

"I'll be there if you need me," he said as we walked in. We got there early, I didn't see any sign of them. I should have asked for a picture, but I guess I thought I'd recognise them somehow. Surely they'd be as nervous as I felt. Everyone already in the coffee shop looked perfectly normal, doing their own thing. Not like they were waiting to meet their long lost daughter. I suddenly started second guessing everything. We should have met somewhere else. This felt like such a mundane setting for something that felt so life changing. In just a few minutes, I'd come face to face with my birth parents. I really didn't know how to process that.

Henry went to get our drinks and then settled me at a table in the back, one that had a bit of privacy. He handed me a mint tea.

"Here, I didn't think you needed caffeine right now."

I gave a nervous laugh. "No, probably not."

"I'll be just around the corner, near the counter, I don't want you to feel like I'm watching you. But text me or come get me if you need me."

"Alright. Thank you Henry."

He just smiled and leaned down to give me a kiss, and then walked back towards the barista counter.

I sat there for a minute, it felt like an eternity, checking my phone every few seconds, thinking they were going to cancel, and fidgeting with my tea cup.

I was staring out the window across from the table when I heard a man's voice call my name.

"Isla...it's really you."

I looked up and saw a man, with a woman standing beside him. He looked awestruck and she looked like she was fighting tears.

He choked slightly, and cleared his throat, "Umm, I'm Simon... Simon Banks. And this is Valerie. We're, umm, well..." He stroked his chin nervously.

"You're my parents," I said quietly, more to myself than to them.

Valerie still didn't speak, but Simon replied, "I'm not sure how much we deserve that designation." He looked down at his shoes.

Finally Valerie spoke. "You're even more beautiful in person. You look so much like my gran when she was your age. But you have my mum's eyes. Green as the moors." Her voice broke and she covered her face with her hands. "I said I wasn't going to cry."

I had been rooted to my chair but in that instant, the tears started flowing and I leapt up from my seat and wrapped my arms around her. Not just as her daughter but as a woman who could only imagine the pain she'd carried all these years.

After a moment we broke from the hug.

"Let's sit down," I suggested.

"I'll give you two women a moment while I go get us something to drink. Are you good Isla?" Simon asked, gesturing to my tea.

"Yeah, I'm good thanks."

He nodded and walked over to the counter.

I looked back at Valerie. She still seemed in a bit of shock, just staring at me but clearly trying not to. I was doing the same. I just wanted to analyse every part of her face to see if I could see my own. She said I looked like her gran and her mum, what part of her looks like them and like me?

Simon came back and sat down next to Valerie. They each stared into their coffees for a moment.

Finally Simon looked up at me and said, "We should have tried finding you sooner."

"We can't waste time on should have's Simon," said Valerie, looking uncomfortable.

"Still, forty years, it was a long time."

"Simon—" Valerie interrupted. It sounded like a warning.

"The timing was how it was meant to be," I said gently.

"You should also know...you have a sister," Simon said quietly.

"A sister? You had another child after me?" I asked kindly. Somehow it comforted me to know that despite how things worked out for the three of us, they were still able to have a life together and raise a child.

"We have a daughter, she's in uni. She's always known she had a sister somewhere, we never kept the adoption a secret," said Valerie.

"She will be here, but we wanted to meet you first," Simon explained. "She's actually quite a fan of yours, and a growing writer herself."

"Really?" I said with curiosity.

Valerie said, "She's studying Creative Writing at Plymouth.

She's part of their Creative Writing Society. I think you actually met there? And before that she attended a signing of yours in Bristol."

Suddenly it all started to click in my head. The girl from the signing, Macey from the society, who contacted me to come speak. The feeling of familiarity I had when we met again in Plymouth. I thought it was because we'd met in Bristol, but no. It was more. She was my sister.

A movement out of the corner of my eye caught my attention, I looked up and walking through the door I saw Macey, holding hands with Ted. She stopped as soon as she came in the door and saw her parents. I watched as she looked at them and then as her gaze shifted over to me. There she was. My little sister. We stared at each other, it felt like an eternity but it was probably only seconds.

She looked unsure.

I smiled.

Then she smiled.

And in an instant I was out of my chair and we were walking towards each other, meeting in the middle ground between us and I wrapped my arms around her. We just held each other for a moment, I don't even know for how long. Time stood still. To think that this brilliant young woman, who I'd been so impressed with when I spoke to her at the uni, was my sister. My full sister. After years of being an only child. I finally have a sister.

Eventually we pulled away and stared at each other. I gently placed my hands on both sides of her face as she gripped my elbows. As I had with Valerie, I scanned Macey's face, looking for similarities between us. Macey seemed to be doing the same for a few seconds then we hugged again, clinging to each other tightly until we both started laughing. I couldn't believe we were sisters!

Finally Macey turned back to Ted.

"I'll come and get you when we're done."

"Okay, I'll be just sitting in the corner if you need me," he said gently, leaning down to give her a kiss on the cheek. He looked to her parents. Our parents. They said hello and he greeted them in return. Then looked at me. "Hi Isla, it's good to see you again," he said with a polite smile.

"Good to see you too Ted," I said kindly, smiling back at him.

He walked off and I invited Macey to sit down. As she sat, Valerie reached out to take her hand and gave it a squeeze. I could only imagine how overwhelming today was for all of them. I know I was feeling overwhelmed, although it felt like Macey had the advantage. She knew our parent's story, I didn't.

I looked at Simon and Valerie, "I know you all have probably already discussed this over the years, but I'd really like to hear the full story. If that would be alright?"

I watched as Simon and Valerie glanced nervously at each other. They each took a deep breath before they began to tell their story.

They took turns, filling in gaps for the other, but basically, they went to secondary school together and began dating when they were 14. Valerie got pregnant when she was 15 and her parents—my grandparents, I thought quietly—insisted on Valerie giving me up for adoption. While part of me was sad to hear this, I honestly couldn't say I blamed them. I can barely imagine being pregnant at age 40. Having a baby at 15 sounded so hard, even under the best of circumstances. She was still a child herself.

Valerie's family moved villages to put distance between her and Simon. I could only imagine what she must have gone through. A new town, a pregnancy, her family making all the decisions, and then losing her boyfriend all at the same time? It all sounded like an impossible situation. I understood the choices her parents made, but I could also hear in her voice and see on her face, how even today she struggled as she remembered how painful it all was.

I was born and adopted, going home to live with my adoptive parents. This is where our stories split. While I went on to have a fantastic childhood with my parents, Valerie had to deal with the after effects of pregnancy and the emotional pain that went along with the adoption, all while she went back to school and finished her education.

She ended up with a place at Durham when she was 18, and

while there she reconnected with Simon who was also going to uni there. They hadn't spoken to each other since they were 15, and Simon really didn't know much except that I had been put up for adoption. They began to date again at uni and stayed together after uni and focused on their careers. They explained they both studied psychology, and both have PhDs. They had Macey when they were 35, seventeen years after they reunited at uni.

They finished their story and we all fell silent for a bit, it was a lot to take in.

"My Aunt Genevieve was my rock during that time," Valerie said quietly. "And in the years after. She was the one who encouraged me to go to Durham and have a fresh start, she allowed me to grieve the pregnancy and the baby I couldn't keep, but also wanted me to not stay stuck in the past."

Simon said sadly, "It was decided almost immediately that we wouldn't be able to keep you Isla. I was devastated to lose both you and Valerie, but at least I was fortunate enough to find Valerie again at uni. Those three years without her were hard."

"Did you have a name for me?" I asked, suddenly curious about how my life might have been if things had worked out differently.

"I would have named you after my aunt, Genevieve," Valerie explained.

"That's my middle name," Macey said quietly.

Valerie smiled at her, then turned to me, "She's passed on now, but she would have loved meeting you. She was the only one who understood me, understood the sense of loss I carried after I gave you up."

"We only ever wanted the best for you Isla," Simon tried to explain quietly. "Recently we decided to try to find you, but it feels so late now."

They all looked so downcast, I hated thinking they felt like they'd failed me somehow. "It's fine. Everything happens at the right time. I don't know how receptive I would have been if the three of you had just dropped into my life even just last year, let alone a few years ago or more. We all have had our own journey to get to this point."

"It's not fair," Macey said sadly.

"Life isn't fair Macey," I said gently. "I've certainly learned that the hard way in my own life. I had a great childhood, but things for me definitely went a bit sideways after grad school and before I started my writing career. Sometimes, bad stuff just happens. What matters is that we're all meeting now."

"You're really not mad at us?" Valerie asked, a little desperately.

I could tell she needed some kind of reassurance. "Valerie, I can barely imagine being pregnant right now, and I'm 40. What you went through, being pregnant at 15, choosing to carry me only to give me up, hoping I'd be raised by good parents…that has to be one of the hardest things a teenager could have to do. Despite how things turned out for me, I certainly wouldn't blame you if you had wanted to make a different choice. You sacrificed a lot for me and I am so profoundly grateful. I will never judge you for the decisions you made or for how you chose to protect your mental health after you gave me up. Valerie, I can't be mad. You and Simon did what your parent's thought was best. No one knows how they would handle that kind of situation until they're in it, and even then I can only imagine the doubt you both dealt with over the years."

"Every single day," Simon spoke softly at first and then said more firmly, "From the moment I found out and Valerie's parents whisked her away so I couldn't see her to the day we got the message from the agency that they'd found you and then finally making contact with you, every single day I've wondered if we did the right thing, if I should have fought harder for you." He roughly wiped his eyes.

I looked around the table, they were all so quiet, everyone lost in their own thoughts. I reached my hand out to both Simon and Valerie, and my other hand to Macey.

"Can we agree that the past is in the past? That from today we move forward?"

Simon and Valerie both gripped my outstretched hand. Then

Simon reached out a hand to Macey. She took it and reached out to take my hand. And we sat like that, holding hands and letting go of the past, for several seconds.

When we each sat back, we all seemed to be lighter, more at peace. I hoped this would be the beginning of healing for both Simon and Valerie. I knew that whatever had happened in the past, it had brought us to this moment and I had a whole new side of my family history unfurling before me. I wanted to get to know these people. I wanted to have a relationship with my sister. My sister! I could still hardly believe it!

We talked for a little bit longer, but about easy stuff. Their lives now, what living in Glossop was like, and how Macey was doing since I last saw her. I told them about Mrs. Russell and my parents and about Georgie and how excited I was about her babies. I also told them about Henry, and that he was here with me.

"He came along for moral support, like I'm sure why Ted came here with Macey. If it's alright though, I'll have you meet him another day."

Simon laughed, "Of course it's alright. You've only just met us. It's only fair that we save meeting the fiancé for another time. But I'm glad you have someone and that you're happy."

"We'll come back to Bath, and soon," Valerie said. "And you both are welcome to come to Glossop. You could stay with us, or if you'd be more comfortable there are some lovely hotels nearby."

"I'd love to come to Glossop, I'm sure Henry would as well. We'll have to see when we can get away, it's a bit hard right now because of his mum's ongoing recovery, but you're welcome in Bath anytime. I have a holiday place, it's not yet on the market but you'll always be welcome to stay there. You as well Macey. It's close to the city centre and not far from my own house. You and Ted could come and stay anytime. Or you could stay at my house," I offered her shyly.

"That would be great," Macey said. "I'd love to come stay with you. And maybe sometime Charlotte and I could come visit you and Beth, we could stay in your holiday house then if that would be alright."

"It's always available for you and your friends, anytime you want a girls weekend away," I said with a smile.

Macey and I said goodbye to our parents—I was still getting used to that—they needed to get their train back up north. It was hard saying goodbye, but I knew I'd see them again soon.

"I need to find Ted," Macey said shyly.

"I'm glad he came with you," I said.

"So am I."

We walked to the other side of the cafe, and as I suspected, we found Ted sitting with Henry.

"This young man and I started talking and realised we had something in common," Henry said with a grin.

"Oh?" Macey said, looking between the two of them.

I wrapped my arm around Macey's waist and gave her a side hug. "Yeah, their girlfriend's are sisters. This is my fiancé Henry. Henry, this is my sister Macey," I said with a smile. I didn't think I'd ever get used to saying that. My sister, Macey.

"Oh wow!" Macey said, looking between me and Henry. "I'm glad he came with you," she said with a smile, echoing what I'd said to her.

"I think you and I both needed backup today."

She smiled in agreement.

"When do you two need to get the train back to Plymouth?" Henry asked kindly.

"Not for a little while," Ted replied. "We weren't sure how long we'd be here and also thought we might wander around Bath a bit. Depending on how things went here and how Macey felt after."

"What do you say we go get a bite to eat? I know it's a bit early, but I'm feeling a bit peckish after all that," I said with a grin.

Macey's eyes lit up, "I'd love that!"

"Do you want to just do a girls thing, or can us gents come along?" Henry asked with a laugh.

"You gentlemen are definitely invited. There's a good place just down the road from here, on the way back to the station. We can get some food and something to drink and hang out there until you need to get your train home," I suggested.

Everyone agreed and we left the coffee shop together. The days felt much lighter and longer now, and the late afternoon sun cast a warm glow on the limestone of the buildings around us. Macey and I walked quietly, both of us lost in our thoughts, as I listened to Henry and Ted talking amiably behind us. I looked up at the sky and took a deep breath. Life really works in mysterious ways. And as we continued down the road, I slipped my arm through Macey's and I felt her lean into me and I heard her sigh contentedly. Whatever happened, things were going to be alright.

EPILOGUE - VALERIE

"Hey Mum!" Macey said, popping her head around the door. "Are you ready?"

"Yes sweetheart, I'll be outside in a moment. Isla and Henry are meeting us at the restaurant, aren't they?"

"Yep, they are meeting us there!" she replied, before wandering off.

There hasn't been a day where I had wanted to stop time as much as this one. Today, we were going out to dinner to celebrate Macey finishing university, and I suddenly felt like I was losing her to the real world. When she moved away to Plymouth for university, it was manageable. And to be honest, we weren't as close back then, like we are now. The past year has seen a lot of change, and growth, in our family. I've been able to bond with Macey since, I've visited her regularly in her final year of studies. I've also been able to bond with Isla, which has been such a blessing. And Simon, well, I've been able to bond with him too.

"You look striking," Simon said, the next one to appear at the door.

I blushed as I finished buckling the straps of my heels and

walked over to where he was standing. "And so do you," I said, taking his arm and allowing him to escort me outside.

We were staying in Plymouth this weekend, in a lovely apartment by the beach. Simon had booked it for him and I online, and I was delighted when we arrived to a sea view. Macey and Ted had met us here to walk to the restaurant together. Macey's official graduation ceremony wasn't until September, but we wanted to do something now, in May, to mark the end of the term. We would come back down in September for those celebrations as well.

"Let me take a photo of you both," I said to Macey and Ted when I exited the hotel we were staying in. The sun was setting, and being right on the water, the view was exquisite.

"Mum," Macey said begrudgingly. "We need to leave. And you're so embarrassing!" she said, laughing.

"Hey, I want to remember this. And how beautiful my daughter and her dashing boyfriend look."

The pair smiled at each other which made for a perfect candid picture, and we headed to the restaurant.

———

"MARIO!" Ted said happily as we were greeted by a gentleman at the front desk.

Macey had mentioned that she and Ted had been here before, on a few occasions, and Ted knew the owner from childhood. Macey then introduced us to him, before we all found our table where Isla and Henry were already sitting.

"Hey guys!" I said excitedly, placing my bag down on the table to hug the both of them. "How are you both doing?"

"Great!" Isla replied. "Excited to see you all and celebrate Macey."

I turned to Henry, "How's your mum?"

"She's doing great," he replied smiling. "Thanks for asking Valerie. She's been walking with only a cane, she's been thrilled to get rid of the walker."

"Georgie's twins have been running circles around her, it gives her motivation to get up and be active," Isla said smiling.

"Are they walking now?!" I asked excitedly. I'd met the twins, two girls, on one of our last trips to Bath, they were delightful.

"Just," Isla replied. "Georgie's already overwhelmed, but Grant is convinced they're going to be football or track and field stars."

We all laughed.

"They're still crawling a lot, but Mum loves chasing after them and they adore her," Henry said laughing. "It's been great for her recovery."

Turning to Isla, "How are your parents?" Simon and I had met them not long after we met Henry after that first meeting with Isla in the coffee shop. It had been emotional, but good to meet them. It seemed to finally close the past and start fresh for the future.

"They're good," Isla said. "They send their good wishes and also a card for Macey."

The conversation with all of my children and their partners was as easy as ever. At one point, Macey went to the toilet, with Isla, and left me alone with the men of our family.

"I feel like I should have gone with them! A girls trip!" I laughed.

"There's actually something I wanted to talk to you about, quickly. I think I have time, Macey usually takes ages in the loos, fixing her makeup and what not," Ted said nervously.

"Am I okay hearing this?" Henry asked, raising an eyebrow.

"Yeah mate!" Ted confirmed, still anxious.

"Is everything okay?" Simon said, taking the words out of my mouth. We both must have looked extremely worried, as Ted was quick to reassure us.

"Don't panic. It's nothing bad! It's actually something very good, at least I hope it will be. I know this is very old fashioned, and though I don't see a reason to do it, I still wanted to, out of respect. I think Macey would appreciate that." He took a deep breath before continuing. "I wanted to ask you permission, for me, to marry your daughter."

I squealed. "Yes! Oh my gosh Ted! Yes!" I repeated excitedly.

Ted turned to look at Simon, waiting for a response from him.

"Of course son. I couldn't have chosen anyone better for my daughter. She loves you very much, we can all see that."

Henry smiled to confirm.

"When?" I added, far too excited to contain myself.

"Not yet, soon." Ted admitted. "Probably in the next few months. I just had to ask you now."

"Oh I am delighted! I promise to keep my mouth shut, however much I want to shout it from the rooftops!"

"Please!" Ted laughed. "I want it to be a big surprise."

"I am sure it will be." I said, still on a high.

Macey and Isla returned, and we continued chatting and catching up, as if nothing had changed. Inside however, I was bursting with excitement. Both of my girls were going to be married soon. Isla already was, and her wedding had been spectacular. She had been walked down the aisle by both her dad and Simon, it was amazing to be included so much in her special day. And now, Macey was to soon be a fiancée. If she said yes of course. But I had no doubt in that. My thoughts were interrupted by Macey tapping on a glass in front of me.

"I'd like to make a big announcement!" she said enthusiastically. I wasn't sure what it could be, considering Ted had only just asked us if he could take her hand in marriage, so I knew it couldn't be a proposal.

"Ted and I are moving. To Berlin."

I gasped. "What?!"

"In a few weeks. I know, it's a little last minute. Well, at least it seems that way. But we've actually had this in the works for a while. We just wanted to wait to tell you, make sure it was all confirmed. It's not forever don't worry. Ted has been offered a job with an international publishing agency, and they need someone in their Berlin office for six months, due to a major project that is based out there. They asked Ted if he would be interested, and when he mentioned it to me, I jumped at the idea. My freelance work, which I am now so busy with, allows me to work from anywhere. I didn't want Ted to miss out on this opportunity for him, but also, for me!"

"That is amazing! Congratulations to you both. I'll definitely be visiting. For the beer of course!" Simon said laughing.

I poked him in the shoulder.

"Mum?" Macey asked worriedly. "You haven't said much!"

"I am so happy for you both! A little taken aback, but so, so, so happy. What about the language though?! You'll have to learn German!"

"Ted actually did A-Level German, and can remember a lot of it. He's already started teaching me, and I'm going to go to some classes when we're out there."

"I am incredibly proud of the both of you!" Isla chimed in. "Berlin, and Germany as a whole, is fabulous. It's so steeped in history. Henry and I will definitely visit. I was actually thinking about basing a novel story there, one revolving around the fall of the wall."

"Oh wow, that would be a fascinating read!" I said, feeling overwhelmed with love for my family. Macey was carving an excellent career for herself, writing for online publications and also producing copy and content for businesses. Isla was already so established in her career, but her upcoming novels were sounding even more daring than the previous ones. I know that Macey often struggled with branching out of her comfort zone, and I had learnt that Isla was similar in that way, so to see them make such shifts in their lives, I was immensely proud. To also see them overcome so much and be happy with their loving partners, meant so much too.

Macey and Ted, Isla and Henry, and now Simon and I, we had all learnt so much in love, and how to make it work. Macey and Ted were significantly younger than the rest of us, but they remind me so much of Simon and I at that age. True love doesn't discriminate. You can find it when you're 15, and you can find it when you're 40, or somewhere in-between. Everyone deserves a chance at it, or even a second, or third. My daughters and I, we've all been on different journeys, with love that is. And despite our generational differences, we've all now experienced love in its purest form.

"I'd like to make a toast," I said abruptly, whilst standing up and raising my glass. "To all of us. To love. From finding it for the first time to learning to love again. It's the same kind of love," I continued, smiling at Simon by my side. "Whatever paths we took to get here, and however all of our paths crossed, it certainly feels like we were all destined to be here together, today. Almost like it was in the stars or just plain, good fortune. Whatever it is, one thing is for sure. It has to be, more than fate."

The End

JOIN THE FUN ONLINE

Thank you so much for reading More Than Fate! We hope you enjoyed it. If you did, please leave a review of this book on Amazon and any other book platforms you're on. Also be sure to recommend it to your friends! Word of mouth recommendations and reviews are like gold for independent authors so we'd really appreciate you sharing the book if you enjoyed it.

Want to know more?

Connect with the *More Than Fate* Community through our Facebook page to learn more about the characters, the authors, and behind the scenes of the book.

https://www.facebook.com/morethanfate

TAMZIN'S ACKNOWLEDGMENTS

First and foremost I would like to thank Andrea. Not only is she my co-writer, she is my soul sister. I am so lucky to have been able to write this book with such a talented woman by my side. Thank you for every part you have played in this journey Andrea, from bringing my original idea for this to life, to writing Isla so beautifully. Who knew when we randomly connected on YouTube over 5 years ago that it would lead to this. Fate. Or more than...

Secondly, I would like to thank my small but tight knit family and in particular, my mum Kas Burch. She always has been and forever will be my inspiration for anything that I embark on. Everything I do in life, I do with the hope of making her proud. She watched me write endless stories growing up, so for me to finally finish one, and publish it, it's kind of a big deal according to her.

Blood doesn't always define family to me, love does, so I also want to thank my Debbie Doodah. There's no label to define what you are to me, except one hell of a woman who I admire so much. Thank you for always having my back and loving me unconditionally. You have uplifted me in more ways than you'll ever know and I am forever grateful for that.

My friends. I want to thank them too! You know who you are.

Thank you for being the most amazing support network and for cheering me on when it comes to any of my endeavours. An extra shoutout goes to both Ellie Kean and Isobel Clark for being such incredible test readers, and for helping shape Macey into who she is.

A special thank you to my lovely Adam Salter, I wish you were still here to see me publish my first ever novel. You were always my biggest cheerleader, and though I am so delighted to see my first book out, it does sting a little knowing that I won't hear what you think. Thank you for showing me that I am capable, and worthy, of another person's admiration. I hope heaven has a good book selection—I'll be disappointed if *More than Fate* is not on the shelf.

To all the people who have encouraged me in one way or another over the years, including my primary school teacher who ignited my love for writing and believed in me all those years ago. Stacey, you'll always be Miss Parker to me! Thank you. There've been a lot of people who have helped bring this book to life, in one way or another. To my online followers who have stuck around for my various endeavours over the years, thank you too.

Finally, thank you to Amelia Bevans for providing illustrations for our cover. We love them!

I hope *More Than Fate* lived up to everyone's expectations, and that you found it relatable in some way. At the end of the day, when all is said and done, love is complicated and different for everyone, yet we all have it in common.

Tamzin xxx

ANDREA'S ACKNOWLEDGMENTS

Writing a book is always an interesting process, this one even more so because for the first time I had a co-writer. Massive thanks to Tamzin for being an amazing co-writer, there's literally no one else I would have gone through this process with. You are my best friend and soul sister and I love you. I can't wait to see what you do next. Thank you for asking me to tell Isla's story.

Thank you to my dear friend Janelle Medders and my mother Judi Severson for being test readers and giving us such great feedback on the manuscript throughout its evolution. Your feedback was invaluable and I'm so glad you enjoyed the story as much as you did. While Tamzin already thanked them, I also want to thank Ellie and Isobel for being test readers and Amelia for her illustration help with the cover. Tamzin and I both appreciated all the help these people provided along the way.

Thanks, as always, to my family and friends for being supportive in my writing journey and always making me feel like I can do this. Writing a book isn't easy and publishing it is very daunting. It makes such a difference to have a support group that truly believes in the work I'm doing...and who enjoy reading the final result!

Thank you to my online community for sharing this journey with me and being so interested in the writing I do. Your support as I go through the writing process and balance all my projects means the world and makes the process feel a little less overwhelming. Your support means more than I can express.

Finally, thank you to the readers. I hope you enjoyed Macey's and Isla's stories. I hope you have found a way to connect to these characters the way Tamzin and I have, and I hope their stories show you that no matter what your age or experience, we all deserve to be loved, just as we are, and that it's never too late to create the life you want.

Andrea xxx

ABOUT TAMZIN

Tamzin L. Burch is from Sheffield, England, and currently resides in her university city, Derby. She is studying for her Bachelors degree in Marketing, Public Relations & Advertising. Having written stories since she was a young girl, it has been a dream of hers to publish a book one day. A strong belief in fate led her to the idea for this book, which is a homage to Tamzin and Andrea's friendship. When Tamzin isn't in Sheffield or Derby, she's travelling at every opportunity, seeing the globe and eating her way around it.

ABOUT ANDREA

Andrea J. Severson lives in Phoenix, Arizona. She has a PhD in English: Writing, Rhetorics, & Literacies. She lived abroad as a child, while her father served in the U.S. Army, and grew up loving and experiencing other cultures. A fateful solo trip to the UK in late 2010 created a love affair with the country, and London in particular. When she's not hanging out in Phoenix, she's usually flying off to London (with side trips to Oxford) where she can be found walking around taking pictures, writing in a coffee shop, or shopping.

ALSO BY ANDREA J. SEVERSON

A Brave Start

Brave With You

Printed in Great Britain
by Amazon

61344167R00190